The Girl from Greenwich Street

ALSO BY LAUREN WILLIG

Two Wars and a Wedding

Band of Sisters

The Summer Country

The English Wife

The Other Daughter

That Summer

The Ashford Affair

The Pink Carnation Series

The Girl from Greenwich Street

A Novel of Hamilton, Burr, and America's First Murder Trial

Lauren Willig

WILLIAM MORROW LARGE PRINT
An Imprint of HarperCollinsPublishers

This is a work of fiction. Names, characters, places, and incidents are products of the author's imagination or are used fictitiously and are not to be construed as real. Any resemblance to actual events, locales, organizations, or persons, living or dead, is entirely coincidental.

THE GIRL FROM GREENWICH STREET. Copyright © 2025 by Lauren Willig. All rights reserved. Printed in the United States of America. No part of this book may be used or reproduced in any manner whatsoever without written permission except in the case of brief quotations embodied in critical articles and reviews. For information, address HarperCollins Publishers, 195 Broadway, New York, NY 10007.

HarperCollins books may be purchased for educational, business, or sales promotional use. For information, please email the Special Markets Department at SPsales@harpercollins.com.

FIRST WILLIAM MORROW LARGE PRINT EDITION

ISBN 978-0-06-343349-6

Library of Congress Cataloging-in-Publication Data is available upon request.

25 26 27 28 29 LBC 5 4 3 2 1

To Harvard Law and to Cravath, Swaine & Moore:
It's been a long, strange road back to the courtroom.

The Girl from Greenwich Street

Prologue

The deceased was a young girl, who till her fatal acquaintance with the prisoner, was virtuous and modest. . . .

—William Coleman, *Report of the Trial of Levi Weeks*

New York City
December 22, 1799

The shadows were gathering in the back of the house in Greenwich Street.

It had been one of those clear, bright winter days, when the sun shone pitiless as the Last Judgment, all light without warmth, but the early winter dusk was finally falling. Elma welcomed it, even if it did make it hard to see her reflection in the scrap of mirror Caty had allowed was permissible to make Elma neat and tidy.

Elma draped a kerchief across her bodice, studying the effect of the fichu. Whatever she did, her calico gown and dimity petticoat looked decidedly provincial. There was only so much one could do with old patterns, cheap fabrics, and a Quaker cousin with an eye for propriety.

Soon. Soon she'd have dresses of fine muslin and gauze, embroidered all about with this season's whimsies; she'd have clocked stockings of sheerest silk, and shawls so fine one could draw them through a ring. Oh, and she'd have the rings too, starting with one tonight. He'd not shown it to her; he wouldn't. Let it be a surprise, he'd said, a surprise for their wedding night. Surely he should be allowed *some* surprises.

She'd surprises of her own, Elma had countered, trying to sound like the lady of the world she meant to become, not the poor cousin from Cornwall, New York, everyone's drudge and morality tale.

She'd taken his hand in hers and kissed each finger, one by one, her eyes on his all the while.

He'd liked it well enough, she could tell, because his breath had quickened, and he'd nodded and said a quick, "Tonight," before a step on the stair behind them signaled—

"Elma?"

The kerchief slipped from Elma's grasp at the sound

of Caty's voice, so rudely intruding into her own private place.

Elma took her time retrieving the kerchief. "Did you want me?"

"No. . . . That is . . ." Caty hovered at the threshold, neither in nor out. Caty was never still: always up and down the stairs, in and out, seeing what needed doing; seeing who wasn't doing what they were meant to be doing.

Watching. Always watching. Pretending concern. *Oh, Elma, thee will take a chill. Let me give thee a kerchief.* Stuffing thick fabric into the neckline of her dress, muffling her in shawls. She'd like to muffle Elma out of existence, Elma had no doubt. The family embarrassment.

Somewhere, far to the south, in Charleston, Elma's father lived with his other family. Elma used to dream he would come and sweep her away, dress her in silks and laces, put her at his right hand. My daughter, he'd call her.

For all she knew he had other daughters. He'd had another family already, that's what Elma's uncle David said. A sinner leading Elma's mother like a brand to the burning. Twenty-three years Elma's mother had been burning, acknowledging and acknowledging and acknowledging her sin, but never any closer to salvation.

Elma's mother had been sixteen when she'd fallen from grace with a soldier in the Continental Army. Six years younger than Elma was now.

Elma was older and she knew better. If Elma were to burn, she'd made up her mind to do it in grand style.

"Which do you like?" Elma held up two handkerchiefs, alternating them against her bodice to show the effect. "This one? Or that one?"

A furrow appeared between Caty's pale brows. "The second kerchief—is that Peggy's?"

Elma shrugged. "Peggy will never mind. Besides, I don't mean to mop my nose with it. She'll have it back none the worse for wear."

By then Elma would have finery of her own, a doting husband to shower her with the niceties of life, not clothe her in calico and set her to drudge like Caty: minding the children, boiling the linens, feeding the boarders, trimming hats in the millinery that supplemented the income of the boardinghouse.

Caty hesitated, and Elma could see her struggling with the desire to read Elma a lecture on coveting thy neighbor's kerchief. Easy enough to divide between mine and thine when one had something of one's own. Elma's entire life had been pieced together like a quilt from scraps begged from others. If there was one thing she'd learned, it was that it was better to take than to beg.

"Thy fichu is crooked," said Caty at long last, and Elma knew she'd won. Caty crossed the narrow room, beneath the slope of the gambrel roof, and with sure fingers tugged the fichu into place, tucking it into Elma's bodice, higher than Elma liked. "Thee are determined to go out tonight?"

Like the good Quaker she was, Caty minded her *thee*s and *thou*s.

"It's a fair, fine night." Elma deliberately misunderstood her.

Caty's fingers hesitated on the linen. "After thy illness. Should thee take a chill . . ."

"Why, you would nurse me back to health. As you did before." Elma looked hard at the top of Caty's bent head, daring her to look up and meet her eyes. "Just as you did before."

"Tonight . . ." Caty took a step back, her work-reddened hands clasping and unclasping, unaccustomed to emptiness. "Hope told me. She told me thee mean to be married."

"It's a fine thing when one's family won't keep a confidence." Elma felt a curious sense of elation. She'd known Hope would never be able to resist telling Caty; Hope would be bursting with it, all self-righteous good intentions. And jealousy. Mostly jealousy, made worse by having to cloak it in virtue.

"You—thee—ought to have told me."

Oh ho, Caty was flustered if she was falling into secular ways, saying *you* instead of *thee*.

"Why? So you could make me my bridal clothes?"

"Thy family—" began Caty, and faltered.

The steps outside creaked and they both jerked toward the door. It was a heavy tread, not Hope's light step or Peg's cheerful bounce. Elma retreated behind the curtain of the bed.

"Where's Elma?" It was Levi's voice, a deep, cheerful baritone. Elma felt her breath release, raising a faint cloud in the cold air.

"She is hid behind the bed." There was no need for Caty to sound so prim about it.

Elma stepped out from behind the curtain. Levi smiled in relief at the sight of her, and she was struck, as always, by the vitality of his presence, the simple, uncomplicated joy. She loved him and hated him for it.

He limped forward, favoring the leg he'd bruised at his brother's timber yard that morning. Elma had plastered it herself, sponging the blood and giving him a good scolding. "Don't mind me. I want you to tie my hair."

"Couldn't your apprentice do that?" Elma took the black ribbon he held out to her, as he turned his back, bending his knees to make himself shorter. His light brown hair was loose around his shoulders, untouched by powder. She gathered it into a queue.

"And have me in knots? You've a gentler touch." He cast a glance over his shoulder at her, inadvertently pulling his own hair. "Ouch."

"Stay still and you won't hurt yourself." Elma could see Caty's eyes going from one to the other of them. Elma hastily tied the ribbon, giving Levi a light push. "There. You're fit for company. Now go away and leave us be."

He looked at Caty, and then at Elma. Elma gave him a slight shake of her head. He took it in good grace. Levi took everything in good grace. He'd never been out of grace, couldn't imagine what it was like. "As you command."

His steps creaked away, up the stairs, to his own room on the third floor.

When Caty was away in September, Elma had stayed in the big room in the front on the second floor, right below Levi's.

But that had been in the last blazing of the summer heat, when the sun burned off the sidewalks, and those who could afford it fled the yellow fever, piling into boats and wagons, off along the Hudson. The world had felt overripe, everything set to burst; one had to grab while one could, while one was alive, while the fruit hung heavy on the trees, abandoned in the half-empty city. What was one to do but pick what one could?

But that was September. The yellow fever had gone; the wagons with their coffins rattling to the graveyard had been replaced with the sound of carriages bringing home the lucky ones who had escaped to the country. The acrid scent of the gunpowder from the cannons fired to drive off the sickness had faded, the tang of the sea blowing again through her window with the cooler air, with just a hint of the stench of the glue manufactory when the wind was in the wrong direction. There were knockers put back on doors, businesses reopened, and life went back to the way it was. Caty, Hope, and the children came home from Cornwall. And Elma retreated to this dark chamber in the back of the house where the shadows fell early and the small windows caught no light.

There were times Elma could scarcely remember the girl she'd been in September, the dreams she'd dreamed in that big front room. When the trees blazed red and gold, one last burst of wonder before the fall.

Now all was gray and sharp with frost. What she did tonight wasn't for passion, but for cold, hard sense. She'd learned her mother's lesson and her own.

Caty looked meaningfully at Elma. "Levi seems in good spirits."

"Yes," said Elma, not trusting herself to say more.

"I had thought, with his leg, he might not be fit to go out tonight."

"It was only a scratch, hardly worth the fuss." Any elation she might have felt was gone. It was no fun taunting Caty. Not now. Elma just wanted to be left alone. Tonight, she'd leave this room, leave it for good. Down the stairs, out the door, to the meeting place in Lispenard's Meadow. She was making the right decision, she was.

But the game of teasing Caty had lost its savor.

From downstairs came the wail of a child, Caty's youngest, one and a half years old. Caty looked distractedly toward the stairs, clearly torn. "Thee promise to keep warm?"

"Oh, we shall." It was too easy to make Caty blush, even after four children.

Caty took refuge in the petty details in which she delighted. "Thy hands—those mittens will scarce keep thee warm. Thee ought to have a muff, to keep off the chill. Elizabeth next door . . . I might borrow it for thee."

"There's no need to fuss," said Elma.

"Catherine! Where are thee?" A masculine voice bellowed up the stairs, in tune with the baby's wail: Caty's husband, Elias, home from Sunday services.

"Back from meeting already?" Elma could see Caty's

mind revolving like the clock in Mr. Baker's Museum, all wheels and gears, checking all the tasks done and undone, tea to be got, children to be minded, boarders to be fed, her husband to mollify, her unwanted cousin to be speeded on her elopement—but with warm hands, a sop to Caty's conscience.

"Catherine!" Elias's voice was high-pitched, querulous. Elma could hear the stomp of booted feet on the stairs, as the sound of the baby's howling grew louder. "The baby wants fixing!"

"Presently!" Caty called. She turned back to Elma. "Thy cheeks—they have turned so pale. If thee be frightened . . . He's a good man, Levi. I shouldn't think . . ."

"I'm not frightened. I'm just cold." Elma moved quickly to the door. "You're right. I'll get the muff from Beth."

Caty trailed after her, a furrow beneath the plain white line of her cap. "Thou will remember to return it? The muff?"

"If I don't, I have no doubt you'll remind me."

Caty was good at that. She was good at reminding Elma that this wasn't her house, these weren't her things; everything she had, she had on sufferance.

It didn't matter now, Elma told herself. It didn't matter. None of it mattered.

Caty could keep her dull house and her dull husband and her runny-nosed children. Elma would be a great lady, like Mrs. Church. Her lover had promised that she'd sweep through town in a coach and four, with plumes in her hair and jewels on her heels. No Quaker meetinghouse for her. She'd attend church at Trinity, in a pelisse tailored in Paris and her head modestly bent over a calfskin hymnbook.

Perhaps she'd come back from time to time, and let the children marvel at her, at her soft, scented skin and her soft, scented silks, at the rustle of her petticoats and the curve of her curls.

Yes, Elma rather liked the thought of that.

Let them know the brand from the burning might be a phoenix in disguise, ready to blaze far above them.

Averting her face, avoiding Elias and the howling child, Elma hurried down the stairs, through the sounds of the boardinghouse—the children shouting, the baby fretting, Caty bustling, journeymen laughing—letting herself out into the crisp, smoky December air. The street was busy with people paying Sunday calls, ironmongers and tobacconists, builders and grocers, bundled against the chill, dodging out of the way of the sleighs that jangled down the center of the street.

She wouldn't miss it, any of it, Elma told herself.

To the south, above the close-crowded wooden

houses, Elma could see the spire of Trinity Church on Broadway, where the houses were of brick, not wood; where the women wore silk from the ships whose masts pocked the sky; where she would have a home of her own where the beds weren't rented out by the week.

Or perhaps they'd board one of those ships out there in the harbor and sail away to a real city, to London. What was New York, after all? Just a jumble of houses carved out of mud and meadow, filled with the refuse of the world.

Like her.

"Elma!" The ironmonger's sixteen-year-old daughter, Fanny, waved wildly at her from the neighboring stoop.

Pretending not to hear, Elma turned sharply to her left, toward Beth Osborn's house, to borrow a muff to wear to her wedding.

Chapter One

On Thursday last was found in a well dug by the Manhattan Company, on the north side of the Collect (but which afterwards proved useless) the body of Miss G. E. Sands who had been missing from the evening of Sunday the 22nd.

—*Greenleaf's New Daily Advertiser*,
January 8, 1800

*New York City
January 6, 1800*

I heard they found her muff floating in a drain in Bayard's Lane."

"No—not a drain. The Manhattan Well."

Greenwich Street heaved with people, shoving, pushing, jostling.

Alexander Hamilton slowed, contemplating this unexpected hindrance. His two clerks had been more than usually slow and doltish this morning, his correspondence more than usually irritating, so he had darted out of his office with the object of buying Eliza a coffee biggin. She'd looked so heavy-eyed at the breakfast table, bouncing baby Betsy in one arm while presiding over the coffeepot with the other. The coffee biggin, Gouverneur Morris assured him, produced a superior, stronger quality of coffee. Whether it did or not, Alexander had no idea, but it would be something to offer Eliza, to take that smudged, hollow look from her eyes.

Soon, he'd promised her. Soon he'd step away from public life. They'd build an idyll in the countryside, near enough to town that they could enjoy the society of their friends and he could lend his aid as needed to his fellow Federalists, consult on the odd legal matter. . . . Soon. But General Washington had entrusted him with the organization of the new army—never mind how President Adams resented it, how he worked to undermine all of Alexander's plans—and with the general in his grave this past month, Alexander felt more keenly than ever how strongly he needed to press the work forward.

Then there was the petty manner of money. Money, always money. Money for the children's schooling; money to build their house in the country. Money to be earned from the legal practice that was suffering sorely as Alexander struggled to build an army that he knew was needed, if only the ignoramuses in Philadelphia could just be brought to see it.

Just a bit longer. A bit longer and he'd be able to move Eliza and their brood to the countryside, and live the life of a country squire, going out with his fowling piece to shoot ducks in the morning mist, his Eliza presiding clear-eyed at their own tea table. Soon. Eventually. Someday.

But for now, he could buy her a coffee biggin.

Or so he'd intended. Greenwich Street was impassable with this inexplicable crowd. Unlike the elegant brick homes lining Broadway, the houses here were of wood, ugly, clumsy structures so newly built that Alexander could practically smell the wood shavings and fresh-mixed plaster. It was a tinderbox of a street, but it wasn't a fire causing this unaccustomed press of people; he would have smelled the smoke before this.

Only a block away, the students of his alma mater, King's College—now Columbia—rushed to class in their flapping gowns, but this didn't have the flavor of a student riot; there wasn't enough Latin being spoken. Besides, the students were enclosed behind the high gates of the college, effectively locking them away from the city around them. When Alexander was in college, there'd been much made of the college's proximity to the so-called Holy Ground, where pleasure could be found for a price and brawls sometimes broke out between customers and madams, or madams and enraged moralists.

But that was on the other side of the college. This was a street of respectable small tradesmen, running their businesses out of the front rooms of their homes: grocers and tobacconists and, most important, an ironmonger who was reputed to make excellent coffee biggins. Alexander could just make out the wooden sign creaking from one of the awnings, right at what seemed to be the epicenter of the excited crowd.

It seemed unlikely that half the city had experienced a simultaneous desire for a coffee biggin.

"Alexander!" A hand clapped him on the shoulder, and Alexander looked up into the face of his old friend and colleague Richard Harison, once his partner in law practice, still his partner in politics. "Or should I say Major General?"

"Never among friends." Or possibly not at all if that ass Adams had anything to do with it, not to mention Aaron Burr and his Republican rabble, downplaying the threat from France, ignoring the dangers of a Revolutionary regime untrammeled, agitating for the disbandment of Alexander's army. The United States Army, that was, or would be, if Alexander was given the supplies and support he so desperately needed.

"How goes the business of the army?"

"Busily," Alexander quipped.

Even to an ally like Harison, Alexander could never admit the fear that it was all for naught, all his preparations and plans, the punishing pace he had set himself and his clerks. That ass Adams had never wanted the army and he'd certainly never wanted Alexander. Alexander had been forced on him, by the one person with the power to do so. The person who had lain cold and still in his grave these past three weeks. Alexander had marched in General Washington's funeral procession; he'd listened to Gouverneur Morris deliver the funeral oration; but he still couldn't quite entirely believe he was gone, that great man who had loved him as his own father never had.

And there was his Eliza with gray in her dark hair, their Philip studying at King's College—not King's anymore, but Columbia—and Harison, who had been in his prime when they had begun their practice together just after the war, now heavy-jowled, the new Brutus hairstyle not hiding the fact that his hair was thinning at the temples, and gray now, entirely gray.

How had they come to this? This wasn't what Alexander had thought his middle age would be, scrabbling after pennies, after favor, after political advancement, surrounded by incompetents and opportunists.

Alexander cleared his throat. "What ruckus is this? Are the apprentices revolting again?"

"The apprentices are always revolting." Harison chuckled at his own tired sally. "You must have heard, surely? About the girl. The girl in the well."

The man in front of him had said something about the Manhattan Well, that misbegotten monstrosity. "Ah," said Alexander, as if he knew more than he did. "Are all these people—"

"Here to view the corpse." Harison shoved his hands in his waistcoat to warm them. "You haven't come to gawp at the girl in the well, have you?"

"I haven't. I came to find a coffee biggin for Eliza. The baby is cutting her teeth," Alexander added.

"Did you try brandy—"

"Rubbed on her gums? Or for ourselves?"

"Either." Harison grimaced in sympathy.

"Neither had the least effect, I regret to say. Poor Eliza has had no peace. And neither have I."

"Cherish it. Cherish her." Harison's face drooped like melting candle wax. He was, Alexander knew, thinking of the much younger wife he'd adored, his Fanny, gone two years now, leaving Harison with their four young children. Alexander couldn't imagine such a future, an existence without Eliza. She was the still center of an ever-moving world. "The time—it goes faster than you know."

"I've promised Eliza to spend more time at home—as time allows."

"Time—or your ambitions?"

That was the trouble with old friends. They felt comfortable asking awkward questions. "You haven't come for the girl in the well, have you?"

"I've come as an officer of the court," Harison said grandly. "And, I admit, out of a certain measure of curiosity. The family's allowing the public in to see the body—fanning the flames. If I'm to sit on the case, I feel it's my duty to see what every other man jack in the city will have seen."

"That's what they're all waiting for? To see the girl's corpse? It's macabre—barbaric."

"It's human nature," said Harison equably.

"Of the basest sort."

"It makes a compelling story," said Harison thoughtfully. "Perhaps because it's such a familiar one. The girl lured . . . seduced . . . discarded. And she's a Quaker, to boot. You haven't read of it in the papers?"

Alexander had been avoiding the papers because the papers refused to avoid him. He'd promised Eliza he'd hold his fire, but it was hard when Republican scandal sheets slandered him and his fingers itched to take up his pen and defend himself.

Like last time. And they all knew how that had gone.

Mercifully, Harison was still going on about the girl in the well. "It's the talk of the town. There are already tales of hauntings. The girl's tormented soul begging justice, all that sort of nonsense. People half expect to see the sheeted dead squeaking and gibbering in the street. You'd know nothing about that."

Harison looked pointedly at Alexander, who had gotten in trouble, last year, over a prank involving a supposed ghost.

More fodder for the papers. A man couldn't arrange a joke with his family without being splattered with ink.

"Have they arrested anyone for the crime?" Alexander asked abruptly.

"Levi Weeks. He's a young carpenter who boarded in the same house. They're saying he got her with child and killed her to keep from marrying her. You'll have heard of his brother—Ezra. He laid the pipes for the Manhattan Well."

That well, that blasted well again. Alexander seethed at the thought of it. Burr had hoodwinked him; he'd hoodwinked all of them. And the worst of it? He'd had Alexander fighting for his Manhattan Company, supposedly formed for the purpose of digging that well, among others. A well to bring clean water to the city, to fight the dreaded scourge of yellow fever. What civic-minded soul wouldn't support that project? Alexander had drafted the proposal, crafted the clauses, sweated ink and effort over it. Not a party matter, Burr had promised him, and offered him seats on the board for Federalists, including one for Alexander's brother-in-law John Church, proof that this was an undertaking meant to benefit the whole.

Except it wasn't.

The well was only a ruse. In the last hours before the bill went up for vote, Burr had inserted another clause, one setting up a financial institution. It wasn't a well he was proposing but a bank, a bank to rival Alexander's own Bank of the United States.

And he'd done it. With Alexander's support.

How Burr must have laughed at him in his mansion, Richmond Hill. How all the Republicans must have chortled to see Hamilton throw his support behind a measure designed to unman him.

Alexander burned at the very thought of it, but there was nothing he could do now. The bill to establish the Manhattan Company had passed—thanks to Alexander's efforts. The Manhattan Company was at this very moment amassing funds and extending credit, a monstrous instrument that pretended to the public good while serving private gain.

For Burr, all for Burr. And the Republican Party.

Harison was still talking. "Young Colden will prosecute, of course. Weeks has retained Brockholst Livingston for his brother's defense. And Colonel Burr."

"They've hired Burr for the defense?" How Burr would enjoy that, posturing in the courtroom in his sleek black frock coat.

He'd have Livingston do the work while he took all the credit. It would play directly to his claim to be the champion of the working man, a vivid image for voters to take with them to the polls: Burr using his eloquence to save a lowly carpenter from the gallows.

Unless . . . A germ of an idea began to form. "What evidence is there against the young man?"

"Precious little, as yet. Rumor and hearsay—the sentiment of the street. They've been baying for his blood. Someone's been handing out broadsides, riling them up. The mob's convinced he did it. They'll settle for nothing less than his neck in a noose."

"That's not justice. That's lynch law." Charles Lynch and the men like him who took it upon themselves to enact vengeance on those they'd condemned without process of law were anathema to everything Alexander stood for. That wasn't the sort of polity he'd fought for, with the sword and with the pen. "What makes them think it was this young man?"

"The family claim he was walking out with her—they've been quite voluble about it."

"Did anyone else confirm that? Were they seen together? Is there any evidence the girl was with child?"

"You sound as though you're taking down the points of the case." When Alexander didn't reply, his friend looked at him sharply. "You're not, are you? Weeks is well defended—"

"By Livingston?"

"He's a very able lawyer in the criminal sphere."

"He'll acquit young Weeks on a technicality and leave his reputation in tatters. In a case such as this, a case that touches on a man's honor, it isn't enough to create a doubt; one must leave no doubt." As Alexander knew, all too well.

Harison looked sideways at him. "And then there's Colonel Burr. . . . That's the matter of it, isn't it?"

Just thinking of the Manhattan Well made Alexander burn with rage. "You know well enough what his methods are."

"I know well enough what yours are." Harison let out a puff of breath, visible in the cold air. "Didn't you just tell me yourself you'd promised Mrs. Hamilton not to exert yourself?"

"My Eliza would be the last to prevent me from exerting myself in a matter of justice," said Alexander firmly, although when he remembered Eliza as she'd been that morning, exhausted, as close to defeated as he'd ever seen her, he wasn't quite so sure.

There'd been a piece in the *Aurora* last week, claiming Alexander had been with his supposed mistress, Maria Reynolds, in Philadelphia. Eliza knew it was nonsense, of course. Alexander was reasonably sure Eliza knew it was nonsense. It was just another Republican dig, another attempt to discredit him, dragging up that old muck, the painful remembrance of his own misjudgment.

A case such as this would provide fodder of quite another kind for the papers. Burr and his Republicans had been making inroads with the lesser sort in the city, the small tradesmen and mechanics. Livingston was an ardent Republican; the two of them defending this Weeks boy would only entrench them as the champion of the little man.

But if Hamilton were joined with them in Levi's defense . . . well, perhaps that might go some way to getting the Federalists the votes they needed to carry the spring assembly elections.

There was also the matter of the house. Ezra Weeks was one of the most sought-after builders in the city. If one were to build a house, one must have a builder. So it was really for Eliza's benefit in the end if Alexander were to offer to Weeks to defend his brother.

And there was justice to be served too. It was really quite economical; he could annoy Burr, improve his own standing, benefit his party, thwart the mob, and forward the project of the house in the country, all at the same time.

"Would you have me leave an innocent to the mercy of the mob—and the eloquence of Livingston and Burr?"

"You know best," said Harison doubtfully.

"Except when I do not?" Alexander clapped his old friend on the shoulder, his spirits rising dangerously; he could feel the excitement building, the thrill of a challenge. "You'll introduce me to Weeks senior? I've had it in mind to build a house for Eliza. . . ."

"Oh, it's about a house, is it?"

"I might just interest myself in his brother's case." Alexander looked seriously at his old friend. "I can't leave a man to the mob, Richard."

"Or the glory to Colonel Burr?" Relenting, Harison took his arm. "Come. We'll leave these ghouls to their gawking. I'll take you to Ezra Weeks."

Chapter Two

I saw the corpse of the deceased twice. I had but a superficial view, however, of it, as it lay in the coffin, exposed to the view of thousands; I examined such parts as were come-at-able—Such as her head, neck and breast.

—From the testimony of Dr. Richard Skinner at the trial of Levi Weeks

New York City
January 6, 1800

"You can see what he did to her—Weeks." Richard Croucher's exaggerated British drawl carried over the slurred consonants of the local Dutch accent.

There were too many people crammed into the frame house on Greenwich Street; Catherine Ring felt as though it were about to split open, like an over-filled barrel. People lined the streets outside, peering through the windows. Caty could hear the cries of vendors hawking oysters and roasted chestnuts, gingerbread and cider, handbills and gossip. People breezed into the house with crumbs and rumor on their lips.

A new wave of visitors shoved past Caty as if she weren't there, as if this weren't her house, her sitting room, her cousin. They ogled the bruises on Elma's throat and breast, trailing their fingers over the dark marks on her neck, lifting her limp hands, pursing their lips in noises of sympathy and horror and glee. Some pretended to expertise, calling themselves doctors, spouting learned words in Latin while they peeled apart Elma's bodice. Others didn't bother to pretend any professional interest. They just stared and speculated, fondling her hair, her dress, making ribald remarks as if it didn't matter, as if her family weren't listening, as if there weren't children there.

Caty wanted to take her broom and sweep them all out of her house. Out, out, out.

Let them see what he did to her, Elias had said, the same words, over and over, battering Caty's ears. What he did to her . . . what he did to her . . .

What Caty had allowed him to do to her. Elias hadn't said it, not outright, but Caty could hear it; she could feel it in the way Elias wouldn't quite look at her, wouldn't meet her eyes, slouched away when he saw her coming.

He couldn't blame her more than she blamed herself.

On that endless Sunday, there had been so many moments when she might have taken Elma by the hand and said, "Thee needn't be married in this hole-and-corner way. Be married from thy own house, with honor. If he persuades thee to run from thy family he wants nothing good of thee."

Elma would have laughed if she'd said such a thing, Caty knew that. And yet . . . *Come back*, she imagined herself calling.

Instead, Caty had tied on Elma's gloves for her.

Caty elbowed through the crowd in the front room; she had to find Elias and make him stop this. Not just because they were letting goodness only knew who into the house, tracking in the refuse of the streets, and she had dinner to make and children to tend—the living still mattered too—but for Elma's sake also. It wasn't decent; it wasn't seemly.

"I saw them—making the beast with two backs." Mr. Croucher's dark head, the hair pulled back neatly into a queue, bobbed up and down. "Shameless, utterly shameless."

Caty wanted to grab him by that tidy queue and yank. Why couldn't he be quiet? Why did he have to keep shouting their shame?

Never there when the rent was due; stickling over

every penny; only a lodger, not a boarder; oh no, Caty's plain cooking wasn't good enough for Richard Croucher—but since Elma had gone and their house had turned into a traveling fair he was all over like mold on cheese, whispering in Elias's ear, shaking his head over Levi's perfidy, sharing scandalous stories of what had gone on while Elma was left alone without female supervision during the yellow fever. . . .

Scandal spurred the sales of silk stockings, Caty thought bitterly. Their tragedy was Mr. Croucher's business opportunity. Share a delicious secret; sell a bunch of garters.

They were all looking at Caty, of course. Caty, who had let this happen in her house. Caty, who had left Elma. Unchaperoned. In a house of men.

During the fever!

Caty had taken the children away while yellow fever raged through the city that autumn; she'd had no choice. She couldn't leave them to sicken. And her sister Hope—Caty needed the help with the children. It made sense at the time to leave Elma in the city in charge of the boardinghouse. She was a woman grown, Elma, twenty-two years old. By the time Caty was her age, she'd been several years married and had two children.

Elma would never marry now.

Caty pressed her lips hard together. If Mr. Croucher

had really seen Elma in bed with Levi, he ought to have said something then, not stored it up to gloat over later. And why hadn't Mr. Croucher told Caty then? Or Elias?

Caty's husband stood behind Elma's coffin, his tall form hunched, giving him a scarecrow aspect, as though he'd folded in on himself. Ever since Elma had disappeared, they'd none of them been themselves, that was fair to say, but Elias had been so strange, so furtive, huddling in corners with Croucher, hurrying out of rooms as soon as Caty entered them, prone to sudden outbursts and brooding silences.

A love fit, that was what Elias had said when two days, then three, then four had passed and Elma still hadn't come home. She must have flung herself in the river in a love fit.

Elias had gone to Captain Rutgers and had him drag the waters around Rhinelander's battery, never knowing, never imagining that Elma's battered body was at that very time at the other end of the city, submerged in a well in Lispenard's Meadow. It was the muff that had led them to her, Beth Osborn's muff, floating on the surface, fished out by a boy and brought home to his mother.

Thou will remember to return it? The muff?

Caty's head ached. The noise. The smells. The press

of people. The effort to hold back tears, to be calm, serene, strong. Hide the tumult she was feeling.

It was the Saturday before Christmas that Hope had come to her, all indignation, to tell her that Elma had told Hope, in strictest confidence, that she was to be wed, in secret, the following night.

To Levi? Catherine had asked.

Who else? Hope had snapped back.

Heaven help her, Caty's only feeling had been relief. Elma—out of her house. Elma married, safely. Levi was a good boy, a good match. He wasn't a Friend, but then, neither was Elma, who had refused, persistently, to countenance coming to meeting.

Yes, Hope was disappointed to see Levi's attentions go elsewhere, but Caty had never liked the idea of seeing Hope married out of their meeting. She'd pretended not to notice as Hope had experimented with *you* instead of *thee*, trying on the language of the godless as Elma might preen in a borrowed kerchief. Levi married to Elma? It was the answer to a prayer.

It must have been the devil whispering in Caty's ear, making her close her eyes and her heart. Why in secret? she ought to have asked. She ought to have told Elias, urged him to remonstrate with Elma. She ought to have spoken to Levi, demanded to know his intentions.

But it had never occurred to her to wonder, or to worry.

Even when Elma had failed to appear that night, when Levi had returned to the boardinghouse without her, pretending ignorance, Caty still half thought it was only one of Elma's tricks, that she'd appear, laughing at them, a ring on her finger. Wasn't it a good joke? Elma would say, her arm around Levi's waist. Didn't I make you wonder?

But Caty hadn't. She hadn't wondered until it was too late. She hadn't wanted to wonder.

She'd just wanted Elma safely married. Was that so wrong? Elma decently married, out of Caty's house. Caty had been five when Elma had been born—the result of Aunt Lizzy's lapse of conscience with a soldier from the Continental Army—and nothing had been the same since. Elma poisoned everything she touched—and Elma touched everything.

Pity her, Caty's mother had advised her. Pray for her. The child cannot help that she was born into sin.

"—with child," someone was saying loudly. "He killed her because she was with child."

Next they'd be calling Caty's respectable boardinghouse a bawdy house.

"The doctors examined her," Caty snapped. They'd cut Elma open and peered at her insides. It made Caty sick to think of it. "There was no child."

The woman gave Caty a nasty look, then turned away and muttered something to her companion. Now they were both staring at her, whispering about her, mocking her in her own house. Caty could feel her cheeks heating beneath her white cap.

Respectable, she'd always been respectable—it was all Elma's fault, always Elma's fault. Couldn't she have just stayed gone?

A sharp cry brought Caty to herself. Her youngest, Eliza, had fallen and someone had stepped on her hand. Eliza's little face was red with inexpressible misery. Caty shoved her way to her and swept her up, bouncing her in her arms, pressing her cheek to Eliza's, murmuring nonsense words. Thank goodness, she seemed more alarmed than hurt; Caty couldn't feel anything broken. Beneath the baby's dress, Caty could feel her clout sagging. The baby reeked of the sour scent of old urine.

Guilt stabbed Caty, her child wet, hurt, while she stood here gawking. "Where is thy aunt Hope? She was meant to be minding thee!"

Elma might be dead, but that didn't mean there weren't still children to tend and boarders to feed. This had gone on long enough. Caty hitched baby Eliza higher on her hip and shoved her way through the waiting throng, ignoring complaints that she was jumping the queue.

Elias stood sentry by Elma's coffin, ignoring his children, his family, his responsibilities to the living. What did he think he could do by this, bring Elma back to life? She was gone, and this did nothing but track refuse across the floor Caty sanded by hand twice a day.

"It is enough," she said sharply, and when he still didn't look at her, she raised her voice to be heard over the throng. "Must we welcome the world into our home, husband?"

Elias muttered something that sounded like "bear witness."

"They sent doctors to prod at her. Wasn't that witness enough? It's not seemly."

"What happened to her isn't seemly." Mr. Croucher was at Elias's side; he was always at Elias's side. Caty would have hated him if she'd had the energy left for it. "Don't you want the world to know what that man did to her? The man needs to be brought to justice."

"Yes, of course, but . . ." Couldn't they just bury her quietly? Bury her quietly and let that be the end of it. The end of Elma. Make her disappear as though she'd never been. In her heart of hearts, Caty wished they'd never found her. If it hadn't been for the muff, floating to the surface . . .

Why had she made Elma borrow that muff?

Caty pushed the horrible thoughts aside, focusing on Elias, trying to catch his eye, to make him look at her, to see her. "To have so many, coming to stare at her . . . to see her shame . . . Why not just display her in the street?"

"Yes." Elias's eyes met hers. There was something about his expression that made Caty's stomach lurch with alarm. "Yes. Let the whole city see what he did."

"I didn't mean— Elias!" Caty clutched Eliza too tightly; the girl squirmed to be let down. "Surely, thee . . ."

Elias had already turned his back to her. "Let them see what he did and make him pay."

"Justice," murmured Mr. Croucher sagely.

Caty ignored him, holding the struggling Eliza as she made a futile attempt to grab her husband. "Elias—"

But he was already spreading the word about, conscripting strangers as pallbearers. They seized Elma's plain pine coffin. One hand flopped, limp, over the side, the nails cracked and broken.

"Gently!" Caty cried. Too late, too late. Always too late.

"Caty!" Her sister Hope pushed past, her cheeks wind-bitten, as though she'd been outside. "What are they doing?"

"Putting thy cousin on the street for all to gawk at,"

said Caty bitterly. "And where were thee? Eliza was nearly trampled! And she wants fixing."

"Hush, my little one." Hope neatly plucked the baby from her sister's arms, making silly faces at her. Eliza wrapped her chubby arms around Hope's neck. Hope looked out at Catherine around Eliza's head. "They've put her on the street?"

"For the world to see. As if enough haven't seen already." Couldn't they just bury her and have done with it?

"We were sorely deceived in that man." Caty's baby sister was a woman grown, twenty years old and taller than Caty, but in her indignation Hope looked ten again.

"But to show her shame on the public street . . ."

"*His* shame." Hope's chin jutted out in a stubborn way that Caty recognized well; it was like their father when he announced that the call had come upon him to go preaching abroad, never mind what he was leaving behind at home. "He was the one who lured her from her home."

Hope's voice cracked. Hope had gone to the charity sermon with Weeks, and to his brother's house; before the fever, before they'd left the city, they'd all thought it was Hope he was courting, not Elma. If *courting* one could call it.

"When she told thee he meant to marry her..."

"Who knows what lies came from his lips?" Hope's face twisted with anger. "He asked me to sign a paper saying he had paid no more attention to Elma than to any woman in this house. He *knew* that was positive lies! Why should he think I'd lie for him?"

"Hope..."

Hope wrenched her head away, and made a show of sniffing at Eliza. "Eliza's soiled her clout. I'll tend to it."

Hope ought to have tended it before. Where had she been? Not in the house.

It had been Elma who used to disappear, sometimes for whole nights, claiming she'd been at the neighbor's, when she hadn't. But not Hope. Hope was Caty's darling, her little sister, as near a child to her as her own children.

But Hope wasn't a child anymore. She was a woman grown. The idea that Hope might have secrets—it was too much for Caty's mind to compass.

The noise from the street had risen to an alarming pitch as Elma's body was brought outside to the delight of all viewers, but the sitting room had emptied along with Elma, leaving behind trails of muck and slush and a long gouge on the wooden floor where someone had dragged the wooden settle out of their way.

Two weeks ago, Levi Weeks had sat on that settle

and Caty had watched him, waiting for some sign to pass between him and Elma.

"I should have stopped it." Caty's voice was low. "I should have done better by her."

Hope bristled. "How were thee to know? How were we any of us to know? He pretended to such virtue."

Outside, the crowd was chanting, shouting for Levi's blood.

Hope lifted her chin. "If Levi Weeks doesn't hang, there's no justice in heaven."

Chapter Three

The Jurors of the People of the State of New-York . . . on their oath present, that Levi Weeks, late of the seventh ward, of the city of New-York . . . on the 22nd day of December, in the year of our Lord 1799 . . . feloniously, willfully, and of his malice aforethought, did kill and murder . . .

—From the indictment of Levi Weeks

New York City
January 7, 1800

It wasn't hard picking Levi Weeks out among the inhabitants of the Bridewell.

Straw crunched beneath Alexander's shoes as he stepped into the cell. His breath misted in front of him; the windows had bars but no glass. The stone walls intensified the bitter January chill, making it colder within than without. Alexander's business sometimes called him to the New Gaol, the debtors' prison on the other side of the Common, with its whimsical cupola—he'd had Eliza's portrait painted by an artist in the New Gaol, and a very becoming portrait it had been too—but that prison, with its shabby genteel inhabitants, resigned but not broken, was a world away from the grim confines of the Bridewell, where pickpockets and murderers brawled over the contents of a bucket of mush and a man wandered mumbling to himself, clad only in such filth as adhered to his person.

"There's Levi," said Ezra Weeks in a low voice, his head turning this way and that, sizing up the room for threats.

Alexander would have known without the telling. The young man had crammed himself against the far wall, his knees drawn to his chest as though he were trying to make himself as small as possible.

His hair, when clean, would be a dark blond or a light brown. At the moment, it hung loose around his shoulders, matted with dirt and straw and what looked like porridge. Unlike some of the others, his shirt and trousers were still largely intact, but they bore dark stains, including some that looked like blood.

They had waited until twilight to come. Yesterday, Elma Sands had been interred in the Quaker burying ground. But before she made her final journey, her family had taken the unprecedented step of displaying her corpse in the street for anyone to come and see. And they had. Hundreds of them. Thousands of them. All shouting for Levi Weeks's blood.

Ezra Weeks had insisted he could ensure his brother's safety, but he hadn't balked at the suggestion that the transfer from prison to home be undertaken quietly, under cover of darkness.

"Levi." Ezra spared a look over his shoulder at the other inmates, then turned back to his brother. "Levi. We're here to take you out."

"Ezra?" Levi squinted up at them, and Alexander could see one eye was swollen to a slit. Dried crusts of blood clung beneath his nose. "Is that really you? I dreamed—" He rubbed his hands across his eyes, or tried to, and winced. "I've had the strangest dreams. I dreamed I was taken to prison."

He shivered violently, wrapping his arms tighter around himself.

"Where's your cloak?" Ezra started to look and then checked himself. "Never mind that. General Hamilton and I have come to take you away."

"General . . . Hamilton?" Levi blinked at Alexander, confusion mingling with awe. "I saw you—in the procession—for President Washington. Why—"

Ezra Weeks pressed a hand on his brother's shoulder, lightening his touch when his brother winced.

"General Hamilton has been kind enough to interest himself in your case."

"My case?" Incomprehension gave way to dawning horror. "They say—they said—Elma— They showed me—they showed me—oh God."

Levi folded in on himself, burying his face in his knees, his back shaking with tears, or cold, or both.

Like Alexander's eldest son, Philip, in the grips of the fever two years ago, so sick that some of the doctors had pronounced him beyond saving. The hours by his bedside, praying. Putting precious chips of ice to his cracked lips. The wonder of the moment when he'd opened his eyes and known Alexander again, weak but safe.

This boy couldn't be much older than Philip. Their features were nothing alike, but there was something of that youthfulness—something of that confusion, that thin line that divided the grown man from the boy—that touched Alexander to the core.

Levi lifted his head from his arms. "Elma—what are they—what do they think—?"

"They say you did it," said Ezra bluntly. "The coroner's jury has brought in a verdict of murder."

"I'm ruined." Levi rocked back and forth on the straw. "When they took me, they showed me—they asked me— Oh God, they'll hang me. They'll hang me. And I never did it, I swear, I never . . ."

Alexander crouched down beside Levi Weeks, ignoring the squelch of whatever lay in the straw. "I will not allow you to hang," he said, the same way he might have once told Philip there were no monsters under the bed. "But we can discuss this in a more congenial setting. Your brother has arranged the payment of bail. Come. Let me help you up."

The younger man's hand was larger than Alexander's and heavily calloused, but he put it into Alexander's like a child, like Philip in his younger days, when he would still hold Alexander's hand. Levi winced as he slowly levered himself off the foul ground. He favored one side, Alexander saw, and his trousers were ripped as well as his shirt.

Ezra's chest swelled. "Who did this to you?"

Levi swallowed hard and shook his head.

"We're honest thieves here!" someone called out. "We don't hold with women-killers!"

"Who said that?" Ezra swiveled, searching for the source of the sound, hands already forming into fists.

Alexander put a hand on his arm. He could feel the heavy muscles. Ezra Weeks might be a man of business now, but he'd put in his share of heavy labor. "A public brawl will only make matters worse."

Ezra hesitated, but after a moment, he nodded curtly and stepped aside, flanking his brother as he and Alexander escorted Levi through the jeering, gibbering mob, down the stairs, and into the cold night air, which might be scented with manure but felt positively clean compared to what they had just departed.

Ezra Weeks had secured a closed carriage, not his own, to bring his brother away. It rattled over the short distance from the Bridewell west to Greenwich Street, while Ezra frowned out the window, keeping an eye out for pursuit, fists opening and closing as though he were itching to punch someone.

When the carriage turned north on Greenwich Street, Levi lifted his head. "We're not going to the Ring house?"

Ezra choked. "Are you mad? They'd tear you limb from limb."

"When you said home, I thought you meant—" The light from the carriage lamps wasn't sufficient to illuminate Levi's features, but Alexander could hear the pain in his voice. "I hadn't thought. I can't go back."

"It's a boardinghouse, not your ancestral acres," said Ezra impatiently. "You were only there since July. Once it's safe, I'll send Demas to fetch your things."

Ezra Weeks's home and lumber yard sat at the corner of Greenwich and Harrison, only a few minutes from the Ring boardinghouse by carriage, but a world away otherwise. Here, the closely built streets gave way to open land—but not for long. Alexander could see the beginnings of new construction on the plot opposite. The city was growing up around Ezra Weeks's lumber yard, creeping toward the open land between the city and Greenwich Village to the north.

In between lay the wilderness known as Lispenard's Meadow. And the well in which Elma Sands had drowned.

A well which Ezra Weeks had dug.

These were exactly the sort of men he needed for the Federalists, Alexander reminded himself. The sort of men Burr had so successfully courted. But this time, he was going to get in ahead of Burr.

A servant came out to light them up into the house, holding the candle as Ezra helped his brother up the steps. The house wasn't what Alexander would have expected for a man of Ezra's growing wealth and stature. The room into which they were taken was no formal parlor but a farmhouse kitchen, with an open hearth and a well-scrubbed wood table. At Ezra's nod, the serving boy threw more wood on the fire—a grand gesture given the price of firewood this winter—and sat Levi in the seat nearest the blaze.

Ezra bundled a pile of plans out of the way. Alexander caught a glimpse of a complicated diagram of doors of various sizes; a sketch of a fanlight.

If he could clear Levi's name, he could build his Eliza a house with a fanlight like that, a house of elegant classical lines that would make Burr's Richmond Hill look outdated and fussy. Alexander's father-in-law had already promised him seasoned logs from the Schuyler lands upstate.

"That's fine work," said Alexander, nodding at the plans.

"That's Levi's work," said Ezra shortly.

Alexander looked again at the boy—no, not a boy, a man. The firelight played off the planes of his face, showing the five days' stubble of his prison stay. "You have a fine sensibility for classical forms."

For a moment, Levi's eyes lighted. "I have a book of designs—*The New Vitruvius*. Elma said—"

The words ended as though choked off. His face went blank.

"Here. Eat." Ezra shoved a plate of cakes in front of him, ripping off the napkin that covered them. "You look half-starved. What did they feed you in that place?"

"Cornmeal mash—with molasses. Some of the men had spoons. The rest of us—" Levi stared down at his fingers, as though he could still feel the grit of it. "These cakes are good."

"Sally made them for you. She was concerned for

you, as were we all." Ezra looked pugnaciously at Alexander, as though daring him to contradict him. "The servants are very fond of Levi. Everyone is very fond of Levi. He should never have been taken to that place."

Levi scratched one arm. Through the rips in his shirt, Alexander could see the raised bumps of bug bites. "There was a man—he called himself Paul—he said he'd been there two years. He said the rats had eaten his shirt off."

"You're not there now and you're not going back. We'll see this sorted." Ezra's knuckles were white on the edge of the table. "It's nonsense, of course. Levi was here with me that night. The night the girl disappeared. John McComb will swear to it. John McComb the architect."

"I am well acquainted with Mr. McComb." Mr. McComb had designed a lighthouse for Alexander—for the government, that was—and done it very well after Alexander had set him straight on a few points. "It's no use his swearing to anything unless it's true."

"Are you implying it's not?" Ezra blustered.

"The prosecution will. Mr. Weeks, you must be aware, sentiment runs strongly against your brother." Alexander held up a hand, forestalling Ezra's protests. "I place no faith in the verdict of the mob, but many do. Our task is that much the harder."

"They've been whipping up sentiment against the boy, using him as a scapegoat." Ezra Weeks's Massachusetts accent was very strong. He wasn't, Alexander thought, that much older than his brother, for all that he affected an air of authority.

Alexander could just remember being that young. He had thought himself on top of the world in those golden days of the Revolution, certain he had all the answers, certain that industry and truth would win the day. It felt like a very long time ago.

"My goal, Mr. Weeks, is not merely to cast doubt on your brother's guilt but to prove his entire innocence so he might walk back into the world a whole man, without a shadow cast upon him."

Ezra grunted. "The entire thing is ridiculous. If that Ring fellow couldn't control his niece—"

"Cousin." Levi looked up from crumbling his cake to bits. "She wasn't his niece. She was his wife's cousin."

Ezra scowled. "Niece . . . cousin . . . What does it matter? Eat your cake."

Levi looked past him at Alexander. Despite the fire behind him, he shook faintly with cold. "They didn't want her. No one wanted her. That was what Elma said. She had a father but she'd never met him—he'd gone before she was born. He'd never married her mother."

Bastard. Alexander had had it flung at him time and again.

Alexander cleared his throat. "Elma Sands's father. Is he still alive?"

Levi nodded. "She told me she had a father in Charleston and someday she'd go to him."

That past June, on a tiny island in the middle of the Caribbean, Alexander's father had drawn his last breath. He'd accepted the money Alexander had sent him twice a year—but he'd never accepted Alexander.

It was foolish, Alexander knew. Eliza's father had taken Alexander in as if he were his own. Alexander had his own children, children who knew how much they were wanted—he'd sat by their bedsides hour by hour when they were sick, played with them, prayed for them. But when he thought of that old man dying alone in Saint Vincent, Alexander felt . . . cheated. He wasn't sure what he'd expected. That someday his father would recognize him, acknowledge him, apologize to him. Say he'd never meant to leave them.

But he had. He'd left them. And now it was too late for amends.

"I don't see how this is relevant," said Ezra sharply. "The girl is dead. What does it matter if she had a dozen fathers or none?"

Alexander ignored him. He addressed himself to Levi instead. "What can you tell me about her?"

"Elma was . . . she was herself." Levi hunched over his tea, cupping his hands around the ceramic bowl for warmth. "When they showed me—I said I recognized the dress and they asked me if I recognized the countenance—but I didn't! I didn't. Elma was—she was so alive. She was like strong tea on a cold morning, or punch that goes to your head. She made you feel awake, alive."

"You know those wild spirits," Ezra said quickly. "One minute they're up in alt; the next they're in the depths of melancholy. The girl probably flung herself in that damned well. Her uncle—pardon me, Levi, her cousin—was telling the whole neighborhood she'd killed herself in a love fit, until suddenly he changed his tune and decided to point the finger at Levi. I don't know what he thinks he gets out of it."

There was something Ezra was leaving out.

Alexander looked at Levi. "Her family says she told her cousin she meant to marry you that night. Was there any truth in that?"

Ezra jumped in before his brother could answer. "Maybe she meant to marry him. That doesn't mean he meant to marry her. She might have fancied herself in love with the boy. He's a fine figure of a lad, anyone would agree. Half the girls in that house fancied him, you told me so yourself, Levi. But that's nothing to the lad's discredit."

"No." Alexander let his eyes rest on Levi. The hot tea and well-stoked fire had brought some color to Levi's cheeks. Rested, clean-shaven, there was no denying he would be a handsome lad. But there was a shadow over his countenance. There was something Levi wasn't telling—Alexander was sure of it.

Had he offered the girl marriage? Had she gone to meet him that night?

Ezra's voice went on, over-hearty. "Who's to say what fits a girl like that might take? Why, you yourself said, Levi, that she'd threatened to do away with herself. With laudanum."

"Did she?"

Levi's voice was hoarse. "It wasn't like that. She didn't mean it—not seriously."

Ezra looked meaningfully at Alexander. "The girl was heard to say she wished she had no existence."

"It's your belief she did away with herself?"

"It's clear, isn't it? That's what I told your colleague Colonel Burr. *He* agreed with me." Alexander frowned at him, and Ezra hastily amended his tone. "Perhaps she did it for love, but if she did, that's not the boy's fault. He never promised her anything."

"Her family claims he did. They claim he promised her marriage." Alexander held Ezra Weeks's gaze, staring at him until he blustered himself into silence. Now was his chance to mark himself as superior to Burr, more strategic than Burr. "This is only what the prosecution will say. If your brother cannot answer me, how can he answer them? Think of it as . . . setting the foundations for a structure. Without the correct underpinnings, the whole will collapse."

"That's not exactly how it works, sir—but I take your point," Ezra said hastily.

"I will defer to you on matters of building if you trust I know how to build a case. I might have need of your expertise someday—as you do mine now." Feeling he had made his point, Alexander turned back to Levi. "Did you mean to run away with her that night?"

Ezra controlled himself with an effort; the force of his disapproval was palpable.

"No," Levi croaked.

"Might she have been disappointed in her hopes of your affections?"

"She—I—no." Levi looked up wildly. "She made a joke of it, that I never asked her to walk out with me—but it was only that I knew she wouldn't! When I asked her—"

"The girl felt slighted," Ezra barked. "You heard what he said."

When I asked her, Levi had said. Asked her what? To walk out with him? To run away with him?

"What do you think, Levi? Might she have done away with herself for love?"

A strange shudder passed through the boy. The words tore out of him. "Not for love of me, sir."

"Then for whom?"

Levi shook his head wordlessly.

"Why would she tell her cousin you meant to marry her?"

Levi hunched his shoulders.

Ezra couldn't control himself any longer. "With a girl like that, who can tell what they might say?"

Alexander ignored him. "Levi?"

Levi shook his head wordlessly. "I can't think."

Ezra pushed back his chair. "You heard him, sir. He's so tired he can't think. The boy needs rest after his ordeal in that hellhole. I wouldn't be surprised if he contracted an ague. If he falls ill, it's the Ring family who will need to answer for it. I should never have sent him to that place."

Slowly, Alexander stood, looking around the shadowy kitchen.

A child's wooden horse lay discarded on the floor,

half-hidden by a washtub. Alexander's own home was constantly littered with such things; with the little ones' dolls and hoops, the older ones' schoolbooks and dirty linen. He'd tripped over Noah's Ark just that morning and barked his shin on a table.

No matter how crowded their hired house at 26 Broadway became, with their own seven children in and out, ranging in age from Philip at Columbia to baby Betsy with her teeth just coming in, Eliza somehow always found room for more. Orphaned nephews, orphaned daughters of old friends; there was always a bed, always a place at the table.

"Why did Levi board with the Rings rather than living here, with you?"

Ezra shrugged. "I've two children of my own and a new one on the way. And it's good for a lad to have a place of his own. My journeymen board there too. It was convenient to the lumber yard. And I don't have the space myself."

"How many of your journeymen board at the Ring house?"

Ezra had to stop and think. "Three—and Levi's apprentice. As I said, it was convenient." His face darkened. "If I'd known, I'd never have let any of them near the place. But it seemed like a respectable house. Mrs. Ring—have you met her? She seemed like a sensible woman. And that there were young women there—well, what's the harm in a bit of flirtation provided it doesn't go too far? Levi was on good terms with all of them. He took—what was her name? the other one—to a charity sermon."

"Hope," Levi said hoarsely. "Her name is Hope."

"He paid more mind to Hope than to Elma. Elma couldn't bear it and threw herself into a well. The family doesn't want to admit it and that's why they're pointing the finger at my boy."

Ezra pounded the words like nails, one after the other, as if he were trying to hammer them into Alexander's skull.

The clock on the mantel said it was well past seven. Alexander had an appointment to keep at eight o'clock, to the north of the city, in the stronghold of his enemy.

"Our first order of business is to stem the tide of public condemnation. I go to meet with Colonel Burr and Mr. Livingston to discuss how best to go about it. After that"—Alexander looked back at Levi, hunched in his seat by the fire—"we can begin to determine the truth of the matter."

"The girl killed herself," said Ezra Weeks firmly. "And that's the truth of it."

Chapter Four

Resolve to succeed and you cannot fail.

—Aaron Burr, 1799

New York City
January 7, 1800

I've come from Ezra Weeks." Hamilton stood in the doorway of Aaron Burr's drawing room, steaming with cold and self-importance.

Never mind a good evening or the other social niceties. The man had demanded this meeting and then arrived late. Why bother to pretend to courtesy?

"How kind you are to honor us with your presence," said Aaron gently. "Do come in. As you see, Brockholst has preceded you."

Hamilton gave a curt nod to the tall man sprawled in Aaron's favorite chair, with the chintz cover, in blue, to match the window curtains. "Livingston."

Brockholst didn't even bother to nod. He just glowered. "Hamilton."

It was going to be, Aaron could see, an utterly delightful evening.

"Forgive me for not offering supper. My Theodosia is indisposed, so I find myself a bachelor, reduced to cold meats."

To his credit, Hamilton looked genuinely concerned. "It's nothing serious, I trust? When Philip was ill—"

"A simple ague." In fact, Aaron's daughter Theodosia was quite recovered, more than well enough to preside at the table, but Aaron had no intention of rewarding the man for pushing in where he wasn't wanted.

Hamilton had insisted upon a meeting; Aaron had determined the place and manner of it.

Richmond Hill was at its best at night. In the candlelight, the pale patches where paintings had once hung were less apparent. Between dusk and dawn, Aaron could imagine Richmond Hill as it had once been, crammed with Turkey carpets and China porcelain, lyre-backed chairs from France and a liquor case from Holland. He missed his inlaid card tables and his marble side tables, each chosen with such care—all sold two years ago in the wake of a disastrous financial loss.

He would buy them back and better. Once he had

recouped his finances. The fledgling Manhattan Company was serving its purpose nicely, but the monies Aaron had redirected to himself from its coffers were just a morsel in the maw of his debts.

Since Hamilton had no interest in polite nothings, Aaron went straight to the point. "I understand you have decided to interest yourself in the matter of Levi Weeks."

Brockholst could be heard to mutter something that sounded like "damned interfering puppy."

Aaron hoped he would contain himself. The last thing they needed was a duel.

Brockholst had been fortunate not to be prosecuted for his last encounter, in which James Jones had publicly tweaked Brockholst's noble Roman nose and been rewarded with a bullet to the groin and a swift trip to the cemetery. Aaron needed Brockholst at his side in the upcoming elections, not immured in the Bridewell like Levi Weeks.

"It's a travesty." Hamilton was wringing his hands, actually wringing his hands, like a third-rate actor playing Lady Macbeth.

What a loss to the stage he was. Aaron spared a moment's regret the man hadn't taken to the boards and let politics be; what a boon to public life that would have been.

"Do sit down," Aaron suggested. "May I offer you a glass of claret? It's just lately arrived from France."

Naturally, Hamilton had no interest in taking a seat. He was too busy wearing a track on Aaron's one remaining Turkey carpet. "The boy has been sacrificed on the altar of public opinion. A thousand tongues of rumor lash him about. Even his fellow inmates in the prison have declared him guilty and wreaked their vengeance upon his unresisting frame. This boy—only a boy—faces the gallows."

"How public-spirited you are to interest yourself in his fate," Aaron murmured.

"Considering he had no representation before," growled Brockholst into his own glass of claret.

Hamilton let that slide off him, as he had let so many things slide off him. Women, for example. "If we are to prevent this boy being sacrificed to the coarse appetites of the common mob, we must discuss our strategy for his defense."

"There's nothing to discuss," Brockholst said tersely. "The girl had a vial of laudanum. A roomful of people heard her say if she could she would swallow it whole."

"And the bruises?" Hamilton countered fiercely.

"Can be accounted for by the effect of submersion upon the corpse." Aaron's patience was beginning to wane. It was time to bring this meeting to a close. Let

Hamilton see they had the matter well in hand. "The doctors who performed the autopsy found no conclusive evidence of violence. They will attest to that."

"I spoke to Dr. Hosack this morning." Of course he had. Aaron might have guessed. Whatever the topic, Hamilton must play the expert.

"Dr. Hosack," said Aaron, "did not perform the autopsy."

"No, but he viewed the body, and saw, in addition to the general discoloration caused by submersion, a series of spots around the windpipe of the sort that might be effected by a hand grasping the throat." Hamilton paused in his peripatetics around the room to draw some air into his own windpipe, his sky-blue waistcoat swelling. "He is firmly of the opinion that the livid marks on her neck could only have been caused by violence."

"Opinion is little better than rumor," said Aaron. "Mere empty air. I wonder that you would give it credence."

"The girl said she would kill herself and she did," said Brockholst.

Hamilton's gold buttons glinted in the candlelight. "Levi Weeks didn't appear to believe so."

"Levi Weeks would do well to believe so. His neck depends on it. Claret?" Aaron tipped the decanter over the glass without waiting for Hamilton's answer. Apparently, their unwanted co-counsel needed to be reminded which side he served. "We can find a dozen people to swear that the girl had a melancholy disposition."

"Levi Weeks described her as lively."

Levi Weeks didn't know what was good for him. Neither did Alexander Hamilton.

Aaron held out the glass of claret to Hamilton. "What can one expect? The girl was a bastard. They are notoriously prone to violent humors."

Hamilton's hand shook on the stem of the glass. For a moment, Aaron thought it would fall, which would be a pity, since it would break up the set. Hamilton managed to retain his grip on the glass, but he couldn't hide the flush that spread up from his cravat straight to the tips of his ears.

Really, the man was almost too easy to goad.

Aaron gave him a moment to stew, and then said smoothly, "In this case, it works to our benefit. If the girl did away with herself . . . why, then, Levi Weeks is saved."

"But if she didn't?" Hamilton's pale skin was suffused with color; Aaron couldn't imagine how he'd endured a tropical climate. "One must entertain all possibilities."

"My dear Hamilton, I prefer to entertain only by invitation."

Brockholst snorted with amusement.

Hamilton's fingers tightened on the stem of his glass. "I should think that justice should be the object of any practitioner at the bar. The girl's associates should be questioned, her circumstances examined. Who was by the well that night? Are there houses near enough that someone might have overheard an altercation—or noted the lack of one?"

"Why not consult the man who carts away the morning soil or the watchman napping in his box?" inquired Brockholst sarcastically.

"Why not, indeed?" murmured Aaron. A delightful prospect was beginning to open itself before him. Hamilton, a victim of his own industry. "If you must satisfy the dictates of your conscience . . . by all means. One wouldn't want to work an injustice to that poor girl or her family."

Brockholst tossed back the rest of his claret. "That's young Colden's obligation as prosecutor, not ours."

"And we may be sure he will fulfill it," said Aaron meaningfully. "Diligently."

"Diligently, yes. Intelligently, no," said Brockholst dismissively. "The boy is like a farmer told to plow a furrow. He'll move forward regardless of what lies in his path."

"Or what comes at him from the side?" Aaron suggested.

Brockholst allowed himself a grim smile. "Colden still believes he won the Pastano case."

"The Portuguese man who stabbed his landlady? I thought you gave that one to him rather too easily."

Brockholst made a face of disgust. "It never occurred to Colden to ask why we never put up a fight—and why all of our testimony was about Pastano's mental state. I've petitioned the legislature to pardon him on grounds of insanity."

"That should unnerve Colden nicely," commented Aaron. For all his maddening habits, it was indisputable that no one knew how to work the more subtle mechanisms of the law better than Brockholst.

Hamilton frowned at them both, clearly not liking the tone of the conversation. Hamilton liked cleverness only when it was his own; for everyone else, he adopted a high moral tone. "That was all very well for Pastano. He was found with blood on his hands. But here—it would do our client a disservice to win by a trick. He deserves nothing less than to have his name cleared of any blot—not to mention the girl, whose soul cries out for justice."

"You sound like a handbill," observed Brockholst dispassionately. "Did you see her sheeted form gibbering by the well?"

Aaron moved between the men under the guise of refilling Brockholst's glass. "Our duty is clear. We must make certain our young carpenter was where he claims that evening. Someone must speak to John McComb—and inquire of the other residents of the street in case they might recollect Levi's comings and goings."

Brockholst snorted. "Would you also ask at the tavern to discover what he imbibed and in what quantities?"

"If it might have a bearing on his actions that night, yes," said Aaron. For a man of his acumen, there were times when Brockholst could be remarkably obtuse. "I would attend to it myself, but I have business that calls me to Philadelphia. . . ."

"I'll go." Really, it was too easy. Hamilton rose to the suggestion like a fish to the lure.

"You might speak to the family as well," Aaron suggested, enjoying himself immensely. "Did Mrs. Ring see young Levi leave with the girl that night? The other boarders in the house—can any of them lend credence to the claim that Levi meant to marry her? The family insists upon it . . . but, then, they would."

"They have the whole town believing it." Hamilton was so lost in the problem at hand, he was entirely oblivious to Aaron's purpose. He spoke as though they were colleagues, consulting. It had been the same with the Manhattan Company. Appeal to the man, flatter his judgment, and he was yours. "Angelica and Eliza say it is the talk of the tea tables. Miss de Hart assured them on the best authority that Levi Weeks was already married to Miss Julianna Sands and, wishing to free himself of the entanglement, flung her into a well."

"Of course they would," said Brockholst with disgust. "It reads like a novel by Mr. Richardson. The virtuous girl seduced and betrayed. . . . We've all heard that tale before. It's the sort of thing girls pass around among themselves and giggle."

Aaron preferred the novels of Mme d'Arblay to those of Mr. Richardson, but he decided to allow that to pass. "Then we must find a different tale to tell them. A piece, printed in one of the papers, suggesting to the public that they suspend their judgment. . . ."

"I'll write it," said Hamilton immediately.

As much as Aaron desired to keep Hamilton busy, the last thing they needed was one of Hamilton's impenetrable screeds, a thousand words where ten were needed, all of them sound and fury, and laden with unnecessary clauses. Besides, Aaron didn't trust Hamilton to deliver the right message, which was that the girl, prone to melancholy, had taken her own life. Entertaining all possibilities was very well—and Aaron was very happy to let Hamilton waste his time entertaining them—but Aaron had a case to win.

"My dear fellow, we have already overtaxed you! We mustn't batten on your generosity of spirit—or take you away from your valuable work defending us from the French."

Ah, he'd hit a nerve there.

"Besides, we have our litigation in Albany to consider. But we mustn't discuss that here, with our opposition in earshot." Taking Hamilton's arm, Aaron led him to the door, casting a humorous look over his shoulder at Brockholst, their opponent in the commercial case of *Le Guen v. Gouverneur and Kemble*. "Alexis will see you out. I look forward to hearing what you discover on behalf of our young friend. You're wise to begin before we need to head north."

Aaron's manservant, Alexis, was waiting with Hamilton's hat, gloves, and cloak. Aaron bid the other man a genial farewell, and waited until the light of Alexis's candle had disappeared down the stairs before returning to Brockholst.

"Will you stay a moment? I have some other matters to put to you."

Brockholst looked past him at the doorway. "That coxcomb puts me in ill humor."

"One tolerates what one must—when one must."

Aaron poured a small measure of brandy into a glass; only the best brandy and the best glass, both from France.

"He'll ruin our case."

"Will he? It seems unlikely he would discover anything which would unsettle the presumption of suicide."

"Unless young Weeks is guilty," said Brockholst bluntly.

"Are you afraid our exuberant Alexander will discover something to our client's discredit? I doubt it. Ezra Weeks is a careful man."

"The trouble with turning over rocks is that one might not like what one finds under them."

"Whatever we find, we'll handle with gloves—and bury it again, if we must," Aaron said soothingly.

Incisively intelligent, incurably erratic, with the broad sense of humor of a schoolboy, Brockholst was an ally who needed careful managing.

But then, who didn't? The only one Aaron could fully trust was his Theodosia.

"I don't like his presumption any more than you do, but it works to our advantage. Let Hamilton weary himself chasing a phantom. We have other fish to fry."

Brockholst scowled over his brandy. "Hamilton has joined Troup in acting against me in the Cooper matter."

"A dispute over land, was it?" Everyone was always

being sued over land speculation. It was a land speculation that had ruined Aaron's finances, stripped his house bare—and Hamilton, who had litigated the case that had beggared him. It was like Brockholst to take it personally. "Hamilton probably needs the fees."

"He's doing it to persecute me. Cooper," added Brockholst pointedly, "is a Federalist. He's misconstrued the whole matter. It's nothing more than a ploy to waste my time and sully my name."

"If it is a ploy, it's a weak one. We'll make them pay at the polls." Aaron deemed it time to get to the heart of the matter, or else Brockholst would stay brooding and drinking his brandy all night. Aaron already owed a formidable amount to his wine merchant. "I had hoped you would do us the honor of putting yourself forward as a candidate for the assembly in the spring elections."

"I don't know...."

"Governor Clinton has agreed to serve."

Brockholst sat up straight in his chair. "I thought he'd resolved never again to enter office!"

Aaron played his winning card. "And General Horatio Gates."

"The hero of the Saratoga?" If any man was revered as much as President Washington for his military prowess, it was General Gates. "He's never run for office."

"He is prepared to rise to the needs of the hour."

In fact, Gates was decidedly undecided, but that, Aaron felt, was a triumph, given the man's well-known reluctance to sink into the pit of politics. He had no doubt he could bring Gates around—with Governor Clinton and a Livingston on the ticket.

"We also have Henry Rutgers and John Broome." Aaron named two more heroes of the Revolution. He licked a drop of brandy off the side of his glass. "Venerable patriots whose love for their country compels them to battle the abandoned and reckless policies of General Hamilton."

"You look like the cat who got the cream," Brockholst mocked, but Aaron could tell he had him, even before he added, "In that case . . . I'll do it."

"Your country thanks you," said Aaron, and held out the decanter to top up Brockholst's glass.

A Clinton, a Livingston, and a slew of war heroes. Let Hamilton top that.

"Who does Hamilton mean to put forward for the Federalists?"

"As far as I can find"—and Aaron had found a great deal—"not many of note. Oh, and our young friend Cadwallader Colden."

Brockholst's eyes narrowed. "Would Hamilton insist upon taking up the case of Levi Weeks only to hand the victory to Colden?"

For a moment, Aaron felt a trickle of unease. But only for a moment. "And risk his reputation in the process? It seems unlikely. No. He wouldn't want to be seen to fail so publicly."

Not to mention that it would be entirely unlike Hamilton to conjure anything quite that subtle. Hamilton was like a child who thought he was being devious in his theft of tarts with the jam smeared all over his face. Actual intrigue was beyond him.

"Hamilton has once again been too clever for his own good. Humiliate Colden—and he humiliates one of his few candidates with any standing. Throw the case to Colden—and he humiliates himself. Which of the two do you think our coxcomb will choose?"

"Hmmm." Aaron could see Brockholst turning the problem around in his mind, looking for unexpected pitfalls.

"I'll start our work in hand before I leave for Philadelphia tomorrow. We lay the foundations of the case, and let Hamilton waste his time as he will."

"I'm still not sure it's wise," said Brockholst, but he heaved himself out of his chair and let himself be led to the door, where Alexis was waiting with his cloak. "What is this business in Philadelphia?"

"Oh, a trifling thing." A trifling matter of wheedling a loan of twelve thousand dollars from a Philadelphia merchant to whom he already owed several times that—but Aaron had no doubt he could convince him that it would be less trouble to make the loan than refuse.

But before he left for Philadelphia, he had a defense to undertake—all the more urgently for the fear that Hamilton might try to write something first.

In his depleted library, surrounded by the books he hadn't been able to bring himself to sell, Aaron pulled up one of his few remaining mahogany chairs to a small table, took out a fresh sheet of paper, and began to write.

The public are desired to suspend their opinions respecting the cause of the death of a young woman whose body was lately found in a well. . . .

Chapter Five

However some circumstances that have been published may seem to justify the horrid imputation of her murder which has been thrown on a certain young man, yet there are others which strongly militate against it, and appear to establish his innocence in an unquestionable manner. We understand he has, contrary to some accounts, the universal testimony in favor of his character. He is a moral, sober, industrious, amiable man.

—Anonymous piece in the *New-York Daily Advertiser*, January 9, 1800

New York City
January 9, 1800

"He has no conceivable temptation to perform such an atrocious action—that's a bald-faced lie!"
"You won't forget David's birthday?" The coffeepot hove distractingly into Cadwallader's line of vision.

Cadwallader Colden, assistant attorney general of the city of New York, moved himself and the *New-York Daily Advertiser* out of the way of the coffeepot.

"*She had several times been heard to utter expressions of melancholy and throw out threats of self-destruction, particularly the afternoon before.*" Cadwallader set the paper down slowly on the table, his eyes still fixed on the page. "They mean to make out the girl killed herself."

"Cadwallader!" The coffeepot plonked down next to him.

Cadwallader ignored it. "*Several other circumstances have come to our knowledge . . .* What circumstances?"

"Could you perhaps turn your mind to the circumstance of your only child's birthday?" Maria's tone was as acid as the coffee. "Which happens to be today?"

Cadwallader shook his head, trying to clear it. *No conceivable temptation . . .* "Of course. Certainly. It's just this matter of the girl in the well. . . ."

An easy, straightforward case. Or so it had seemed. Until today.

"There's also the matter of your son's third birthday."

"Yes. Certainly. They might have had the decency to make themselves known, whoever it was who wrote this piece." Cadwallader picked up the paper again, giving it an irritated flap. "It might be Colonel Burr—

Josiah told me Weeks retained Livingston and Burr for the defense. Livingston didn't put up much of a show in the Pastano case . . . and this doesn't sound in his style . . . but Burr. It might be Burr."

Livingston he'd faced off against before. The man was formidable—formidable and cutting—but one felt like one knew where one stood with him. Burr was slippery, tricksy. Look at the way he'd turned the Tammany Society from a philosophical society to a political organization. Cadwallader still felt sore over that. He'd enjoyed the old days of Tammany, when they debated topics like the true nature of man, not how many votes could be got for Burr's Democratic-Republicans. Was man fundamentally good or evil? These were questions that deserved proper consideration; the nature of man called for as much study as Cadwallader's botanist aunt would give to the veining of a leaf.

But these days, there was no room for abstract argument: there was only partisan combat and sharp elbows.

It would be just like Burr to place anonymous insinuations in the paper. "*She was not, as it was said, pregnant, nor can it be proved that he was under an engagement to marry her.*" It was true that the autopsy had established that Elma Sands wasn't pregnant, but to claim there was no engagement . . . "What kind of proof do they expect? A written bond?"

"My father and Ben and Susanna will be here at four," said Maria in a clipped voice.

That was the thing to do. Talk to the family, verify their testimony. "I'll need to speak to the family," said Cadwallader decidedly. "I wonder if there was anyone else to whom she might have spoken about her plans to be married. . . . One of the neighbors, perhaps."

Marie tossed her serviette down on the table and pushed back her chair with an audible scrape. "Be here at four," she said sharply. "And don't forget to stop at Monsieur de Singeron's confectionery to pick up the plum cake I commissioned."

Cadwallader looked up from the paper. "You commissioned a plum cake?"

The door of the dining parlor slammed behind his wife.

For a moment, Cadwallader considered going after her, apologizing, before deciding, on the whole, that it was probably easier and more comfortable to let her work out her spleen on her own. He thought wistfully of the early days of their marriage, when Maria had entered into his interests and the breakfast table had been a place of domestic and intellectual harmony. But then had come a string of disappointments—that was what Maria called them, disappointments—and with each, Maria had withdrawn a little further from him, spending more time with her parents and siblings. When David had been born, all had been happiness for a bit—but David's safe delivery proved the exception rather than the rule. They'd had another disappointment that autumn, close on the heels of the death of Maria's mother in August.

Cadwallader had suggested a visit to the country, a sojourn in the south, a spa, a European tour—but Maria didn't want to risk David to the vagaries of travel or to his father's sole care at home. No use to point out David had a perfectly good nursemaid and a house full of servants. Maria refused to countenance the prospect.

Vaguely, Cadwallader thought it would be quite a good thing if they had another child. It would give Maria someone else on whom to practice her ideas of Republican motherhood. Not that she wasn't a wonderful mother to young David. And David—if a man were to have only one child in this life, it were well that it be one like David, so clever, so sunny-natured. Most of the time.

If Maria were feeling more herself, she would understand what this case meant. They were already saying that Cadwallader wasn't fit for office, that he'd been given this position only because his late sister's husband, Josiah Hoffman, was the attorney general. And perhaps that was so, but that didn't mean that Cadwallader couldn't make a success of it.

It was just that he hadn't managed to make a success of it quite yet. There had been that embarrassing business of the woman found strangled in a cistern in December. Rose Malone. A widow, remarried a week. Cadwallader had been so sure the new husband had done it—it was usually the husband—until the husband proved to have been unimpeachably elsewhere. With no other suspects, they'd quietly released the husband from the Bridewell and dropped the case.

At least Cadwallader had Pastano to point to. Of course, Pastano wasn't anything to brag about. The man had been discovered in the act of stabbing his landlady. But still. It was a mark on the correct side of the ledger.

But this—this was different. This was no widow stuffed into a cistern or a Portuguese landlady stabbed by her compatriot. This was a young woman in all the hopeful blush of youth, shamefully betrayed.

Cadwallader's fingers itched to write a scathing rebuttal—but a fragment of rhyme he had been reading to David last night from his worn copy of *A Little Pretty Pocket-Book* played through his head: *Think ere you speak, for words once flown, / Once uttered, are no more your own.*

David had made faces and demanded they move on to *Jack the Giant-Killer*—and perhaps there was a metaphor too, given the stature of the two men Cadwallader was facing. Burr could write circles around him any day. Livingston's grasp of the niceties of the law was unparalleled.

No, what he had to do was build a case they couldn't knock down, a towering edifice of evidence. Jack had outsmarted the giant, and so could he. Cadwallader smiled to himself at the notion, picturing David in his nightdress, his face fresh-scrubbed, his curls still damp around the edges. David wouldn't understand yet that this was a form of giant slaying too, but someday he would, and would be proud. Cadwallader would make him proud. And Maria too.

Maybe, if he could dispel this miasma of failure that hung about him, Maria would be happy again, and stop slamming coffeepots at the breakfast table. She'd broken the handle of the last one. Not that Cadwallader minded the cost—they could afford the porcelain—but he'd like to see her happier.

Rolling the offending paper into a tight cylinder under his arm, Cadwallader called for his gloves and his greatcoat and set out for Greenwich Street.

He felt recently as though he were always a few furlongs behind; he was wrong-footed in the courtroom, wrong-footed with Maria. Everything he touched went subtly wrong. And he couldn't for the life of him figure out why.

This was the turning point, Cadwallader told himself, as he knocked at the front door of the Ring boardinghouse. He would bestride the courtroom like a colossus. Or something like that.

Mrs. Ring answered the door herself, a child clinging to her leg, her cheeks flushed with the heat of the kitchen, and flour smeared in the auburn hair that escaped her cap. At the sight of Cadwallader, her expression veered between consternation and hope.

"Mr. Colden, has thee news for us?"

None that would cheer her. Levi Weeks had been released on bail from the Bridewell and his lawyers were spreading rumor and innuendo about Elma.

Cadwallader decided not to share that bit.

"It's your sister Miss Hope Sands, I wish to see," he said soothingly. "Just a trifling matter of ascertaining some details."

Mrs. Ring's face fell, but she regained control of herself rapidly. "If thee will sit in the front room? Hope is at work in the millinery. I shall fetch her to thee."

The child, younger than David, with the plump

fingers of babyhood, peeped out from behind Mrs. Ring's gray skirt. Cadwallader wiggled his fingers at her. The child smiled back before ducking away again.

"Eliza!" Mrs. Ring scooped the girl up in her arms. "Come. Let us fetch thy aunt."

Eliza snuck another look at Cadwallader over her mother's shoulder, one thumb stuck in her mouth.

The front room was painfully spare, a stark contrast to his own parlor, which was hung with chintz and adorned with portraits of Cadwallader's grandparents and flower drawings by his aunt Jane, the celebrated botanist. It was very hard being the least distinguished member of a distinguished family, a family bursting with statesmen and scholars. Some, like his grandfather, had managed to be both. It was true that his father hadn't done anything very particular—other than choose the wrong side of the recent conflict—but he'd got out of it by dying, leaving Cadwallader with the burden of trying to live up to his family's legacy.

Mrs. Ring ushered in Miss Hope Sands, excusing herself with apologies that were backed by the smell of something burning in the kitchen.

Cadwallader hovered, waiting for Miss Sands to be seated. "I fear I must ask you some . . . delicate questions."

Miss Hope Sands seated herself on the settle, straight-backed, her hands pressed into a knot in her lap. Her hair was a nondescript light brown instead of her sister's auburn, but there was something about the set of her chin and a certain light in her eyes that marked her as a person not to be ignored. "I will answer whatever thee need ask."

Cadwallader felt inexplicably reassured by that firm alto voice. Here was a witness who would say what she said and mean it. "Did Miss Elma Sands—did your cousin—did she ever utter expressions of melancholy? Or threats of self-destruction?"

Miss Sands's lips pressed tightly together. "It was only the once."

"Do you mean to tell me she did utter expressions of melancholy? The sort that anyone might utter upon a trying occasion?" Cadwallader asked hopefully.

Miss Sands looked past him, at the mantelpiece, which was bare except for a simply carved mantel clock. "It was only one of Elma's tricks."

Cadwallader sat down, and wished he hadn't. He could feel the hard edge of the settle digging into the backs of his thighs. "What sort of trick?"

Miss Sands released a long sigh. "My cousin had an illness last autumn. It left her in a great deal of pain—she said." Her lip curled in a way richly indicative of her feelings toward her cousin. But girls often bickered to no purpose. Cadwallader remembered his sisters sparring in their youth. Both now dead, taken from him and each other too soon. "Dr. Snedecker left a vial of laudanum with her. One night, as we were gathered here, in the front room, Elma made a show of holding up the bottle and pretending to drink from it. She said she should not be afraid to drink it whole."

"Only pretending?"

"The stopper was in." There was a fine note of irony in Miss Hope Sands's voice that made her sound older than her years. "Elias said, 'Foolish creature, it would kill thee,' to which Elma replied she wouldn't mind if it did, or something to that purpose. It was just for the attention. She hadn't any intention of drinking it. Not more than the prescribed drops."

Cadwallader didn't like the sound of this at all. He could only imagine what Burr would make of this—and of him—on the stand. "You're quite certain of that?"

"If she had meant to drink it, she would," said Hope firmly. "She only wanted us to beg her not to."

"Was anyone else present?" Of course, someone must have been, or how else would the author of that piece in the paper have heard? But perhaps whoever it was had heard only a whisper, a rumor, and not the whole of it. . . .

"My sister. Elias. I don't recall whether Levi was

present. I don't believe he was." Cadwallader had a moment of relief, before she added, "Oh, and Timothy Crane, one of our boarders."

Cadwallader had an unpleasant sinking feeling. "Isn't he one of Ezra Weeks's journeymen?"

"Most of our boarders are," said Miss Sands. "We've only two who aren't."

A house full of men dependent on Ezra Weeks, at least one of whom had witnessed Elma Sands threaten to take her own life. This got worse and worse. "She held the whole vial to her mouth."

"In jest! She only meant to tease us."

"A strange sort of jest."

"She was angry Caty hadn't sent for the doctor when she was ill in November," said Hope Sands, in a forthright way that impressed Cadwallader. He hoped it would impress a jury as well. "She wanted to make us see how much she suffered."

"Why did no one tell me this before?" demanded Cadwallader, aggrieved.

Miss Sands set her chin. "Because it had nothing to do with anything."

He hoped she was right. "Do you believe your cousin might have taken her own life?"

"No."

"You seem very sure."

"I've never been more sure of anything—except my redeemer," she added as an afterthought. Her father, Cadwallader remembered, was rather famous as a preacher. He wondered if that would lend her testimony more credence. "Elma would never have done anything to harm herself. She intended to have a grand future, she told me—married to Levi."

"And you're quite sure she said she was going to be married to Levi?"

Hope Sands paused slightly before answering. A shadow crossed her face. Remembering her cousin, thought Cadwallader approvingly. It was a becoming show of emotion.

"Yes," she said at last. "She told me the week before. We were trimming hats. I ran a pin through my finger when she told me."

She rubbed her thumb absently against her finger as though she could still feel the remembered wound.

"She—she told me she was to be married the following Sunday. She told me I wasn't to tell, not even Caty. He'd wanted complete secrecy—she wasn't to have told me, but—but she thought I ought to know."

"Why so much secrecy?"

"We know that—now—don't we?" Hope spoke in short bursts, her hands curled in fists in her lap. The passion in her voice made a mockery of the sober gray of her dress. "If she hadn't told me—if I hadn't told Caty—she might have disappeared and none the wiser. He could have stayed here—talking, laughing, pretending to goodness—and all the while, Elma—"

Cadwallader gave her a moment to compose herself before asking, "On the day of her, er, wedding . . . did she seem—apprehensive? Unhappy? Melancholy, even?"

"*Melancholy?* She was elated," said Hope Sands fiercely. "She *bedecked* herself for him. She put on her finest clothes—she borrowed Peggy's handkerchief—she adorned herself like a sacrifice for the altar."

A memory stirred. Cadwallader's Loyalist father had sent him to be educated in England; he remembered sitting in the Drury Lane theater, watching the legendary Kemble as Hamlet. Sarah Siddons had played Ophelia. He'd imagined himself in love with her, like half the bucks in the audience. What it had been to be sixteen years old, thrilling to imaginary tragedy, not stumbling through the aftermath of the reality of one.

"*I thought thy bride-bed to have deck'd, sweet maid / And not have strew'd thy grave,*" murmured Cadwallader.

"Is that what they're saying in the papers?"

"No, it's—never mind." Cadwallader got hold of himself. Perhaps Ophelia wasn't the best comparison. Ophelia had drowned herself.

Cadwallader forced his attention back to the matter at hand. "You are quite positive your cousin had no idea of drowning herself?"

"My cousin," said Hope Sands, rising to her feet, "had no idea of anything but Levi Weeks. She thought to go to her bridal bed—and he drove her to her grave."

Chapter Six

QUESTION BY PRISONER'S COUNSEL: Did not Levi pay as much attention to Hope Sands, as he did to Elma?

ANSWER: Yes, I think he did and more too.

—From the testimony of Margaret (Peggy) Clark at the trial of Levi Weeks

New York City
January 9, 1800

Hope stayed in the front room after the lawyer had left, staring at her own hands, empty and idle.

She should go back to the millinery. Peggy and three other girls were hard at work; Hope had left her own work half-finished. The millinery, like the boardinghouse, was Caty's idea, and like everything Caty put her mind to, she had made a success of it. At their busiest times, they had as many as twenty women shaping straw, sewing on beads and blond lace, securing flowers and feathers.

Hope could sew on a feather so it stayed—but Elma had a genius for the work. She could take a bit of white crepe and shape it into a turban, or find an old black beaver hat, add a gold chain and a single feather, and turn it into the latest word from London.

Sometimes Elma would try them on, modeling her creations for the others—the same way when they were little she'd take a handful of flowers and weave them into crowns of bugleweeds and touch-me-nots, Turk's-cap and tiger lilies. She'd woven Hope crowns too, in those long-ago days when they'd been girls together, escaping their chores in the fields outside the house in New Cornwall.

Hope's mother had looked sadly at them, and spoken of the ways of the flesh and frippery. The confiscated crowns had frizzled on the grate, reduced to ash. Elma's mother hadn't said anything at all, only looked down and gone on sanding the floor, board by board.

After that Elma had kept her fripperies to herself.

Hope hadn't told about Elma's cache of discarded finery: ripped lace, stained silk, a broken comb, a fan and embroidered stomacher Granny Mercy had worn to local assemblies before Father had convinced them to turn Quaker and renounce such things. Hope had never told anyone about the purloined paper on which Elma sketched flowers and people and landscapes, some real, some fantastical, palaces and princes, and, over and over, a man in the dark blue coat of a Continental Army officer.

Hope had always kept her secrets for her.

Until Levi.

You mustn't tell, Elma had said, that day in the millinery, just as if they were children again, and Elma enlisting Hope's aid in something they both knew to be forbidden. Jumping in the creek; tearing blank pages from the back of one of Father's books to draw on; borrowing Caty's comb and then claiming she hadn't.

If I mustn't tell, then why tell me? Hope had demanded. She wasn't in a mood to play confidante.

But Elma went on anyway, leaning close, her breath tickling Hope's ear. *Don't tell Caty. I'm to be married on Sunday.*

To Levi? Hope had blurted out, and then wished she hadn't. Of course to Levi. It had always been Levi, ever since they'd come back from the country. Levi who had sat by Elma's bed hour by hour when Elma had been taken ill, refusing Hope's offer to take a turn tending her. Levi who had private jokes with Elma, ones Hope couldn't follow.

Elma had only smiled in that dangerous way she had when they were little, when she was about to propose something truly dreadful, and held up the hat she was working on. *What do you think? Do I look like a bride?*

Thee looks like thee has three hats to trim and only an hour until the light wanes, Hope snapped back, and Elma leaned over and kissed her on the cheek.

When I am married and have a home of my own, you will come to me, and wear silk and eat iced cakes.

A fine castle in the air thee has built thyself, Hope mocked, but she had to drop her eyes quickly over her hat to hide the pang the words had given her: Elma, married to Levi, in that fine house he always talked of building.

One day, he'd said shyly, as he and Hope had walked to the charity sermon together, one day he'd build a house to his own design, with a curving stair and a classical pediment. She didn't think him foolish for it? His brother thought him foolish, told him to concentrate on his work and stop scribbling.

No, she didn't think him foolish.

But it was Elma who would someday run up that curving stair, Elma's children who would play in the fine, bright nursery Levi planned on his imaginary top floor. There had been a time—walking with Levi in the crisp December night, sitting down with him at his brother's table, holding his niece on her knee—when Hope had imagined herself into that home. Not for the silks and iced cakes, but for Levi, for the light in his eyes when he smiled at her, the feel of his hand on her elbow helping her over a slick patch in the street, the endearing boyishness as he confided his dreams of designing homes like John McComb, but better.

That whole long week after Elma told Hope had been an agony, going through the motions of daily life, knowing that a week from now, five days from now, three days from now, Elma would be Mrs. Levi Weeks.

As they bent over their work, Elma would lean to Hope and murmur things like, *Maybe I'll commission you to make one like this for me when I'm married*, and *You haven't told Caty, have you?* and Hope would have to pretend not to hear.

Sidelong glances, murmured comments. A conspiracy of which Hope had no desire to be a part. *Should I wear this for my wedding? I hope it will be fair weather Sunday night.*

Every word a pinprick. Hope had gone to meeting and prayed for peace, prayed for generosity of spirit, prayed for kindness and understanding, but jealousy had squirmed in her like maggots on meat.

"Hope?" Hope started as Peggy's cheerful face appeared in the doorway. She and Elma and Peggy—how they'd laughed together. Before Levi came and cut up all their peace.

"Did thee need me? I didn't mean to leave thee with all the work. Thee can scold me if thee like."

"I don't mind. You can do mine tomorrow." Peggy glanced behind her, lowering her voice to a hiss. "You've a caller."

"A caller?"

"I'll not be far if you want me." Peggy whisked out of the way and past her stepped Levi.

Hope's chest felt tight; she couldn't breathe. He stood there, in the doorframe, his hat in his hand, that rip in his breeches Elma had mended for him, looking at her like there was no one else in the world, and she couldn't help it: she felt that sudden surge of joy that always attended his appearance.

He wasn't quite the same. His nose skewed slightly off-center, destroying the symmetry of his face, and there was a fading bruise next to one eye. It ought to have made him look raffish, but it didn't. The morning sun caught the golden lights in his hair, the broad planes of his cheekbones, the line of his throat beneath the crooked ties of his shirt.

"How dare thee show thy face here!"

"I had to see you."

Once she would have thrilled to those words. "Why? So thee can ask me to sign another *paper*?"

"That wasn't my idea, it was my brother's; you know it was my brother's." Levi took two eager strides toward her, stopping abruptly as Hope flinched away. "You know I would never have hurt her."

"Do I?" It wasn't fair that he could still look so appealing. If the form revealed the soul, his face should be dark and cankered; worms should crawl from his lying tongue; his hair should writhe with snakes. "I thought I knew thee. I was mistaken."

How dare he look so sorrowful? "You know there was nothing of that sort between us."

His lies gave her strength. Hope drew herself up to her full height. "I know thee was alone in her room with her with the door locked and not a candle lit between you."

Levi stared at her, his hat hanging forgotten on one hand. "I—how would you—"

Hope's eyes flickered sideways. "Dr. Snedecker bid me fetch Elma."

It was only a little lie. She'd been sitting on Elma's bed with her, talking about something she didn't remember, when Levi had come to the door—and Elma, out of Levi's sight, had arched her brows at

Hope, jerking her head slightly to the side. Hope had taken the hint and left. But at the bottom of the stairs, she'd removed her shoes and tiptoed back up.

She'd stood there, her ear to the door, hating herself, hating them, but all she'd heard was the sound of their whispers, muffled by the wood.

And then there had been a knock at the door below and she'd hastily run back down to find Peggy admitting Dr. Snedecker, there to check on Elma. She'd taken Peggy up with her to get Elma—as witness, she supposed, although why she should want a witness she wasn't quite sure.

Hope stared belligerently at her cousin's lover. "What did thee want with her in the dark with the door locked, Levi?"

Levi ran a hand through his hair, making a bit come free from his queue. He was always doing that. Hope used to find it endearing. And Elma would cluck and tie it back for him. *Destroying my handiwork*, she'd complain. *Why should I care when you'll only tie it back for me again?* he'd tease. And Hope would stand there, a fixed smile on her face, pretending she didn't feel an awkward third to their banter.

Levi didn't have Elma to tie back his hair for him anymore. It stuck out in wisps around his face. "It wasn't—if you had seen, you would know—it wasn't for courtship, but only for conversation!"

"If it were for conversation, why could thee not converse in the sitting room like any other person in this house? Do thee always lock the door for conversation? Thee didn't need a closed door to converse with me."

"For your honor . . ." Levi stammered.

"But not Elma's? Thee had no care for Elma's honor?" The color was rising and waning in Levi's cheeks, as changeable as an autumn leaf. Hope took courage from his discomfiture. "Richard Croucher says he saw thee together—in a way that could not be mistaken. Thou must have forgot to lock the door."

Levi scowled at her. "Richard Croucher would say anything against me. He holds a grudge."

"Because he spoke out for Elma? Do I hold a grudge against thee? Does Caty?"

"You didn't have to be so quick to judge me!"

"So quick? It's months I've watched thee!" Hope wished the words back the moment she said them, but it was too late. In a low voice, she added, "I would have had to be blind not to know what was between thee."

"It isn't what you think. I swear it."

"What use is thy swearing? Thee swears and forswears thyself as easily as thee draws breath."

"I never lied to you." Levi took a step forward, his eyes never leaving hers. She felt his gaze like a touch. "I never kept anything from you that was mine to keep."

He looked so earnest, so true, that Hope almost felt herself weakening. Almost.

"When Elma didn't come home on Monday—thee told Caty thee had no doubt it would turn out better than we thought. Why did thee say that?"

Levi's eyes dropped. He shook his head, silent.

Hope could feel the rage building in her. "How could thee? How could thee pretend thee didn't know? *If I knew something I would tell thee*, thee said." She took a cruel satisfaction from the way he flinched at her savage mockery of his words. "But Elma didn't keep thy secret. We *knew*."

"I never knew she told you we meant to marry!" he cried. Quickly he amended, "Because we didn't. I was never with her Sunday night. I was at my brother's—he'll swear to it."

"Did thy brother refuse to let thee marry her? Did he want thee to marry higher?"

Hope looked closely at Levi, watching his mouth open and close, as he stuttered and failed to speak. "She might have brought a suit against thee for breach of promise. A fine thing that would look for thy brother—and thee."

Levi made an inchoate noise of frustration. "She wouldn't marry me! She wouldn't even walk out with me! You know that better than any." His voice dropped. "It was you I asked to walk with me, Hope."

His eyes were light blue, like a rain-washed sky.

She could remember walking with him, large and warm and safe beside her. Sitting with him at the table in his brother's house, as his brother's wife poured her tea, and the baby made them all laugh crawling up onto Hope's lap. And she'd looked at him, and found him looking at her, and felt a warmth spread through her that had nothing at all to do with the tea.

"Thee left with her that night," Hope said stubbornly. "Just after eight. She waited until thee came and then thee both left."

"I left a little after eight but I never left with Elma. You would have known if you'd been here to see."

Hope put her chin up. "Caty said thee did. She said she heard thee whispering on the stair and then the door closed behind thee both."

Levi looked seriously at her. "Where were you that night, Hope? When I came home and asked for you, you weren't there."

Hope hesitated a moment. "I was at meeting. Thee knows that."

"Until midnight?"

"What would thee know of our meeting?" Hope snapped.

Levi looked at her searchingly, as though she were a beam he was scrutinizing for woodworm. "I know that Elias came back well before you did. He was here before I went out. Where were you, Hope?"

Hope gasped for breath, feeling the way she had when Elma had dared her to jump in the creek, and there had been that horrible moment when the waters had closed over her head and the sodden weight of her skirts had wrapped around her, before she scrabbled choking back to the surface. "Thee cannot mean—"

"If you quarreled—if there were an accident—"

"What would I be doing with Elma in Lispenard's Meadow? When she had said she was gone to be married to thee?"

"When *you* said she was gone to be married to me." The room felt horribly still. The boarders were all out, at work. Even the dust motes caught drifting in the afternoon sun seemed to slow and stop. "She never said anything to anyone else."

"Because thee enjoined her to secrecy!"

"It's your word—and your word only."

"Is that thy brother speaking too?" Hope asked bitterly. "Thee knows I'm only a woman—and a Friend. I cannot swear as thee do—or forswear myself neither."

Levi turned his hat around in his hand. "You weren't so particular once—when you came to church with me, and my brother's house."

"I wish I had been," spat Hope. "I wish thee had

never entered this house. I wish thee had never had an existence!"

Levi stared at her, the bruises around his eye livid against his white face, his eyes blazing.

"You may well get your wish." He turned to go, and then paused, the words torn out of him. "Will you watch when they hang me? Or will you be at *meeting*?"

"Go," croaked Hope. "Go before I tell Elias thee had the gall to cross his threshold. He's said he'll shoot thee if he sees thee."

"So he can avenge Elma's honor?" Levi gave a strange laugh, that turned into something like a sob. "Oh, Hope. *Hope.*"

She couldn't bear it, couldn't bear the way he was looking at her.

"Go," she said fiercely.

And he did.

Chapter Seven

Had it been true, that I had left every thing else to *follow the Drum*, my delinquency would not have been so great. But our military establishment offers too little inducement and is too precarious to have permitted a total dereliction of professional pursuits. The double occupation occasioned by these added to Military Duties, and the attentions which circumstances call me to pay to collateral objects, engage my time more than ever . . .

 —Alexander Hamilton to Rufus King,
 January 5, 1800

New York City
January 18, 1800

"Forgive me for receiving you like this." Elizabeth Weeks made an effort to push herself up against her pillows, wiggling into something closer to a sitting position.

Her husband dove forward to help her. "You know what the doctor said. You're to stay lying down."

"I can't lie down all the time." From the edge of annoyance in her voice, Alexander had the impression this wasn't the first time they had had this conversation.

"We lost the last one," said Weeks bluntly. "The doctor says we'll lose this one too unless she rests."

"We will impose upon you as little as possible," Harison said soothingly. "General Hamilton and I both know what it is to be in a delicate condition."

Elizabeth Weeks looked like she had thoughts about that, but she subsided against her pillows.

"Mr. Harison is here in his capacity of recorder of the city of New York to take your testimony in the event that you are unable to appear in court," Alexander explained carefully.

They all knew that what he really meant was that they were there to record Elizabeth Weeks's testimony in the event that she die in childbirth before Levi's case came to trial.

"I am happy to do whatever is needed to free Levi from this terrible charge," she murmured.

Alexander could hear the clock ticking, and not just the delicate porcelain clock on the mantel, decorated with gilt and cherubs.

It had been nearly two weeks since he had chosen to

interest himself in Levi Weeks's affairs, two weeks in which good intentions had bowed beneath the weight of obligation. What with planning a military academy, sorting out the shape of hats for his soldiers, berating James McHenry by letter, and plotting Burr's political downfall, there had been very little time to hunt down witnesses to establish the innocence of Levi Weeks.

It was suicide, Livingston insisted, and Burr agreed.

But it wasn't enough to assert that and leave it at that, even if Alexander agreed, which he didn't. There were reports, more reports than could credibly be dismissed as imagination or scandalmongering, of cries of distress from the vicinity of the well at a little before or after nine o'clock on the twenty-second of December.

Levi's time on that night needed to be accounted for, which was why Harison had accompanied Alexander here, to the Weeks house, on a Saturday, even though at the house on Broadway Alexander's three middle boys and Eliza's nephew were home from school in Staten Island for the day, bringing dirty linen and clumsy Latin translations and sending little William wild with the joy of having his older brothers at home.

It would, Eliza had made clear, be nice to have Alexander home while the boys were home, particularly since he meant to depart so soon for Albany and would be away for goodness only knew how long . . . but Elizabeth Weeks's baby might arrive at any time, depriving them of a key witness, and Alexander keenly felt how little time he had devoted to Levi's defense, how scattershot were his efforts, sandwiched between his other obligations, in the sleepless fog of the baby's nightly howling.

Elizabeth Weeks's testimony was crucial and her time limited.

Alexander pulled up a slipper chair by the bed. The upholstery was French silk, so rich that he could feel himself sliding off again. If the rest of the house was little more than an extension of the lumber yard, this room was an unexpected treasure hoard, in which Ezra Weeks had showered his bed-bound wife with all his growing prosperity could offer. Mahogany and fruitwood, gilt and silk; porcelain dishes holding candied sweetmeats and spiced nuts.

A one-legged wooden doll that lay forgotten on the brocade coverlet provided a homely touch amid the unexpected opulence.

"If I might?" Harison flipped the tails of his coat, seating himself at a small table Ezra Weeks had placed close by the bed, with paper and ink set out for writing. After going rapidly through the business of taking her oath, he asked, "Can you tell us what you recall from the evening of the twenty-second of December?"

"Levi was here with us," Ezra said immediately.

"Mr. Weeks," said Alexander, striving not to alienate the future builder of Eliza's house, "we must have it in Mrs. Weeks's own words."

Harison nodded reassuringly. "Now, my dear lady, you were saying?"

Elizabeth Weeks glanced at her husband. "We dined with my parents."

"Daniel Hitchcock—the lumber merchant," Ezra interposed. Given the price of wood, it seemed likely Ezra Weeks's father-in-law was a prosperous man.

"Levi came to us when we were drinking tea, just before candlelight. He often does. The children like to see their uncle." Elizabeth grimaced, shifting slightly.

Harison set down his pen, asking conversationally, "How many children do you have, Mrs. Weeks?"

"Two, George and Mary Ann. There was another boy before Mary Ann, but—"

Ezra Week took his wife's hand. "There'll be others."

Alexander had children of his own waiting for him. "When did Levi leave?"

Harison gave Alexander a reproachful look.

Elizabeth Weeks recalled herself with an effort. "Levi drank his tea with us—and then John McComb and his wife came in. Levi stayed for a time, but the McCombs didn't seem to be going, so . . ."

"The house clock had just struck eight when Levi left," said Ezra Weeks briefly. "The McCombs stayed for twenty or twenty-five minutes. I lighted them out, and by the time I returned Levi was at the table."

"Mrs. Weeks?" Alexander tried not to grit his teeth too audibly.

"Levi came back, oh, very shortly after the McCombs left." She exchanged a look with her husband. With the air of someone reciting a lesson, she said, "They left about twenty-five minutes after eight and Levi was back by the time Ezra returned from lighting them to the corner. He stayed with us for supper."

"My apprentice, Demas, will say the same," said Ezra.

Alexander had no doubt he would. "How did Levi's appetite seem to you?"

"What does that matter?" demanded Ezra Weeks.

"He ate a hearty supper," said Elizabeth Weeks. "He talked about the work for the next day. My love—tea—do you think—for our guests? I ought to have thought . . ."

"You're not to get up."

"I didn't mean to make the tea myself. Perhaps Sally . . . ? I'm so parched. . . ."

Ezra Weeks surged toward the door. "I won't be a moment. Don't overexert yourself."

Through the thin walls, they could hear him shouting for Sally. Elizabeth Weeks, Alexander thought, might look mild, but she had her own ways of managing her spouse.

"Ezra thinks the troubles brought on my illness," she said softly. "He fears this business with Levi will make us lose the babe. Levi—Levi feels terrible to have brought this trouble upon us. Not that it's his fault," she added quickly, looking alarmed. "Ezra wouldn't want you to think this was any of Levi's making."

Ezra, thought Alexander, had a great many strong opinions. "How did Levi seem to you that evening?"

"As ever." Her brow wrinkled, as if thought were a great effort. "He'd cut his leg that morning—I believe it still pained him. George likes to grab him around the leg. It's a game they have together. But other than that . . . he seemed cheerful. I think."

"Why did he go back to the Ring house at eight?"

Elizabeth Weeks smiled weakly. "If you're acquainted with John McComb, you know he can go on. Levi was waiting to get instructions from Ezra for the day's work—he does that every evening—and when it looked like John would never leave he took his hat and went back to the Ring house. There's so little space here," she added distractedly. "Ezra means to build our house . . . but he's in such demand, and there's so little time."

The city was expanding rapidly and a good builder was hard to find. All the more reason to resolve the Weeks case speedily in Levi's favor. "Did Levi say anything about being married to Elma Sands?"

Elizabeth Weeks looked at her swollen hands. The fingers had puffed so large that her rings were lost in the folds. "No. . . . Not to me. I had always thought—he seemed more interested in the other one. Hope. He brought her to us once." She showed a little more animation at the memory; Alexander could see a hint of the woman she must have been before this pregnancy sapped her strength. "She drank tea with us. Ezra—he had hopes Levi would look higher, but Miss Sands—Miss Hope—seemed a decent, well-mannered girl."

There couldn't be more than a few years between Hope Sands and Elizabeth Weeks—a few years and four pregnancies. They were all so young, thought Alexander ruefully. Young as he and Eliza had once been, a thousand years ago.

"Was Levi courting Miss Hope Sands?" If they could make a strong case it was Hope, not Elma, who had attracted Levi's interest, there went half of Colden's case, right there.

"I had thought—Levi—he's a kind boy, but not always—not the most firm-natured of souls. Ezra worries he's easily led." Elizabeth Weeks seemed to be having trouble catching her breath. "He needs a strong-natured wife—someone with sense—who can guide him."

Ezra strode in, his gaze fixing immediately on his wife. He didn't like what he saw. "Sally will be in with the tea. What's this about guiding him?"

"I was just saying—I had thought Hope Sands—the right sort of strong-minded girl—for Levi."

"He could do better," said Weeks, but his concern was clearly for his wife, not his brother. "You're not well."

"My head hurts," she said apologetically. "I can't seem to think."

"This was too much for you."

"We'll just read the statement and have Mrs. Weeks sign it," said Harison quickly. "About candlelight, or a little after, John McComb and his wife came in; Levi Weeks was then in the room, and remained with the company until after the house clock struck eight and then went away; to the best of your knowledge and belief, Mr. and Mrs. McComb left the house about twenty or twenty-five minutes after eight; after your husband lighted Mr. and Mrs. McComb out, before he had time to sit down, Levi Weeks came in, and remained with you, conversing on the business to be performed the next day—appeared cheerful, ate a hearty supper, and went off to his lodgings—"

"It must have been about ten o'clock," Elizabeth Weeks said faintly.

"As you believe, about ten o'clock." Harison added a note. ". . . saw no particular difference in his conduct or behavior. . . . Is that all correct, Mrs. Weeks?"

"Yes." Elizabeth Weeks wasn't paying attention to Harison. She struggled to sit up, all her interest focused on the door, through which a high-pitched voice was shouting, "Pull me! Pull me faster!"

Levi Weeks came into the room with a small boy attached to his leg and a toddler girl clinging to his neck. "Look, I've got a shackle around my ankle." He laughed, making a game of dragging his nephew along behind him.

His smile faded as he saw Alexander and Harison. He stopped short, leaving his nephew to howl, "Pull me! Pull me!"

"Mama!" The little girl wiggled to be put down. She made a dash toward the bed, and was firmly caught by her father.

"Don't climb on your mother," he said.

"I don't mind it," said Elizabeth Weeks, holding out her swollen hands to her daughter. "I've got your dolly."

Levi Weeks was staring horrified from Alexander to Ezra. "I didn't mean— About the shackle—"

"That will be the only sort of shackle you need bear. Don't worry. We have it all well in hand," Alexander said grandly, if not entirely truthfully. He was rewarded by Ezra Weeks's fierce nod of agreement. "We'll leave you now. I have shackles of my own home from school."

"Thank you, Mrs. Weeks," said Harison, and bowed gravely over her swollen hand. In a lower voice, he added to Alexander as they walked out of the house, "It seems hard to think that nice boy could have shoved that girl into the Manhattan Well."

"We can only hope a jury will feel the same way," Alexander said wryly. "Walk with me a way?"

"How far a way?" asked Harison warily. He had taken less exercise since Fanny had died.

"To the Manhattan Well. I want to see how long it takes to walk from here." If John McComb left the Weeks house at twenty-five past and Levi were back no more than ten minutes after that, then he would need to have gotten to the well, strangled his paramour, and made it back to his brother's kitchen table in the space of under half an hour. The operation would require efficiency, dispatch, and sheer ruthlessness—and even then, it might not be possible.

Harison considered the matter from a comfortably stationary position. "At least fifteen minutes, I would think. Maybe more—if it were dark or the weather were ill. And no, I'm not pacing it out with you now, even if the day is uncommon mild. Didn't you say you had promised to go home to your shackles?"

"I also promised Ezra Weeks I'd see his brother without one." Alexander had promised too many people too many things. "I leave tomorrow for Albany to argue for Le Guen before the Court of Errors."

"Tomorrow? Merciful heavens, man! You should certainly go home to your family! I can hire someone to pace the length to the well and back."

"That might be best. If an impartial party can show that it was impossible . . ." Then Alexander could go off to Albany with a good conscience.

"I take it Burr and Livingston will be in Albany with you?"

"On either side of the question." Alexander and Burr had been retained by the Huguenot merchant Le Guen against the firm of Gouverneur and Kemble, represented by Brockholst Livingston. The litigation had been fought out, with increasing acrimony, over the course of four years and multiple causes of action. Alexander was looking forward to unleashing his spleen and collecting his fee. "At least it keeps them from their intrigues here."

"Yes, but it also gives young Colden a free hand. You know he'll be busy in your absence."

"It doesn't matter how busy he is if Levi Weeks couldn't have got to the well and back," said Alexander firmly.

Chapter Eight

I live opposite Ezra Weeks's lumber yard, and on the night when the deceased was lost, I heard the gate open and a sleigh or carriage come out of the yard about eight o'clock. It made a rumbling noise, but had no bells on it, and that it was not gone long before it returned again.

—From the testimony of Susanna Broad at the trial of Levi Weeks

New York City
January 20, 1800

"You're sure you saw a sleigh come out of Ezra Weeks's yard." Cadwallader tried not to bounce in his enthusiasm. Respectable assistant attorney generals weren't meant to bounce. But Cadwallader felt like bouncing.

A sleigh. He'd never considered a sleigh.

"Running without bells it was." The lappets on

Susanna Broad's cap nodded along with her. "It was the night that girl went missing, round about eight o'clock."

"You're certain it was about eight o'clock?"

The lappets swayed again. "My son and daughter was gone to meeting and meeting is always done about eight o'clock. I saw the sleigh right about when they came home."

"And you're sure it had no bells."

The elderly woman gave him a look that had undoubtedly intimidated stronger men. "If it had bells, I would have heard them, wouldn't I? There was no bells on that sleigh. Proper hazard it was," she said darkly, "running about on a dark night with nothing to let folks know they need to get out of the way."

No one took a sleigh out at night without bells. It was the common courtesy of the road. Unless, of course, someone wanted to travel unremarked. A man eloping. Or a man on his way to do away with an inconvenient encumbrance by strangling her and flinging her in a well and hoping no one would see.

Cadwallader could have capered like a boy, but for the fear that Mrs. Broad would undoubtedly thwack him across the calf with her sturdy walking stick, which rested next to her chair. Besides, it would be unbecoming the dignity owed to his office.

On the outer edges of town, the Broad house was one of the few with a view of Weeks's home and lumber yard. Cadwallader had called in the faint hope someone might have seen Levi walking back from the direction of the well. He had never expected anything like this.

"What about a light?" he asked, trying to control his excitement.

"No light." Mrs. Broad pursed her lips. "It's a wonder they didn't trample some poor soul. Lots of folks on the street that time of night, coming back from meeting. I'd have been at meeting myself but I can't get about the way I used to—not like you young folks, gadding this way and that, picnics in the meadow, turtle feasts, don't know what all."

"Yes, yes." Not that he was that young, really. Only in comparison with his learned opposing counsel. He was thirty-two, a time at which a man should be trusted to make a name for himself—and he felt increasingly confident he might. "Mrs. Broad, can you show me where you were when you saw this sleigh?"

Mrs. Broad groped for the handle of her stick. Cadwallader obligingly handed it to her. "You might lend me an arm."

Cadwallader suspected that if he'd lent her an arm, she would have asked for her stick, but he obliged her all the same, supporting her uneven steps toward the

Dutch door of the house. At her directive, he unlatched it and pushed it open.

Mrs. Broad leaned her elbows on the bottom half, resting her weight on the sturdy wood. "I like to set here and watch for my boy to come back from meeting. Make sure he gets home safe. He's still my boy even if he's a man grown."

Cadwallader looked out over her white head. Nothing had ever been as beautiful as the winter-blasted landscape: the muddy, pitted road; the pigs rooting in the garbage by the side of the street; and a clear view straight over to Ezra Weeks's lumber yard, workshop, and stable.

"That's the gate over there? The gate you heard open that night?"

"And what other gate might it be? The pearly ones?" She cackled at her own wit. "I'm not aiming to see those yet for some time, my boy. Those are the gates, right enough. You can see 'em with your own eyes."

"How often do they take the sleigh out at night?"

"I can't say as how I've heard that gate open at night before. That's why I remarked it. And then when I went to help poor Catherine Ring lay out that poor drowned child, and that man who lodges with 'em was telling us how Levi Weeks had done led her astray, I bethought me of that gate."

"That was very astute of you, Mrs. Broad. Very wise, I mean." Cadwallader's brain was racing. "Did you hear the sleigh come back again?"

"The way that gate creaks? I should say I did! It wasn't gone long before it returned again." She looked significantly at him. "Short trip, it was."

To the Manhattan Well and back. In a sleigh, the ground could be traversed much more quickly than on foot.

The Van Nordens, who lived nearer the well than anyone, had claimed they heard a cry at eight or nine at night. They couldn't narrow the time to anything more specific than that. Catherine Lyon, a neighbor of the Rings, had done better. She had come forward immediately, saying she had been helping a woman who had fallen in the street outside the Ring house just after eight when Elma had stopped and spoken to her. A male voice—no, she hadn't seen him, it had been dark—had said, "Let's go," and Elma had gone. Less than half an hour later, Catherine Lyon had heard Elma cry out for help from the fields around Lispenard's Meadow.

If Elma and Levi had walked together to the sleigh and then taken it on their supposed elopement they could have been at the well within that half hour . . .

"Did you see who was in the sleigh?"

Mrs. Broad snorted. "On a dark night with no lights

on the sleigh and none of the streetlamps lit? You need to talk to them fancy friends of yours and tell them no one's cleaned the streetlamps since they been set out—nor lit them neither."

"You can be sure I will, Mrs. Broad," said Cadwallader sincerely. If he ever had anything to do with city administration, fixing the lamps and getting rid of those disgusting feral pigs would be among his first priorities. He had many thoughts on the matter. "Would you be willing to come to court and say there what you've said to me here?"

"I'll do what's needed to help that poor girl. I helped lay her out, you know."

"So you said." Cadwallader paused, struck by a thought. "Did your son or his wife see the sleigh?"

"I don't know as they did—it left before they were home—but there'll be others abroad who did." Her mouth set in a thin line. "A sleigh without bells! Even if he didn't kill that poor girl, he shouldn't be allowed to drive reckless."

With that, Cadwallader sincerely agreed. It was all he could do not to kiss Mrs. Broad's withered cheek and spin her around in a jig, but he suspected she wouldn't approve of either.

A sleigh without bells . . . She was right, someone else would have remarked on it. But where to find them? A notice in the paper, perhaps. His first impulse was to go running to Josiah, to tell him of the marvelous news and ask his advice, but Cadwallader checked himself.

Bad enough that he'd had that embarrassment over the Malone woman who'd been found strangled and stuffed in a cistern, when he hadn't even been able to pull together enough evidence against the woman's husband for an indictment.

He couldn't go running to Josiah for everything. Cadwallader wished he had Josiah's effortless talent, his incisive mind, and his broad knowledge of the law. It had stung last fall when General Hamilton had insisted that Josiah prosecute the case against the publisher Frothingham personally—instead of leaving it to Cadwallader.

Well, he would show them, thought Cadwallader staunchly. This time, he'd blaze into the courtroom with an unassailable case and impress them with his brilliance. Starting with a sleigh without bells . . .

He thought of going home, but Maria had one of her meetings this afternoon, the Society for the Relief of Poor Widows with Small Children, and the parlor would be filled with women, including Mrs. General Hamilton and Josiah's mother, Mrs. Hoffman, who always looked at Cadwallader as though his boots were muddy, even when they weren't.

On an impulse, Cadwallader abruptly switched course and hurried into the Old Coffee House instead. On the middle of a Monday, it was only half-full, the green baize curtains marking off the private booths drawn back. A cluster of foreign merchants murmured over their coffee; a country cousin come to town smoked a pipe and slowly perused a paper. A group of men had moved on from coffee to cherry bounce and were talking merrily in one corner.

The proprietor, John Byrne, put down the rag he'd been using to sop up a spill of coffee. "It's not a lodge night, is it, Mr. Colden?"

The commerce of the city might have moved to the new Tontine Coffee House, but the members of the Grand Lodge remained loyal to the Old Coffee House, holding their meetings in the long room upstairs.

"No, I was just in need of convivial company. Mrs. Colden is holding a meeting of the Society for the Relief of Poor Widows with Small Children."

Mr. Byrne reached for a pot and a cup. "I'll add a tot of rum to your coffee, then, shall I?"

Cadwallader looked at the merry group in the corner. "No, just the coffee—but might I beg a favor of you?"

"I'd never say you nay, Mr. Colden. I know you'd never ask anything to my dishonor," joked Mr. Byrne.

Unless he wasn't joking. He actually seemed quite

serious about it. Cadwallader suspected that made him very dull. It might be nice, just once, he thought wistfully, to be the sort of person who asked mad and impossible favors, who became embroiled in duels and raised notices in the papers.

Like Brockholst Livingston. Or Alexander Hamilton.

Sadly, Cadwallader resigned himself to a life of unremarkable virtue. "Would you mind asking if anyone saw a sleigh running without bells on Sunday before Christmas? That would be the night of the twenty-second of December."

The Old Coffee House might no longer be the hub of commerce it once was, but a broad array of people still wandered through those old doors.

John looked up from filling the pot. "The night of the twenty-second of December? That's the night that girl—"

"It is. So you see why it might be important."

John raised his voice. Over the assembled chatter of the company, he bellowed, "Gentlemen! Anyone here see a sleigh running without bells the Sunday before Christmas? There you are," he added to Cadwallader, passing over his tray. "Well, then. You! You look like you've something to say."

The man Cadwallader marked as a country cousin took his pipe from his mouth. "I didn't see a sleigh, but

I saw a sleigh track, hard by the Manhattan Well—up the new road Colonel Burr had built. Monday before Christmas, it was."

Monday before Christmas. The day after Elma Sands disappeared. Depending on the time of day, it might be relevant. Or it might not. "What kind of track was it?"

"A one-horse sleigh. I noted it because it ran so close by the well. Mind you, I said to my wife, that sleigh drove so close by the wall it's a wonder it didn't turn over."

"Where did the sleigh track go?"

"Up toward the balloon house. I thought somebody had missed their way because there's no road there—dangerous sort of driving."

Especially in a sleigh with no lights or bells. If it was the sleigh with no lights or bells. They'd have had no need to drive up to the balloon house, unless Levi had needed to go up that way to turn the sleigh around—or the horse had got spooked and got away from him.

Cadwallader wasn't entirely sure this had any bearing on his case, but he did his best to hide his disappointment. "I thank you, sir. And your name is?"

"William Lewis." After a pause, the man added, "I noted there was a board off the well. Left a gap, it did. Maybe as much as a foot across. Careless, I thought it."

A large man, part of the happily inebriated group in the corner, unfolded himself with some difficulty. "I think I saw your sleigh. Running without lights or bells? It nearly ran me down."

"The Sunday before Christmas?"

"I'd been called out to a christening at Dr. Pilmore's church—"

"Christ Church on Ann Street?" commented a man at another table. "I tried to hear one of his sermons once, but there wasn't even room to stand at the back! He's a powerful preacher, that one."

"And a lengthy one," said the man who'd been to the christening, raising a general laugh from his friends, who appeared to have had enough cherry bounce to find just about anything funny. "It was late when we made our way out. I took up two friends in my sleigh, and we'd just made it up the Bowery, as far as the middle stone, and then down to Broadway, when a sleigh came on at a full gallop—no bells to give warning, running full tilt right down the middle of the road."

"Is there room for two sleighs to pass there?" asked the man who hadn't been able to hear Dr. Pilmore preach.

"Hardly! It took some pretty fancy driving, I tell you," boasted the driver. "They didn't even slow, not even when we huzzahed at them. And it was a dark horse too. We didn't see a thing until they were nearly upon us. I thought we were going to go over for sure."

"Did you see who was in the sleigh?" Cadwallader asked eagerly.

"I was too busy trying not to land in the ditch. There were two or three people in it, but that's all I can say. You can ask my friends if you like—they weren't so busy with the reins."

"I'd be much obliged if they'd call on me at 47 Wall Street. Anyone with any information about a sleigh on that night can call on me at 47 Wall Street."

"I'll put the word about. We all want to do what we can for that girl. It was all anyone was talking about here for days." Byrne paused for a moment and then added, slowly, "Ezra Weeks has a horse for sale. He put up a notice here in the coffee shop."

"When did he put it up for sale?"

"Not so long ago." Byrne's eyes met his. "I hear it's a dark horse."

Cadwallader thanked him again and stumbled out, feeling drunk though he'd touched only coffee and not the rum he'd been offered. At that, he didn't even remember drinking his coffee, although the sour taste in the back of his mouth and the grit between his teeth told him he had. He walked home in a daze and had to read *Jack the Giant-Killer* three times before David was satisfied.

He needed to see that horse.

What with one thing and another it wasn't until the following afternoon that he was able to make his way to upper Greenwich Street, having first managed to put Maria in a temper, misplace several important documents, and burn a hole in the back of his frock coat standing too near the fire.

It wasn't until he was halfway up Greenwich Street that Cadwallader realized the folly of his actions. He couldn't pretend to be thinking of buying the horse; Ezra Weeks knew exactly who and what he was. And to ask to see the horse outright would tip his hand and give them time to prepare their answers and hide any evidence of the sleigh's having been taken out without bells that night.

Cadwallader slowed, contemplating the lowering prospect of returning home empty-handed, the hour's wasted effort, the sense of having failed again. He was weighing the advantages and disadvantages, wondering which way to go, when a woman hurried up to him, dragging a small boy behind her.

"Mr. Colden?" Her breath showed in great puffs in the cold air.

"Yes?" He didn't think he knew her. She looked like

she might be one of Maria's widows. Her shawl and apron were clean but neatly patched, and the boy's coat was too short in the wrists.

"I saw you from my window and came down as fast as I could." She drew in a deep breath. "My name's Margaret Freeman. My husband told me you were asking about a sleigh without bells. He was at the Old Coffee House yesterday. Stop tugging at me, Henry!"

Henry gave Cadwallader a resentful look.

"You saw the sleigh?" Cadwallader looked at her with more interest.

Despite John Byrne promising to ask his patrons, not a single other person had come forward yet with any credible word of the sleigh, although one not entirely sober person had told him he'd seen a sleigh bearing the Archangel Michael with a flaming sword. On recollection, though, the Archangel Michael's sleigh had bells, the man had decided. What sort of madman drove a sleigh without bells?

"It was that night—the Sunday before Christmas. I was on my way home from meeting with my children—yes, Henry—and I had to pull them out of the way as the sleigh went past us. There were two men and a woman in the middle, all laughing very loud."

"*Two* men and a woman, you say?"

"I saw them clear," she said. "They were all talking and laughing very lively, particularly the woman."

"What time was it?"

"A quarter past eight," she said decidedly.

"Might it have been any later?" Cadwallader asked, but without much hope.

It was the wrong number of people in the sleigh and there wasn't any way Levi could have got Elma to the stable and into the sleigh that quickly. They hadn't left the Ring house until nearly a quarter past. It seemed strange there would be two sleighs without bells that night, but it was quite possible that this woman just hadn't noticed the bells in the general din of the street.

The woman was firm on the point. "I know particular because I looked at the clock on the mantel as soon as we were inside—meeting ran long and I needed to get the children to their beds."

Unless . . . A second man, waiting in the sleigh—holding the horses, harnessed and ready to go. All Levi would have to do would be to lead Elma out and into the sleigh, wherever it was waiting.

"Mr. Colden? Sir?"

Cadwallader bowed formally. "Mrs. Freeman, I can't tell you how helpful you've been. You, as well, young man."

The boy stuck out his tongue at him.

Cadwallader didn't care. He could see the case unfolding before him. He had the why of it and now the how. Levi Weeks had courted Elma Sands; he had enjoyed her favors; he had lured her to the well under promise of marriage, spirited her off in his brother's sleigh, and cruelly and foully murdered her.

Just one last question puzzled him. Who was the second man in the sleigh?

Chapter Nine

One day my master said to me, "You must not think it strange of my keeping Elma's company—it is not for courtship nor dishonor, but only for conversation." One night I pretended to be asleep, and the prisoner undressed himself, and came with the candle and looked to see if I was asleep or not. Supposing I was, he went downstairs in his shirt, and did not come back until morning.

—From the testimony of William Anderson, apprentice, at the trial of Levi Weeks

New York City
January 22, 1800

"It's only to collect my master's things."
Catherine watched stony-faced as William Anderson sidled past her toward the stairs, the key that had been Levi's clenched in his hand. He tripped on

the bottom step and bumped against the wall, wincing as much with shame as with pain.

"Give it me," said Caty shortly. "I'll let thee in."

Meekly, Levi's apprentice followed her up the stairs to the room he had shared with Levi. No one had entered since Levi had been taken up by the constables nearly a month before. Levi's spare shirt hung on a peg on the wall; his sketches littered a small table; and an untidy heap of blankets lay snarled on the pallet where his apprentice had slept.

"I—I am sorry," the boy stammered. "About Elma—Miss Sands."

"Take what thee came for." If he was looking for exoneration, Caty wasn't going to provide it.

She stood there, in the doorway, as the boy hastily gathered together Levi's belongings: his clothes, his few books, his papers, the shaving kit that sat next to a basin and ewer still filled with weeks-old dirty water.

She'd have to clean that. She'd empty and scrub and re-let the room to someone else. But right now Caty could only stand there, consumed with emotions she couldn't even begin to name as she watched Levi's apprentice creep about, removing his things as though he'd never been there, never caused them this shame and grief.

"Did thee know?" The words tore out before she

could stop them. "Did thee know what thy master and Elma planned?"

The boy paused, a clumsy pile clutched to his chest. "I—no. No, they never told me."

But he might have guessed. Caty knew it wasn't fair to unleash her frustrations on this child, only a boy, with his skinny neck and arms, his hands and feet too large for his frame, his voice still squeaking. But he was there and Levi wasn't. Levi hadn't dared come back himself.

"Did thee know they were courting?"

Courting. Such a dainty term for what had been going on in her house, beneath her roof. Richard Croucher had told everyone about their "courting" in lurid detail. He made it sound as though Caty had been running a bawdy house instead of a respectable boardinghouse.

"Did thee? Did thee know what they were about?"

William Anderson flushed a deep, beet red, straight up to the tips of his ears. "I—I might— There was one night—he thought I was asleep—"

"He had Elma—in here—with thee?" Caty thought she might be sick. In her own house, where her babies slept below. Where she was meant to be keeping Elma safe.

"No!" The boy looked genuinely distressed—for her. He was trying to comfort her, Caty realized, and didn't know whether to be touched or offended. "Levi left the room—in his shirt—and didn't come back until morning. But I didn't know where he went. He might have been walking. Or sitting."

Or lying. With Elma.

"It wasn't anything—I might have been mistaken. And when I asked him—" The boy stuttered to a stop, realizing he was damning himself with every word. "When I asked him if he meant to—to marry Miss Elma, he said I mustn't get the wrong idea."

"I see," said Caty, her voice glacial.

"He said it wasn't for courtship—or for dishonor—but only for conversation."

The boy looked at her eagerly, as though that could make it all better. Only for conversation. The sort of conversation that occurred lip to lip, and thigh to thigh.

"Get thee back to thy master," said Caty hoarsely. "Take his things and get thee back."

The boy hurriedly shoveled Levi's belongings into a small trunk, smashing them any which way. Caty itched to pull them from his hands and put them into order. But she forced herself to stand and watch, his movements growing more and more clumsy beneath her unwavering stare.

"Thee forgot that." She pointed to a scrap of black on

the floor. The ribbon Elma had used to tie back Levi's hair one month ago today. "Thy master's ribband."

The boy lunged for it, shoving it into his pocket. "I thank you, Mrs. Ring. I wish—Elma—she was always kind to me."

With another mumbled word of thanks, he scurried past Catherine, down the stairs.

Caty let him go.

Levi's key burned like a brand against her palm. The room was only a room now, the bed slightly askew, a month's dust dulling the floor. Levi couldn't have entertained Elma in that bed, not with his apprentice sleeping on the floor. Caty remembered William that night, the night Elma disappeared, drowsing on the front room settle, waiting for Levi to come home and let him into their room, following him like a faithful hound up the stairs to bed.

Had Levi crept out in his shirt at night and met Elma in her room? Just the once, William said, but what did William know? He was a boy and boys slept sound.

Only for conversation.

There had been that other night, the night Elma had said she had slept at the Watkinses' house, but when Caty had tasked Elizabeth Watkins with it, with letting Elma catch a chill sitting up too late by the stove with her daughter Fanny, whispering and giggling, she said she didn't know anything about it; Elma had never been with them.

This wasn't the country. A boy and girl couldn't slip out and spend the night behind a hedgerow—as Aunt Lizzy had done with her soldier. Besides, it had been December and cold, too cold for trysting outdoors.

Did they have a place they repaired to? A secret place of their own? Had it been just the once? Or had there been other nights, nights Caty didn't know about?

She couldn't attend to everything, Caty thought, aggrieved. There were her own four children, on top of the work of the boardinghouse and the millinery. At nine, Rachel was a help already, but four-year-old David was a boy with a boy's energy, Phoebe, at six, couldn't be trusted not to tease David and provoke him to trouble, and baby Eliza had careened from one bout of drippy-nosed misery to the next this winter, constantly sick and sneezing.

Caty had been so busy and so tired, and yes, maybe she ought to have noticed, but Elma was a woman grown, and how could she be expected to see everything, always?

It would be different if Elias took on more of his share of the burden, but—Caty cut off that disloyal thought. She could manage well enough on her own, just as her mother had before her. Men were different, that was all. They had different concerns. Like her father, answering the call to bring the word to the people of England, the German states, and wherever else he felt he might be needed. Last they'd heard, he'd been in Ireland, visiting Friends in the vicinity of Dublin, with plans to journey into Ulster.

He didn't even know Elma was gone.

Caty went slowly to the bottom of the stair and shut the staircase door behind her, resting her head against the wooden boards that enclosed the stair. She had stood here that night, just where she was standing now, and listened for Elma and Levi to come downstairs.

Caty heard Elma all the time. She heard Elma's step on the stairs, racing up too fast for decorum. She heard Elma laugh; she heard Elma whisper; she heard the floorboards creak above her head. Looking out the window, Caty would see a flounce of a calico skirt and run out, searching for that elusive form in the crowd, only to find it was someone else entirely. Her bread burned and her stitches snarled. She snapped at Phoebe and forgot to change the baby's clout, only to grab them tight and hug them so hard they demanded to be let down again.

One month ago, Elma had been alive.

It seemed impossible that time should stretch on and

Elma should be gone. Buried. A name on a marker in the graveyard. Not even their own graveyard in Cornwall, but the Friends burial ground here in the city, a place of strangers.

Perhaps Elma might prefer being buried among strangers—although not among Friends. She had never wanted to be a Friend. It had been a source of ongoing frustration to Caty's father that he could convert the heathen of Rhode Island and Connecticut, but not his own niece.

Caty had thought that living with her and Elias, Elma might change. Elma could live in the city, the teeming, exciting metropolis for which she'd always yearned. Under Caty's loving guidance, she'd free herself of her frivolous desires, meet a nice boy at meeting, and set her mind to a life of happy industry.

But it hadn't worked out that way. By the time Elma had been under her roof a year, Caty would have been happy for Elma to have married anyone, just so long as she was out of her house.

That night, Caty had stood by this stair and heard their whispered voices: Levi and Elma. She had retreated hastily to her room, so they wouldn't catch her listening. From her room, she'd heard the front door open and close. The relief of it, the incredible relief of it, knowing Elma was gone . . .

Caty jerked back as steps clattered down the stair. Not Elma's tread, never Elma's tread again, but Elias's heavy clump and the mincing click of the heels of their lodger Croucher. They opened the door, nearly walking right into Caty in their absorption.

They made such an ill-assorted pair: her husband in his homespun, his baggy trousers and loose shirt; their lodger in a tightly fitted bottle-green frock coat over a waistcoat of cream brocade embroidered with birds of paradise.

"Mrs. Ring." Croucher tipped his hat to her. He contrived, as he always did, to make her feel like a scullery maid in her own home.

"Mr. Croucher. Does thee plan to do us the honor of gracing our table?"

"I've other arrangements," said Mr. Croucher vaguely, by which, Caty knew, he meant he would call on acquaintances at the dinner hour and wrangle an invitation to eat, rather than paying the highly reasonable rate she charged to feed her boarders. "It's such a busy season."

"Catherine." Elias cleared his throat, looking somewhere past her rather than at her. "Mr. Croucher was just telling me that he is to be married—to the Widow Stackhaver."

"I wish thee happy. I suppose that means thee will be not much longer with us?"

"Oh, there are affairs to set in order," Croucher said airily, waving one of his long, thin hands. Dull red glinted from a ring on his finger, not a gem, but polished stone. He looked meaningfully at Elias, raising all of Caty's worst suspicions. "We shan't be married for some weeks. You needn't fear. I don't mean to leave you without a lodger quite yet, Mrs. Ring."

That wasn't what she feared.

Swirling himself in a greatcoat with no fewer than five capes, Mr. Croucher took himself off, undoubtedly to batten at someone else's table. Five capes! Caty could make breeches for David and cloaks for all three girls out of that material.

Elias would have gone too, turning toward their room on the other side of the stair, but Caty stepped in front of him, trying to put words to her misgivings. "That Croucher—thee are constantly in company together."

Elias hunched his shoulders. "Is it so strange a man would want for companionship in this house of women?"

Most of their boarders were men. But that wasn't what Elias was talking about, she knew. It was the millinery. He deeply resented the millinery, and the dozen girls who came and went, trimming hats, dropping bits of ribbon, and making more money for them than any of his projects had in a year.

Caty stepped up to him, tilting her head to look up into his face. She could see the stubble on his chin, where he hadn't shaved since yesterday, the brown tinged with gray. "He has not persuaded thee to anything, has he?"

Elias's expression went blank. "I don't know what thee might mean."

He was a terrible liar, her Elias.

"It's the store, isn't it?" Caty doggedly kept pace with him as Elias strode toward the bedroom, trying to avoid her.

She wouldn't let him avoid her any longer, not if he meant to embark on another of his ill-fated business ventures, with Croucher as a partner. When they'd first come to the city, Elias had opened a dry goods store in the space that Catherine now used for the millinery. It had failed miserably.

Caty caught up with Elias as he fumbled with the lock of their door. "If he wants thee to go into partnership for his frivolities . . ."

He dropped the key, lurching inelegantly for it. "If I did, that would be my business, not thine."

Caty looked at him, thinking how different he

looked from the man she'd married, the first marriage in the new meetinghouse. She'd been so proud. So proud to be a harbinger of future joy. So proud of the man she'd married, so sure he was destined for great things, that they were destined for great things together. She'd been seventeen, and he'd been thirty-one, and it had seemed wonderful to her that a man of his industry and vigor and obvious powers could take an interest in a girl like her.

Her father had blessed the match; her mother had made the fruitcake. The whole community had garlanded them with flowers.

She would always remember Elias like that, standing in the sunshine outside the new meetinghouse, the light bringing out the glints of red in his brown hair, standing tall and sure, his hand extended to her—to her—as they started their life together.

But that had been before the mill that failed . . . and the dry goods store that failed . . . and the patent waterwheel that Elias had sworn and sworn would make their fortunes, bringing clean water to the city . . . until the Manhattan Company had passed his plan over, the same way every other investor he'd approached had passed his plan over.

It galled him that the boardinghouse kept their children fed and clothed, the boardinghouse and the millinery Caty oversaw when she wasn't cooking and scrubbing and mending, and she didn't mind it, she didn't mind it at all, if only Elias would stop dreaming and help just once in a while. She'd been telling him for weeks now the front door stuck, but he was too busy paying good money to stick advertisements in the paper for a waterwheel no one wanted.

It's not money wasted when it makes our fortunes, he'd snapped, but the only fortune Caty saw was the amount they were spending on wood to heat the house through the winter. The cost had risen to sixteen dollars the cord, thanks in no small part to Ezra Weeks buying up every available log to make pipes for the Manhattan Well. That horrible, horrible well.

Was he now to enter into business with that Croucher, the man who had been spreading their shame throughout the city? The man who'd rather wear silk and beg his bread than dress in wool and pay for an honest meal?

"I don't like that man," Caty said doggedly. "I don't trust him. He wears finery but he's always late paying his rent."

"What does thee know of it—of anything?" said Elias dismissively, and turned the key in the lock.

It was all too much. Caty followed him into the bedroom, the children's trundles pushed neatly under the bed. She followed him as he yanked his cloak off the hook in the corner. "Did he tell thee—that Croucher? Did he tell thee he saw Elma and Levi together while I was in the country?"

She could see Elias's hands clench, his knuckles very white against the dark wool. That was it, wasn't it? Caty didn't know whether to be angry or relieved. It was why he couldn't meet her eyes. He'd known. He'd known and he'd done nothing.

When she'd been in the country a month, he'd sent her a letter, begging her to come back to the city. At the time, she'd felt a perverse satisfaction over it, that he'd realized he couldn't manage without her, that he was finally seeing all the work she did, unnoticed, unthanked. She'd decided to make him stew, to see just how much she was worth, and stayed another two weeks in the country before coming back.

Not just to make him stew, of course. The children were so happy in Cornwall with her mother, and her mother was so happy with the children. But letting Elias miss her was part of it too.

Caty took the edges of Elias's cloak, drawing them together over his chest for him. "Was that why thee wanted me to come back?"

Elias's eyes slid away from hers as Caty fixed his cloak at his neck. "It was thy place to be at my side."

Caty's hands stilled on the careful bow she was tying. "He told thee. Or thee saw."

"What does it matter—now?" She could feel the vibration in his chest as the words tore out, raw and horrible.

"It matters because—" Because she might have stopped it. Because Elias never told her anything anymore. Because they had stood up in the presence of God and their families and pledged to be loving and faithful so long as they both should live. Because she was meant to be his helpmeet, living in the Light of the Lord, and one couldn't very well be a helpmeet when one's husband never told one anything.

This wasn't what they had promised each other ten years ago in the new meetinghouse, the bees buzzing happily in the flowers her mother had planted outside, the scent of sawdust still fresh in the air, the nails Caty herself had carried over from the smithy at New Windsor gleaming brightly, holding the whole together. She'd thought her marriage would be as solid as the new meetinghouse, as pure and bright, nailed together with true respect and affection.

Her voice low and unsteady, Caty said, "Does thou rate me so low that thou cannot share thy troubles?"

His finger brushed her cheek, the barest trace of a

touch. Like when they were courting and he would cup her face in his hands, looking down at her as if she were all the riches of the world and his hope for salvation.

Caty leaned her cheek into his palm. "I might have shared thy burden. If I had known...."

Elias's hand dropped, his expression turning ugly. "What thee means is that thee would have answered the problem better. Does thee think thyself so subtle? Thee make no secret thee think me a poor excuse of a man."

"Elias—I never—"

"Didn't thee? When was the last time thee shared my bed?"

"We've four children in the room with us!"

"Thee ran off to thy mother at the first opportunity—"

"—to spare the children from the fever—"

"Thee judges me, flaunting thy industry. 'Oh, Elias, look how many hats!' Hats! I might have brought fresh water to the city! And thee taunt me with hats!"

"*Might* doesn't put bread on the table." Caty clapped her hand over her mouth but it was too late; the words were out.

Elias's lips twisted into a sneer. "There's the truth of it. Straight from thine own lips."

"Elias—wait. Please. We can leave—go back to

Cornwall—" Back to the fields of her youth, to the meetinghouse where they'd been married, to the smell of snow and bread baking and green things ready to grow. Her mother would be there to help with the children; the children would have their cousins, her brother's children. Elias could tinker with his inventions to his heart's content, Caty wouldn't care so long as they were home again, away from this horrible place. "Think how happy we might be there. Back in the Cornwall meeting . . ."

"And have thee telling everyone of my failure. No. We'll stay where we are."

"And have thee giving our hard-earned coin to Richard Croucher?" Caty shouted after him.

But it was too late. Elias was gone, slamming the door of their bedroom behind him so hard that her cloak fell from its peg in a sad heap on the ground.

"Mama?" Rachel stuck her head through the door. Her cheeks were pink from the kitchen hearth. Hope had fixed her hair that morning; her shining braids were slightly crooked. "I heard shouting."

"It's nothing, my lovely." Caty gathered the first child of her marriage into her arms, resting her cheek against the top of her head. Her hair was no longer wispy fine like Eliza's; she was nine already, Rachel, and growing so fast. Ever since Elma died, she'd looked so solemn all the time, as though she'd aged a decade in a month. "Nothing to concern thee."

Caty would see that it wasn't.

When it came to her children, she would do whatever was needed to protect them.

Chapter Ten

Attend the Court of Errors and hear the Arguments of the adversary—Hamilton is desirous of being witty but goes beyond the Bounds and is open to a severe dressing. . . . Col Burr is very able & has I see made considerable Impression.

    —From the diary of Gouverneur Morris,
    February 11–12, 1800

Albany, New York
February 11, 1800

"You might wish to protect yourself," murmured Aaron, as he walked with Hamilton down the crumbling steps of the Albany Stadt Huys into the February evening.

They'd spent the day in the room of the old state house that doubled as the sitting place of the Court of Errors, playing out the latest stage of the long-running—and highly lucrative—squabble between the merchants Le Guen, Gouverneur, and Kemble.

The commercial case, for which Aaron and Hamilton had first been retained in 1795, had burgeoned into no fewer than eight separate actions in multiple different courts, with suits and countersuits, and allegations of fraud.

Aaron found it a reliable source of fees; Hamilton, on the other hand, had taken the cause of Le Guen extravagantly to heart, laying about at the opposing counsel as if they were barbarians at the gates and not honorable colleagues. He'd all but accused them of arson and barratry and had probably refrained from that only for want of time.

So acrimonious had the case become that Isaac Gouverneur had brought in his honored kinsman Gouverneur Morris. The man hadn't litigated for years, but his eloquence was legendary, his stature as a statesman undisputed, his alliance with Hamilton of long standing. Aaron could have told them that wouldn't work; when Hamilton's blood was up, friend became foe with the same ease with which a bit of judicious flattery could turn one from foe to friend again. Hamilton had savaged Morris without compunction but with a great many extraneous adverbs.

Even for Hamilton, his performance had been extreme; one might even say, intemperate.

The air here was crisper than in the city of New York, the color of the sky a deeper hue. Aaron breathed in appreciatively. "Gouverneur Morris has expressed his desire to give you a severe dressing."

"He doesn't mean it," said Hamilton, with undue confidence. Aaron strongly suspected that if there had been a horsewhip to hand, Morris would have applied it with the outraged panache of a French nobleman lashing an impudent upstart.

Morris had so far lowered himself to demand of Aaron if Hamilton were in his cups.

No, Aaron had replied wryly. Merely drunk on his own oratory.

That had earned him the reluctant appreciation of Gouverneur Morris—an event to remember in itself—and the curt advice to rein in his co-counsel before someone gave in to the temptation to give him a damned good thrashing.

Aaron estimated that Hamilton's oratory had kept him from his supper by an hour—but it had lost Hamilton at least one ally, so perhaps one might make allowances.

"Comparing Isaac Gouverneur to Shylock might

have been a bit extreme." Aaron couldn't resist twisting the knife a bit. "You brought Robert Troup nearly to tears."

"Robert Troup! A creature it is almost a vice to name."

That was a fine way to dismiss one of one's oldest friends. Troup had followed Hamilton about like a faithful puppy ever since their days rooming together as students at King's College. Right now Troup was a whipped puppy.

A whipped puppy might bite his master.

It had been, Aaron thought, really quite a useful day's work. Hamilton had eviscerated their opposition and, in the process, alienated two of his closest allies, allowing Aaron to position himself as the sensible voice of reason in contrast to Hamilton's intemperate ravings.

Men remembered that sort of thing when it was time to go to the polls.

"If you continue upsetting your friends at such a rate," said Aaron mildly, "you will have no one with whom to dine."

"Better a dinner of herbs than a stalled ox and hatred within," said Hamilton stubbornly.

Hatred, was it? The man was as changeable as the weather, while thinking himself constant as the tides. He had been spending too much time in Hamilton's company, thought Aaron grimly, if he was beginning to think in such labored metaphors. He would have to spend some time reading Voltaire to clear his mind, a literary purgative.

"I can offer you better than herbs if you wish," said Aaron, knowing it was a safe offer. Hamilton always stayed with his wife's parents when he came to Albany.

"Mrs. Schuyler is expecting me," said Hamilton promptly.

He didn't invite Aaron back to share the bounty of General Schuyler's table. Aaron hadn't expected he would. Schuyler had had little love for Aaron ever since Aaron had relieved General Schuyler of his senate seat nine years ago.

The Schuylers knew how to hold a grudge.

That didn't matter. Against Hamilton's Schuylers, Aaron had Brockholst's Livingstons. Where once the Schuylers might have been royalty here in Albany, their power was waning, the old general consumed by gout, beggared by bad land deals, increasingly dependent on his brilliant but erratic son-in-law.

The Livingstons, on the contrary, had only continued to expand their influence. General Schuyler was of the old school, tied to the land, to a patroon system of feudal patronage that was fast evaporating. He was the past. It amused Aaron to see Schuyler cling to Hamilton as the rising star who would revive his fortunes, as Hamilton flung himself into the bosom of the Schuylers in a desperate attempt at legitimacy.

They would both lose.

But there was no reason Aaron couldn't be generous in victory. Hamilton was useful—in his way. When he wasn't carried away by the charms of his own voice.

If only one could stow him in a cupboard and take him out when needed. Aaron amused himself with the image: a pocket Hamilton, to be set to work as desired, drafting contracts and formulating bills, and then shut away again as his tiny voice grew too shrill, like the homunculus of the Renaissance alchemists.

"When do you return to New York?"

"As soon as our arguments are concluded. I told Eliza I plan to leave on Sunday and hope to be with her by early next week." Hamilton's ruddy face glowed as he spoke of his Eliza, like a boy in the first throes of calf-love.

How quickly the affair of Maria Reynolds was forgotten.

"Your military work calls you, I imagine," said Aaron casually. He didn't think it had occurred to Hamilton to arrange anything like the organization he had put in place preparatory to the election—but the thought of Hamilton bustling uncontested through the city while Aaron pursued allies elsewhere in the state gave him a bit of pause.

"Yes, and the Weeks matter." It took Aaron a moment to recall what Hamilton was talking about; the case of Ezra Weeks's amorous brother was not one of his priorities. "We've only a month until trial and still know little more than when Ezra Weeks first came to us!"

Us, was it? Aaron gave a delicate cough.

Hamilton was too busy speaking to notice. "I took Harison with me to speak to Elizabeth Weeks before I left for Albany—but there are still some points on which I wish to be satisfied. I hadn't time before I left to get to the truth of the matter."

It was just like Hamilton to set himself up as the arbiter of truth, a stone statue on a pedestal, undoubtedly holding gilded scales. And blind. Dangerously blind.

"Truth," said Aaron delicately, "is the daughter of time, not the product of the courts. Our remit is to establish our client's innocence, not the truth of the matter."

"Aren't those one and the same?" demanded Hamilton, as if it weren't quite plain they weren't the same thing at all. If he didn't know that by now, Aaron wasn't going to be the one to explain to him. But then, as Aaron had learned over the course of their very long acquaintance, Hamilton had a remarkable capacity for self-delusion.

"Ezra Weeks is the man who pays our fee."

"We owe a greater debt to justice. Don't you think the girl deserves as much? What if it were your own Theodosia?"

Privately, Aaron felt quite secure his Theodosia would never be in such a position. He had raised her to be superior to the rest of her sex in judgment and reason. Not to mention that she wasn't a common girl of no breeding and less sense; she was mistress of Richmond Hill.

For so long as he managed to retain Richmond Hill.

No, even if he failed to recoup his debts, his Theodosia was not unprotected. She was hardly some little Quaker milliner to be used and cast aside.

Not that blood and position were always a protection. There had been that business of Nancy Randolph . . .

But his Theodosia would never be such a fool. It was absurd. Aaron blamed Hamilton for putting ridiculous thoughts in his head. Apparently, foolishness was catching, like the grippe.

If he could deliver New York into the hands of the Republicans, his influence would be assured; it would be a short step from there to the vice presidency. It was what he and Jefferson had agreed.

No one would dare presume to take advantage of the vice president's daughter, no matter how fathoms deep in debt he might be.

"Do you see your Angelica in the role?" Aaron asked idly.

"It might be anyone's daughter," said Hamilton, which was palpably untrue. Elma Sands wasn't anyone's daughter. She was the illegitimate child of goodness only knew who, which made her, in a way, no one's daughter.

Rather like Hamilton.

"By that logic, might not Levi Weeks be anyone's brother? The boy is personable; the girl is dead. Witnesses—many witnesses—saw her threaten to drain a bottle of laudanum."

"If a thing is to be done, it should be done right," said Hamilton stubbornly. And by *right*, as Aaron knew all too well, Hamilton meant his way. If there was one thing of which Hamilton was assured, it was that he was right and everyone else was wrong, co-counsel be damned. "To merely acquit the boy isn't enough; we ought to bring the guilty to justice."

"Unless," Aaron pointed out, "the girl was the means of her own destruction."

Hamilton's chin jutted out. His nose was very red in the cold and beginning to drip. "If the girl was the instrument of her own destruction then Weeks has nothing to fear by my investigations."

It was truly impressive how quickly Hamilton had gone from inviting himself to participate in the case to taking charge of it. Or so he thought. Aaron was willing to allow him to think so. Up to a point.

It was a delicate balance. On the one hand, it was very useful to have Hamilton occupied. On the other. . . . It was well that the prosecution was being headed by Cadwallader Colden, who could be trusted to see only the obvious, and that only if it was put directly in front of him.

"My dear Hamilton, your eloquence has persuaded me." In truth, it was less his eloquence, and more the chill, which was making itself felt beneath Aaron's greatcoat, jacket, and waistcoat. His current lodgings were uninspiring, but they were warmer than the steps of the Stadt Huys. And there was work to be done, a great deal of work. "I believe I see the general's sleigh."

General Schuyler had sent his own sleigh to carry his son-in-law to the family homestead, as if Hamilton were an errant schoolboy being brought home.

"My regards to the general and Mrs. Schuyler." Nothing annoyed people more than courtesy from a foe.

Hamilton looked at him uncertainly. "Might I offer you a ride to your lodgings?"

The poor man; the courage it took him to offer the hospitality of his father-in-law's sleigh.

Aaron might be in debt to creditors from Philadelphia to Boston, but at least he was his own man. "The walk is short and the night is clear. I'll see you here tomorrow."

On nights like this, Albany was full of ghosts. If Aaron closed his eyes, he could be back nearly twenty years ago, in the large but inconvenient house to which he'd brought his Theo as his bride. They'd married here in Albany, he in his old coat, Theo in borrowed ribbons. Even the parson had been borrowed. They had been married in a double ceremony with Theo's half sister Catherine and Dr. Joseph Browne.

But that was all in the past. Theo had been gone these six years now, and he refused to give way to mawkish sentimentality. Theo would have mocked him for it more than anyone, more even than he mocked himself.

The veil between past and present was too thin; he missed her unbearably.

It would pass.

There was a summation to write for tomorrow—let everyone see how cool and reasonable he could be compared to his excitable co-counsel—and lists to draw up of potential donors to his Republican faction. Oh yes, there was plenty of work to occupy him—and a letter to write to his Theodosia scolding her for not writing more frequently in his absence.

Aaron set his face against the wind, trudging down the road to his lodging house as a brightly lit sleigh jingled past him in the darkness.

Chapter Eleven

Mr. Williams testified that at the request of the Attorney-General, he had made an experiment in what time a man might drive a horse the most usual route from Ring's to the Manhattan Well, and from there back again to Ezra Weeks's down Barley-street, and that although the roads were bad, he performed it once in 15 minutes and once in 16, without going out of a trot.

—From Coleman's report of the trial of
 Levi Weeks

New York City
February 24, 1800

Cadwallader pulled out his watch as the sleigh jingled to a stop just a few yards away from Ezra Weeks's property.

John Williams, from the livery stable, stood up in the seat, shouting, "The time?"

"Fifteen minutes!" Cadwallader called back, and a cheer went up from the motley crowd of onlookers who had somehow assembled as John Williams and Sylvester Buskirk had raced a sleigh—as close in kind to Ezra Weeks's as Cadwallader could find, pulled by a horse of similar power—from the Ring boardinghouse to the Manhattan Well to Ezra Weeks's lumber yard.

He felt a moment of misgiving that this experiment had become so public. He knew it had always been a risk running it right under Weeks's nose and had deliberately picked a day when he knew Weeks and his crew to be at James Cummings's house. It had never occurred to him that the sight of a sleigh pounding ventre à terre down Barley Street, not once, but three times, might eventually draw a crowd. Some even clutched hot cups of mulled wine. Vendors had followed the sounds of excitement, turning Cadwallader's sleigh trials into an impromptu public outing.

But he had the results he needed.

"Told you I could go it in under fifteen minutes," said John Williams smugly, jumping down from the sleigh and handing the reins to his colleague.

It was technically at fifteen minutes, not under, but Cadwallader wasn't going to deny him his triumph.

In the crowd, money was changing hands. High-spirited young lads would bet on anything, thought

Cadwallader indulgently. When he was a boy at school in England, he had once bet a quarter's allowance on who could hop first on one foot three times around the classroom. It had seemed a perfectly reasonable venture at the time.

Was that Hamilton's nephew there, clapping his friend on the arm? Cadwallader hoped not. Not that he had any hope of keeping this secret—he wasn't sure why he had thought he could—but he had felt more comfortable with the idea that he could gather his evidence quietly while they were all occupied elsewhere.

General Hamilton had returned to the city a week ago now—Cadwallader knew because Maria had taken tea with Mrs. Hamilton—but as far as anyone could tell had been utterly preoccupied with his work for the army, a state of affairs that suited Cadwallader perfectly.

Not that it mattered what he or any of the lawyers for the defense did or discovered; Levi Weeks had done it and Cadwallader could prove it.

Cadwallader forced his attention back to Williams, who was justifiably waiting for praise. "And not out of a trot?"

"I might have given her her head a bit on that straight stretch . . . but no. Not out of a trot. Not for more'n a moment, anyway." Williams gave the horse an affectionate scratch behind the ears. "She's a good 'un, she is."

Cadwallader lowered his voice so the gathered onlookers couldn't hear. "Could Ezra Weeks's horse do the same?"

Sylvester thought on it for a moment. "He stood in my stable for sale this past month—I think he could."

Cadwallader felt a glow of satisfaction. They had him. The jury had to see how suspicious it was how quickly Ezra Weeks had taken steps to extract the horse from his own stable. It was only surprising Weeks hadn't also found a way to quietly remove the sleigh.

Cadwallader pressed a coin first into Williams's hand, then Sylvester's. "My thanks to you both. You've been of more assistance than you can know."

"Shall we give you a ride home, sir?"

"Why not?" said Cadwallader giddily. He felt like a Roman emperor being borne through the streets in a triumph, only somewhat more comprehensively clothed.

They'd done it. They'd proved, conclusively, that even on a bad road, the trip could be undertaken between the time Levi was known to have left the Ring boardinghouse and the time he supposedly returned to the Weeks kitchen.

Of course, the defense was sure to argue that it had

been night; one could drive faster by day; the horse was sturdier; whatever they could say to discredit the results, but he, thought Cadwallader proudly, was prepared for them.

There'd been a moon that night, making it easier to see. Any delay from the dark would be more than discounted by the comparative lack of traffic on the road. He'd even made sure to have a second man in the sleigh to more closely approximate the weight the horse would have been pulling that night.

He still hadn't any idea who the second man in the sleigh might be. William Anderson, Levi's apprentice? Demas Meed, Ezra Weeks's apprentice, who had charge of the sleigh? Ezra himself? No, Ezra's time was accounted for by the McCombs, and McComb was a man of stature, not the sort who might be easily bribed or shaken.

Pleasantly occupied in these musings, Cadwallader bade farewell to Sylvester Buskirk and John Williams and bounded up the steps to his own door, bursting to tell Maria his triumph. Happily unloading his cloak, gloves, and hat on a waiting servant, he burst into the parlor, only to be stopped short by the sight of his brother-in-law, perfectly turned out in the latest sort of frock coat and a pair of very well-tailored breeches, building houses out of books with David. Cadwallader recognized *Blackstone's Commentaries*, now turned building block.

"Ah, Cadwallader." Josiah rose effortlessly to his feet. The edifice of legal thought collapsed and David set up a wail of disappointment.

"I'll take him out," said Maria. There was a set to her mouth that made Cadwallader very nervous.

Indeed, there was something in the way that Josiah looked at him that made Cadwallader's mouth go dry and his palms go damp. He was very aware that he was covered in the dust and grime of three sleigh trials and ought perhaps to have washed his hands and face before presenting himself in the parlor. Had he remembered to scrape his boots at the door? Cadwallader wasn't quite sure.

He wished Josiah didn't always make him feel such a hulking oaf. It hadn't been so bad when he had been in his twenties, just home from his studies in England, but he was past thirty now, and might have reasonably expected to pick up some of the polish and poise his brother-in-law carried so effortlessly.

Of course, he couldn't help his face. The square face and crooked nose that had looked so distinguished on his grandfather, the famous colonial governor, only made Cadwallader look more like an unsuccessful pugilist than a distinguished member of the bar.

Cadwallader had never quite understood why Maria had agreed to marry him. He was beginning to fear that Maria didn't either.

Josiah shook out a paper that was lying on Maria's tea table. "Have you seen today's *Commercial Advertiser*?"

"Not yet." Cadwallader felt a growing sense of unease. Josiah didn't usually call to discuss the day's news. He was also wearing an expression that fell somewhere between pity and exasperation.

Wordlessly, Josiah handed the paper to Cadwallader.

PASTANO PARDONED

A dozen images darted through Cadwallader's mind. Pastano, on the stand, pouring forth a flood of rapid Portuguese, Rabbi Seixas patiently translating. The corpse of Mary Ann De Castro, cruelly stabbed again and again. Brockholst Livingston, looking down the length of that impressive Roman nose, forbearing to offer any defense—because Pastano was guilty, because they all knew he was guilty, no one could deny he was guilty.

"He was guilty. He was indisputably guilty. He was discovered in the act of stabbing his landlady in the neck. With a knife!"

"It is an instrument generally used for stabbing," said Josiah drily.

"Mr. Livingston didn't dispute his guilt. He didn't dispute any of it. The jury declared him guilty. He *was* guilty."

"No," said Josiah wearily. "Brockholst wouldn't waste time disputing the indisputable. But you left his argument undisputed, and that's how he caught you."

What argument? Cadwallader didn't remember him making much of one. There had been various witnesses to Pastano's character—although what they hoped to prove given that the man had been caught in the act of stabbing his landlady Cadwallader wasn't quite sure—but all they said was that the man had behaved oddly.

Josiah retrieved the paper and folded it under his arm. "Brockholst made a convincing case that the balance of his mind was disturbed, a case you made no effort to refute."

"It was immaterial," said Cadwallader blankly. "Insanity offers no immunity from a charge of murder. It was his hand that committed the crime regardless of whatever was within his disordered brain."

Josiah's mouth twisted. "The legislature feels otherwise. They see him as a proper object of mercy. Based on the undisputed fact that the balance of his mind was disturbed, the legislature has passed the pardon and the governor has signed it."

The governor was Brockholst Livingston's brother-in-law John Jay. Not that Cadwallader could throw stones, given that he owed his present position to his brother-in-law, but it rankled a bit all the same.

Cadwallader felt vaguely sick. He sat down heavily on one of Maria's too dainty chairs, ignoring the ominous cracking sound it made. "Do you think—do you think that this was Mr. Livingston's strategy all along?"

"Given the line he took at trial and the fact that he made no effort to argue for his client's innocence—yes," said Josiah drily. "He had this determined before the jury sat."

Cadwallader stared at the mud on his boots, feeling as though he'd been boxing and someone had landed a punch straight to his stomach. Or possibly lower. Pastano had been his one success since taking up the role of assistant attorney general, the one conviction he could point to. And now it was gone, signed away by an act of legislature because Brockholst Livingston had played a long game and Cadwallader hadn't spotted it.

"I don't need to tell you," said Josiah, although apparently he did feel the need to tell him, thought Cadwallader despairingly, since he was doing it, "how important it is that we achieve the conviction of Levi Weeks. Ah, thank you, my dear."

Maria had returned without David, but with a maid bearing a tea tray. The maid set it down upon the table, on the spot where that damnable newspaper had lain. Maria busied herself with the important act of preparing the tea.

Cadwallader grasped after some of the euphoria he had been feeling a mere quarter of an hour ago. "I ran a sleigh trial today," he said incoherently. "From the Ring boardinghouse to the Manhattan Well and back to Ezra Weeks's lumber yard. I can prove that Levi Weeks had access to just such a horse and sleigh—that the horse and sleigh were seen the night of the murder—and that Levi Weeks could have accomplished it in the time allotted."

"With surety?" asked Josiah. "If one link in the chain were to come undone . . ."

"I can prove every one." And so he could. But he had proved each step in the Pastano case too, and look what had become of that.

"Thank you." Josiah accepted a cup of tea from Maria. "New York is looking to us to bring this girl's family justice. The entire country is looking to us."

"I know," said Cadwallader hoarsely. Maria handed him a cup and he took a large gulp, scalding the back of his throat and making himself cough.

His brother-in-law looked at him doubtfully. "All of them seek to use the courtroom as a theater in which they can display their skills in advance of the election." No need to say which election; it was the April New York elections which consumed everyone. "If they cannot sharpen their wits on each other, they will whet them instead on you."

The burned skin on the top of Cadwallader's mouth prickled. "Sir, I cannot try to match them in skill or eloquence, but I believe we have justice on our side. I *know* we have justice on our side."

His brother-in-law delicately sipped his tea. "Brockholst will try to unnerve you."

"He already has," muttered Cadwallader.

"Burr will skewer you on points of law—and Alexander will talk in circles until you're half-distracted," Josiah added fondly.

Josiah and General Hamilton were old friends, of such close association that five years ago, General Hamilton had nearly fought a duel as a consequence of coming to Josiah's aid against one Commodore Nicholson.

"We can't afford to show them any weakness in our argument."

"No, certainly not." Cadwallader felt like David without a slingshot, or Hercules facing down the Nemean lion without his club. Or his strength.

Josiah looked at him keenly. "Is there anything to this story the girl might have taken her own life?"

"No." On this, at least, Cadwallader was able to speak with conviction. He could feel Maria's eyes on him, judging him. "There was no history of melancholy. Miss Sands fell ill in early December with a"—he tried to remember exactly what Catherine Ring had told him—"with an acute disorder of the stomach. Cramping and such. She was given laudanum for the pain."

"Was she known to take it with more frequency than her illness would warrant?"

"As far as I can gather, she was only known to have spoken of taking it the once," said Cadwallader. "And it was really by nature of a jest."

"A jest?"

"She was a high-spirited girl. I can find a dozen people who will attest to that. The defense is only seizing on the idea of suicide because they have nothing else to offer. But we have people who swear they heard cries of murder from the well at somewhere between eight and nine on that night. No one planning to make away with herself cries murder."

"One would assume not."

"The case couldn't be more clear," said Cadwallader firmly. He resisted the urge to sneak a glance at Maria to see if she was impressed. "Another boarder saw Levi

Weeks and Elma Sands engaged in illicit relations as early as September. The whole family attests to his attentions to Elma. During her illness early in December he personally tended to her—he wouldn't allow even her own cousin to take his place by her side."

"But she wasn't with child?"

"No." That would have made the case against Levi stronger. "But he did promise her marriage. She told her cousin Hope Sands that they were to leave to be married at eight on that Sunday night. A little after eight, Levi returned to the boardinghouse and collected her. That night, a sleigh was seen running without lights or bells and"—Cadwallader finished triumphantly—"a neighbor can testify that she saw the sleigh leaving Ezra Weeks's yard just about eight, returning not long after."

"Just be sure you have the evidence to prove what you claim," Josiah warned, setting down his cup as he rose from his chair.

"If I have to, I'll interview every man in the city," declared Cadwallader recklessly, as he showed his brother-in-law back out into the frosty day.

When he returned to his own hearth, Maria was standing by the tea table, her mouth pinched into a thin line, staring at him over her new silver teapot.

"Every man in the city," she said. There was a fine, sharp edge to her voice.

"And women too." Cadwallader was not sure how he'd upset her, only that he had. That seemed to happen a great deal these days.

"Elma Sands's illness—what do you think it was?"

It was nice that Maria was taking an interest in the case. It had been so long since they had shared anything. "Who can tell with these disorders of the stomach?" Cadwallader said expansively. "The doctor said it came on suddenly. He wasn't called until several days later, which makes it harder for him to tell. But it's not really relevant, except insomuch as it explains the laudanum."

Maria stared at him as though she had just seen something unpleasant crawling out of his cravat. Cadwallader reflexively smoothed down his hair. "You told Josiah she was seen in an indelicate situation with Levi Weeks in September. In December she had an illness that involved 'cramping and such.'"

"Yes?" Cadwallader had no idea what she was getting at.

Maria closed her eyes tightly. "We've suffered five disappointments, Cadwallader. *Five.* We've had five disappointments and you don't even recognize the signs?"

"But—she wasn't with child. The doctors examined her insides."

Maria breathed in deeply through her nose, staring at the fine plasterwork of the ceiling. "Just because she wasn't with child at the time doesn't mean she hadn't lost a child. I'm not with child, am I? And I've lost and lost and lost."

"Maria—" Cadwallader reached out a tentative hand to her. "We'll have another."

Maria flinched away, her skirts swirling with her. "Will we? You say that, but you're not the one who has suffered *acute disorder of the stomach*. Five times!"

In the face of her grief and rage, Cadwallader had no idea what to say, so he ventured the first thing that came to mind. "You think Elma Sands lost Levi Weeks's child?"

Maria slammed the door so emphatically behind her that the teacups rattled in their fashionably shallow saucers.

Cadwallader sank down into the chair vacated by his brother-in-law and absentmindedly helped himself to the rest of his tea, now stone-cold and exceedingly bitter.

If he went after Maria she'd only pretend nothing had happened; she didn't like to display excessive emotion. He didn't know that he could bear her mouthing polite nothings to him with a face like a marble mask.

Just because she wasn't with child doesn't mean she hadn't lost a child.

He'd never considered the possibility that Elma Sands might have lost Levi Weeks's child, that her illness— her cramps of the stomach—might have been anything other than the sort of disorder anyone might suffer.

You don't even recognize the signs, Maria had accused him. And he ought to have. Now that she'd said it, it seemed so plain. Catherine Ring's refusal to send for the doctor until the danger was past. Levi Weeks's attentiveness during Elma's illness—his refusal to allow anyone else, even her cousin Hope, to nurse her.

Had he hoped she would die then and free him from his embarrassments? Had he given her something to induce her to lose the child?

Cadwallader realized that he'd been holding the teapot over the cup for several seconds and nothing was coming out, although he appeared to have managed to dribble the last dregs down his leg. He scrubbed absently at the stain on his fawn-colored breeches, thinking hard.

There was no way he could prove any of it. Not unless Catherine Ring was willing to testify that Elma had been with child—and, from what he'd seen of her, he doubted she would admit it, even if she'd known. She must have known.

But what it told him was that Levi Weeks was even more of a cad than he'd previously imagined.

Was it once she'd lost his child that he'd promised to marry Elma—and began planning her murder?

Cadwallader extracted himself from the too small chair. It was time to forge the links of the unbreakable chain of evidence with which he would see Levi Weeks hang.

But first he needed to find some breeches without tea stains on them.

Chapter Twelve

I cannot be a general and a practicer of the law at the same time without doing injustice to the government and myself.

—Alexander Hamilton to James
McHenry

New York City
February 24, 1800

> It is very certain that the military career in this country offers too few inducements and it is equally certain that my <u>present</u> station in the army <u>cannot</u> very long continue under the plans which seem to govern . . .

The pen was a good one, the ink fresh, but Alexander felt like he was writing the letter in his own heart's blood, each word squeezed out unwilling. His aide-de-camp, George Izard, had asked his advice about staying in his current position with Alexander or taking up an offered post as secretary to the minister plenipotentiary to Portugal.

It was galling having to put down on paper the truth Alexander had been avoiding as long as he could: his army's hours were numbered.

Since returning from Albany, Alexander had flung himself into the army's business, as if he could remedy by industry what others lacked in interest. But it wasn't enough, it was never enough—they had halted enlistment, and he knew what that meant. It was a preliminary step to disbanding it entirely, everything Alexander had worked for, planned for, neglecting his family, his law practice, pouring out reams of correspondence, leaving his Eliza to drill the troops, enduring leaky tents and inadequate supplies, dipping into his own pocket to entertain dignitaries, badgering that idiot Adams for pay for his troops....

For nothing. All for nothing.

Alexander could feel an abyss yawning beneath him. On the one side, all his plans: a military academy, a naval academy. Had anyone else given serious thought to how many steps per minute were ideal in a march? On the other, a howling void, all he'd built knocked down with the glorious unconcern of a small child building a block tower only to shatter it down again. Only this wasn't a child's toy, this was the republic they'd fought for with the lives of their comrades. Had they all forgotten so soon? If General Washington were still alive . . .

Grief oppressed him. Grief for the lives lost, for the lives still to be lost. General Washington, gone. His father-in-law, once a vibrant, powerful man, now plagued with illness. Alexander hadn't wanted to worry Eliza, he had tried to make it sound as nothing, but during his stay in Albany his father-in-law had taken a turn so bad they had sent for Eliza's youngest sister, Kitty. He'd rallied, thank the Lord, but it had struck Alexander to his core, the contrast between the Philip Schuyler he had so admired, a soldier, a statesman, a lord of the North, to a querulous old man in a bath chair who looked to Alexander to solve his financial and political difficulties.

And Alexander was happy to do so! His mind was constantly whirring, seeking sinecures for Angelica's husband, so that Angelica might continue to cut a dash, and financial remedies for his father-in-law, so he could reign, as he had always reigned, from his seat in Albany. Raise Eliza's brother's son, get Eliza's sister Peggy out of scrapes. All of that, Alexander would do all of that; he would raise an army, he would file motions, he would badger his friends with letters to stop Burr's ambitions, but if he paused, even for a moment, it would all come crashing down and he would be left naked and shivering, revealed as the poor forked creature he was.

Retire, Eliza urged. Live the life of a country squire. But without occupation, what was he? Nothing but a bastard from an island so small it was barely a dot on the map. All his achievements—they felt so fleeting. He had come from nothing and in a moment he would return to nothing, and where would that leave his Eliza, his children, who trusted him, who believed in the myths he had spun around himself?

The door crashed open and Philip Church breezed in, red-cheeked with cold, and a faint smell of rum about him.

"Where have you been?"

Philip rubbed his cold hands together. "Betting on sleigh races. Cadwallader Colden paid some men from the livery stable on Broadway to race a sleigh to the Manhattan Well and back again. I won half a crown off Peter De Hart."

"Sleigh races," Alexander repeated, trying to still his annoyance at Philip, annoyance that wasn't the boy's fault but the world's. He had been twenty and high-spirited once.

Sometimes it was hard to look at Philip and not think of the compromises he'd made, the bargains he'd struck, to keep John Church in employment so that Philip might wear a coat of the latest cut and waste half a crown on sleigh races.

Sleigh races.

Alexander set down his pen, his attention suddenly very focused. "What is Cadwallader Colden doing holding sleigh races?"

Philip, cheerful with cherry bounce, was unperturbed by Alexander's sharp tone. "They're saying Levi Weeks carried Julianna Sands off in a sleigh and this proves it."

"Gulielma. Gulielma Sands." The rumormongers could at least get the girl's name right. It was the sloppiness Alexander found so offensive.

"Julianna sounds more romantical," said Philip cheerfully.

"This isn't a romance. It's a woman's life—and a man's," said Alexander sharply. He'd never thought of a sleigh. He'd hired Rhinelander to walk to the well and back, timing his progress, and had been comfortably assured he'd done what he ought, but this put a different complexion on matters entirely.

If Weeks was guilty . . . Alexander felt obscurely that this was all Aaron Burr's fault. If Burr hadn't been defending Weeks, Alexander would never have volunteered to join his defense, but here he was, facing two unpleasant options. Either Weeks was guilty, and Alexander would have to swallow his scruples and defend a murderer, or he was innocent, but with such damning evidence against him that it would take a momentous effort to defeat.

Burr wasn't going to do anything about it and neither was Livingston; they were both off on their own affairs, and, goodness knew, Alexander should be busying himself with his.

Alexander looked at the pile of memoranda on his desk, the unanswered correspondence, the half-written letter to George Izard.

"I'm going out," he said abruptly. He jabbed a finger at the pile of correspondence. "Reply to that."

He jammed his hat onto his head and strode out of his office, making for Greenwich Street. The cold air hit his face like a tonic, quickening his step, sharpening his thoughts.

If there had been a sleigh, the neighbors might have seen it. Alexander had meant to speak to the neighbors, but there had been no time before he'd left for Albany, and after his return he had been utterly preoccupied with the affairs of the army.

Alexander's chest ached at the thought of his

army, but he forced himself not to think of it, to keep moving, down Greenwich Street, the same path he'd taken that fateful day two months ago on his way to Joseph Watkins's shop to buy Eliza a coffee biggin.

"Jos. Watkins, Ironmonger," read the sign above the door.

Inside were the usual wares of the ironmonger, nails and tools and cooking pots of every description, including a row of the coffee biggins he'd intended for Eliza. A young woman, about Alexander's daughter Angelica's age, was wrapping a parcel for a customer. Alexander paused to examine the coffee biggins—there was one with lion handles on the side that he rather fancied for Eliza—waiting until the door closed behind the customer before approaching the girl.

"Miss Watkins?" It was a safe guess. These businesses were usually family concerns. "I was wondering if I might have a word with your father."

The girl didn't ask who he was or what he wanted. She raised her voice and shouted, "Pa! Gentleman to see you!"

A man in a leather apron bustled through the door that separated the shop from regions beyond. He had the same prosperous appearance as his shop; his graying hair was neatly cut. "How many times must I tell you, Fanny—General Hamilton! You honor us with your custom. How may I be of service to you?"

It was very gratifying being greeted with that sort of enthusiasm.

This, thought Alexander, was the very sort of tradesman they needed for the Federalists. He turned the full force of his charm on the ironmonger. "I'd intended to buy a coffee biggin for my wife—and very fine ones you have here. But I fear it's other business that brings me here today. The matter of Levi Weeks."

"Ah." The tradesman's expression turned wary. "We'd imagined someone would be around about that, sooner or late. Would you like to come through, sir? My wife can give you a dish of tea. Or coffee from our own biggin."

Alexander put his hat under his arm. "That's very kind of you."

"Fanny," said Watkins. "Tell your mother we have a distinguished visitor."

"But, Pa . . ." The request was clearly too great an imposition to be borne.

"Now," her father said firmly.

With a swish of her skirt, the girl departed. Alexander could hear her shouting, "Ma!"

Watkins looked resignedly after her. "My apologies for my daughter. She used to be a great help in the shop, but she's of an age . . ."

"I have one of that age myself," said Alexander, although he couldn't imagine his sweet Angelica behaving so.

"This affair next door," said Watkins, still clearly feeling some excuse was needed. "It's unsettled her. It's unsettled us all, to be honest."

"Your house adjoins the Rings' boardinghouse?"

"It does," said Watkins guardedly. He untied his leather apron.

Alexander watched him closely. "The night Miss Sands disappeared—did you see anything in the street? Hear anything?"

Watkins seemed to relax a little. "Not that night, no."

"You didn't see a sleigh?"

Watkins took his time hanging the apron on a hook by the door. "I saw any number of sleighs. But I didn't see Elma Sands climb into one."

"You've heard, then," said Alexander, wondering how long it would take for the whole town to know that Levi Weeks had abducted Elma Sands in a sleigh.

"It would have been hard not to. Mr. Colden began his trial just outside our door. My boys rushed out to follow the sleigh. But no, I didn't see Elma in a sleigh that night." A shadow crossed Watkins's face. "I was there when they found her. It's a sight that will haunt me to my dying day."

"How did you come to be there?"

"Elias Ring told me the muff Elma had been wearing that night had been found in a well. He wanted someone to go with him. So I went." Watkins's face was gray. He recalled himself with an effort. "Here, it's foolish to be standing in the shop with a dry throat when I might offer you coffee in comfort."

Watkins led Alexander through the door that separated the shop from the house's living quarters, into a comfortable front room containing somewhat more the usual amount of ironware. Candles stood on iron holders, an iron-and-tin coffee biggin sat on the table, and an iron stove warmed the room. A heavily pregnant woman not in her first youth was pouring boiling water into the coffee biggin.

"Let me, my dear," said Watkins, and took the kettle from his wife.

"Ha," said Mrs. Watkins, "showing off your good manners for your distinguished visitor? Sir," she added, dropping a clumsy curtsy to Alexander.

"Thank you for receiving me," said Alexander. "I'm afraid I'm here to talk to you about the sad matter of Elma Sands."

"We've heard you're to save Levi from the gallows," said Mrs. Watkins, who apparently had no thought that didn't make its way to her lips. She jerked her head toward the wall. "You've made no friends over there."

"In the Ring house, you mean?" That was no news. When Alexander had attempted to interview Catherine Ring, she had accorded him the respect due his station, but made it quite clear she viewed him as being of the devil's party.

"They're not bad neighbors," said Watkins vaguely.

His wife didn't seem to share that view. "People constantly coming and going, that Mr. Croucher oozing over here at dinnertime trying to sell me stockings and goodness only knows what fripperies, and that Elma—"

Alexander raised his brows, looking from one to the other. "That Elma?"

"She wasn't the companion I'd have chosen for my girls, that's all," said Mrs. Watkins, and busied herself with the coffee biggin.

Alexander nodded his thanks as she handed him a cup of extremely strong coffee, and made a note to remember to purchase Eliza her biggin before departing.

"Elma was an associate of Fanny's," said Watkins, choosing his words carefully. "She had a way about her—Fanny was mad to fold her kerchief the way she did and copy the way she dressed her hair."

"Elma was trouble," said his wife flatly, handing Watkins a cup. "Remember that time she told Catherine Ring she'd been here with us when she hadn't?

And Catherine blaming us for Elma catching a chill."

"She wasn't a bad girl. The little ones loved her. She always had time for them, even when Fanny didn't. She'd play with their toys with them and listen to their stories." Mr. Watkins looked down at his coffee cup. "She used to tell me she wished she had a father like they did."

"You just liked her because she flattered you," Mrs. Watkins accused her husband.

"No—I think she meant it. She needed a father, that poor girl."

Alexander could feel the coffee energizing him, sharpening his wits. "You say she told Mrs. Ring that she was here with you when she wasn't?"

Watkins looked troubled. "She did come and stay over here now and again. They've a lot of coming and going at that house; boarders there for a few weeks and then gone."

Mrs. Watkins snorted. "Catherine Ring would rent out her own bed if it would make her a penny."

Her husband sent her a quelling glance. "Elma used to say there were nights when she hardly knew where she was to sleep or whether there'd be a bed for her."

"As if we have that many beds here with six of our own and your apprentices!" Mrs. Watkins let out a long breath. "There was a time or two that Elma stayed for supper and stayed on after—I'd hear her and Fanny up whispering to all hours and goodness only knows what they were talking about, the two of them! But there was a night she said she was here that she wasn't."

"Maybe Catherine Ring misunderstood her," said Watkins.

"I think Catherine Ring understood her very well," his wife retorted. "After what she got up to in September—"

She broke off, biting down hard on her lip.

"More coffee?" she asked, lifting the biggin.

Alexander wasn't to be distracted. "What did Elma get up to in September?"

The ironmonger and his wife exchanged a long look.

Mr. Watkins said slowly, "As you may have seen, our house shares a wall with the Ring house. The wall is only a plank partition, plastered and lathed on both sides."

"My husband made it himself—and might have made it thicker," Mrs. Watkins said pointedly. It was clearly an old argument. "You can't sneeze in here without them over there hearing it. We've no privacy at all."

"And nor have they," admitted Mr. Watkins. "I hardly like to say it. . . . It may have been nothing at all. But I imagined one night I heard the shaking of a bed and considerable noise there, in the second story, where Elma's bed stood."

"Imagined, ha! If you imagined it, I imagined it too." Mrs. Watkins turned back to Alexander. "He said to me, Joseph did, she'll be ruined next. Elma, that is."

It was just in keeping with this thoroughly awful day that his investigation would yield information damning for Levi Weeks, thought Alexander grimly. Previously, only Richard Croucher had been willing to attest to relations of a sexual nature between Elma and the accused. Perhaps Burr and Livingston had the right of it; perhaps he should have insisted the girl committed suicide and looked no further. Perhaps he should never have involved himself in the case at all.

"And you have no doubts as to the nature of the noise?" asked Alexander.

"There was no mistaking it," said Mrs. Watkins firmly. "I was of two minds about letting Fanny associate with her after that, but we knew it wouldn't go on after Catherine came back from the country—and Elma did have a winning way about her," Mrs. Watson allowed grudgingly. "But once Catherine Ring told me Elma was saying she was here when she wasn't, I knew it was starting up all over again—and we would have said something—but we didn't want trouble—it's never good to have trouble with your neighbors—and who knew it would come to this?"

Who, indeed. Alexander asked himself that on a daily basis about the army, about his legal practice, about his expenses, about the state of the country. How had it come to this? He forced himself to return his attention to the Watkinses. If this information was true, then it was time he had a long talk with Levi Weeks, who had claimed that he had visited Elma "only for conversation." If he had lied about that, what else might he be lying about?

"You are quite certain you heard Elma Sands in a compromising position with Levi Weeks?"

A curious stillness seized both the ironmonger and his wife. Watkins froze with his coffee cup half to his lips; Mrs. Watkins's lips opened as though to speak, but no sound came out. She looked to her husband.

"We heard Elma Sands in a compromising position, yes," said Watkins slowly. "But . . ."

Mrs. Watkins gave her head a brisk shake. "Go on. Tell him. What's the use of hiding it now? It's bound to come out anyway."

Watkins hesitated, looking a decade older than his years.

Alexander drew himself up, embodying all the

majesty of the law. "If you have some information that has a bearing on the murder of Elma Sands, it is your bounden duty to share it so that justice might be served."

Watkins set down his coffee cup. "It wasn't Levi Weeks I heard through that wall with Elma. It was Elias Ring."

Chapter Thirteen

During [Elma's] indisposition [Levi] paid her the strictest attention, and spent several nights in the room, saying he did not like to leave her with Hope—my sister—fearing she might get to sleep and neglect her; and in the night he wanted to go for a physician, but I discouraged him, thinking she would get better by morning.

—From the testimony of Catherine Ring
at the trial of Levi Weeks

New York City
March 1, 1800

"Have thee seen Elias?" Caty hissed, catching Hope just as Hope had almost made it to the door.

"No," Hope lied.

She had seen him leave an hour earlier, heading in the direction of the tavern by the corner of Greenwich and Barclay. Her sister's husband had become a frequent patron there. Hope wasn't sure if it was for the numbing properties of their rum or to get away from the tension emanating from Caty like one of Mr. Franklin's experiments with lightning.

"Elias's great friend Mr. Croucher has brought his intended to see his room—and her serving maid to clean it for him." Caty's voice vibrated with indignation. She straightened abruptly at the sight of someone over Hope's shoulder. "Mrs. Stackhaver. Was the room to thy liking?"

It was evident Mrs. Stackhaver was a faithful purchaser of Mr. Croucher's wares; Hope recognized the lace fichu, too thin and fine for March, and the silk that made up the widow's turban. Mr. Croucher sauntered behind his betrothed, looking well pleased with himself. They made a striking couple, both brilliant in brocade, utterly out of place in the simple environs of the boardinghouse.

"We need water and rags," said Mrs. Stackhaver imperiously. Beneath her carefully cultivated tones, Hope could hear a strong trace of a rural Dutch accent. "I'll set my girl to cleaning."

"Mr. Croucher's room," said Caty tightly, "is cleaned as often as anyone else's."

"Which is not enough," sniffed Mrs. Stackhaver. "Margaret!"

A girl appeared behind her, all big eyes and thin wrists, her brown hair modestly braided beneath her cap. She looked hardly older than Rachel. "Ma'am?"

"Mrs.—" Mrs. Stackhaver looked blankly at Caty. Mr. Croucher leaned over and whispered into her ear. "Mrs. Ring will bring you what you need to render that room habitable."

"Habitable," muttered Caty, as she turned toward the kitchen, to get the desired materials. "Habitable, she says. As if it weren't his mess that was the trouble. Dropping his clothes on the floor, expecting me to pick up after him. . . ."

"Caty." Hope cut in before the rant could develop further. "Caty, I'm going out."

"Out?" Her sister looked at her sharply, panic in her face. "And who's to mind Phoebe and Eliza while I'm minding Mrs. Stackhaver?"

"Rachel is with them," said Hope soothingly. "I've finished the hats Peggy left to trim and I've fried the oil cakes thee asked me to make. I thought I would bring a basket of oil cakes to the Widow Broad—thee are always saying what a sad thing it is she gets so few visitors and her son never takes any notice of her."

"Ye-es," admitted Caty. "It's a fine Christian thing and it was kind of thee to consider the notion, but . . ."

"Mrs. Ring!" bellowed Mrs. Stackhaver.

"I won't be long," said Hope reassuringly, and bolted before Caty could call her back.

The door made its usual prolonged creaking noise as Hope pulled it firmly shut behind her. Safely out in the street, Hope slipped expertly into the shuffling gait that marked her as a true New Yorker. She'd barked her shins on protruding stoops and pump handles more times than she cared to count when they'd first come to the city, but now she knew just how to weave around obstacles and avoid the wild pigs that periodically charged through the streets.

Hope breathed in deeply. With the slight thaw, the air stank of refuse both animal and human, but it was still preferable to the close confines of the boardinghouse.

Ever since Elma had disappeared, Hope could scarce go to meeting without Caty pacing in front of the door until she got back. *I'm not Elma,* Hope had told her, but Caty had only looked distracted and said who knew what dangers were out there and was that the stew burning?

The cakes for the Widow Broad bumped in their basket against Hope's hip. Hope's breath came faster, making puffs in the air. The Widow Broad lived just across Greenwich Street from Ezra Weeks's lumber yard. From Levi.

Hope hated herself for what she was doing, but she couldn't seem to stop herself. The day they'd buried Elma, she'd snuck out and hurried down to the Bridewell. It was a foolish thing, really; she should have known she'd have no sight of him. She'd turned around and rushed home again, just in time to see Elias organizing the removal of Elma's coffin into the street.

And then, of course, there had been Levi's visit to the boardinghouse. Hope had turned over every word that had passed between them, miserably certain she had made a poor show of herself, that if she had it to do again she would do it differently: be more immune to his charm, steel herself against his lies, force him to admit what he'd done.

How *dare* he imply that she might have harmed Elma? She'd loved Elma.

She just hadn't liked her very much those last three months, and it was Levi who was to blame for that.

Levi who was, impossibly, alarmingly, hauling a large plank of wood into his brother's workshop. He lost his grip on his burden at the sight of her, futilely grappling to keep it from falling on the damp ground.

He hauled it up again, staring at her with such mingled hope and trepidation that Hope began to wish she hadn't come after all or, having come, had simply gone on walking at the sight of him.

"Hope. I hadn't dared wish—"

Hope drew away. "I've come to bring cakes to the Widow Broad. If I'd known thee were here I would never have come near."

Her conscience twanged. Lies, all lies. She'd come just for this but now she was here she couldn't remember what she'd wanted of him. To look at his face and see if it bore the mark of the murderer? To berate him as she had done before in the hopes he would, at last, break down and confess?

If only he'd just *admit* to what he'd done, then she might be able to put him from her mind. Not her heart, she told herself fiercely. She'd long ago put him from her heart.

"I'll leave you to your act of mercy, then," he said. There was something different about him. It wasn't just the effect of the gray light of the strange season that wasn't quite winter but wasn't yet spring. His face was thinner, his cheekbones sharper, and there was a bitter edge to his voice that hadn't been there before.

It pricked Hope, that he should sound so aggrieved, when he was the source of all their sorrows. "Thee had best hope for mercy," she said sharply, "from He who has the power to give it."

"Why? So I can take the blame for something I never did?" He took two quick steps forward, and Hope was struck by the wiry strength of him, the corded muscles in his arms, the heat that steamed off him.

"Thee knows thee could tell us of Elma if thee would!" she tossed back, refusing to be intimidated, trying to ignore the uneasy notion that this man—this man she once thought she knew—had already once committed murder and might again and there was no one to hear her but the Widow Broad, old, infirm, and increasingly deaf.

"You want me to tell you of Elma?" There was a dangerous edge to Levi's voice. "There are things I could tell of Elma. But they're not what you think. And you wouldn't thank me for telling them."

Hope was breathless with indignation. "Has thee the gall to imply thy crimes are of my cousin's making? I know thee shared a bed with her. Even Elias has admitted he heard thee together when we were away in New Cornwall."

In New Cornwall, where Hope had, like a ninny, spent the days daydreaming of a handsome carpenter, peeling the skin off apples and throwing them over her shoulder to see if they made a letter *L*.

"*Elias.*" Levi's voice was rich with loathing.

"Did thee think he would hold his tongue? Like thee thought Elma would hold her tongue about thy marriage?"

"There was no marriage!" Levi shouted. He controlled himself with an effort, his chest rising and falling rapidly beneath his worn work shirt. Abruptly, he said, "You want the truth? I did ask Elma to marry me. But not that night. And not for the reasons you think. If I could turn back the clock and change what happened, I would—but *it's not what you think.*"

Hope's throat hurt. "Thee said thee never asked her to marry thee."

Levi closed the space between them, leaning his arms on top of the fence that enclosed his brother's yard. "I said I didn't go to be married to her that night."

"Thee argue like a lawyer," Hope said bitterly.

"Hope . . ." The fury had leached from Levi's face, leaving only regret—and something like pity. "Hope, there are things you don't know."

"I know enough. I know thee to be false as a March thaw." Hope stomped up to the fence, shaking with rage and frustration. "First thee said there was nothing between thee and Elma, nothing more than fellowship, and now thee say thee asked her to marry thee. Thee claim she never left with thee—but a month from now, will thee say otherwise?"

"I've never lied to you. I've only kept those secrets that weren't mine to share." Levi straightened, his eyes on hers. "If you want to know the truth, apply to your sister."

Hope gawped at him. "Caty? Caty has no secrets from me."

The idea of Caty—Caty!—keeping secrets was absurd. Caty didn't have time for secrets; her every moment was occupied with the boardinghouse and the children and the millinery.

"Ask her." Levi grasped her arm; Hope could feel his touch burning through the thick wool of her sleeve. "Ask her about Elma's illness—her cramping of the stomach. Ask her why she wouldn't let me go for the doctor."

Hope stared down at his fingers. She drew in a long breath, saying, as steadily as she could, "Thee are hurting me."

Levi dropped her arm, looking horrified. "I would never hurt you."

"Is that what thee said to Elma?" Hope asked smartly, and turned away before the devil could seduce her further.

Chapter Fourteen

ELIAS RING: At this time, when my wife was gone into the country, Levi and Elma were constantly together in private. I was alone and very lonesome and was induced to believe from their conduct that they were shortly to be married.

DEFENSE: Were you not the friend and protector of Elma?

ELIAS RING: Yes.

—From the testimony of Elias Ring at the trial of Levi Weeks

New York City
March 1, 1800

The devil made work for idle hands, that's what Caty always told her daughters, but here she was, lurking by the door, waiting for Elias, even though there was dinner to be cooked and rooms to clean—because apparently she didn't get her rooms clean enough, even if her hands were raw and calloused and her back hurt from the endless bending.

Maybe if Elias didn't disappear goodness only knew where, maybe if he took on any of the work of the boardinghouse at all, people wouldn't feel they had to bring their future wife's servant to see their room properly cleaned.

Caty knew pride was a sin, but it hurt her all the same. She'd heard what people were saying about her establishment. Disorderly. Ill managed. It didn't help that the front door still stuck. Couldn't Elias even take the time to fix the door? She'd only been asking him for the past three months. But no. He was too busy pursuing businesses that came to nothing, too important to complete the homely tasks she begged him to take on. It was all too homely for him.

Caty was too homely for him.

Caty pushed that thought aside. She could hear Elias's voice through the open top of the door, raised in greeting to someone—and not altogether steady. It was the distance that was slurring his words, she told herself, and retreated into their bedroom, just behind the door, so it wouldn't look as though she was waiting for him, so she could come bustling out and pretend surprise.

So strange to see thee at home! I had thought thee had gone abroad.

No, too bitter. Not the best start for a helpful conversation about ways in which Elias might participate more in the work of the household, while delicately intimating that she knew he was going to the tavern when he said he was going to meeting but was prepared to ignore it as long as it didn't happen again.

It was this business with Elma. It had shaken all of them.

But soon—within the month, Mr. Colden said—the case would go to trial, Levi would be hanged, and they could start again as they meant to go on, with all of this behind them.

Why, Elias! I had hoped thee might help me. The shutter in Mr. Lacey's room is askew. . . .

The front door opened with a prolonged groan. Caty took a deep breath and prepared to plunge forward, but before she could another pair of footsteps slapped sharply across the floor.

"Ah, Elias," said Mr. Croucher. "One would begin to think you were avoiding me."

Elias stopped short. Caty could hear his labored breath through the crack in the bedroom door—another thing Elias had failed to fix.

"I don't want to talk to thee," Elias muttered, and Caty felt a surge of relief. Maybe, just this once, Elias had heeded her words and had realized that entering into a business with Mr. Croucher would bring nothing but trouble and debts. "Why won't thee leave me be?"

"Why, Elias," chided Mr. Croucher. "You know why."

"Isn't it enough?" The anguish in Elias's voice pierced the warped wood of the door. "I've done as thee said. I've forsworn myself again and again."

"Hardly." Mr. Croucher sounded amused. "How can you forswear yourself when your creed forbids you to swear? Besides, none of it is outright lies. You've only . . . implied."

"I told the lawyer I heard Elma at it." Elias was whispering, but he was as bad at whispering as he was at running a dry goods store; Caty could hear him as clearly as if he'd shouted. "I told him I found her clothes lying in the room on the second floor when there was no one in the house but her and me and Levi."

Caty fitted her eye against the crack. She could see Mr. Croucher's hand on Elias's arm, a red stone shining dully in the ring on his finger. "You told perfect truth. You did hear her—and you did see her clothes lying where they'd been pulled off her. You simply neglected to add that it was you there with her yourself—enjoying her favors."

The wood of the door scraped Caty's cheek. No. She couldn't have heard what she thought she'd heard. She'd misunderstood. The idea of Elias—with Elma—no. It wasn't possible. Mr. Croucher—he was worldly, a sinner, he judged everyone by his own standards. He might have seen—oh, Elias talking to Elma, as a good brother should.

Only as a brother! Yes, Elma had a taking way about her, and, yes, Elias enjoyed her sallies, but it was no more than he might have exchanged with Hope. It was just high spirits on Elma's part and indulgence on Elias's.

"Must thee needs remind me?" Elias hissed.

"I wouldn't have you forget yourself—or what you owe me. But for me, they'd be on you now, you know. It would be all over the city, what you did—with her. You might have remembered to close the door. Or were you that eager to tup her that you forgot?"

"I would I'd never been born."

Croucher clapped Elias on the back. "Come, it was a bit of sport. It's what they're made for, the pretty jades. Without women, hell would be like a lord's great kitchen with no fire in it. You'd be a fool not to warm yourself by the blaze when it's offered."

Elias made a strangled noise.

Caty felt like her own throat was frozen, all of her was frozen, turned to a pillar of salt, like Lot's wife. What was Sodom and Gomorrah to this? Her own husband . . . her own cousin! No. It was lies. It had to be lies.

Croucher went on, persuasively, "How were you to know the girl would get herself murdered by a jealous lover? No one need have known—and no one need know so long as you're careful. I'll see to it for you. If you abide by the terms we agreed."

"I'll do as thee says." Elias's voice was so low, Caty could hardly hear him. "What other choice have I?"

"None," agreed Croucher genially. "You could tell the truth and shame the devil—but I don't think they'd take well to that sort of thing in your meeting, do you?"

The stairs creaked beneath his tread as he ascended, whistling.

Elias yanked open the door to the bedroom and saw Caty standing there, white-faced. An expression of sheer panic crossed his face, so familiar and so strange. She had cupped that jaw. She had kissed those lips. She had stroked that hair.

And so had Elma.

Caty could scarcely force her lips to move. "Is it true?"

Elias pushed past her, making for the hook to hang up his cloak. "I have no idea what thee mean."

"Elma—thee—" Caty couldn't make herself say any more. It was too vile for words. Lies—it had to be lies.

But then why hadn't Elias said so? Why hadn't he fought back?

A hundred unbidden memories rushed in on her from the past three years. Elma, laughing up at Elias. Elma, lifting her skirt to show the steps of a dance and a good flash of ankle besides. Elma, asking Elias to help her tie the ribbon of one of the hats she'd trimmed so she might show it to them, and Elias chucking Elma under the chin and saying he hoped the face it adorned would be half so pretty as hers.

It had made her uneasy, but there'd been nothing in it, Caty was sure of it. How could there be? It was just Elma's way, and the sooner she was safely married the better. And if she'd half wondered, there'd been nothing to give her pause when she came back to town. If anything, Elma had avoided Elias, leaving the front room as soon as he entered, stepping behind the curtain of the bed when she heard his step on the stair.

Elma—skulking out of her way. Caty had thought it was because she'd scolded her for the state the house was in.

Elma—disappearing the second Elias entered a room.

Elma, holding up a vial of laudanum and locking eyes with Elias, only Elias, as she threatened to drink it whole.

Caty could feel herself starting to shake, as though she had the ague. She was hot and cold all at once. "Elias..."

He had his back to her, his shoulders bent, his hands clenching and unclenching at his sides. He turned, and there was something in his face she had never seen before.

"If thee had been here where thee were meant to be," he said viciously, "none of this would have happened. Does thee know how lonely it was with everyone gone away? Thee went away and left me."

"I—" Caty's lips moved but the sound wouldn't come out.

"I begged thee to come home." Elias advanced toward her. "I wrote to thee and I begged thee. But no. Thee was too busy basking in the country air to attend to thy own husband."

Caty licked her dry lips. "Elma was a girl—in our care."

"She was a woman grown. She knew what she was about. Thee left me here with her."

"Not with her—" Just to manage the boardinghouse. Not to share her husband's bed. Caty covered her mouth with her hand, unable to bear the image.

"See?" Elias loomed over her, forcing Caty to crane her neck back to look at him. "Thee knows what thee did."

Caty felt like a shattered cup, all sharp-edged pieces. "I didn't leave because I wanted to. It was for the children. . . . Our children."

Rachel and David and Phoebe and Eliza . . . their little trundles lined up so neatly beneath the bed.

"It was only six weeks," Caty said desperately. "We were only gone six weeks."

"Only. Even when thy body is here thy spirit is absent. Thee never has time for me. Everyone is more important to thee than thine own husband. At least Elma—"

He broke off, the import of what he was saying clear to both of them.

Elma wasn't cooking and cleaning for thee, Caty wanted to say. Elma wasn't making sure thy children were clothed and thy bills paid. But she knew if she did they would cross a bridge over which they could never return. And she wanted, so badly, to go back to an hour ago, before she knew.

"Elma listened to me," he finished.

She'd done more than listen.

Caty bit her lip hard, the pain anchoring her. "Richard Croucher—how does he come to know this?"

"He saw us," Elias said briefly.

"He saw her with thee. Not Levi." Caty remembered the way Richard Croucher had smirked at her, and now she knew why.

Elias made an impatient gesture. "For all thee know, he saw her with Levi too. No one misses a slice off a cut loaf. Why does thee think Levi would sooner kill her than marry her? He knew what she was."

"What thee made of her." The words were out before Caty could stop them.

Elias's face hardened. "She was a daughter of Eve. And thee—if thee had been a proper wife to me, I would never have had to look elsewhere. This is thy doing, Catherine, thine and none else's. Let that be a lesson to thee."

"I never meant . . ."

"No, thee were headstrong and proud. If thee had been guided by me, none of this would have been visited upon us."

But it hadn't been visited upon them. This wasn't divine retribution. Elias had made the choice to share her cousin's bed.

What else might Elias have done?

"Elias, thee didn't . . . hurt her?"

"What does thee take me for? It was Levi. It was Levi who killed her. Thee knows it to be true. What? Do thee think I pushed her in the well? I was by thy side that night." He seized her by the shoulders, his fingers digging into her skin through the thick layers of linen and wool. "Thee knows I was in the house. Thee will attest to that in court, because thee knows it to be true."

Elias slouched so these days that Caty had forgotten how tall her husband was, how strong his hands. He'd helped build their meetinghouse, hauling those boards, hammering nails. He'd grown soft in their city life, but that old strength was still there in his fingers.

"Yes," she choked out. "Thee were here. With me."

Except when he wasn't.

Elias released her, so abruptly that she staggered.

"What happened before—it was nothing to do with anything. We will never speak of it again, does thee understand me?"

Caty nodded, not trusting herself to speak.

"Good," he said, and turned to go.

"Elias?" Caty's shoulders hurt where his fingers had pressed. Or maybe that was her imagination. He hadn't held her so hard.

"Yes?"

"The front door—" she said tentatively. "It still sticks. If thee might find the time to fix it?"

His eyes met hers. Caty used to love his eyes. She used to love the way he looked at her. Now he was staring at her narrow-eyed, as though gauging her intentions.

He gave a short, brief nod. "All right. I'll do it today."

"I thank thee—husband," Caty said, and tried not to think of Elma.

Chapter Fifteen

I had taken my passage for this day, and anticipated the pleasure of dining with you on Saturday. But—but—these buts—how they mar all the fine theories of life! But our friend Thomas Morris has entreated in such terms that I would devote this day and night to certain subjects of the utmost moment to him, that I could not, without the appearance of unkindness, refuse. . . . But, again, more buts. *But* after I had consented to give him a day, I sent to take passage for tomorrow and lo! the stage is taken by the sheriff to transport criminals to the state prison. I should not be much gratified with this kind of association on the road, and thus I apprehend my journey will be (must be) postponed until Friday, and my engagement to dine with you until Monday.

—Aaron Burr to his daughter,
Theodosia, March 5, 1800

New York City
March 11, 1800

Aaron Burr sat in a ramshackle office on Water Street and contemplated murder.

It was Shakespeare, if Aaron recalled correctly, who had blithely urged, "Let's kill all the lawyers." That seemed a bit extreme. Aaron would happily limit the carnage to one General Alexander Hamilton, who, not content with wasting his own time, was intent on wasting Aaron's as well.

After an exceedingly tedious journey, delayed by one annoyance after another, Aaron had returned home in happy anticipation of a joyful welcome from his Theodosia and instead had discovered Theodosia gone to visit her half brother John Bartow Prevost, leaving an empty house which Hamilton had attempted to fill with a barrage of agitated correspondence, all demanding Aaron's immediate presence for news of great moment.

This news appeared to have something to do with the sexual habits of the residents of the boardinghouse on Greenwich Street, a topic which Aaron viewed as entirely insufficient for dragging him down to Hamilton's office on Water Street when he had far more urgent matters to attend to, including, but not limited to, Theodosia's disregard of his intentions, the conduct of the coming elections, and the state of his coffers.

Aaron's creditors were showing an unsettling tendency to desire the return of their money.

Thomas Morris—he had been terribly apologetic about it, but he had suffered reversals of his own. Morris's reversals, Aaron was quite sure, were nothing compared to the amount Aaron had lost through the ill-fated Holland Land Company. The thought of the hundred thousand acres he'd had to default on made him feel sick. Theodosia was still angry at him for dragging his stepson John Bartow into bankruptcy.

There were few people for whose good opinion Aaron cared, but Theodosia was one. Perhaps the only one.

John Bartow would recoup his fortunes—they would all recoup their fortunes—as soon as these elections were won. Power, patronage, emoluments. What were a few trifling debts to those?

And it was all his, provided this prancing nuisance in front of him could be kept sufficiently distracted. Aaron had no doubt that if he faced any threat to his ambitions at all, it was from Hamilton. He could only be grateful that Hamilton's obvious talents were counterbalanced by his poor sense.

For example, expending his energies hunting down rumors about the amorous peccadilloes of Quakers.

Aaron broke into Hamilton's monologue. "Can one truly identify a voice heard through the wall—under such circumstances?"

"The walls are mere lathe and plaster. And it wasn't just the once. The neighbor said he heard it as many as fourteen times, in the time of the sickness—from the middle of September until Mrs. Ring returned in October."

"If this is the case," Aaron asked skeptically, "why did he not come forward before?"

"He didn't want to make trouble for the Rings." Hamilton was so excited that he didn't even bother to enhance his words with his usual flowery decoration. "You know how these small tradesmen are. They keep to themselves. He said Catherine Ring is a nice woman and doesn't deserve the shame. And he thought it ended when Catherine Ring came home from the country."

Brockholst was sprawled on a chair far too small for his large frame; it looked in imminent danger of reverting to the bare slats from which it had been formed. "Are you saying that the Quaker killed her? Doesn't their creed forbid violence?"

"The doors of hell—and the halls of our prisons—would gape empty if men abided by the strictures of their creeds," Hamilton countered. "Is not a Quaker yet a man?"

"If you prick him, does he not bleed?" murmured Aaron. "Never mind. Go on."

Hamilton needed no encouragement. "When Elma Sands first disappeared, Elias Ring insisted she had killed herself in a love fit and engaged a local waterman to drag the area around Rhinelander's battery. It wasn't until her body was found in the Manhattan Well"—there was a pause as the hated name was uttered—"that he began to level accusations at Levi Weeks and do so most vehemently."

Thank goodness for the Manhattan Company. Without it, Aaron would be even now in debtor's prison. "Your point being?"

"Why change his tune so abruptly? Why unless he feared the girl's body would show signs of violence—that he himself had inflicted?" Hamilton didn't wait for Aaron to respond; it might interfere with his enjoyment of his own voice. "We know Elias Ring returned to the boardinghouse before Elma departed that night—two boarders have remarked on it—but we have only his wife's word that he remained there. He might easily have slipped away at the same time as Elma or a little after."

"Mere speculation." Even as he said it, Aaron had to admit that there was something in the story Hamilton was telling. He just wasn't sure he wanted there to be something in it. His instructions from Ezra Weeks had been clear; the case, simple. "What proof have we other than the word of this neighbor?"

"The neighbor's name is Watkins, Joseph Watkins, a very accomplished ironmonger. He makes an excellent coffee biggin," Hamilton added.

Aaron failed to see the relevance of that statement. "Did he tell anyone else of what he heard?"

"He did. He told one man. Richard Croucher." Hamilton pronounced the name as though it was meant to signify something to them.

Aaron raised a brow, pretending he had any idea who Hamilton was talking about.

"The lodger." Brockholst frowned. He might claim to be giving the case little attention, but Aaron knew Brockholst of old; he always did all the assigned reading, and then read the gloss and the commentaries to boot. Brockholst had time for such things. Brockholst didn't have lists of voters to compile before the coming elections; he had Aaron to do that for him. He had only to ride Aaron's efforts to victory. "He claimed he caught Levi Weeks in flagrante delicto with Elma Sands."

"Precisely." Hamilton jabbed a finger in the air. "He is the only one who claims to have seen Levi Weeks engaged in carnal relations with Elma Sands."

"There is nothing to preclude both of these being

true," said Aaron drily. "She might have been distributing her favors broadly. She was a bastard. They are notoriously prone to hot blood."

Hamilton didn't even hear him. He was too busy extolling his own brilliance. "Think of it. Who has more reason to do away with Elma Sands? The young man who felt for her nothing but affection or the married man with four children who could see his entire existence rendered as nothing if she reveals their affair to his wife?"

"This could work to our cause," said Brockholst thoughtfully. "Even if the Quaker didn't kill her, this will raise doubt in the minds of the jury. This Watkins. He's prepared to testify?"

"As is his wife, a most respectable matron. And there's more."

"A confession, perhaps?" Aaron asked sourly. Hamilton was meant to be off chasing wild geese, not catching and bringing them home dressed and stuffed for supper. It didn't at all suit Aaron's purposes to have Hamilton the savior of Levi Weeks, the man who single-handedly flushed out the true killer of Elma Sands.

"Near enough," said Hamilton seriously. "Before we were called to defend Weeks—"

Aaron gave a dry cough. Once again, Hamilton rewrote history to suit his own fancies.

"Before we were called to defend Weeks, a campaign was already being waged against him, designed to impress the conviction of his guilt so firmly in the minds of the public that no amount of evidence would be sufficient to remove it. We were told that he was engaged to Elma Sands; we were told that he left with her to be married that night; we were told all this as incontrovertible truth. Whence did these so-called truths spring? This was a tale carefully crafted, deliberately told, not the random meanderings of idle speculation." Hamilton drew himself to his full height, undoubtedly to avoid the pain of sitting. Hamilton's chairs were a thing of penance. "Not only can we prove that the true killer of Elma Sands was Elias Ring; we can also provide evidence that Levi Weeks, far from being a killer, was the victim of a concerted campaign of slander and misdirection, persecuted by cunningly contrived rumors."

"Slander hardly equates to murder," Aaron pointed out.

"Who has the motive to prove another's guilt but the man who bears that guilt himself? Rumor may have a thousand tongues, but the source of these stories has only one." Hamilton's face had the flush others might acquire from the enjoyment of a fine wine. "I spoke to all the other tradesmen in the area. None of them saw anything of Elma that night, or of Levi Weeks, but they all say Mr. Croucher has haunted their establishments, spreading slanderous stories about Levi Weeks. I believe that when Watkins told Croucher of his suspicions of Elias Ring's improper behavior with Elma, Croucher saw for himself a business opportunity. His silence and collusion in exchange for . . ."

"Money, one presumes." Brockholst was sitting up straighter in his chair, clearly intrigued.

"This is all speculation," said Aaron flatly. "All airy nothing."

"Until we prove it. Mrs. Forrest said something very curious. Wait. Let me find it." Hamilton turned out his pockets, providing an edifying assortment of scraps of odd paper scribbled on both sides. The one he was looking for appeared to be scrawled on the sort of brown paper usually reserved for wrapping parcels. "The Forrests keep a grocery establishment next to the Ring house. According to Mrs. Forrest, Croucher was in her shop with Elias Ring and told her that he'd passed by the well that very night—but not at the right moment. He repeated, several times, what a pity it was that he hadn't happened by at the right moment, because he might have saved her."

"By Jupiter," said Brockholst.

"And Minerva and her all-seeing owl," said Hamilton smugly. "You see it too, don't you? I believe he did go by the well that night. I believe Richard Croucher saw Elias Ring murder Elma Sands."

If this was so—if Croucher would reveal as much on the stand—Hamilton would be unendurable.

It might not be true. Hamilton always spoke as though his conclusions were the only conclusions and all other possibilities delusions. But if it was . . . then there must be some way yet to reclaim this for Aaron's own benefit.

They had only a month until the elections.

"What was this Mr. Croucher doing out there in the middle of nowhere after dark that he witnessed Miss Sands by the well?"

"He says"—Hamilton consulted another much-abused scrap of paper—"that he attended a birthday party at the home of a Mrs. Ann Ashmore—or possibly a Mrs. Ann Brown—and his way home led him through Lispenard's Meadow."

This caught Brockholst's attention. "You spoke to him?"

"Naturally. He tried to sell me stockings for Eliza."

Brockholst's brows drew together. "Never mind the stockings. You didn't mention your suspicions, I trust."

"No." Hamilton much preferred giving instructions to receiving them; Aaron could tell he was offended by Brockholst's abrupt tone.

"Does Colden know anything of this—of Elma Sands's relations with Elias Ring?"

Hamilton hadn't expected his news to be received in this way. "Not that I know of. Watkins said he hadn't told anyone else. As for Mrs. Forrest—I don't believe Colden spoke with her either. That's not to say he won't."

"He won't. He has the bit between his teeth about Levi abducting a girl in a sleigh. Ha!" Brockholst looked expectantly at his colleagues. "The bit between his teeth? Never mind. The important thing is that Colden remain in ignorance. If we can surprise him at trial . . ."

"Isn't the important thing that we bring the murderer of Elma Sands to justice?" declared Hamilton grandly.

What he meant, Aaron knew, was that he was picturing himself revealing the murderer, to the accolades of an adoring public.

"That," said Aaron, "is Cadwallader Colden's affair. However—one could make inquiries. Discreetly."

"Very discreetly," warned Brockholst.

"I was going to speak to Ann Ashmore—or Brown," said Hamilton. "To determine whether Mr. Croucher might have left at such a time that he would have passed by the well at the crucial moment."

Aaron exchanged a look with Brockholst. For once,

they were largely in agreement. If Hamilton was correct in this, they would have to ensure he not take the credit for it—or apprise Mr. Colden of this new theory of the case.

"Allow me," Aaron said. "I believe I know the house—and it can be done in such a way as to leave Mr. Colden entirely in ignorance."

Chapter Sixteen

The Sunday before the young woman was missing, I saw a young man sounding the Manhattan Well with a pole. I went up to him and asked him what he was about. He said he made the carpenter's work, and that he wanted to know the depth of the water. He measured it in different places and found it five foot five inches, five eight inches, and six foot.

—From the testimony of Matthew
Mustee at the trial of Levi Weeks

New York City
March 21, 1800

Cadwallader Colden couldn't believe his good fortune.

"You're certain it was the Sunday before the young woman went missing?" he asked the man in front of him.

The man heaved a barrel down off the back of his

wagon. It bore the legend "FINEST BRANDY." "Couldn't have been any other day, since it's Sundays I have free of my toil."

"And you saw a young man at the well." Cadwallader dodged out of the way of another barrel, which, no longer braced by its fellow, showed a disturbing inclination to seek its own exit.

The man fielded the barrel with the expertise of long experience, setting it safely on the ground outside the tavern. "With a pole."

"And he was sounding the depths, you say?"

The man paused, leaning on one of the barrels. "He said he'd done the carpenter's work, and wanted to know the depth of the water. He made it between five feet five inches and six foot. Deep enough, he said."

Deep enough. The words had an uncanny ring to them.

"And this man—do you think you might recognize him if you saw him again?"

"I'd recognize his jacket, for sure. Red as a robin's breast."

Clothing could be changed. "But his face—his voice—do you think you could pick him out in a courtroom?"

"Depends how many is in the courtroom," quipped the carter, but when Cadwallader didn't laugh, he thought about it and said, "Might do."

"It would be a great service," said Cadwallader seriously.

More service than this man knew. It chilled Cadwallader to the marrow to think of Levi Weeks testing the depth of the well, prying off the board, luring Elma with promise of marriage.

A crime of passion one could understand, if not condone. Actions taken in the heat of blood and then regretted. But this . . . It was monstrous, foul. No wonder people claimed the ghost of Elma Sands haunted the well, crying for justice. If ever justice was owed, it was here.

Levi Weeks might seem all that was amiable. But this was a man who took the time to sound the depth of the well before he dragged his lover, pleading for mercy, across the frosty ground and flung her into the unforgiving waters.

It shocked even Cadwallader.

He'd always supposed that the driving force came from Ezra Weeks, the stronger-willed of the brothers. But what if it was the other way around? What if it was Levi himself who had decided to rid himself of his unwanted encumbrance, and his brother, after the fact, who closed ranks around him?

A man could smile and smile and be a villain.

"I take it the young man was of assistance?"

Cadwallader turned to the man beside him, whose presence he'd nearly forgotten. "Mr. Croucher, I cannot thank you enough. Your aid has been invaluable."

The Rings' lodger shrugged modestly. "I was in Mrs. Wellham's grocery and heard him say he'd seen a man by the well. I'd thought it might be of use."

"Of use indeed," said Cadwallader warmly, as they fell into step together down Greenwich Street, back toward the boardinghouse. "If you could discover for me who might have been in the sleigh with Levi Weeks that night, I'll have all I need to send the murderer to the gallows."

"Ah, if only I could. If only I'd passed by the well at the right time that night, I'd be able to tell you all—or better, have stopped it before there was anything to tell." Mr. Croucher sighed heavily. "It haunts me, Mr. Colden. If I'd known—if I'd been there—"

A sentiment that Cadwallader felt fully, that sense of always being one step behind, failing those one most wished to serve.

"All we can do now is bring her justice," Cadwallader said soberly, "and hope it serves as a warning to other men who might seek to rid themselves of unwanted lovers in such a way."

"There was that Malone," mused Mr. Croucher, expertly navigating his way around a protruding pump. "I knew her, poor lady."

"You knew Rose Malone?" Cadwallader had never met her in life, only in death. They had found her stuffed into a cistern, curled up like a baby. The doctors might disagree about what killed Elma, but they'd been certain about Rose Malone: she had been strangled.

"I have customers throughout the city. She bought stockings from me for her wedding, poor lady. When I heard the news, I felt I'd had some part in it, sending her to her death silk-shod. It was the husband who did it, they said."

"The papers say a great number of things."

"Did he ever come to trial?"

"No." Cadwallader had been so sure her husband had done it, but William Malone had a dozen friends who could testify he'd been with them at a lodge meeting that night and not one of them would say otherwise.

Pastano—released. Rose Malone—her murder unavenged. Cadwallader's failures haunted him. He'd failed Mary Ann De Castro and Rose Malone.

But not Elma Sands. He'd bring her killer to justice, whatever it took.

"Ah, well," said Mr. Croucher. "They say the mills of the gods grind exceeding slow."

"But they grind all the same." The other man had stopped on the corner, and seemed inclined to turn rather than go on. "Do you not return to the Ring house?"

"No, I'm on my way to my bride's. The Widow Stackhaver—soon to be a widow no longer." Mr. Croucher swelled with pride. "She has a house on Ann Street and we're looking to buy the house next door as well, to make into a shop for my wares. We're to be married next week."

"My congratulations." It was nice that someone had joy to look forward to in the midst of the death and bleakness that had enveloped the Ring boardinghouse. "Has she any children?"

"An adopted daughter of sorts—but she's an unruly wench." Croucher tapped his nose. "Came of bad blood. I've told my wife she'd best be rid of her or there'll be trouble to come, but what can I say? The girl's insinuated herself in her confidence."

"Perhaps she's just young and will mend." A thought nagged at Cadwallader. The defense, he knew, planned to level that same notion of bad blood against Elma. Now, there was a topic for a paper, if Tammany Hall were still the discussion society it had been: Were men or women born bearing the sins of the parents? How was character formed and was it inherited or made? But the courtroom was no place for such musings, only for solid certainties. "Elma Sands—did she strike you as being of an unruly disposition? Possessed of bad blood?"

"Oh, no. I wouldn't say that. Elma was a sensible girl." Mr. Croucher's lip curled. "But for her infatuation with Levi Weeks. When it came to him, she wouldn't hear a word. She thought he was an Adonis."

It was Mr. Croucher who had seen the two of them together, in flagrante. "Did you say anything to her about him? Try to warn her?"

"Of course. She didn't thank me for my pains." Mr. Croucher shook his head. "I was courting my dear bride-to-be, and perhaps I didn't try as hard as I might. But who would think this would be the end of it? These violent delights . . ."

"Have violent ends," Cadwallader finished for him, and watched as the other man strode off in the direction of Ann Street, away from the Ring boardinghouse.

The Ring house seemed a different place in the March sunlight, with the promise of spring in the air. A little shabby, perhaps, but not a sinister place of violent delights and violent ends. Just another of the rather ramshackle frame houses that had sprung up as the city had spread.

Elias Ring was at the front door, doing something to the hinges. He paused his work as Cadwallader stepped up.

"Mr. Colden. Did thee want me?"

Cadwallader resisted the urge to tell Elias to stop his work on the door. It was by the sticking of the door that Catherine Ring had known that Levi and Elma must have gone out together.

Why shouldn't he fix his own door? In a week, the judges would sit for the quarter sessions; a grand jury would indict Levi Weeks; and his case would be brought forward to trial. It was right for the family to move on, to try to rise above the sorrow Levi Weeks had brought upon them, not save a squeaking door as a relic of tragedy past.

"I only came to tell you all that the quarter sessions sit next week and Levi Weeks will be taken up soon after. You'll be called to testify, of course."

"Thee knows I cannot swear."

"Don't worry; there are ways of dealing with such things. You'll be affirmed rather than sworn. All you need to do is go in there and tell the truth."

The Quaker's broad hat cast a shadow across his face. "*Ye shall know the truth and the truth shall make thee free.*"

"So we hope," said Cadwallader.

But the Quaker wasn't done with the verse. He seemed to be speaking more to himself than Cadwallader. "*Jesus answered them, 'Verily, verily I say unto you, whosoever committeth sin is the servant of sin and the servant abideth not in the house forever.'*"

"Well, I hope this house will once again be a pleasant place to abide once the trial is done. Is Mrs. Ring in?"

"She's in the kitchen." Elias jerked his head toward the back of his house.

Cadwallader went around to the small yard that was behind the house, trying to remember if there were any references in the scripture to kitchens. With his father-in-law a bishop, he felt he ought to know these things. Presumably, if there had been one, Elias Ring would have quoted it for him.

Toiling and spinning did seem to be represented here, and also the fruits of the field. Washing hung in lines, and someone had begun turning the ground for as large a kitchen garden as the small space would allow.

She was truly an excellent woman, Mrs. Ring. Cadwallader admired her industry tremendously. Country-bred, of course. That accounted for it.

Inside, he found as charming a scene as one could imagine. Hope Sands sat at the table with one of the Rings' daughters, holding a hornbook in one hand and the girl on her lap as the girl struggled to sound out the letters. Mrs. Ring's back was to them as she bent over a large kettle, which filled the air with a savory smell. Fresh loaves of bread sat covered with a cloth.

It might have been a painting, a Dutch domestic

scene—Cadwallader was rather fond of Dutch domestic scenes—of the house in good order, both women neat in their brown dresses and white aprons and caps, the milk in its jug, not a dish out of place, so different from the way the house had been when Cadwallader had first called on them in January: the house overrun by curiosity seekers, Hope Sands's anger, Mrs. Ring's grief. This, he thought, must have been what it had been like in the house in Greenwich Street before Levi Weeks had shattered their peace.

He couldn't bring Elma back to them, but perhaps he could give them this.

"Mr. Colden!" Mrs. Ring dropped her spoon at the sight of him. "Is there—have thee news?"

Cadwallader leaped forward to get it back for her. "Calm yourself, Mrs. Ring. All is well. I've only come to tell you your ordeal will soon be over. The quarter sessions begin next week and Levi will be called to trial shortly after."

Mrs. Ring clutched the spoon to her chest. "Over. Truly?"

Cadwallader felt an almost unbearable swell of sympathy for the bereaved family. Elma had disappeared on December 22. Their ordeal had stretched on for months now. "The defense will try to raise what misgivings they can, but I have no doubt justice will prevail. More evidence against Levi Weeks appears by the moment. A man came forward just today who says he saw Levi sounding the depth of the well the week before he eloped with Miss Sands."

Hope Sands's face went very white. "He sounded the well?"

"It is the purest example of villainy," Cadwallader said happily. Belatedly, he remembered Levi had lived with them for months, been part of their household. There were rumors that Hope Sands had been fond of him, or he of Hope. "But how were you to know? He appeared—he still appears—as amiable a young man as one could imagine. We will rip the veils from him and reveal him to the jury as the monster he is. The force of the evidence against him is such that nothing can stand against it."

Hope set her niece from her lap and stood, her knuckles white against the unvarnished wood of the table. "There's no doubt, then? There's truly no doubt?"

"Of course there's no doubt." Catherine Ring looked as though she hadn't slept in weeks. Her auburn hair was lank beneath her cap and her cheekbones had a hollow look to them. "There's never been any doubt."

Cadwallader rushed to confirm her words. "Levi Weeks sounded the well. He promised your cousin marriage. His brother's sleigh was seen leaving the lumber yard at eight o'clock, running without a light or bells. That same sleigh, without a light or bells, was seen heading in the direction of the well. And you, Mrs. Ring. You saw them leave together."

"Yes." Mrs. Ring shoved a lock of hair back under her cap. "I didn't exactly see them leave—but I heard their steps on the stairs."

It was enough. "Why would Levi come back here at eight o'clock but to keep his assignation with Elma? There was no reason for him to come to your house to sit ten minutes and then go back to his brother's house. He came to meet Elma and he spirited her away in his brother's sleigh."

"And then he returned here and pretended he knew not what became of her," Mrs. Ring said bitterly. "He left us all wondering and worrying. But for that muff I made her borrow—"

She covered her mouth with her hand, her whole body shaking.

Cadwallader couldn't blame her. It was a sickening prospect, the girl's body in the well, rotting, undiscovered, while her murderer feasted at her family's board. Months, perhaps years of uncertainty as they wondered what became of her, not knowing if she'd run off, or if she'd killed herself in a love fit.

"But the muff was found," said Cadwallader bracingly, "and so was your cousin. We can bring Levi Weeks to justice. And we will. Mrs. Ring, I'll call you to the stand first. Then you, Miss Sands."

"Thee wants me to speak first?" Mrs. Ring looked more alarmed than the occasion warranted, but Cadwallader supposed that for the non-lawyer, court was a fearsome thing.

"As the person who knew Elma best," said Cadwallader reassuringly. "And you, Mrs. Ring—you were the last person to see her alive."

Chapter Seventeen

While to my opponents it belongs as their duty to exert all their powerful talents in favor of the prisoner, as a public prosecutor, I think I ought to do no more than offer you in its proper order, all the testimony the case affords, draw from the witnesses that may be produced on either side all that they know, the truth, the whole truth, and nothing but the truth.

>—From the opening statement of Cadwallader Colden at the trial of Levi Weeks

New York City
March 21, 1800

"Other than Levi," said Hope quickly. She didn't like the way Caty looked at all. But then, she hadn't liked the way Caty looked for weeks now.

"Of course," agreed Mr. Colden hastily. "But the

workings of the law do not permit us to bring Levi Weeks to the stand. And even if we did . . ."

"He'd lie," Hope finished for him.

The way he'd lied the night he returned without Elma and said he'd no idea where she was. The way he'd lied when he wanted Hope to sign a paper saying he'd paid more attention to her than to Elma. The way he'd lied when he tried to make her think her sister knew something about Elma she didn't.

"Precisely." Mr. Colden seemed relieved that she'd understood him so readily. Since their dress was simple, he seemed to think they must be simple too. "All we need of you, Mrs. Ring, is to tell the jury exactly what you've told me. How you helped Elma get ready, how you saw Levi come for her, how you waited for her return. . . ."

"Yes," said Caty woodenly. "Yes, I can do that."

"As the first person the jury hears, you're the one who will make the deepest impression on them." Mr. Colden looked at Caty, and Hope saw her sister through his eyes: a respectable matron in a modest dress with work-reddened hands. The mother of children. A Quaker. The epitome of all that was honest and good.

They wouldn't know that Caty hadn't been herself recently, that she jumped at shadows and snapped at the children. Not that it was strange, Hope told herself.

They'd all been changed by this. Elias had become surly, Caty anxious. And Hope? Hope wasn't sure what she'd become but she didn't like it.

"What you say will set the tone for the entire trial. You have the ability to create the story, Mrs. Ring. Not that it's a story! It's all truth."

If you want to know the truth, apply to your sister.

"The attorneys for the defense will try to discomfit you. They'll question your words, your memories. They'll twist what you say. They'll try to make you doubt yourself and the evidence of your own eyes. They are," Mr. Colden said ruefully, "very good at that sort of thing."

They weren't the only ones who were good at that sort of thing. Hope could see Levi leaning against the fence, his eyes fixed on her, compelling, so compelling, making her doubt herself, making her doubt Caty—Caty! It was absurd.

Mr. Colden was right. It was nothing more than an attempt to create mysteries where there were none. And she was as simple as Mr. Colden seemed to think them for heeding Levi even for a moment.

"What do we do when they do that?" Hope asked.

Mr. Colden beamed at her. "Don't let them shake you. Hold firm and tell the truth as you know it. We know they mean to claim that Elma was melancholy, that she threatened to take her own life."

"She was only melancholy after her illness," said Caty tightly. "I don't even know that I'd call it *melancholy*. Being ill would make anyone low. She was right again by the middle of December."

Ask her about Elma's illness—her cramping of the stomach. Ask her why she wouldn't let me go for the doctor.

"Anyone will tell thee Elma was of a cheerful disposition," Hope said loudly, as if she could drown out the sound of Levi's voice in her head.

"Yes, her illness." Mr. Colden perked up, looking meaningfully at Caty. "I gather Levi was very, er, solicitous of Elma in her illness?"

Caty poked at the hotchpot on the hearth. "He was always very attentive to anyone who was sick."

"But especially to Elma—when she had the cramps in her stomach?"

"She was much troubled by cramps in her stomach," said Caty, concentrating forcibly on the stew pot. "She'd been troubled by cramps for nearly a year."

But that wasn't true at all.

Hope should know. They'd been bedfellows most of their youth; they'd had their courses together; they'd washed their linens together. There were times, when the boardinghouse was too full to hold everyone, when they'd shared a bed as they had as children. If Elma had suffered from cramps in the stomach, Hope would have known. Elma would have told her. In great detail.

A wave of fierce grief shook Hope. It always surprised her, the grief. Hating Levi tended to distract her, but then, out of nowhere, something would come that reminded her of the old Elma, the Elma from before Levi had divided them, and Hope would be left gasping, like the time she'd let Elma talk her into jumping into the pond in their shifts and been submerged in freezing water.

Elma had bobbed up laughing, shaking the water out of her face.

"Don't you like it? Don't you want to do it again?"

"Never," Hope had shot back.

Never, never, never. This time Elma hadn't come up laughing. She was gone, gone forever, and Hope would have given anything to have her back, in all her moods.

You shouldn't have jumped in that pond, Elma, she wanted to say. *You shouldn't have gone off that night to meet Levi.*

Hope couldn't shake the feeling that she had helped cause this; that if she'd been nicer to Elma those past months, she never would have felt she had to run off. But her feelings had been hurt at coming back from the country and finding Levi so intimate with Elma. And so she'd turned her back on Elma, pointedly focused on Caty and the children, made it clear who her family was and wasn't.

She would give anything to take it all back.

"Did Levi come to breakfast as usual the next morning?" The lawyer was still talking, taking Caty through the events of that night, the night Elma disappeared. Caty's voice was stilted, hesitant, not like herself at all.

"Yes."

"Was anything said about Elma at breakfast?"

"No, nobody mentioned her." Poor Caty looked utterly crushed, miserable at the clear imputation that she had failed in her duty.

"About ten or eleven o'clock the day after Elma went missing, I met Levi alone upstairs and attacked him about Elma," Hope broke in. "He denied knowing anything of her, although from his looks I was confident he did."

Mr. Colden coughed slightly. "When it comes time for trial, Miss Sands, you must wait until called to give your testimony. You may discover things you wish to add to your sister's testimony, or there may be statements other witnesses make that you know to be frankly untrue, but you may not answer unless you yourself are on the stand, and then only to reply to the questions that are put to you. That is why it is so important to think now of everything you might wish to say—and every possible question the defense might put to you—so you may answer clearly and not regret anything left unsaid."

Statements one knew to be false, like Elma having suffered from recurring cramps in the stomach for a year, when it had only begun in early December.

Hope glanced at Caty, who had her hands twisted together at her waist, her entire form stiff with tension.

"I know it is an ordeal, but it will soon be over. All that is required of you is the truth, the whole truth, and nothing but the truth," Mr. Colden said encouragingly. "If I may, Mrs. Ring, I'll come to you the day before trial to go through what you remember and make sure it's fresh in your mind. Mr. Ring too."

Caty's face looked like that of a much older woman. "I'll make sure Elias is here."

When the lawyer had gone, Caty took a bucket of water and some rags. "I'd best attend to my chores. Mr. Croucher leaves us to marry, but he wishes to keep his room to display his wares."

"Why not tell him to go elsewhere? Thee never liked his running a store from our home."

"What choice have we? Who would take a room here—now?" Caty's voice cracked. She turned quickly away, hiding her face. "I'd best go clean before he sees fit to send that girl again to do my work for me."

"At least Elias fixed the door." Hope's mind wasn't on the door; it was in the road outside the Widow Broad's house, Levi calling after her. "Caty? When Elma was ill, why wouldn't thee let Levi call the doctor?"

"What does that matter now? I have work to tend to. And thee too," Caty added tartly.

"But why?" Hope followed her up the stairs, toward Mr. Croucher's room. "Why didn't you want the doctor?"

"Words are cheap, but physicians cost money. Levi hasn't children to feed."

And never would now. Not if they hanged him.

Hope followed Caty into Mr. Croucher's room. "Why did thee tell Mr. Colden that Elma suffered from cramps of the stomach for a year?"

Caty set her bucket down with a thump, dipping her rag in the water. "It felt like a year. Thee would think no one had ever been ill before."

But that wasn't true either. Elma hadn't made a fuss—not until later, with the laudanum, and that had just been the once. She'd had the laudanum vial, but hadn't taken it, not even the few drops prescribed by the physician, not after those first few days when she'd been so ill that Levi had pleaded with Caty to call for the doctor now, before it was too late, and Hope had been barred from the room.

Mr. Croucher's room was stuffy, thick with the scent of the dyes used on the fabrics he sold and the expensive snuff he took pinch by pinch from an enamel-and-gold box. "Why did Mr. Colden look at thee like that when he spoke of Elma's illness? Why wouldn't Levi let me stay with her? Why won't thee tell me?"

"There are some subjects not suited to thy years."

"I'm older than thee when thee married Elias! In a year, I'll be older than Elma will ever be."

Caty twisted the water out of the rag as if she were wringing the neck of a chicken. "If thee must know . . . thy cousin was with child."

"With *child*?" Hope gawked at her sister. "But—"

They'd come back from Cornwall toward the end of October, and Elma—Elma had left only a few days later, visiting friends in the country. Hope had missed her and been relieved all at the same time, because Elma in the country meant Levi to herself.

When Elma had returned, they hadn't spoken much. Elma had been at her most provoking, returning any attempt at intimacy with mockery. She'd always, Hope realized, been infuriating when she was unhappy.

And Hope hadn't seen it. Or hadn't wanted to see it. All she'd seen was the way Elma leaned toward Levi, the way she whispered in his ear, the solid bar of Elma's bedroom door closing behind them.

"The baby—was it Levi's?"

Caty slapped her rag against the sill. "Who else?"

Hope shook her head, too sick for words. Of course it was Levi's; it couldn't be anyone's but Levi's. But it was one thing to know they'd gone into that room alone together, one thing to hear Mr. Croucher whisper of what he'd seen, and another to be presented with the proof of it.

A baby was such a solid thing.

"I should have known she'd be just like her mother. Father warned me. Born of sin, he said. A daughter of Eve." Caty scrubbed at the grime on Mr. Croucher's windowsill with quick, angry movements. "I wish she'd never been born."

"Thee can't mean that!"

Caty slammed the rag down. "We were happy before she came."

"It wasn't Elma's fault," said Hope hotly. "We were happy before *Levi* came. Caty?"

Caty buried her face in her hands. It took Hope a moment to realize she was crying, her whole body shaking with sobs. Hope couldn't remember ever seeing Caty cry before. Not when they were children; not when people robbed their father's short-lived store; not when Elias's businesses failed; not when Elma didn't come home.

Tentatively, Hope put an arm around her sister. She always thought of Caty as so sturdy, but her bones felt as small and fragile as Rachel's. "Please, don't cry, Caty."

"If only she hadn't—" Caty choked on the words. "Why? Why? *Why?*"

"It must have been the baby," Hope said, feeling sick. "That must have been why he killed her, because he didn't want her to tell anyone about the baby."

Caty made a horrible noise, deep in her throat. She shook off Hope's encircling arm. Yanking a handkerchief from her sleeve, she wiped her ravaged face.

"We do not speak of this again," Caty said in a strangled voice. She straightened her cap on her tightly plaited hair. "If thee hasn't hats to trim, then there's Mr. Lacey's room to clean."

As if they could scrub it all away.

The bloody cloths in a bucket. Levi, begging Caty to send for the doctor.

Hope felt as though she'd just been through a tempest and emerged to find the world made unfamiliar with fallen branches and shattered glass. What else had she failed to see? What other secrets had Caty kept from her?

Poor Caty, always taking on everyone's burdens, trying so hard to spare everyone else.

Hope held out a hand to her sister. "Caty—thee

needn't bear it all alone. I'm a woman grown. I'll help thee carry thy burdens."

Caty slapped the rag into her palm. "If thee want to share my burden, clean this room. I haven't time to stand here all day gossiping like thee and Peggy."

With that, she pushed past Hope and out of the room, leaving Hope standing in Mr. Croucher's room with a damp rag dripping in her hand.

Chapter Eighteen

When my wife returned, I asked who went out? She said, "Elma and Levi." I answered that it was wrong, [Elma] would get sick. She replied, "He will be more careful of her than I would be."

—From the testimony of Elias Ring at the trial of Levi Weeks

New York City
March 21, 1800

"I mended the door for thee," Elias said.

Caty dropped her rag into her bucket, placing her hands on the small of her back, which ached something fierce.

After Mr. Croucher's room, she'd gone on and cleaned Mr. Lacey's and Mr. Russel's rooms, venting all her emotion into the grime and soot beneath the cracks. Sometimes it seemed like all the filth of the city found its way within their walls.

Caty hated herself for breaking down in front of Hope. She'd tried so hard to put up a strong front for the children. Hope might claim to be grown, but she was Caty's child too, her little sister, hers to protect. To have Hope questioning her . . . offering to share her burdens . . . when she had no idea just how hard Caty had worked to protect her, to keep her in happy ignorance . . . it was all too much to bear. Caty wanted to sink down on the floor, cover her head with her apron, and howl like Eliza.

And now Elias wanted thanks for a task she'd first asked him to complete months ago.

"I thank thee," she said.

Elias hovered in the doorway, casting a long shadow across the floor. He waited while Caty gathered up her bucket of filthy water, her dirty rags. He didn't offer to take it from her.

When she went to leave, he stood in the doorway, blocking her path. "What did the lawyer want with thee?"

"Mr. Colden?" She knew just who he meant, but she was tired and sore at heart.

"He was with thee for some time."

"Only to tell me of new evidence against Levi—and advise me how to speak at trial." Meanly, Caty added, "I'm to tell the whole truth and all will be well."

There was a petty satisfaction to watching Elias flinch. "Thee won't. Will thee?"

Caty's bucket was very heavy and her temper was short. The scene with Hope had been bad enough. She didn't have the energy to soothe Elias's sore conscience. She hoped it pricked him like a thousand fiery pitchforks. "Would thee have me lie in a court of law?"

"There are things they have no need to know. . . ." Elias put a hand on the wall behind her, his voice low and urgent. "Thee would not betray me."

"As thee betrayed thy marriage vows? Thy children?" Including the child who had never been born. By Caty's calculations, the baby would have been due in May. By now there would have been no hiding it, no matter how many extra petticoats Elma wore. "What would thee have done if Elma had carried thy child to term?"

Elias took a step back, his expression wary. "What child? There was no child."

"Thee didn't know?" Even as she said it, the full truth hit her. Of course he hadn't known. He was a man. He didn't have to know such things. He just did what he'd wanted and ignored the consequences. It was Caty who had borne the consequences for him, just as she always bore the consequences for him.

The laughter tore out of her, high and hysterical.

She couldn't seem to stop it, any more than she could stop the sobs.

It was just like Elias. Do what he would and let someone else clean up after him.

"Did thee think Elma's illness merely a distemper of the stomach?"

He had. She could see it in his face. Come home, he'd written her, and she'd come home and solved his problems for him.

"At the autopsy," he said. "They said there was no child."

"Was." Caty drew a shaky breath. "Fortunate for thee she lost it before they cut her open."

Lost. What an utterly inadequate term, as though Elma had misplaced her baby, instead of being scoured from the inside out with blood and fever. If Levi hadn't sat by Elma's side, hadn't guarded her and sponged her forehead and held her hand and demanded preparations of willow bark and broth, Elma might well have expired with her baby.

"It might not have been mine," Elias muttered.

Caty looked at him. She felt as though she was seeing him clearly for the first time: the weakness hidden by the strong features of his face, now beginning to sag as he passed his fourth decade. She remembered being sixteen, listening rapt to Elias as he told her of his plans and inventions, of the fools who stood in his way, who didn't appreciate his genius. It wasn't his fault; nothing was ever his fault.

It wasn't that he had changed; it was only that she had finally realized what he was.

Elias put a hand on her arm in a clumsy attempt at solicitude. "Tell me what I can do to make it right with thee."

Go back and change it all, she wanted to say. *Be the man I thought you were, rather than the man you are.*

Caty said the only thing she could. "Thee might carry my bucket for me."

Elias drew back, offended. "Don't make mock of me. I meant it truly."

"So did I," she said, and stepped past him, into the hall. Carrying her own bucket, filled with everyone else's filth. Just like always.

She could hear Elias behind her. "Catherine . . ."

She used to thrill to his calling her Catherine. At home she was always Caty. When Elias called her Catherine, she'd felt like someone so much older and more mature than her sixteen years, the person he wanted her to be.

She was tired of being Elias's Catherine, the excuse for all his failures. She just wanted to be Caty again.

Caty stopped in front of the door of the room that had once been Elma's. "I will not share thy secret."

Caty could see the gears turning in Elias's mind, like one of the machines he designed, and just as effective. "If they ask thee..."

It hadn't occurred to her that they might. But it did make sense. Levi knew. Why wouldn't he tell the men working for his defense? The idea of her family's shortcomings being exposed to the world made Caty feel ill.

"I will not expose thee but I will not lie for thee."

It wasn't what Elias wanted. "Thee are my wife."

"Good of thee to remember that."

Elias's hands clenched into fists. "Will thee never let me put that behind me?"

They were the subject of hundreds of handbills and broadsides. They were about to stand in a courtroom in front of the eyes of all New York and pray the worst of their shame wasn't aired. And Elias thought she should put it all behind her?

Caty was so angry she could barely speak. "Thee has no notion of what I've done for thee."

"Haven't I?" Gone was all attempt to be conciliatory. "Thee tells me often enough! Thy ceaseless industry keeping us from the poorhouse...."

"I never minded about the money!" Caty shouted.

Elias stared at her. Caty would have stared at herself.

She'd never heard such a tone emerge from her own throat before, never imagined it could. She'd prided herself, always, on being calm and reasonable, the one who kept harmony in the household, just like her mother before her.

"My father was always far from home, spreading the word," Caty said in a low voice. Her throat felt scratchy and raw. "I wouldn't have cared if thee had never earned a cent if only thee were here with me and the children."

She admired her father tremendously, but she'd wanted a husband who would be more than occasional bulletins delivered by post, someone who would stand by her, sharing life's pleasures and burdens.

Elias stared at her in complete incomprehension. "It was thee left me to go away into the country."

Caty felt weary to the bone. "Would thee have come away with me and the children if I'd asked thee?"

His eyes shifted away from hers. "Someone had to mind thy precious boardinghouse."

No. Elias wouldn't go back to Cornwall and live in her mother's house, even for a month. Not even for the sake of his children's health, or his wife's. It had suited him better to preside over an empty kingdom with Elma as concubine.

Caty could picture them last summer before she'd

left for Cornwall, Elias sitting next to Elma on the settle in the front room, regaling her with tales of his wondrous waterwheel. Just as Caty had once listened to him, wide-eyed, when she'd been sixteen and had no children to mind, no boarders to feed.

What a fool she'd been, to think that if she tried hard enough, worked hard enough, she could make their marriage what it ought to be, what they'd pledged in the new meetinghouse. Elias had never wanted a wife, not a real wife, the sort of wife she had tried to be.

It had all been for nothing, all of it.

"That night," Elias said hesitantly. "The night Elma didn't come home. Thee gave me the child to fix."

"Eliza." He couldn't even be bothered to use his own child's name. "Thy youngest child's name is Eliza."

"I know my own child," he said impatiently, although Caty wasn't at all sure he did. "Thee remembers? If they ask thee—thee gave me the child."

"To fix and put to bed." Caty was still smarting over Elias's failure to use his own child's name. His legitimate child. "But that was after Levi had come back already. What thee did before that I have no notion."

Elias bristled. "What does thee mean by that?"

"Exactly what I said."

Elias loomed over her. "Thee knows I was here with

thee. Thee came into the sitting room and I asked thee who had gone out and thee said Elma and Levi."

"And then thee went too," Caty said relentlessly. "And I had no more sight of thee until I brought thee the child to fix."

"I didn't go out—only into the garden to have a pipe!"

"For two hours? In the dark and the cold?" Caty's father had forbidden the use of sugar and tobacco in their household because it was the fruit of the labor of their enslaved brethren, which meant that Elias had got in the habit of sneaking outside for his evening pipe. But it didn't take a man that long to smoke a pipe.

Elias's expression turned ugly. "How would thee know? Thee weren't here when I came in."

"Because I was putting *thy* children to bed."

"I looked in and saw them asleep—but thee were nowhere to be seen. I heard the door," he added ominously.

"The door thee hadn't fixed?" Caty spread her arms wide, daring him to look at her. Hope took after the tall side of the family, the Sands side, but she and Elma were both slight, like their grandmother Mercy. "Thee had best go tell Mr. Colden to call off the trial. Thee has found the true murderer. I lured Elma to the Manhattan Well—under what pretense only thee can imagine.

I lured Elma there and I pushed her in over the side. Go. Tell thy children their mother is a murderess."

"Don't be absurd," Elias muttered.

It was all absurd, from the piles of handbills in Mr. Croucher's room, making up all manner of stories about Elma's restless ghost, to the fact that her husband had betrayed her with her own cousin in her own house.

Caty didn't understand how she had gone from simply trying to make a home for her family, to be a good wife and a good mother and a good sister and abide by her father's strictures as best she could, to this. It was the Lord testing her, sounding out her weaknesses, her hidden pride, her hidden resentments.

She'd always hated Elma, from the time Elma had first entered and upended their household by being born.

They'd been a proper family before then. It was only after Aunt Lizzy had fallen pregnant that her father had felt the call to preach in the farthest reaches of New England, abandoning them to make their own way as best they could in the midst of a war in which they were suspect and mocked for her father's refusal to fight.

If he'd been there, her father might have used his eloquence to spare them the slights they'd endured. As it was, they'd had to beg him to send a letter, attesting that they weren't loyalists. It had taken months to arrive, and in the meantime, they'd been robbed, spat on, threatened.

All because of Elma.

The Lord couldn't have found a harsher trial to test Caty than her husband betraying her with Elma.

Why was she being punished? It was Elias who had sinned. Elias and Elma.

"It was thee came to me with thy unquiet conscience," said Caty mercilessly. "It was thee wanted me to lie for thee. Are thee so lost to all feeling that thee would put thy crimes on thy wife?"

"Not my crimes!" Elias cried. "My only sin was of the flesh. It was Levi killed her; we all know it was Levi killed her. Thee saw her leave with Levi."

"I thought I heard her leave with Levi," Caty corrected him. "I didn't see them."

"But thee knows it was he Elma meant to meet." It was dangerously satisfying watching Elias grovel.

Caty lifted her chin. "I know what Hope told me. I never heard it from Elma's own lips."

Elias's face looked like a skull. "Thee will not say that—in court."

"Maaaaaamaaaaaaaaa," Phoebe called from downstairs.

Caty took a quick, sharp breath. What had she been thinking? The children. Elias was their father.

The only peace they'd ever have was if Levi was convicted for Elma's murder and soon.

"Coming!" she called, and then faced her husband. "No. I'll not say that in court. Thee has the right of it. We both know it was Levi killed her."

"Thee shouldn't have teased me," he said sternly, masking his fear under an air of authority.

"No, husband," she said, and turned to go down the stairs to Phoebe.

"Catherine?" he called. He held out the bucket of dirty water to her. "Thee forgot this."

It was with extreme strength of will that Caty prevented herself from emptying it over his head.

Chapter Nineteen

On Friday last, Croucher came running into the store and said, "What do you think of this innocent young man now? There is material evidence against him from the Jerseys, and he is taken by the High Sheriff, sir, and carried to jail; he will be carried from there, sir, to the court and be tried; from there he will be carried back to jail, and from thence to court again, sir, and from thence to the place of execution, and there be hanged by the neck until he is dead."

—From the testimony of David Forrest at the trial of Levi Weeks

New York City
March 28, 1800

"She lost the baby." Levi slumped in a chair in the room the governor of the Bridewell had so kindly allowed Alexander for his conference with his client.

Unlike the last time Alexander had visited him in the Bridewell, Levi was clean-shaven and neatly dressed. He'd only just been brought back to prison, having been taken before the grand jury and indicted on a charge of having with force and arms assaulted Gulielma Sands, and feloniously, willfully, and of his malice aforethought, cast, thrown, and pushed the said Gulielma Sands into a certain well, and there choked, suffocated, and drowned the said Gulielma Sands.

In case that weren't enough, a second count had been added, accusing Levi of having cast and thrown the said Gulielma Sands upon the ground, beating, striking, and kicking her, with mortal strokes, wounds, and bruises, in and upon the head, breast, back, belly, sides, and other parts of the body.

That, Alexander thought, was overreach. The medical evidence didn't support a charge of battery. Strangulation, possibly. But the bruising on the rest of her body had been such as might have been caused by immersion in the water, not a brutal beating.

Levi had sat through the litany of horrors like a man in a nightmare. He'd scarcely seemed to hear the words, so engrossed was he in his own private terrors.

When prodded, Levi had said, "Not guilty," but the statement had lacked conviction.

"The baby?" These were the first words Levi had

spoken of his own accord since he had been fetched from his brother's house, and Alexander had no idea what he was talking about.

"Elizabeth." Levi looked at him with red-rimmed eyes. He looked as if he hadn't slept in a week. "Elizabeth lost the baby."

It took Alexander a moment to remember Ezra Weeks's heavily pregnant wife, now pregnant no longer.

It was, he thought, a very good thing they had taken her deposition when they had.

Now that Levi had spoken, the words flooded out in a deluge of grief. "The doctors despair of her life. Mary Ann keeps asking for her mother. I don't know what to tell her. None of us know what to tell her. Ezra sits by Elizabeth's side hour after hour, never sure if the next breath will be the last."

That hit Alexander in the gut. Six years ago, Eliza had nearly died of a miscarriage. Alexander had been away from home, in the wilds of Pennsylvania, leading troops against the insurgents who had taken up arms against the whiskey tax; it had been left to others to visit Eliza and send him word. He'd rushed back as soon as he'd heard; he'd immediately resigned his post at the Treasury. But it still haunted him, the thought that his Eliza might have perished while he was elsewhere.

"Childbirth is a dangerous thing for women," Alexander said soberly.

Levi shook his head wildly. "I brought this on them. If it weren't for me, Elizabeth would never have lost the baby. It was the strain—that was what they said—the strain of the charges against me—"

He gulped for air, his face contorting into gargoyle shapes.

"I never meant to hurt anyone. Oh God, Elma—and now Elizabeth—"

Alexander patted his hand. "With good care and God's grace, she'll see this through and there will be other children."

"Unless she dies." Levi refused to be comforted.

"It will worry them more if they hang you," Alexander pointed out. "The best thing you can do for your family now is prove your innocence in a court of law."

Levi gave a short, bitter laugh. "What hope is there for me? They're all in league against me. That Croucher has been spreading stories that there's evidence against me come from the Jerseys—"

"Why from the Jerseys? Have you connections there?"

"No! My family is from Massachusetts!"

The insinuation that he might be from the Jerseys seemed to distress Levi as much as his own impending execution.

"He and Elias Ring—they've been stirring everyone up against me. Ring has been telling everyone he'll shoot me on sight." Levi shoved his hands into his hair, making it stick out wildly around his face. "I was a prisoner long before they brought me back here. Ezra forbade me to leave the yard for fear someone would take justice into his own hands. They say I touched Elma's corpse when they found her and her drowned face wept tears of blood."

The sign of a murderer.

"What did I do to bring this on myself—on my family? What did I do more than any other man has done?" Levi demanded hysterically. "All I did was talk to a pretty girl. . . ."

"What about Ring?" Alexander demanded, breaking into Levi's lament. "From all accounts, he did far more than talk to her. You were there in the house with them this autumn. Did you know?"

Levi stared at him like a startled rabbit, frozen in a field.

Alexander looked at him with exasperation. "Why didn't you tell me of Ring and Elma? The basis of the prosecution's case—the center of all the rumors against you—is that you seduced an innocent girl with promise of marriage. If the world knew that Elma was sharing her favors with Ring . . ."

"I didn't want to shame Elma," Levi muttered.

"Elma is beyond shaming," said Alexander gently. "You, however . . . You're not beyond saving. If not for your own sake, for your family."

Levi dropped his face into his hands. "She asked me to keep her secret for her."

"Would she wish you to keep it at the expense of your own neck?"

"I know. I know. I've been a fool. If I said it now, who would believe me? He's a Quaker. And he's made the world believe that Elma had eyes for no one but me. When she never wanted me at all," he added resentfully. "Not like that."

"What was it like?"

"I thought it was such luck when I found that there were three pretty girls at the Ring house," Levi said bitterly. "Not for dishonor. Just for . . ." He waved his hands helplessly.

"I know. I was young once." Alexander could remember being a young lieutenant colonel in General Washington's household, overwhelmed with his choice of beautiful women at the Morristown assemblies. "A bit of flirtation adds spice to the supper table."

Levi nodded. "There were the three of them, all so different. Peggy was a game girl and she had tongue enough for two sets of teeth, but there was nothing in it. Hope, now—" His lips tightened over whatever he had meant to say. "And then there was Elma. We went to Mr. Baker's museum once, Elma, Hope, and I. Elma had a way of walking, as if she owned the cobbles beneath her feet."

Looking at him, Alexander thought it was a good thing that defendants weren't allowed to speak in their own cause. Anyone seeing the expression on his face would have no doubt that the young man had been hopelessly smitten with Elma Sands.

"Somehow, we got to talking about the building, and the style of it, with those arches and the cupola sticking up out of the middle of the roof. I'd thoughts on it—and Elma had too. I drew a sketch for her, of how I'd have built it, if it were mine to make." Levi's throat worked. "My brother—he's all for my being part of the family trade; he's worked hard to train me in it—but as a builder, not an architect. He treats my designs as one step away from writing poetry, a dilettante's game. But Elma, she would look at my designs with me. She'd suggest improvements too."

"She had an interest in architecture?" Alexander knew he sounded skeptical, but it seemed unlikely the girl from the countryside had been studying Vitruvius. On the other hand, he was a boy from an island in the middle of the Caribbean Sea.

"She liked fine things. No, that sounds wrong. What I meant was, she had an eye for line and form. They set her to making hats, and she was good at it, or so they tell me," he added, with masculine indifference to haberdashery. "If she'd been a man, she might have been an artist. She'd taught herself, she told me. Her family didn't hold with such things. They didn't hold with a lot of things—including Elma."

"Because she was a bastard."

Levi nodded. "Mrs. Ring never let her forget it. She'd make comments about Elma dressing too gay, and how she ought to be grateful for their kindness. She was always at her to come to meeting, but Elma insisted she wouldn't profane their presence by forced attendance without a true conversion."

Alexander was beginning to get a sense of this Elma, a forceful young lady with a somewhat dangerous sense of humor. A talented, restless girl, constrained by her birth, unable, as a man might—as he had—to break out of her circumstances.

"When did you first know of Elma and Ring?"

Levi grimaced. "When the others went away during the fever. . . . It was hard not to notice what was going on. Isaac Hatfield had taken the room below mine, but he was away more than not, and while he was gone— they used his room. I don't know. Maybe Ring didn't want to take her in his wife's bed. Maybe the bed was better. It was right below me, and the floors aren't thick."

"Did you say anything to Ring—or to Elma?"

"I didn't know what to say! It was ruin for her, anyone could see that. Mrs. Ring disliked her enough already; she made no secret of it, for all she thought she did. I've three sisters of my own," he added abruptly. "Mercy, Sally, and Kate. I thought, what would I do if it were one of them? So I found Elma in the kitchen when Ring was out of the house and told her I'd heard them."

"What did she say?"

"She asked if I meant to tell of them. I told her no, of course not, but had she thought of what she was doing." Levi bit his lip. "She said it was no matter, Caty—that's what she called her cousin—Caty was gone to the country and liked it there better anyway, and their marriage was only a marriage in the eyes of the meeting, and if he were to leave the meeting, he'd be free to marry again."

Alexander knew little enough of Quaker marriage vows, but he didn't think that sounded particularly likely, and said so.

Levi made a helpless gesture. "I'm not sure what he promised her and what—what she imagined. Men will say things when they—you know."

"I know," said Alexander grimly.

"Sometimes she'd talk of their going away, to Charleston, where her father was. Ring said they didn't appreciate him in New York, so Elma had this idea they'd go elsewhere, start over somewhere where no one knew them."

"It must have been a shock to her when Mrs. Ring came home."

"It was like seeing a ghost, all the life knocked out of her. I got her to agree to visit friends in the country. I took her down to the docks myself, to make sure she wouldn't change her mind. I thought that would be the end of it—maybe that she'd even decide to stay on in the country. I didn't know what to do other than getting her away as quickly as I could."

"Why you?"

"She didn't have anyone else," said Levi simply.

"When Elma came back, what happened then? Did she and Mr. Ring resume their intimacies?"

"No. I don't know what he'd said to her before Mrs. Ring came back, but whatever it was—it wasn't kind. If she saw him coming, she'd leave the room." Levi frowned. "I don't think he even knew about the baby."

There were times when Alexander had trouble following Levi's line of thought. "According to the autopsy, there was no baby."

"Not by then there wasn't. Mrs. Ring—I think Mrs. Ring gave her something. Or maybe she would have lost the baby anyway." Levi rubbed his hands along his arms, as though he'd felt a chill. "I was afraid to leave her alone. I didn't trust Mrs. Ring with her. It sounds mad, doesn't it? But I was afraid of what Mrs. Ring might do."

Alexander could feel the hairs prickling on his arms beneath his layers of linen and wool. A baby—now, that was a motive for murder. For Elias Ring—or for Catherine. "Did she know it was her husband's child?"

"I don't know," said Levi helplessly. "I've never seen so much blood. I wanted to send for the doctor—I begged Mrs. Ring to send for the doctor—but she wouldn't let me. I think she would have been just as happy for Elma to die along with her child."

There was a difference between failing to provide aid and actively causing harm. Had Mrs. Ring crossed that line? Alexander doubted a jury would believe that the good Quaker housewife had first attempted to poison her cousin, and then, when that failed, pushed her into a well.

And yet . . .

"I couldn't tell anyone. Not Ezra, not Hope." Levi was lost in his memories, long lines carved into his tanned face. "I offered to marry her. She laughed at me and told me not to throw myself away on the likes of her. She said my brother wouldn't like it and that I deserved better than to be shackled to the village ledger."

Alexander raised his brows. "She called herself a whore?"

"Only because Ring made her believe herself one, General," Levi said earnestly. "What she did, she did because she thought he loved her. You have to understand what it was here, during the sickness. Sometimes it felt like we were the only people left in the world, like Robinson Crusoe on his island."

"There were cannibals on Crusoe's island," Alexander said.

"Sometimes it feels like there are cannibals in the Ring house too," said Levi bleakly. "They were ready enough to devour Elma, and now they're trying to tear the flesh from my bones. They'll do it too."

"Not if we convince the jury otherwise." Alexander was trying to make sense of what Levi had told him, balancing it against what the prosecution would throw at him.

The revelation of Ring's liaison with Elma would certainly raise doubts in the minds of the jury. Ezra Weeks and John McComb would testify that Levi couldn't have made it to the well and back in the requisite times. But there were two points still weighing heavily against Levi.

"Why did she say she was going to be married to you?"

"I don't know. Truly, I don't! When Hope told me—I thought the earth was opening up underneath me."

The only people to claim that Elma had gone to be married to Levi were Catherine Ring, whose husband had been sleeping with Elma, and Hope Sands. "Might Mrs. Ring have made it up, to cast the blame on you?"

"Mrs. Ring might have—but Hope wouldn't. Elma had something in train that night," Levi said reluctantly. "You could tell just by looking at her. She'd put on her best dress and she borrowed that muff from Beth Osborn."

"Mrs. Ring claims that Elma said she was going to meet you at eight—and you came back to the house at eight. Why did you come back at eight?"

"John McComb was at my brother's house, and I didn't know how long he'd stay. When he starts to prose on . . ." Levi caught Alexander's eye and flushed. "All right. I came back because I was worried about Elma. Since Ring threw her over and she lost the baby—it's as though she didn't care what happened to her anymore. I'd tried all day to get her to tell me what she was planning, but all she'd do was tell me that I'd see."

"Your brother thinks she threw herself in the well."

"No," said Levi immediately. "She was . . . excited. She was happier than I'd seen her for weeks. She'd talked so often about running off to her father in Charleston. But why would she go at night? It made no sense. And I wondered . . ." He caught himself, his eyes shifting away from Alexander.

"You wondered?"

"Who she was going to meet," he said, although Alexander was fairly certain that wasn't what he had been about to say. "I followed her out. I thought if she wouldn't tell me . . . But although there was a moon, the light was uncertain and I lost sight of her before she left Greenwich Street. So I went back to my brother's. When I came back, I asked if she'd come in, and Mrs. Ring told me no, that she'd thought Elma was with me."

They had better hope that no one had seen Levi follow Elma out—if the boy was telling the truth. Alexander thought he was. That air of bewilderment might be feigned, but if so, he ought to be treading the boards rather than sawing them.

"You have no idea where she went, or who she went to meet?"

Levi shook his head. "She stopped confiding in me after—"

"After?" Alexander prompted.

Levi hunched his shoulders. "It's no matter."

"You have just been indicted on a charge of murder," Alexander said with some asperity. "Don't you think it's time you told me the truth? We would be much farther forward if you'd told me all this two months ago. Why did Elma stop confiding in you?"

Levi pressed his eyes shut. "Elma stopped confiding in me after I came upon her embracing Croucher."

Chapter Twenty

> [Burr] kept open house for nearly two months, and Committees were in session day and night during the whole time at his house. Refreshments were always on the table, and mattresses were set up for temporary repose in the rooms.
>
> —From the diary of Benjamin Betterton Howell

New York City
March 30, 1800

"Did you visit Mrs. Ashmore?"

As usual, Hamilton wasted no time on polite nothings. With the trial of Levi Weeks called for the following morning, counsel had met for one last conference to prepare their strategy.

"I did," said Aaron.

They were once again in Hamilton's office, in the chairs with no padding, with the salt-scented wind whistling through the cracks in the wood. March appeared to have decided to go out like a lion as well as in like one.

As for Aaron, he was busy playing the lamb. He had allowed Hamilton to convene this meeting at his office; he graciously ignored the fact that Hamilton was ordering him about as though Aaron were one of his clerks. He had his own reasons for not wanting Hamilton anywhere near Richmond Hill.

Let Hamilton crow; he'd have his wings clipped soon enough.

Brockholst was bristling on Aaron's behalf, but Aaron answered calmly, "I called on Mrs. Ashmore at 884 Bowery Lane yesterday. Mrs. Brown, as she sometimes prefers to be called. The house is a distillery—with other diversions to be had."

"It's a brothel?" said Brockholst, diverted.

"Not as such," Aaron replied. "At least, not officially."

Brockholst gave a barking laugh. "Did you sample the wares?"

"Only the brandy," said Aaron blandly.

Although there had been one engaging piece by the name of Eliza Brown who had offered him a cordial, quite cordially. Not a relation of Mrs. Ashmore, alias Mrs. Brown, he'd been informed. It was remarkable what a wide array of unrelated persons named Brown one might encounter.

Mrs. Ashmore, as far as Aaron could tell, catered to a clientele of small tradesmen, men like Richard Croucher. She provided a veneer of respectability and a great deal of home-brewed brandy.

While he might not have sampled all the wares, Aaron considered his visit to Mrs. Ashmore an afternoon well spent.

Mrs. Ashmore herself couldn't vote in the upcoming elections—a fact his Theo had so frequently deplored—but many of her clientele could. Men in their cups tended to be suggestible. Mrs. Ashmore had provided several valuable pieces of information—not about the Weeks affair, which was largely beside the point, but the political and personal preferences of her visitors.

They had parted well satisfied with each other—although not so well satisfied as some of Mrs. Ashmore's customers.

Back at Richmond Hill, Aaron had added the details Mrs. Ashmore had given him to his growing roster of the name, political leanings, financial situation, and temperament of every eligible voter in the city of New York.

Even now, as he sat here in Hamilton's office, docilely letting Hamilton order him about, the list was being divided among Aaron's corps of volunteers. Theodosia was hard at work, providing refreshments and endless streams of coffee, with pallets on the floor for those who might need to rest from their labors. Among his volunteers, he had Dutch speakers, German speakers, French speakers; he had elegant young men and forthright farmers. Whatever the nature of the man, Burr would find someone who could persuade him.

Hamilton might have his army, but Burr felt that his election apparatus was an altogether more military arrangement, and likely to be of longer standing.

Hamilton, in happy ignorance, was brooding on the Weeks affair. "So Croucher might have passed the well that night."

"Mrs. Ashmore was insistent that he hadn't left the party—but I would take her word for what it's worth."

"And what's that?"

"Whatever you're willing to pay for it." In a house where everything was for sale, information was just another form of coin.

"Do you think he's bribed her?"

"I think," said Aaron, "that he is a client of such long standing that it would ill behoove her to contradict him."

"What does it matter?" demanded Brockholst, trying fruitlessly to find a more comfortable position in a chair designed for a much smaller man. "Are we to ascertain the whereabouts of every one of the prosecution's witnesses? I hear Colden has bound over seventy-odd persons."

"Not just a witness." Something appeared to be worrying Hamilton; he lacked his usual bombast. "I spoke to Levi Weeks. He says he saw Richard Croucher embracing Elma."

"It seems a great many people embraced Elma," murmured Aaron. "One can hardly claim it as a distinguishing characteristic."

"This may yet be of use to us," said Brockholst thoughtfully. "Our primary argument, of course, is that the wench did away with herself. Failing that, we open the prospect that one of her many other lovers had cause to do away with her."

"How many are we up to now?" inquired Aaron.

Brockholst counted them off. "Weeks, Ring, Croucher—and the neighbor claims the girl was away of nights and lied about her whereabouts. The prosecution will attempt to stir the emotions of the jury by painting her as a virtuous woman seduced and betrayed. They'll be less sympathetic to a loose woman."

"She was a bastard, after all," said Aaron.

"She was a woman betrayed by the men who promised to care for her," said Hamilton abruptly. "She deserves better from us."

Levi Weeks deserved the defense for which his brother was paying dearly. Elma Sands, on the contrary, deserved nothing from them at all. "My dear sir," said Aaron, "you have done all in the service of justice which a man can possibly do."

The diversion had served its purpose. Investigating Elma Sands had distracted Hamilton from Aaron's other activities. Now it was time for Hamilton to stop before he complicated their case.

"This doesn't change anything, I suppose." Hamilton was still occupied with his own line of thought. "If Croucher knew of Ring's affair with the girl—and we know he knew—then he might have been moved to take advantage of her himself. That Levi saw Croucher embracing Elma doesn't preclude Croucher from having seen Ring push her in the well. The rest all follows as before."

"As one argument among many." Aaron held up a hand. "I know you hold the prospect of suicide in distaste, but the jury must at least be provided the option."

Particularly since Ezra Weeks had made it clear he expected them to insist the girl had committed suicide and Ezra Weeks had a great deal to offer in the coming election if he so chose, in both money and influence.

Hamilton immediately took umbrage. "All those people heard cries from the well. . . ."

"Would you do the prosecution's work for them?" asked Brockholst in exasperation.

"We have," Aaron reminded him gently, "three doctors ready to testify that there were no marks of violence upon her, only such as might have been occasioned by drowning."

"That does the girl an injustice—" began Hamilton.

"The girl seen embracing three men?" Brockholst barreled on before Hamilton could speak again, outlining the plan that he and Aaron had worked out the night before, without Hamilton to distract them. "I propose we proceed as follows. We open by introducing the possibility of suicide. *Then* we show the impossibility of the prosecution's case: to wit, that there was no intimacy amounting to courtship; that even if there was intimacy, the girl was equally intimate with any other number of men; and finally, that the evidence shows that Levi never took out his brother's sleigh and could not possibly have been at the well at the crucial time."

"Why not begin with Ring?" Hamilton's ruddy face was troubled. "We know he was heard to have relations with her; we believe Croucher to have seen them together at the well. . . ."

"Because it is Levi on trial, and unless we refute any case against him, we leave ourselves open to failure. We have no proof against Ring, only speculation.

Certainly," said Aaron temperately, "we will put the proposition to the jury—but as one of many elements."

"Yes. I suppose." Hamilton didn't like it, he clearly didn't like it, but he knew enough to know Aaron was right. "Is that what you mean to put in your opening statement?"

"*My* opening statement?" Aaron repeated.

The opening statement was the junior position, to be given to the less senior of the attorneys; the closing statement the position of honor.

"I had assumed you would wish to open our case," said Hamilton innocently. "Unless Livingston would prefer to do it?"

Aaron and Hamilton had both been admitted to the bar in 1782, but Aaron had been admitted in April; Hamilton in October. Brockholst had been a year behind them. By strict precedence, Brockholst should open; Aaron should close. And Hamilton shouldn't be here at all.

"And the closing statement . . . ?" inquired Aaron delicately.

Hamilton produced two closely written sheets of paper with a flourish. "I've already begun it."

For Hamilton to deliver the closing oration made a powerful point, one that wouldn't be wasted on the voting public when they went to the polls later in the month.

Aaron took the papers delicately by the edge. As usual, Hamilton had been writing with a pen with an indifferent nib and had watered his ink to the point of illegibility. But the words jumped out all the same.

> *Gentlemen of the Jury, I know the unexampled industry that has been exerted to destroy the reputation of the accused, and to immolate him at the shrine of persecution without the solemnity of a candid and impartial trial. I know that hatred, revenge and cruelty, all the vindictive and ferocious passions have assembled in terrible array and exerted every engine to gratify their malice. The thousand tongues of rumor have been steadily employed in fabrication . . .*

It was classic Hamiltonian flourish, all self-righteousness and hyperbole. But powerful. There was no denying the sheer force of it, the way it moved the emotions just as he claimed the enemies of Levi Weeks had manipulated the emotions of the public.

> *We have witnessed the extraordinary means which have been adopted to enflame the public passions and to direct the fury of popular*

> resentment against the prisoner. Why has the body been exposed for days in the public streets in a manner most indecent and shocking?—to attract the curiosity and arouse the feelings of numberless spectators.

"Such dreadful scenes," Aaron read aloud, "speak powerfully to the passions; they petrify the mind with horror—congeal the blood within our veins—and excite the human bosom with irresistible but undefinable emotions. When such emotions are once created, they are not easily subdued."

No, they weren't. They weren't at all. Anyone seeing Hamilton delivering this speech would indeed have undefinable emotions stirred.

> In cases depending upon a chain of circumstances, all the fabric must hang together or the whole will tumble down.

What was that but a veiled reference to the state of the country itself? A country fractured and fractious, in which Hamilton sought to position himself as the heir to General Washington, the man who could hold their fragile republic together in the face of forces seeking to break it apart.

Here was Hamilton, the champion of truth and reason, standing against artifice and base motives.

No, Aaron didn't like it at all. Unless . . .

"Burr should close," said Brockholst, spoiling for a fight. "He's the most senior of us."

As a point of order, he was right. But order was one thing and policy another. Aaron had the glimmer of an idea which might work even better to his advantage.

Aaron held up his hand. "Must we quibble over matters of precedence?" To Hamilton, he said, "Might I have a copy, so I might look it over at leisure?"

"Certainly." Now that he'd gotten his way, Hamilton was all generosity. "I'll have one of my clerks copy it for you. Philip!"

Philip Church sauntered in. Aaron had fought a duel with young Church's father last year, but there was no malice on either side. Church said a civil hello and took away the draft to copy.

"With your good grace," said Aaron to Brockholst, "I will attempt the opening statement. With your advice and guidance, of course."

Brockholst looked like a kettle about to boil over. "You shall have that, of course. Although I feel strongly that you should—"

"I thank you." Aaron looked meaningfully at Brockholst. "It is, after all, the opening that sets the tone of the case."

Brockholst subsided, giving Aaron what he fondly assumed to be a subtle nod. They were agreed on that, at least. Hamilton must not be allowed free rein to bungle the defense of Levi Weeks.

There were other reasons, as well. But those were Aaron's business and no one else's.

"As to the cross-examination of witnesses . . ." Hamilton began.

"I believe we should share that equally," said Aaron. "With deference to Brockholst, who has the most experience in these matters."

Brockholst bowed, a decidedly ironic expression on his face.

"We shall wish, of course," Aaron said smoothly, "to emphasize the harms that can be worked upon a man's reputation even where guilt has not been assigned. Brockholst had that case a few years ago, a rape case . . ."

"Lanah Sawyer." Brockholst could always be distracted by past trials. "Yes, she accused Henry Bedlow of rape. He was acquitted after only a few moments' deliberation, but Sawyer and her family so inflamed the public against him that he was hounded into poverty and debtors' prison. The mob threatened to pull down my house for my part in defending him."

"That is precisely what we must fight against," Hamilton said excitedly. "The thousand tongues of rumor . . ."

"As you so eloquently say in your closing statement," said Aaron gravely. "Ah, thank you."

Philip Church had returned, offering Aaron a hastily written, ill-blotted copy of Hamilton's oration.

Aaron folded it carefully, tucking it into the pocket of his waistcoat.

"I wish we had more time," murmured Hamilton. "I feel there's something I'm missing, something I ought to have seen. . . ."

There was. But it wasn't what Hamilton was thinking; Aaron was quite certain of that.

"Brockholst, you will walk with me?" Aaron stood, taking up his hat and gloves. Now that this farce of a meeting was over, it was time for the real work to begin. "Gentlemen, I shall see you tomorrow in court."

Chapter Twenty-One

[A] very clear day but very blustery.... The trial of Levi Weeks for the murder of Miss Sands came on this morning—scarcely anything else is spoken of.

—From the journal of Elizabeth De Hart Bleecker, March 31, 1800

New York City
March 31, 1800

"Hang him!"

"Hanging's too good for him! Crucify him!"

There hadn't been such a mob around Federal Hall since President Washington's inauguration ten years ago, when New York was still the nation's capital and the building around which the crowds were thronging the seat of government. The crowd, however, was in far less sanguine a mood than they had been that day.

In fact, thought Cadwallader Colden, rather than sanguine, they were sanguinary. It was a clever turn of phrase; he would have to remember it to repeat to Maria later, that evening, once Levi Weeks had been pronounced guilty.

"What is the matter? Why have we stopped?" Catherine Ring leaned forward, trying to see out the window.

Cadwallader had taken the precaution of fetching the Rings and Hope Sands in his own carriage. It had been a strange atmosphere in the Ring house that morning, everyone in their Sunday best, some coming to be called by the prosecution, some the defense.

Of Richard Croucher there had been no sign. He had married his widow the day before, and left his room at Mrs. Ring's to spend his wedding night with his bride before coming to beguile his honeymoon testifying against Levi Weeks. Cadwallader hoped he made it to the court in a timely fashion, although he would have to fight his way through the press of spectators to get there.

Elias Ring stuck his head out the window. "They're clearing the street."

Constables with sticks were pushing the people back, making way for a phalanx of city militia and volunteer guards. In the center, closely guarded all around, marched Levi Weeks, back straight, head up, staring straight ahead.

"Murderer!" The crowd had sighted him and surged forward again. "Devil!"

"For Elma!" Someone lobbed a clod of dirt—or possibly something other than dirt—at Levi, hitting one of his guards instead.

From his high position in the carriage, Cadwallader saw Levi flinch, but his head never turned.

"Stone him!" One enterprising soul was attempting to pry a cobble from the street, and was overborne by members of the volunteer guard—paid by Ezra Weeks, Cadwallader had no doubt.

"It's the people, raising their voice in your cause," said Cadwallader, trying to keep the excitement from his voice.

Surely thousands of New Yorkers couldn't be wrong? The jury would be made from New Yorkers such as these.

Hope Sands lifted her chin. "Good for them. Levi Weeks is a positive villain and it's only fit the whole world knows it."

"I only want it to be over," said Mrs. Ring faintly. "The children . . . I don't like to leave them."

Her sister reached out and took her hand, squeezing it. "Mr. Colden's maid has them well in hand. They won't miss thee for the one day."

No neighbors had been found who were willing to mind the Rings' four children while all the family and the boarders were at court. No one wanted to miss the trial. They were all going as either witnesses or spectators. So Cadwallader had brought with him one of his own housemaids, with strict instructions to stay at the Ring house as long as was needed.

That had been Maria's idea, of course.

"Polly will mind them as if they were her own," said Cadwallader heartily, although in truth Polly was only thirteen. But she could at least be trusted to change the baby's clouts and make sure the little boy didn't burn down the boardinghouse.

The carriage rattled into motion again. "Make way for Mr. Colden!" his coachman bellowed. "Make way for the attorney general!"

A cheer rose from the crowd, from a thousand throats, shouting his name. Admittedly, interspersed with cries of "Hang Levi!" and "Justice for Elma!" but his name all the same, with a grand huzzah such as he'd never thought to hear.

The steps clunked down and the coachman opened the door, grinning broadly. Dazedly, Cadwallader stepped out, and the cheering rose to a crescendo.

"Huzzah for the attorney general! Hang Levi!"

Cadwallader bowed to the crowd. He rather hoped Maria could hear. Was she in the courthouse? She'd said she meant to attend with Josiah.

A light cough from the interior of the carriage reminded him of his duties. Cadwallader handed down Catherine Ring, her gloved hand cold in his. He'd never seen her in gloves before, always with bare hands, engaged in a domestic task—and then Hope Sands, who stepped lightly from the carriage like a lady born.

Elias Ring clambered down by himself, his broad hat and baggy trousers drawing some guffaws from the crowd. It was not the best start, Cadwallader thought, as he hurried them under the grand arched loggia into Federal Hall. Cadwallader had meant to call Elias directly after his wife, but now that he thought about it, perhaps it might be better to call Hope Sands second, and push Elias Ring back to third. He wasn't needed for much, anyway. His primary purpose was to testify to the relationship between Elma and Levi while Mrs. Ring was in the country, and to confirm Mrs. Ring's account of Elma's mental state on the day she disappeared.

Catherine Ring and Hope Sands, on the other hand, in their Quaker brown and gray, made just the impression Cadwallader desired. Mrs. Ring's nervousness was only what one would expect of a common person confronted with the grand workings of the law. An honest woman, a good wife and mother.

He could see her eyeing the soaring ceiling, surmounted by L'Enfant's grand glass cupola, which bathed the lobby in light—the light of truth, Cadwallader thought poetically.

He took Mrs. Ring by the arm as he maneuvered them around the crowd. "Try not to be overawed by the grandeur of your surroundings. The jurors will be good citizens like yourselves."

Elias Ring glowered at him from under his broad hat. "And why should we be overawed? Awe we owe only to the Lord, not the children of Mammon."

If he was going to take that sort of tack, he wasn't going to make a good impression on the stand. Ring appeared determined to be displeased and displeasing. Cadwallader reassured himself that Elias Ring could be hustled on and off the stand as quickly as possible. He was only a side character in this drama.

"Pardon—excuse me—" Cadwallader employed his elbows to clear a path into the courtroom, almost unrecognizable for the press of bodies. Every inch of space was jammed with people, shoved together on the benches, hanging from the balconies, pressing forward nearly to the bench itself, where Chief Justice Lansing, Mayor Varick, and Richard Harison, recorder of the court, sat clothed in majesty and their robes of office.

"Hear ye, hear ye!" bellowed the clerk of the court. "All manner of persons that have business to do at this court of oyer and terminer, held in and for the county of New York, let them draw near and give their attendance and they shall be heard! If they can," he added, sotto voce.

Chief Justice Lansing banged his gavel. "Bailiff! Clear the court of unnecessary persons!"

Cadwallader shepherded his little group closer to the front of the room as the bailiff pushed people out the door, some putting up more protest than others.

"Ah, Colden, there you are!" called Brockholst Livingston, from the table where the defense sat, all looking annoyingly unruffled. "Thought you'd changed your mind!"

"I was delayed by the people raising their voice in Elma's cause."

"The mob, you mean," said General Hamilton. He raised his voice so all could hear. "When once you let the mob have their voice, there is no hope of justice."

Was that to be their tack? Well, they had to have something, and the evidence was all quite firmly on Cadwallader's side. On Elma's side, he meant.

With the room cleared, the prisoner was called to

the bar, taking his place in the dock. Someone—Burr, perhaps? Or Brockholst?—had made sure Levi had been given a clean coat and that his hair was brushed and neatly tied. The only signs of his weekend in the Bridewell were the circles beneath his eyes and a faint smattering of bug bites.

The clerk, Coleman, called forward the panel of jurors. "Levi Weeks, prisoner at the bar"—his sonorous voice turned the rote invocation into grand theater—"hold up your right hand and harken to what is said to you. These good men who have been last called and who do now appear are those who are to pass between the people of the state of New York and you upon your trial of life and death."

A delightful shiver went through those who had been permitted to remain. Cadwallader spotted Maria in one of the galleries, in her new paisley shawl, sitting by Josiah. He resisted the urge to wave.

"Gentlemen of the jury." Coleman faced the jurors. "The prisoner at the bar stands indicted in the words following, that Levi Weeks, laborer, not having the fear of God before his eyes, but being moved and seduced by the instigation of the devil, in and upon one Gulielma Sands, feloniously, willfully, and of his malice aforethought did cast, throw, and push the said Gulielma Sands into a certain well. . . ."

Cadwallader had to stop himself from mouthing the words along with the clerk. He had crafted this indictment, chosen the charges, alleging two counts: first that Levi Weeks had pushed Elma into the well, causing her to drown; second that Levi Weeks had assaulted Elma Sands.

"Upon this indictment, the prisoner at the bar hath been arraigned, and on his arraignment hath pleaded not guilty."

Levi Weeks stood stony-faced at the bar.

"He is now to be tried by his country, which country you are, so that your charge is, gentlemen, to inquire whether the prisoner at the bar is guilty of the felony whereof he stands indicted, or is not guilty, so sit together and hear your evidence."

Catherine Ring clasped her hands in her lap. Elias Ring slouched down so he was all but invisible beneath the brim of his hat. Maria's paisley shawl was a splash of color in the gallery.

"Mr. Colden?" Cadwallader started as the chief justice pronounced his name. "I believe you may wish to open your case."

Cadwallader lurched to his feet, sending his copy of State Trials tumbling to the floor, and the pages he'd marked with it. He hastily scooped it back up.

"Yes, Your Honor, as it please Your Honor. Gentlemen of the jury . . ."

Cadwallader fumbled in his pocket for the closely scribbled pages on which he had written his opening statement. Thank goodness it was still there. He knew that neither Hamilton nor Burr would read—no, nor Brockholst Livingston—but he had thought hard about it and decided there was no point in pretending he was their equal as a rhetorician. The whole point was that he wasn't their equal as a rhetorician. He was just a simple man, a journeyman lawyer, with truth as his standard.

Cadwallader settled himself firmly on his feet and faced the jury, twelve men who knew they were participating in the most momentous trial of a generation, all looking to him. It was just as he'd told Mrs. Ring two weeks ago. All he needed to do to win was tell the truth, because the truth would hang Levi Weeks.

"Gentlemen of the jury, in a cause which appears to have so greatly excited the public mind, in which the prisoner has thought it necessary for his defense to employ so many advocates distinguished for their eloquence and abilities, so vastly my superiors in learning, experience, and professional rank"—Cadwallader bowed to the trio of eminent attorneys clustered at the defense table—"it is not wonderful that I should rise to address you under the weight of embarrassments which such circumstances excite."

There was a decidedly sardonic expression on Brockholst Livingston's face. As always, it was impossible to tell what Colonel Burr was thinking. General Hamilton, however, seemed to genuinely enjoy the praise.

Cadwallader hastily addressed himself to his paper. "But, gentlemen, although the abilities enlisted on the respective sides of this cause are very unequal, I find some consolation in the reflection that our tasks are so also. While to my opponents it belongs as their duty to exert all their powerful talents in favor of the prisoner, as a public prosecutor, I think I ought to do no more than offer you in its proper order, all the testimony the case affords, draw from the witnesses which may be produced on either side all that they know, the truth, the whole truth, and nothing but the truth."

He lifted his head, making sure to look all around the room: at the spectators in the gallery, Weeks in the dock, the jury in their box. No tricks, no legal feints. Only the truth. This was what he pledged them.

He could see Josiah nod, just once, but it was enough.

"Levi Weeks, the prisoner at the bar, is indicted for the murder of Gulielma Sands. The deceased was a young girl, who till her fatal acquaintance with the prisoner, was virtuous and modest, and it will be material for you to remark, always of a cheerful disposition, and lively manners, although of a delicate constitution."

That was why they were here. For a girl who would never have a chance to be a woman. A girl seduced and betrayed. A girl whose murderer sounded the depths of the well in which he meant to drown her.

"We expect to prove to you that the prisoner won her affections, and that her virtue fell a sacrifice to his assiduity, that after a long period of criminal intercourse between them, he deluded her from the house of her protector under a pretense of marrying her, and carried her away to a well in the suburbs of this city and there murdered her—"

Cadwallader's voice broke. He took a moment, letting the image haunt the jury as it haunted him.

"No wonder, gentlemen, that my mind shudders at the picture here drawn and requires a moment to recollect myself. I will not say, gentlemen, what may be your verdict as to the prisoner, but I venture to assert that not one of you, or any man who hears this cause, shall doubt that the unfortunate young creature who was found dead in the Manhattan Well was most barbarously slain."

In the galleries, he could see enterprising souls scribbling away, recording his words for later publication. He was suddenly very glad Maria had insisted on his wearing his new coat and tying his cravat for him.

But this wasn't about him. This was the story of a girl betrayed.

Cadwallader gestured grandly at a tidy woman in brown, her auburn hair covered by a neat white cap.

"For our first witness, the people of New York call . . . Catherine Ring."

Chapter Twenty-Two

The first, and perhaps the most material evidence on the part of the people, was Mrs. Ring.

> —*An Impartial Account of the Trial of Mr. Levi Weeks for the Supposed Murder of Miss Julianna Elmore Sands,* by James Hardie, A.M.

New York City
March 31, 1800

Caty rose clumsily to her feet.

"Mrs. Ring," Mr. Colden said gently. "Do you solemnly declare and affirm that the evidence you shall give shall be the truth, the whole truth, and nothing but the truth?"

"I do." The words were ashes on her lips.

This was Elias's doing; it was he who forced her to— not lie. She wasn't going to lie. But to withhold. She could feel her soul soiled by it. She wished she could scrub it clean the way she did the washing.

General Hamilton stepped forward, resplendent in a sky-blue coat, the candlelight glinting off the red in his hair.

"Your Honor," he said, in a voice that seemed to bounce into every corner of the courtroom. "The defense moves that Mr. Elias Ring be removed from the room while his wife gives her testimony."

"What?" Elias exclaimed.

"Your Honor—" began Mr. Colden.

Caty felt sick with fear. Elias was arguing; the jury was whispering; the spectators were humming with the excitement of it all. The lawyers had convened in a huddle by the bench.

They knew. Why else would they ask? Levi had seen—Levi had told. Mr. Colden had explained to her—Levi wasn't able to speak in his own case. But what would she do if his lawyers asked her about Elma and Elias?

Lie. She would have to lie, and then burn in hell eternally after.

Justice Lansing gave a smart rap of his gavel. "The prisoner has a right to it, of course, if he requests it. So ordered. Constable, will you escort Mr. Ring from the room?"

"It's just their attempt to unsettle you," Mr. Colden murmured, as though she were a skittish horse, needing to be soothed. For the jury, he asked, "Mrs. Ring, when did Levi Weeks first come into your household?"

Caty could feel Levi's eyes on her. "In July last, Levi Weeks came to board in our family."

Seventh month. She ought to have said seventh month. It was against her religion to use heathen names. Already she was displaying her fall from grace.

Caty's hands felt strange and clumsy in the white gloves Hope had tied on for her, so similar to the gloves she had tied on for Elma the night she disappeared. "Soon after, he began to pay attention to Margaret Clark, till about the twentieth of the eighth month, when she went into the country. About two days after her absence, Gulielma asked me—"

"If you will pardon me." Colonel Burr stepped forward. He wasn't glowing in silk like General Hamilton. His frock coat was of sober black. Somehow, the black-and-white perfection of his tailoring made him even more sinister. "This, Your Honors, is a clear case of hearsay testimony, and does not come within any of the exceptions within the book."

Caty looked to Mr. Colden, mute with confusion. How was she meant to respond to this?

Mr. Colden was already advancing on the bench. "Your Honors will agree that in the case of a person deceased—"

Colonel Burr was there before him. "No one seeks to deny that the declarations of a deceased person may be sometimes received as evidence against a prisoner, but as the assistant attorney general well knows, that rule applies only when such statements are made in the moments after the fatal blow—not several months before," Colonel Burr said drily. "Unless he can show that Gulielma Sands was in apprehension of death as early as August? Such statements are only admissible in the deceased's final moments, when he must be supposed to be under an equal solemnity as an oath."

Mr. Colden rallied. "Your Honor, Miss Sands is no longer here to speak on her own account—because she was most cruelly and foully murdered."

Mr. Livingston unfolded himself from his seat. "Objection."

"Anyone with conscience *should* object to the murder of a young girl. Your Honor will surely agree that this is one of those cases where such evidence must be admitted upon necessity." Mr. Colden seized triumphantly on one of the books on his table. "I refer, of course, to State Trials 487 and 488, Leeche's cases, Bacon 563, and Skinner's Reports."

Caty had no idea what he was talking about, but it sounded suitably impressive.

The attorneys for Levi Weeks, however, were less impressed. "Are we to acknowledge the authority of the English courts, when we have so lately secured our independence from their yoke?" Brockholst Livingston mused. "State Trials has no precedential effect here, and even if they had, my colleague would do well to refresh his recollection of them. The case of Leech articulates the exact opposite principle than that contended by the prosecution."

Mr. Colden began thumbing through the pages. "Your Honor, if you look at Skinner . . ."

"This question," said Colonel Burr, stepping in front of Mr. Livingston, "is larger than the case at hand. Our nation is a young one, as are our courts. What we determine today sets a pattern not just for the evidence in this case but for thousands—nay, hundreds of thousands—of cases to come. We must not let expedience blind us to the needs of the law."

They'll try to trick you, Mr. Colden had warned Caty. But this was something different entirely. Caty felt useless, helpless. She'd thought she was ready for any challenge they'd toss at her but she'd never imagined they'd use the law to brick shut her mouth, to stop her saying anything at all.

"To reply specifically to those cases raised by the *assistant* attorney general, the witness in the first case to which he referred was suffered to proceed without interruption and no point was made to the court respecting it." Colonel Burr smiled pleasantly at Mr. Colden, who was paging through his book with increasing agitation, grabbing at little slips of paper. "As to the second case, it was in the court of sessions in Scotland, and cannot be considered any authority here."

He bowed to the judges and stepped back.

"The testimony," said Justice Lansing, "is ruled inadmissible. Mrs. Ring, you may proceed, but without reference to whatever Elma may have said to you, only what you yourself said and observed."

"But—" Caty didn't know what to say.

Mr. Colden looked pleadingly at her. "You were telling us of what happened when Margaret Clark went to the country."

Caty wet her dry lips, trying to remember the words she'd rehearsed and rehearsed with Mr. Colden, now with a great hole cut out of the middle of them. "After Margaret Clark had gone to the country a few days, Levi became very attentive to Elma, to whom I mentioned it, and she did not deny it. She and Levi were left together with my husband either the tenth or eleventh of the ninth month."

General Hamilton bounced up. "Which room did Elma sleep in while you were in the country?"

What did that have to do with anything? "In the front room on the second story."

Elma had slept in so many rooms while Caty was away.

"After I had been absent about four weeks, I received a letter from my husband, desiring me to come home as he was very lonesome." It was hard to keep the bitterness from her voice, to say it matter-of-factly, as if it were what it seemed. "I at first determined to return immediately, but I always thought Levi a man of honor, and that he did not intend to promise further than he intended to perform; therefore I stayed two weeks longer, and I came home six weeks to the day."

"What was their conduct like upon your return?" Mr. Colden prompted.

"I saw an appearance of mutual attachment—but nothing improper. During her indisposition, he paid her the strictest attention and spent several nights in the room, saying he did not like to leave her with Hope, my sister, fearing she might get to sleep and neglect her. And in the night he wanted to go for a physician, but I discouraged him, thinking she would get better by morning."

And she had! They needn't look at her like that, as

though she'd been neglectful. She'd been trying to protect Elma, to hide her shame. If someone had helped Aunt Lizzy as she'd helped Elma, Aunt Lizzy might have been married now, in her own household.

And there would have been no Elma to seduce Caty's husband and destroy her peace.

The noises had escalated. People were standing and pointing. Caty felt the hair on the back of her neck prickle.

Caty raised her voice over the murmurs of the crowd. "One night, after she had got much better, choosing to sleep alone, she went to bed, and, as I suppose, Levi was gone also."

Behind her, she could hear heavy, labored breathing and smell the familiar mix of wool and sweat and her own homemade soap that belonged only to Elias.

"Your Honors!" It was General Hamilton. "Mr. Ring has reentered the room!"

Chief Justice Lansing gave a smart rap of his gavel. "Constable, remove Mr. Ring."

Elias grasped her shoulder. "Thee didn't tell?" he hissed.

Caty stared at her husband, riven with horror and anger. How could he be such a fool? Did he need to scream his guilt to the world?

Two constables grabbed Elias by the arms. He

struggled in their grip. "What God has put together, let no man put asunder! She's my own wife! Why can't I hear what she has to say?"

"Because you, Mr. Ring," said Chief Justice Lansing, with considerable irritation, "are here not as a husband but as a witness in a murder trial. You will leave this room and not return again until you are told to do so. If you attempt to interrupt your wife's testimony again, you will be sent to the Bridewell to cool your heels. Do you comprehend?"

"Oh, I comprehend," snarled Elias, glaring at Levi's lawyers.

"Constables!" snapped Justice Lansing. "Remove him. Mrs. Ring, you may proceed—as soon as the door has closed behind your husband."

"Mrs. Ring," said Mr. Colden, sounding a bit desperate, "can you tell the jury about the events of the twenty-second of December?"

"Of the—yes." Caty was having trouble catching her breath; specks like dust motes danced before her eyes. "On the twenty-second of December, my sister Hope went to meeting and Levi went to his brother's. In a short time, he returned, having fallen and hurt his knee. Sylvanus Russel said, 'Levi, you won't be able to go out today.' He answered, 'I am determined to, tonight.'"

There were the sounds of a scuffle outside the

courtroom. Caty could feel the clammy sweat gathering at her brow, beneath her cap. She rushed on, pouring the story out in a jumble, how Elma had asked her which kerchief to wear, how Caty had insisted Elma go to a neighbor to borrow a muff—here Caty's throat locked, but she pushed forward. How Levi came in just at eight, and, a minute or two after, as if at a signal, Elma had gone upstairs to get her hat and shawl.

"I took the candle and went upstairs; she had her hat on and her muff in her hand." In that moment, when Caty had thought Elma was going to be married, Caty had come closer to feeling fond of Elma than she ever had before. "I observed she looked rather paler than usual, but I thought it a natural consequence and told her not to be frightened."

A murmur rose from the galleries.

"I went down and left her just ready to follow. Levi took his hat—"

"How long do you suppose it was from the time Levi came in, till they went out?" demanded Brockholst Livingston.

Caty clasped her cold hands together. "Elma might have remained in the room two minutes. In the whole, I don't think all the time from Levi's coming in till they went out exceeded ten minutes."

"Pray, Mrs. Ring, in what situation did you leave Elma upstairs?" prompted Mr. Colden.

They'd discussed this. This was the key point, that Levi had left with Elma. "I left her just ready to come down," said Caty promptly. "Levi instantly took his hat and went into the entry. I heard a walking on the stairs and a whispering near the door at the bottom of the stairs. The front door was opened and the latch fell. I took up the candle and ran to the door to see which way they went. It was moonlight, but having a candle made it darker."

It was Brockholst Livingston who interrupted her again. "Mrs. Ring, are you *sure* you shut the door before?"

As if she were the sort of slattern who would leave her door open at night! "I am positive. It stuck much and it was difficult to shut it. It was something out of order, which made a jarring noise, and it stuck a good deal."

Mr. Colden stepped in again. "Are you sure about the sound of steps going out?"

Caty looked defiantly at Levi's lawyers. "I am very positive. I heard the steps very distinctly."

Chief Justice Lansing looked down at her. "Did Levi return to his lodgings the same night?"

"As I was going to tell, about ten o'clock he returned."

Caty wasn't afraid anymore, only annoyed. She would tell them all this if only they'd let her get on with it. "He sat down and said, 'Is Hope got home?'"

Another murmur from the galleries.

"Then he asked, 'Is Elma gone to bed?' I answered, 'No—she is gone out, at least I saw her ready to go, and have good reason to think she went.' He said"—Caty looked at Levi—"he said, 'I'm surprised she should go out so late at night and alone.'"

One of the other judges spoke up, Mr. Harison, the city recorder. "Did you express any alarm to him?"

"No." Caty knew how it made her look. But they didn't understand how it was. "Feeling very uneasy and agitated, I thought I would speak to Levi more particularly than I had done. I went to his door twice, but seemed as if I had not power to enter. I thought perhaps Elma might be sitting by his stove."

Mr. Harison asked, "Was anything said about Elma at breakfast by anybody?"

"No. Nobody mentioned her until Levi came in, saying, 'Is Elma got home?'" Caty could feel her voice breaking. "I answered no. I said, 'Indeed, Levi, to tell thee the truth, I believe she went out with thee, she told me she was to, and I have good reason to think she did.' He—he looked surprised and said, 'If she had gone out with me, she would have come with me, and I never saw her after she left the room.'"

"Was there anything uncommon in his manner?" inquired Mayor Varick.

"There was to be sure," said Caty fiercely, "more than I can express. Nothing more was said until afternoon, when myself and my sister, being so distressed, we determined to stand it no longer and said, 'Stop, Levi, this matter has become so serious, I can stand it no longer. She told me that night at eight o'clock you were going to be married.' He turned pale, trembled to a great degree, was agitated, and began to cry, clasping his hands together, cried out, 'I'm ruined—I'm ruined—I'm undone forever unless she appears to clear me.'"

She should have known then. She should have gone straight to the constables, to someone. No one could blame her more for it than she blamed herself.

"Two days later, Levi, seeing us much distressed, sat down and endeavored to console us, saying, 'Give her up, she is gone, no doubt—it's my firm belief she's now in eternity.' I answered, 'Why does thee say so?' He replied, 'Why, I heard her say she wished she never had an existence.' I replied, 'If thee recollects, I don't doubt thee has heard me say so.'"

"Pray, Mrs. Ring," drawled Mr. Livingston, "did you say you had wished you never had an existence?"

"Yes! I dare say I have!" Caty glared at him, too angry to be afraid. "In this very case, I might say, 'I wish I never had an existence to witness such a scene.'"

A faint smile spread across Mr. Livingston's lips, and he bowed, acknowledging the point.

"Pray, Mrs. Ring," said Mr. Colden, "I wish you would be particular as to her temper and disposition on the twenty-second."

"I never saw her pleasanter in her life," Caty said honestly. "She was more so than usual."

"What was her general temper of mind?"

"Very lively, open, and free."

Colonel Burr stepped in. "Was it not more so than is usual among Friends?"

"I always thought her disposition rather too gay for a Friend—but she altered her dress and behavior to please me," Caty added hastily.

"How old was she?" asked Mr. Colden.

"About five years younger than myself. She was about twenty-two at the time of her death." Caty squeezed her eyes shut, surprised by grief. It was Hope's voice, crying that she would soon be older than Elma would ever be. It was the memory of Elma, that last afternoon, the Elma she might have been, married and no longer Caty's burden. "I regarded her as a sister."

"When was the body found?" asked Mr. Colden.

Her voice hoarse, Caty said, "The twelfth day after she left our house, or the second of January."

"No further questions," said Mr. Colden.

Caty, her eyes stinging, would have stepped down, but Colonel Burr asked, "What was the character of Levi Weeks while he boarded with your family?"

"It was such as to gain the esteem of everyone in the family," said Caty bitterly.

"Did you observe the prisoner after this affair of the twenty-second eat his meals as usual?"

This affair? As if it were a package gone astray and not a girl dead. "I believe he did."

"Did Levi ever walk out with your sister Hope?"

Caty blinked. "He went once to a charity sermon with her, and Elma was to have gone too, but the going was wet and she was not very well, and I would not suffer her to go."

"What was the state of Elma's health generally?"

Mr. Colden had warned her they would try to bring up the laudanum. "For about a year past, she was at times rather unwell," said Caty cautiously.

General Hamilton jumped in. "Had she any habitual illnesses?"

Caty fell back on the old explanation. "She was at times rather troubled with the cramp in her stomach."

"Where was her usual lodging room?"

Caty didn't understand these questions at all. Why the concern about Elma's room when she had died in a field on the outskirts of the city?

"In the front room. She at first slept in the third story before she went into the country, but for the three weeks before her death, she slept in the back room in the second story."

"Was it not next to Mr. Watkins's bedroom?"

Caty didn't know where Mr. Watkins's bedroom was. When she visited with the neighbors, she tended to stay downstairs. She hadn't Elma's habit of visiting bedrooms. "It was next, I believe."

"Did you ever ask Levi whether he was engaged to Elma?"

"Never till after her death."

"Nor said a word about it to him," General Hamilton pressed.

"No." She knew how it looked, but she couldn't help it.

General Hamilton's voice rang out through the room. "Had you any reason to suspect that any other person but Levi had an improper intimacy with her?"

There was a ringing in Caty's ears. She looked him right in the eye and lied. "No."

She braced herself for the inevitable rejoinder, the direct question she couldn't ignore. But instead he asked, "Do you know of what materials the wall between your house and Watkins's is composed?"

Did he think she was a carpenter? "I don't know."

"No further questions," said General Hamilton, smiling at her as though she had told him something he wanted to know.

What had she said?

Nothing. Nothing but what she and Mr. Colden had practiced. And they hadn't asked her about Elias. The relief of it made her light-headed.

At the back of the room, she could see the doors opening, as Elias was readmitted. He jerked his head at her. Caty gave a little shake of her head. Their secret hadn't come out.

Yet.

Chapter Twenty-Three

Here let us remark the collected composure of [the prisoner's] manner, and the open expression of his countenance. His appearance interested us greatly in his favor. We waited with anxiety for the testimony—convinced that if his was not the expression of conscious innocence, he was indeed a man incapable of feeling.

—A Brief Narrative of the Trial for the Bloody and Mysterious Murder of the Unfortunate Young Woman in the Famous Manhattan Well, taken in shorthand by a gentleman of the bar

New York City
March 31, 1800

"For our next witness, the people call Miss Hope Sands."
Hope rose from the bench, and walked with as much dignity as she could muster to the witness box,

where Mr. Colden waited for her. She felt transformed by rage: against Levi, Levi's lawyers, and most of all, with Elias, who didn't have the common decency to let his wife testify in peace.

It was just like Elias, Hope thought furiously as she took her place at the stand. He was always throwing his weight around when it was least convenient and never there when Caty actually needed him. He kept bringing up fixing that door as though he'd built a palace in a day, as if Caty hadn't been begging him for a year to do something about it.

Levi had offered to fix it, but Caty had demurred, saying she wasn't going to burden one of her boarders; Elias would see to it. Eventually.

Now that squeaky door was a key piece of the evidence in condemning the man standing there in the dock. Levi Weeks.

Will you watch when they hang me?

Hope forced herself to look straight at Levi, really look at him, this man she had thought she loved, who she had never really known. He was a beast, she told herself, a beast masquerading as a man.

"Miss Sands," said Mr. Colden. Hope could see him nervously fingering the fobs dangling from his watch chain. "When were you first made aware of the intimacy between Elma and the prisoner at the bar?"

"The first time I knew them to be together in private was about two weeks after I and Caty came back to town. I was in her bedroom with Elma when Levi came in, on which Elma gave me a hint. I immediately went out, he followed me to the door, shut it after me, and locked it."

Brockholst Livingston rose. "Did you ever tell Mrs. Ring of this?"

"Yes, I told her the same evening," Hope said promptly.

"How did the prisoner at the bar seem to you after Elma went missing?" asked Mr. Colden.

Hope looked at the lawyer in surprise; this wasn't what they'd practiced. She'd thought he'd meant to ask her about Elma's plans to marry. Then she saw, over his shoulder, the trio of lawyers for the defense, General Hamilton with his vivid coat and lively expression, Colonel Burr in sober black, Brockholst Livingston looming over them both. All waiting to pounce if she gave them an excuse.

They would adore another chance to rip Mr. Colden to shreds over hearsay.

Hope found herself determined to thwart them. She'd give them no excuse to tear more strips off poor Mr. Colden, who was only doing his best, alone.

"On Monday, the day after she was missing, about

ten or eleven o'clock in the forenoon, I met Levi upstairs alone. I attacked him about her—he denied knowing anything of her, though from his looks I was confident he did. He soon began to use all possible means to convince me of his innocence."

"*All* possible means?" one of the jury whispered to another, with a coarse laugh.

Hope lifted her chin. She couldn't help the color in her cheeks, but she refused to let them unsettle her. "The Sabbath evening after she was missing, he came to me, saying, 'Hope, if you can say anything in my favor, do it, for you could do me more good than any friend I have in the world to clear me; therefore, if you can say anything, do it before the body is found—'"

All the betrayal and revulsion she felt surged up through her throat, choking her. How could he? How could he refer to Elma as "the body," as though she were nothing more than a collection of bones?

Hope straightened, looking at the men in the jury box, the spectators in the galleries, Levi's lawyers. Let them know the sort of man they were defending. "He said, 'Do it before the body is found, as after it will do no good. But if the body is found a good way off that will clear me, as I was not a sufficient time from my brother's to go far.'"

For the first time in the whole miserable proceeding, Hope saw Levi flinch, and was glad of it.

"He then pressed me very hard to go to the alderman's and see him. I refused, upon which he gave me a paper he had drawn, wishing me to sign it." Loathing dripped from her words like poison. "The purport of the paper was that he paid no more particular attention to Elma than to any other female in the house—that nothing had passed between them like courtship or looking like marriage."

Colonel Burr stepped forward, full of feigned sympathy. "Was not Levi as particular to you as he was to Elma?"

Hope looked directly at Levi. "No. He was not."

"Was not Levi very much liked?"

There was no point in lying about it. "He was, very much. All spoke well of him."

Colonel Burr exchanged a quick word with his colleagues. "Did Levi ever walk out with Elma—or with you?"

They knew this already. Caty had told them. "He went once to the museum with me and Elma. He went once to church with me of an evening; Elma was to have gone, but she was sick."

"Did you not stop at some house on the way to church?"

"Yes, we did." Hope's voice was firm and clear. That night, she had thought . . . Well, it didn't matter what she had thought. "We stopped at Ezra Weeks's, the brother of Levi."

The three lawyers briefly huddled together. When they emerged, Colonel Burr said only, "No further questions."

What did they mean, no further questions? Hope was ready to answer whatever they asked. She wanted to look into Levi's eyes and have him know how much she knew he'd betrayed them. She wanted the jury to know how much he'd betrayed them, this man who looked so appealing but was so rotten at the core.

"Miss Sands, you may step down," said Mr. Colden.

They had kept Caty up there for the better part of an hour or more. Reluctantly, Hope stepped down. As she made her way back to the bench, she could feel Levi's eyes on her. Hope turned and locked eyes with him.

Would she watch him hang? Gladly.

"Mr. Elias Ring," Mr. Colden called.

Hope took the seat Elias had vacated next to Caty.

"You did very well," Caty whispered. "I wish I had your strength."

"You have your own," Hope said, surprised, but Elias had made it to the stand and there was no time to say more.

He mumbled his way through his affirmation, making clear he felt this whole process beneath his dignity.

Hope had never much cared for Elias, had never understood why Caty had chosen to marry him when she might have had so many others, but recently her vague distaste had bloomed into full-blown dislike.

It was, she realized, that she'd generally been able to ignore him. Caty ran the household and Elias slouched in and out as he pleased. Hope dealt with him as little as possible. But Elma's murder had forced them all together, had brought these divisions into the open. To fail to repair a door was one thing; to humiliate Caty in court was another.

Mr. Colden began with the same question he'd asked Hope. "Mr. Ring, when did you first become aware of an intimacy between Elma and the prisoner at the bar?"

"Levi Weeks was a lodger in my house," said Elias brusquely. "In the ninth month—"

Brockholst Livingston broke in. "What is that month called?"

"I don't know it by any other name," said Elias contemptuously. "Thee can tell."

Mr. Colden was jingling his watch fobs again, all three of them. "Mr. Ring, you were saying. In the ninth month?"

"When my *wife* was gone into the country"—Elias looked reproachfully at Caty—"Levi and Elma were constantly together in private. I was alone and very lonesome and was induced to believe, from their conduct, that they were shortly to be married. Elma's bed was in the back room, on the second floor," he added, directly contradicting Caty.

Hope took Caty's hand, freezing even in her gloves, and squeezed.

"The front room had a bed in it, in which Isaac Hatfield slept about three weeks," Elias continued. He nodded to Hatfield, jammed in among the witnesses yet to be called. "Hatfield during this time was occasionally out of town. I slept in the front room below, and one night when Hatfield was out of town, I heard a talking and noise in his room. In the morning I went up into the room and found the bed tumbled and Elma's clothes which she wore in the afternoon lying on the bed."

"Did you see her in the room?" inquired Colonel Burr pleasantly.

"No, I saw nothing, but I have no doubt she was there."

One of the jurymen called out, "Did Elma, do you suppose, get up from her bed and go away naked? You say she left her clothes."

Snickers and guffaws broke out throughout the room at the image of Elma prancing through the house naked.

Hope turned in her seat, glaring at them. How dare they? Her cousin had died and they were making mock of her.

"She left part of her clothes," said Elias shortly. "She had two suits and this was part of the best, which she had on the day before, being First Day."

Hope stared down at her own skirt, gray and plain. Elma's Sunday dress had been her pride: a calico gown over a white dimity petticoat. She had labored over it, trying to make it look like the ones the ladies in the fashion papers wore, over Caty's protests that the calico was too gay, the cut too risqué, the overall impression too bold.

Elma had loved that dress.

Elma had died in that dress.

Mr. Colden made a valiant effort to reclaim the floor. "Did you see anything improper or immodest in the behavior of Elma, until she was acquainted with the prisoner?"

"No. Never."

"Thank you, Mr. Ring." There was no disguising the relief with which Mr. Colden ended his questions; Hope wished Caty could be done with Elias as easily. "If the defense has any questions?"

"We do." General Hamilton bounced up on the balls of his feet, but Colonel Burr cut neatly ahead of him.

"Mr. Ring, did you ever see any intimacies between the prisoner and Margaret Clark?"

Elias looked from one man to the next, as if suspecting a trick. "I have seen, formerly, some familiarities between them," Elias said cautiously.

Hope could have told them that meant nothing at all. Peggy was familiar with everyone. It was what made her such good company, and so entirely unreliable. Not like Caty, who kept everything locked inside, but was true to her core.

Colonel Burr continued, conversationally, "Did you ever hear any noise when Hatfield slept in the room over you?"

"No," said Elias, relaxing a little.

"Did you ever know that the prisoner and Elma were in bed together?"

There was a pause. "No."

General Hamilton pushed past Colonel Burr. "What materials is the partition made of between Watkins's house and yours?"

Elias blinked. "It is a plank partition, lathed and plastered."

"Is Mr. Watkins a clever man and a good neighbor?"

"Yes, he is."

Colonel Burr gently eased past General Hamilton. "Do you remember how Elma appeared on the twenty-second of December?"

Elias's chin stuck out pugnaciously. "She was as cheerful and gay as I ever saw her."

"Pray tell what you remember particularly about that day."

Elias expanded under Colonel Burr's regard. "On the twenty-second of December, I had been to meeting in the afternoon." Once everyone had sufficiently admired his piety, Elias went on, "I returned and found Elma dressing and my wife helping her in dressing. About eight o'clock, Elma went out. I saw her go out of the room, and I heard the front door open and shut about three or four minutes after. My wife took the candle and was gone about two minutes."

"Did you hear her go upstairs?" inquired Colonel Burr as if it were a matter of only idle interest.

"I am not certain that I heard anybody go upstairs," said Elias dismissively. "When my wife returned, I asked, 'Who went out?' She said Elma and Levi. I answered that it was wrong, Elma would get sick. She replied"—Elias gave Caty another resentful look—"he will be more careful of her than I would be."

Hope could have shaken him.

"Did Mr. Weeks return that night?"

Elias made clear what he thought of this "Mr. Weeks" business. "About ten o'clock Levi came in. He asked if Hope had got home."

It was foolish, but that still gave Hope a strange feeling in her stomach, every time. She felt exposed, raw, even though she knew Levi had only been using her as a cloak for his real actions, and not genuinely concerned about her whereabouts.

"He asked, 'Is Elma gone to bed?' My wife answered, 'No, she is gone out.' He observed it was strange she should go out so late and alone."

A shaft of afternoon sunlight lit General Hamilton's hair, making him glow like flame. "Have you not threatened the prisoner at some time since this affair began?"

Elias gaped at him. His mouth opened and closed, frog-like. "I never threatened him—that I know of," he sputtered.

He'd threatened to shoot Levi. Hope had heard him. So, apparently, had many other people. Maybe, thought Hope angrily, if he'd spent less time drinking at the tavern and more time at home helping Caty, he wouldn't have been so loose with his words. Or so foolish as to try to lie about them!

Elias twisted like an animal in a trap. "I had a conversation with him! In which he asked me if I had not said certain things about him, respecting Elma being missing."

"A conversation?" repeated General Hamilton, his voice ripe with disbelief.

"It was he threatened me!" Elias protested shrilly. "He said if I told such things of him he would tell of me and Croucher!"

Chapter Twenty-Four

And here I observe, before I enter upon the evidence on either side, that it is not my intention to give even a detail of all the different testimonies. Many of them appeared to have no sort of connection with the point in question.

—An Impartial Account of the Trial of Mr. Levi Weeks for the Supposed Murder of Miss Julianna Elmore Sands, by James Hardie, A.M.

New York City
March 31, 1800

A surge of elation rushed through Alexander. First Ring's attempt to interfere with his wife's testimony and now this—what further proof did they need that Ring was guilty?

Colden quickly jumped in, trying to direct attention

back to Levi. "Did you not tell the prisoner at the bar you believed him guilty? How did he appear?"

Ring hastily followed his lead. "I did, and he appeared white as ashes and trembled all over like a leaf."

Instead of going back to the question of what Ring and Croucher had to fear from Levi, Burr asked, "What was the character of the prisoner previous to this, and how was he liked in the family?"

Alexander frowned at him. They were losing the advantage he'd won. They needed to push forward against Ring, not fall back on Levi's character.

"His character was very good, for anything I know," said Ring sullenly. "His behavior was such that he was generally esteemed."

Alexander pressed forward. "Were not you the friend and protector of Elma?"

Ring's eyes darted to the bench where his wife sat. "Yes."

"Did you ever speak to her about her *improper intimacy* with Levi?"

"I never did," Ring said reluctantly.

Because it had never existed. It had been Ring with Elma in Hatfield's room, not Levi. Alexander opened his mouth, prepared to say just that, but there was Burr again, cutting in with irrelevancies.

"On the night of the twenty-second, did you hear

any whispering in the entry or anybody come downstairs?"

Ring looked from Burr to Alexander, clearly suspecting a trick. "I did not, for I set in the corner and was not attentive to these things."

"Thank you, Mr. Ring," said Burr. "The defense has no further questions."

"What do you mean, no further questions?" Alexander hissed, as Mr. Ring stepped down, amid a flurry of whispers and speculation. "He was unsettled—we could have got him to admit to his intimacy with Elma! Or more!"

"Would you place all your wares in the shopwindow?"

"Yes, if they're there to be sold!" They might not get such a good chance at Ring again. Opportunity was seldom a lengthy visitor, as Alexander knew all too well.

"Then you cheapen yourself and them." Burr abandoned the mercantile metaphor, saying briefly, "We must keep to the point, not be distracted by irrelevancies."

The point. Did he mean the shaky argument of suicide? It was absurd. Why have ammunition if one wasn't to use it?

"You, sir," murmured Alexander, "are too subtle for me."

Burr bowed, as if Alexander had just paid him a compliment.

Alexander hadn't missed the way Burr had used the hearsay argument to frame himself as the arbiter of law for the new nation, setting the pattern for the future. Burr talking about not letting expedience bend to justice struck Alexander as ironic in the extreme. This was the same man who had claimed the law was anything boldly asserted and plausibly maintained.

"Did you not observe a very particular kind of attention in the prisoner, to Elma?" While Alexander was distracted, Colden had called Margaret Clark to the stand.

"I can't say I did. I can't say there was anything looked like courting her." Peggy Clark wasn't a Quaker. Her dress was a brightly patterned calico. Her hat sported a broad bow, beneath which bobbed carefully contrived curls. "After I returned, he and she appeared more intimate together, which I suppose was from their having been together while I was in the country."

Poor Colden looked utterly nonplussed. Alexander wondered why he hadn't confirmed what his witness meant to say before he called her to the stand.

"Did you ever know of their being locked up together?" Colden asked hopefully.

"I knew once of their being locked up together in the

bedroom—afterwards Levi told me they were in the bedroom together," Margaret Clark added cheerfully, robbing the statement of any value for Colden. "That was the Monday evening before she was missing. Another time, I saw him standing in her room when she was sick, but I thought nothing of it because he was always attentive to anyone who was sick."

Colden was looking rather sick himself. "Pray, how long did you live in the house, do you suppose?"

"I might have been absent about half the time," she admitted.

Burr asked smoothly, "Did not Levi pay as much attention to Hope Sands as he did to Elma?"

Margaret Clark didn't pause for a moment. "Yes, I think he did, and more too."

There was a rustling as people turned to look at Hope Sands, who was sitting very straight on her bench.

"Thank you, Miss Clark," said Mr. Colden in a strangled voice. "If I might call Mr. Richard Croucher to the stand. . . ."

Alexander watched intently as a tall, thin man rose from the benches. He was dressed with continental care, his cravat tied in an intricate arrangement, his waistcoat of floral brocade. His hair was dark, his features thin and angular. He was not a particularly handsome man—one might go so far as to call him ill-favored—but his clothes and bearing gave him a certain air.

This, then, was the mysterious Mr. Croucher who had been so busy about town spreading rumors of the guilt of Levi Weeks—the man whom Levi had caught embracing Elma the week before she died. The man who might implicate Elias Ring as her murderer, if pressed the right way.

Mr. Croucher bowed to the judges in their robes, as if they were meeting at an assembly, and not a trial for murder. "May it please the court and gentlemen of the jury, I was a lodger but not a boarder in Mrs. Ring's house. I remained at the house all the time of Mrs. Ring's absence and paid particular attention to the behavior of the prisoner and the deceased, and I was satisfied from what I saw, there was a warm courtship going on."

"When you say a warm courtship, Mr. Croucher..."

Mr. Croucher shook his head, as though it pained him to proceed. "I have known the prisoner at the bar to be with the deceased Elma Sands, in private frequently and all times of night. I knew him to pass two whole nights in her bedroom."

This was more to the taste of the crowd. The people who had begun to slump in their benches sat up straighter.

Mr. Croucher leaned forward, drawing the whole room into his confidence. "Once, lying in my bed, which stood in the middle of the room and in a posture which was favorable to see who passed the door, and which I assumed on purpose—I had some curiosity—I saw the prisoner at the bar come out of her room and pass the door *in his shirt only*, to his own room. Once, too, at a time when they were less cautious than usual, I saw them in a *very intimate* situation."

"Seducer!" someone shouted at Levi. "Murderer!"

Alexander thought he saw a hint of a smile play about Mr. Croucher's lips before it was hastily replaced with an expression of carefully cultivated sorrow.

"Did you ever tell anyone of this?" asked Mr. Colden.

"I never took notice of it to anyone." It was not, Mr. Croucher's manner seemed to imply, the occupation of a gentleman to inquire into the affairs of another.

"Thank you," said Mr. Colden. "If the defense has any questions?"

"Pray, what countryman are you?" inquired Burr.

Mr. Croucher drew himself up. "An Englishman. I have been in this country since January 1799."

Alexander wasn't going to let Burr waste any more time on irrelevancies. "Where, sir, were you on the night of the twenty-second of December 1799?"

"I supped that night at Mrs. Ashmore's—but that's not her real name." Mr. Croucher allowed himself a slight smirk. "It is 884 Bowery Lane. It was the birthday of her son. She has had a good deal of my money, and I thought I would go and sup with her."

"Did you go anywhere else that evening?"

Mr. Croucher gave an elegant shrug. "I crossed twice or three times from Greenwich Street to Broadway and was once at the Coffee House. I went out to the Bowery and returned to Mrs. Ring's."

A busy man, Mr. Croucher. A busy man and a strangely precise one. "What time did you return home that night?"

"It was my agreement with Mrs. Ring to be home at ten o'clock of nights, but on this occasion I stayed out until eleven or half past eleven."

"Do you know where the Manhattan Well is?"

"I do." Suddenly, Mr. Croucher was a great deal less talkative.

"Did you pass by it that evening?"

"I did not—I wish I had." Mr. Croucher arranged his sharp features into an expression of wistful regret. "I might, perhaps, have saved the life of the deceased."

He was lying; Alexander was sure of it. He would stake his reputation that Mr. Croucher had passed by the well that night. "Have you not said you did?"

Something flickered behind Mr. Croucher's eyes. "No. I might have said I wished I had."

"Have you ever had a quarrel with the prisoner at the bar?"

"I bear him no malice," Mr. Croucher said guardedly.

"But have you ever had any words with him?"

"Once I had—the reason was this, if you wish me to tell it—" Croucher paused. Alexander had no doubt he was contriving his story as he spoke. "Going hastily upstairs, I suddenly came upon Elma, who stood at the door. She cried, 'Ah!' and fainted away."

There was a hooting from some of the men standing at the back.

"I wish pretty women fainted at my feet!"

"You think he's so ugly he made her swoon?"

Mr. Croucher waited until the general hilarity abated. "On hearing this, the prisoner came down from his room and said it was not the first time I had insulted her. I told him he was an impertinent puppy. Afterwards, being sensible of his error, he begged my pardon."

In the box, Levi was shaking his head furiously, looking like it cost him all his power not to burst into speech.

"And you say you bear him no ill will?" inquired Burr.

"I bear him no malice, but I despise any man who does not behave in character," said Mr. Croucher with dignity.

Character. That was the crux of it all, wasn't it? The character of Elma. The character of Levi. The character of the man standing before them in the witness box.

"How near the Manhattan Well do you think you passed that night?" Alexander asked.

Mr. Croucher gave it some thought. "I believe I might have passed the glue manufactory."

The glue manufactory was out of his way, on the opposite side of the well. There was no reason for Mr. Croucher to have passed anywhere near the glue manufactory. "Do you not know what route you took?"

"I do not." Croucher ought to have stopped there, but his unease betrayed itself in a flood of words. "I cannot certainly say, I might have passed by one route or another. I go sometimes by the road, sometimes across the field."

"Was it dark?"

"I believe there was a little moonlight. The going was very bad." That much Alexander believed to be true. It would have been dark and cold. It wasn't far from 884 Bowery Lane to the Manhattan Well. Far closer than the Rings' boardinghouse or even Ezra

Weeks's lumber yard. But the paths would have been rutted and pocked with frozen mud and uneven turf.

A strange route for a man to choose to take home on an icy, cold night.

Except that Croucher hadn't gone home. Not until far later.

The discrepancy struck Alexander. Why would Croucher have been passing the well at the crucial time? It made no sense for him to have left Mrs. Ashmore's, crossed to the well, and gone back again. Unless he had gone to Mrs. Ashmore's later than he claimed? Or unless he was at the well by appointment. As Ring's accomplice?

Colden took advantage of Alexander's distraction to bring everyone's attention back to Levi's guilt. "Have you ever heard any noise in the room of the prisoner at an uncommon time of night, since this affair happened?"

"Yes, sir, I have." Mr. Croucher seized on the change of subject with alacrity. "The night the deceased was missing and the next night and every succeeding night while he stayed in the house, I heard him up whenever I waked at all times from eleven o'clock at night until four in the morning, and a continual noise, almost. I thought then his brother had some great work on hand and that he was drawing plans, but since I have accounted for it in a different way."

He looked meaningfully at the jury. It was pure melodrama, thought Alexander—but effective nonetheless. It was a potent image, the murderer, driven by an unquiet conscience, pacing the floor night after night, tormented by guilt.

"Mr. Croucher," said Alexander, raising his voice so it could be heard in all corners of the room, "were you ever upon any other than *friendly* terms with Elma?"

"After I offended the prisoner at the bar, who she thought was an Adonis, I never spoke to her again."

"Thank you, Mr. Croucher."

Burr stepped up, dismissing the witness, cutting off Alexander's line of inquiry.

"I had more questions for him," murmured Alexander, keeping a pleasant expression on his face for the sake of the jury. "You overstep yourself, sir."

"And you," said Burr, smiling as if they were exchanging pleasantries, "are overplaying your hand—our hand. You might wager wildly on your own account, but not on mine."

"This isn't a wager. It's a man's life."

"How good of you to recall that. If we spend less time on wild theories and more time on defending him, he might emerge with his neck intact," said Burr pleasantly. "Shall we?"

Chapter Twenty-Five

He is a grave, silent, strange sort of animal, inasmuch that we know not what to make of him.

—Aaron Burr on Aaron Burr

New York City
March 31, 1800

In his zeal to have the glory of finding Elma Sands's murderer, Hamilton was going to see Levi Weeks hanged, and jeopardize Aaron's fee in the process.

Ezra Weeks was not looking pleased. He looked even less pleased as Colden called the next witness to the stand: Levi's apprentice, William Anderson.

"Did you notice your master pay particular attention to Elma?" asked Colden, who apparently proceeded under the principle that if he asked the same question often enough he might eventually get the answer he wanted.

"I never saw anything to make me suppose that

my master was more particular in his attentions to Elma than to the other two, Margaret and Hope." Young William looked appealingly at Levi, like a puppy hoping his master might pet him. "One day my master said to me, 'You must not think it strange of my keeping Elma's company. It is not for courtship nor dishonor, but only for conversation.'"

That statement was met with the derision it deserved. Everyone, thought Aaron grimly, was now entirely convinced that Levi had been carrying on a torrid affair with Elma. If they hadn't believed it before, that comment about conversation had clinched it.

"Did you ever know your master to be in private with Elma? You are under oath," Colden reminded the boy when he hesitated.

Young William looked from Colden to Levi and back again. "One night I pretended to be asleep, and the prisoner undressed himself and came with the candle and looked to see if I was asleep or not. Supposing I was, he went downstairs in his shirt and didn't come back till morning."

"Did your master always sleep with you?"

"Yes," the boy said quickly.

"How did he rest the night after Elma was missing, and the next?"

"He slept as well as usual the night Elma was

missing, and Monday and Tuesday nights, but on Wednesday night, near day, he sighed out in his sleep, 'Oh! Elma!'"

"Was Elma of a lively and cheerful disposition?"

"Yes, she was that." William Anderson caught sight of Ezra Weeks's scowl and ducked his head. "But less so the day before she was missing."

The boy stepped down, his future employment in jeopardy if the look on the senior Weeks's face was anything to go by. Aaron hoped the boy had talent with his tools, because he didn't with his tongue. He'd done more to condemn his master than anyone else so far.

This was not going well.

Yes, they'd succeeded in excluding Mrs. Ring's evidence about Elma's intentions; Mr. Ring had obliged them by making a scene; and they'd rattled Colden. But they'd entirely failed so far to counter Colden's testimony about Elma's state of mind—cheerful, gay, too gay for a Quaker; everyone agreed. It was going to be a hard thing to convince the jury that Elma had flung herself into the well under the influence of melancholy.

Perhaps if Hamilton had spent a little more time following the agreed line of questioning and less chasing after his own theories, they might be in a better position. A jury needed a clear line of reasoning to follow, not scattershot accusations.

They had been having somewhat more success making out that Levi had flirted with everyone, and not just Elma. That he'd taken Hope Sands to his brother's was a nice touch. But it was flimsy, all of it. And William Anderson had just dealt them a blow from which it would be hard to recover.

Which left them with one line of defense. They needed to prove, beyond a shadow of a doubt, that Levi Weeks had never been near the well that night.

Colden's next witness was an elderly woman, who made her way with difficulty to the stand, leaning heavily on her stick and batting off the well-meaning attempts of the assistant attorney general to help her.

"I live opposite Ezra Weeks's lumber yard, and on the night when the deceased was lost, I heard the gate open and a sleigh or carriage come out of the yard about eight o'clock. It made a rumbling noise but had no bells on it, and it was not long before it returned again."

"How did you know it was eight o'clock?" Aaron asked her.

The old woman looked at him as though he were a half-wit. "Because my son and daughter was gone to meeting and meeting is done about eight o'clock."

"When was this, Mrs. Broad? What month was it?"

Mrs. Broad bristled. "I don't know the month. I know it was so."

"Was it after Christmas, or before Christmas?" Aaron asked patiently.

"It was after, I believe." Mrs. Broad thought about it before announcing, "It was January."

There was a stirring and rustling through the jury and the galleries. Colden's mouth dropped open as an expression of sheer horror crossed his face.

"That you are sure of?" Aaron asked. "It was in January, you say?"

"Yes, I am sure it was in January," said Mrs. Broad firmly.

"Did you ever hear this gate open before?" Aaron asked gently.

"No, gentlemen." Belatedly, Mrs. Broad realized that something was wrong. Taking offense, she demanded, "Do you think I came here to tell a lie?"

Aaron glanced casually at Colden as he asked, "When did you first remember about this sleigh's being taken out?"

Mrs. Broad scowled at him, aware that she was being manipulated, but not sure how. "When I saw this young woman at Mrs. Ring's and helped to lay her out."

Desperately, Colden tried to salvage something from his witness. "Did you observe any marks of violence when you laid her out?"

Mrs. Broad pursed her lips. "I found no bruises except on the right shoulder, when I felt and it was soft—but I thought her neck was broke," she added.

No bruises. No sleigh. And this was Colden's own witness. This, thought Aaron with grim satisfaction, was how it was done. Not chasing after will-o'-the-wisps, but methodically destroying the prosecution's evidence, point by point.

It was just like Hamilton to go after a dramatic solution and ignore the basic work that needed to be done.

Mercifully, Hamilton had retreated into abstraction, attending with only half an ear to the testimony. All of his attention was on the bench where Mr. Croucher sat next to a woman in a gown of brocade too rich for court in a color which did not become her. Periodically, he would glance from Mr. Croucher to Elias Ring and back again, like a clock where the second hand had become stuck and stuttered back and forth between the same numbers over and over again, never advancing.

That, from Aaron's point of view, was just as well. It left him free to get on with the real work. One by one, Colden called his long list of witnesses, building his story of the abduction by sleigh. One by one, Aaron and Brockholst tore their testimony to shreds.

The woman who claimed to have seen Elma on the street that night had to admit that she never saw the supposed Elma's face, and certainly hadn't seen any sleigh. Another woman, who claimed to have seen Elma in a sleigh, admitted she couldn't identify the sleigh and the moon had been obscured.

Candles were brought in, branches of them, set around the courtroom. It had to be well past the supper hour now. Some of the spectators slunk off in search of sustenance. And still Colden went on, calling witness after witness.

The mood in the courtroom had begun to change. Subtly, but Aaron could feel it. The crowd had come in baying for Levi's blood. But now . . . they weren't so sure.

Buthrong Anderson testified that he had seen a one-horse sleigh on a full gallop heading toward the well, pulled by a horse the same size and color as that owned by Ezra Weeks.

Brockholst was in his element. "Do you pretend to distinguish the color of a horse in the night?"

"Not exactly—but I knew he wasn't light-colored."

Brockholst turned to the jury, inviting them to join him in his skepticism. They were all, he seemed to imply, men of experience, and could spot nonsense when they heard it. "Can you determine the size of a horse when he is on the gallop, and, as you say, on a full gallop?"

"I think he was such a horse as I have described him," said the witness sulkily.

Mr. and Mrs. Van Norden, whose house was nearest the well, both testified to hearing a woman cry out, "Lord have mercy on me! Lord help me!"

"I got out of bed to hear and see what I could," said Mr. Van Norden, "and I looked out of the window toward the well. I can see the well from my house, and I heard this noise that I tell you of, and I looked then to the well, and I saw a man walking near the well, about the well."

"Did you see a sleigh at the time?" Brockholst asked.

"No," said Mr. Van Norden. Clearly, the thought had never occurred to him.

"Might there not have been a sleigh there which you could not see from your chamber window?" Colden suggested desperately. "I'll put the question a little more particularly—is not the make of the ground such that if a sleigh was standing near the fence at the well, you would look over it from your window, in looking at the well?"

"I don't know," Mr. Van Norden said, flummoxed by the question. "I never minded."

Colden's next two witnesses, mere boys of eleven and thirteen, didn't even make it to the stand.

"Do you know what an oath is?" Justice Lansing inquired. "Dismissed as incompetent."

The candles were guttering in their holders. It had to be nearly midnight, and still there were witnesses slumped next to the walls in the hall outside, waiting to be called.

Colden's broad face was haggard, his cravat askew. He looked like he'd had several rounds in the boxing ring and come out the worse. "But, Your Honor, those boys..."

"Are not competent to testify," said Lansing wearily.

The next witness knew what an oath was, but admitted his testimony was all hearsay.

"I know nothing about this affair of my own knowledge—only what I've been told."

Lansing turned the full force of his offended majesty on Colden. "Is this a joke, Mr. Colden? Do you intend to call everyone in the city of New York to testify? Perhaps a baby in the cradle?"

"My apologies, Your Honor. I only meant to be thorough...."

"It is past midnight, Mr. Colden." Justice Lansing sighed. "Call your next witness."

With a certain amount of trepidation, Colden called William Blanck to the stand.

Justice Lansing regarded him with a jaundiced eye. "Your witness appears very young, Mr. Colden. How old are you, child?"

"About thirteen, sir."

"Do you know what an oath is?" asked Justice Lansing wearily.

"No, sir—but I went to school and they taught me my prayers."

Aaron exchanged a small, amused smile with Brockholst.

"Dismissed. How many more witnesses do you have, Mr. Colden?" demanded Justice Lansing, in awful tones.

"Ten. Or possibly eleven," Colden admitted. "The prosecution still needs to show—"

Justice Lansing held up a hand, stopping him. "And you, counsel for the defense. I presume you have witnesses to call?"

"We do have a few," said Brockholst, grinning. Despite their political differences, he and Lansing were old friends.

There was a murmuring on the bench as the three judges consulted. "—might go on until tomorrow evening," Harison was saying.

"What's happening?" demanded Ezra Weeks.

Aaron went to stand beside him. "The court is trying to determine whether to adjourn. There is no precedent for a trial going into a second day."

Ezra Weeks had no interest in precedent. "What does that mean for Levi?"

Aaron wasn't sure. The exhausted jurors were clearly frustrated with Colden, and his increasingly irrelevant and inadmissible parade of witnesses. On the other hand, they might convict Levi out of sheer exhaustion.

"On the whole," Aaron said, "I believe it would be to our advantage if the court were to adjourn."

The little surprise he had planned for Hamilton could easily wait another day.

A hush fell over the room as Justice Lansing cleared his throat. "The court is prepared to sit as long as necessary."

"It's two in the morning!" protested one of the jurors, the same one who had been so amused earlier by the prospect of Elma gallivanting in the nude. He didn't sound amused anymore.

"Sir," said the foreman, speaking on behalf of the whole. "We're agreed that if we were to stay, we wouldn't be able to give this business our full attention. Garrit there has already fallen asleep."

"Huh, what?" Garrit mumbled.

"We can't let you go home," said Justice Lansing irritably. "Having been sworn, you must be kept away from anyone who might sway your opinion."

"They might sleep on the floor of the portrait gallery," suggested Harison, who was clearly longing for sleep himself. "We could assign two constables to keep them together until morning—and another to bring them some blankets and refreshments."

"For want of any better suggestions, so be it," said Lansing. "Constables! See the jurors brought to the portrait room and bring them what they need to make them comfortable. The prisoner at the bar will return to the Bridewell until morning."

A sound escaped Levi's lips, the first sound to pass them all day. Despite himself—and his private conviction that the boy might well have done exactly what Mr. Colden claimed—Aaron was moved.

"What about us?" asked Catherine Ring. If anyone seemed as distressed as Levi by the adjournment, it was she. Aaron noticed that she pulled away from her husband, moving to stand before the bench herself.

Justice Lansing raised his voice to be heard throughout the room. "As to the rest of you, go home and get what sleep you can. Court will adjourn until ten o'clock tomorrow morning."

Chapter Twenty-Six

But if our minds revolt with horror at the idea of murder, it unfortunately happens that this crime may frequently be committed in such a manner as to render it impracticable for us to obtain direct and positive proof against the guilty.

—An Impartial Account of the Trial of Mr. Levi Weeks for the Supposed Murder of Miss Julianna Elmore Sands, by James Hardie A.M.

New York City
April 1, 1800

It was supposed to be done by now.
Creeping into the boardinghouse in the dead of night, Caty felt like a stranger in her own home, in her own body. Her fingers were clumsy on the ribbons holding her gloves; she fumbled with the strings of her bonnet.

Did it even make sense taking off her dress to sleep? She'd only be putting it on again in three hours when she woke to coax the fire back into life and put the water to boil for tea and coffee and stir the porridge.

She needed to put the oats on the coals to cook, she reminded herself. It seemed strange to think that in this endless night there were still the usual rituals to be observed.

She wished Justice Lansing had held firm and insisted they stay.

But that was selfish of her. Caty felt a surge of guilt thinking of Rachel and Phoebe and David and Eliza. Bad enough they'd gone to sleep without her there. What would they have thought when neither of their parents came home? At least they'd wake up and see her tomorrow morning and she could hug them and hold them close before going back to that horrible place where the lawyers in their fancy clothes played their nasty games and stopped honest women from speaking the truth.

Mostly honest women. Mostly the truth.

In the bedroom, the children were all in their beds, Phoebe snuggled up against Rachel, David sprawled on his back with the covers kicked off, Eliza in her cot.

Eliza would be two in just four days. Caty felt tears sting her eyes. It was April—fourth month—

tomorrow—no, today already. For the past three months, since Elma had been found, through the long, hard, miserable months of winter, she had thought of nothing but Levi's trial. They just had to get to the trial, that's what she'd told herself, and then it would all be over and they'd all be back to normal.

Except it wasn't. And they weren't.

Elias banged into the room and began the noisy process of disrobing.

"I'm going to set the porridge to cook for morning," said Caty, and left the room. The idea of being in there, with him, suddenly seemed unbearable.

In August they would have been married ten years.

In the kitchen, Mr. Colden's maid had nodded off in front of the fire. They'd forgotten all about her and so had Mr. Colden. Gently, Caty shook Mr. Colden's maid awake. Mr. Colden hadn't told her what to do with the girl. The girl didn't seem to know either.

"He told me I'm to stay until the trial's over," she said confusedly.

A trial that lasted more than a day. Who had heard of such a thing? Caty felt a surge of frustration, with Mr. Colden, with everyone, with all these men who talked and talked and then left her to deal with their mess.

"There's a bed upstairs for you," Caty said. She was hardly going to send the girl to walk back at three in the morning. "The third door to your right on the second floor."

Elma's room. The room she'd slept in after she'd come back from the country. Just a room now, empty.

They'd asked such a lot of questions about which room Elma slept in.

The girl thanked her and stumbled up the stairs. That would be another for breakfast tomorrow morning, Caty thought, in that part of her mind that was always calculating the number of breakfasts to be cooked, whether they had enough clean sheets to last until Monday wash day, and was there room in the hem to let down Phoebe's dress if she grew again before spring.

It *was* spring, Caty realized, with a horrible lump in her throat. In Cornwall, the daffodils would be coming out already in the meadows, the trout lilies would be sprouting up by the river, and in the woods, there'd be the delicate pink and white of spring beauty. It was only here in the city that the seasons lurched from frost to fever with no in between.

Why had they ever left Cornwall?

Because Elias had wanted to. Cornwall was too small for him. He'd had grander things in mind. Elias—refusing to name the month, glaring at the jury from under his hat. This was his fault; he'd brought them to this. This nightmare she couldn't seem to wake from.

"Mama?" David staggered out to the kitchen, his face blurred with sleep. He was thinning out, growing up, starting to look more like a boy than a baby, but at times like this, he looked like the baby he had been, his cheeks still soft and round.

"Thee needs thy sleep," Caty said, but she couldn't resist holding him close, resting her cheek against his soft curls, red like hers.

It was horrible to think he'd grow up and be a man like Elias or Levi, taking what he wanted, not caring who he hurt.

"I told him to go back to bed." Elias loomed in the doorway, exhausted and annoyed. "If thee coddle him . . ."

Did Elias think the children had no idea what was going on in this house? Caty wasn't sure what they'd guessed or understood, but they knew their cousin had gone and never come back. Murdered. They needed comfort too.

Or maybe she was the one who needed comfort.

Caty gave her son one last squeeze. "I'll be in presently," she murmured to him. "Go now. I'll be here when thee wakes in the morning."

"And make me oil cakes?" David asked hopefully.

"If thee are good." He'd learn soon enough that being good brought no rewards. She'd tried and tried and look what it had brought her. Let him enjoy while he could.

David scampered off to bed, excited at the prospect of a treat. Elias moved aside to let him pass, advancing on Caty.

"Come to bed," Elias commanded.

"I've the oats to set." There had been a time she'd found his arrogance wildly attractive, a sign of his authority. Now she knew it for what it was. The sort of man who'd lie to his wife and make a scene in court. "Why didn't thee tell me that Levi had threatened to tell of thee?"

Elias shrugged. "It wasn't for thee to know."

Not for her to know, but he'd shout it to the world in Federal Hall. "Does thee think those lawyers don't know of thee and Elma? They were toying with thee—and thee gave thyself away! The *friend and protector of Elma*!"

Elias cast a quick look over his shoulder. "Hush. Do thee want to wake the boarders?"

He'd not been so careful of the boarders when he'd been having his way with Elma with the door open. "Did Levi see thee together?"

"He might have." Which meant he had.

Caty remembered Croucher standing up there in court, with that nasty smirk on his face, talking about

Elma's lover being so wild for her he hadn't bothered to close the door. "Why didn't thee just couple with Elma in the front room for all to see?"

"It was only the once—and no one saw," Elias hissed back, and then realized what he'd said.

"In the front room?"

"Thee were away!" Elias dropped his voice. "Isn't it enough? Isn't it time thee stopped throwing this up against me?"

There were no words to contain her emotions. Caty turned her back. "I have to set the oats," she said in a strangled voice.

If he'd come to her, if he'd apologized—but he didn't. He wouldn't. She heard him turn and go, his steps heavy on the uneven boards of the floor. Caty tossed oats into the pot with a shaking hand.

"Caty?" Hope stood in the doorway in her shift, her feet bare, her light brown hair in a long braid over her shoulder. "Is it true? What he said? Did Elias—?"

"Thee shouldn't listen at doors."

"I wasn't listening—I came down because I wasn't sure if thee had remembered the oats!"

As if Caty weren't the one who remembered everything in this house. Hope only helped when she felt like it and then felt a glow of virtue. No, that wasn't fair, Hope did her share, but Caty wasn't in the mood to be fair.

"I'm setting the oats now." Maybe she should just curl up on the hearth and sleep next to the fire.

"What Elias said—about Elma—did Elias and Elma—" Hope's voice cracked. She sounded painfully young.

Caty dropped the scoop into the barrel of oats and slammed down the lid. "Thy cousin wasn't chary with her favors."

"But Elias . . . He's your husband!"

"I know he's my husband!" Hadn't she borne the weight of him these past ten years? Caty shoved at the iron arm to position the pot on the stove. Like everything else in this ramshackle house, it didn't work the way it ought. "Go back to bed, Hope."

Hope folded her arms across her chest, looking as self-righteous as only a woman without responsibilities of her own could look. "Not until thee tell me the truth."

"The truth is that thy cousin was a blight on our home from the day she was born!" Caty lowered her voice, so she wouldn't wake the children or, worse, Elias. "What thee heard—what happened before, while we were in the country—that was nothing to do with anything. Thee knows Elma meant to be married to Levi that night. Thee told me thyself."

"She told me she meant to be married," Hope said slowly. "It was I who said to Levi."

"Does thee think she ran off to be married to Elias and he pushed her down the well? As thee said, he's married already." Never mind she'd wondered it herself. "It was with Levi she went. Thee *know* that. Thee know every word I said in court today was true."

Hope gave her a long, thoughtful look. "Thee said Elma was troubled by cramps in her stomach."

"And she was," said Caty in frustration. Elma had had cramps for weeks after, her body revolting against her sin.

Hope took a step toward Caty. "The baby—was it Levi's baby? Or was it Elias's?"

"I ought never to have said anything to thee." Exhaustion seeped deep into Caty's bones. She ought to have known Hope was too young to understand. "As far as thee or the world knows, there was no baby."

The light of the fire sent strange shadows flickering across Hope's face. "I wondered why Levi wanted me to know of it. But if the baby was Elias's . . ."

"What do thee mean, Levi wanted thee to know of it?" Horror and rage surged through Caty. She grabbed her sister's wrist. "When did thee speak to that man?"

"He told me if I wanted to know the truth to ask thee. . . . Ouch! Caty!"

Hope tried to pull away, but Caty held fast. "Thee spoke to Levi. When did thee speak to Levi?"

"It was when I went to bring bread to the Widow Broad—"

No wonder Hope had been struck by a sudden fit of Christian charity. Caty released Hope so abruptly that her sister staggered. "Thee are as bad as Elma, sneaking and lying."

"I wasn't sneaking! I told thee where I was going—"

"To meet thy cousin's killer!" Everyone abandoned her; everyone betrayed her. What had Caty done to bring this on herself? All she'd ever tried to do was be a good wife and mother and sister. . . . "I should never have brought thee here. I should have left thee home in Cornwall and never let this place corrupt thee."

"Corrupt *me*? When Levi told me that thee knew something—"

Caty wanted to lift her face to the moon and howl like a dog. "Why would thee listen to him? Thee knows what he is!"

Hope stepped back, pale and remote. "I thought I did. I'm not sure now."

"This changes nothing," Caty said shrilly. It was like telling the children to put on their shoes; she felt like she'd said it over and over and over until the words had no meaning. "Everything I said today was true. Everything Mr. Colden said today was true. Thee knows Levi and thy cousin consorted behind locked doors.

Thee knows Elma said they were to be married. Thee knows Levi came back for her that night. . . . And the way Levi behaved when we taxed him of it, wanting thee to sign that paper, saying Elma might have done away with herself. . . . Is that the behavior of an innocent man?"

"He told me there were things I didn't know—and he was right," Hope said in a low voice. "He told me the truth when thee didn't."

"Only to cause strife between us! He only wants to confuse thee." Elias's betrayal had hurt, but this was worse. This was her sister. "He left with her that night. I *heard* him leave with her that night."

Hope only shook her head. "Could thee be easy in thy conscience if thee were wrong?"

"I'm not wrong," said Caty, but she was speaking only to the flickering fire and the oats that would never be steeped by morning.

Hope had gone.

Chapter Twenty-Seven

I discover more and more that I am spoiled for a military man. My health and comfort both require that I should be at home—at that home where I am always sure to find a sweet asylum from care and pain in your bosom. . . . You are my good genius; of that kind which the ancient Philosophers called a *familiar*; and you know very well that I am glad to be in every way as familiar as possible with you.

—Alexander Hamilton to Elizabeth
Schuyler Hamilton, November 1798

New York City
April 1, 1800

It was gone past two by the time Alexander made his way to his own stoop.

Along Broadway, the houses were all dark. Even the strange little wooden house where the German candlemaker, Slidell, resolutely kept his workplace despite the fine brick mansions grown up around him was nothing more than a blot in the darkness, without the man himself in his accustomed place on his wooden stoop, in his apron and cap, defiantly smoking his pipe.

In a few hours, smoke would begin to emerge from chimneys, servants would creep out to sweep the stoops, Slidell would hang out his candles, and the carts would begin to rumble down the street, bearing casks to taverns and goods to market, but for now all was still, an artist's etching, all line and shadow, with no people to mar the scene.

A single point of light came from one of his own windows. Betsy's teeth must be bothering her again.

Alexander let himself in, discarding his hat and gloves. He'd thought he'd been as quiet as he could, but Eliza met him on the stairs, a shawl over her nightdress, shading her candle with one hand. "Shhh. I just put Betsy back down. Did you win your case?"

"Levi Weeks is back in the Bridewell."

"Convicted?" Eliza's hand dropped and the strong light fell across her face. "But your speech . . ."

"Not yet uttered. Colden is still calling witnesses. We've been adjourned until tomorrow. The jury is sleeping in the picture room." Alexander hadn't realized how tired he was, or how much every bone in his body ached, until that moment.

"Have you had anything to eat?" Eliza didn't wait for an answer. "I saved supper for you."

He followed her as she rummaged in the larder, retrieving a plate covered with a napkin, with slices of cold roasted mutton, turnips, and potatoes, placing it before him on one of the table mats she had woven with her own hands.

Alexander poked at a piece of mutton. "I'm worried I've done the boy a disservice."

"Your oration is brilliant," Eliza said indignantly.

"You heard it often enough," said Alexander ruefully. Eliza, as always, had been his first audience and critic, listening and suggesting while she mended torn breeches, kissed bruises, and doled out bread and butter.

Eliza stood over him, the candle in her hand. "If you won't believe me, then what about Betsy? Betsy approved."

"Betsy drooled."

Eliza's lips turned up on one side. "That is her way of showing her regard."

"Some of the jury were drooling by the time Lansing called for an adjournment," Alexander admitted, "but I doubt it was a sign of their regard. Our defense is a shambles."

Eliza gave up any notion of going back to bed. She set the candle down and sank into the seat across from Alexander. "Why do you say that?"

"The girl never took her own life; it's plain to anyone. But Burr and Livingston—they say our business isn't to find who killed Elma Sands but merely to show that Levi Weeks didn't." Alexander lifted his face from his hands. "Eliza, you remember the Bedlow case. The jury acquitted him but he was hounded all the same."

Brockholst might have won the day in court, but it was Alexander he had retained later on, to try to clear his name. Admittedly, the methods Alexander had used might not have been the most orthodox—he had concocted a letter in the girl's name—but none of it need have happened if the case had been conducted properly in the first place.

"If we can't give the mob the true villain—what sort of life will this boy have? And he is a boy, barely more than a boy, not much older than Philip. What boy that age doesn't make a fool of himself with the wrong woman? Think what scrapes I might have got in if I hadn't had the good fortune to find you."

"Hmmm," said Eliza. In the shapes cast by the candle, Alexander could practically see the long shadow of Maria Reynolds.

"And then there's the girl," said Alexander. "Elma. Brockholst would be content to savage her reputation and forget that she was the one who was grievously and mortally wronged. What do they know about the shifts forced upon women who are preyed upon by the men who were meant to protect them?"

Like his mother. His brilliant, determined mother, who had been punished again and again for the crime of surviving.

"If they spent any time with the Society for the Relief of Poor Widows with Small Children," said Eliza firmly, "they would understand better."

Her goodness shouldn't surprise him, but somehow it always did. "Not all the world has your heart."

"Only you," she said, saying it before he could. "And our children."

"And the widows and orphans," said Alexander. He toyed with a piece of mutton. The smell of it was too strong; it made his stomach turn. "Someone killed that girl, Eliza—but I haven't the means to prove who! If I had given this the care I gave Le Guen—if I had given this the care I gave the army—if I had only had more *time*—"

He ought to have listened to Eliza. He ought to have listened when she counseled against taking on too much. But it always seemed like a good idea at the time, all of it, every post, every case. Until it wasn't.

"You were right. I took on too much and I'm doing none of it well."

"If you weren't there to stand up for Elma Sands, who would?" Eliza twitched her shawl closer around her shoulders. "Last winter, we delivered meals and medicine to a hundred widows and their families. Only a hundred. But those were a hundred who were kept from the poorhouse. Should I stop serving the hundred because there are four hundred more I failed? We do what we can, imperfect as we are."

Alexander had never seen anything more perfect in his life, his Eliza, heavy-eyed with exhaustion, her hair half in a braid and half out where Betsy had tugged it, and a slight smell of sour milk about her person.

"I can make a case that Elias Ring did it—the cousin's husband," Alexander said slowly. "He took advantage of the girl—of Elma. We have witnesses to swear to it. He has a wife and four children and only the wife's word to swear he was home that night. Ring forced his way into the courtroom when his wife gave her testimony."

"For fear of what she might say?"

"Yes, but fear of what? Was he afraid she would tell of him and Elma? Or something more?" Alexander cast his mind back on Ring's performance in the courtroom, his hat stubbornly jammed on his head, chin jutting out beneath. "He was sullen and furtive on the stand and when we tasked him—when I tasked him—with threatening Levi, he burst out that Levi had threatened to tell of him and Croucher."

"Croucher?" Eliza stifled a yawn with the back of her hand.

"A lodger. Levi told me last week he'd also come upon this Croucher embracing Elma. Livingston seized on that, as you can imagine. More proof the girl was a wanton." Alexander couldn't keep the bitterness from his voice. "From what Levi said, I'd thought he'd caught them only the once, but on the stand, Croucher said that Levi had accused him of insulting Elma not for the first time."

To embrace a woman once might be a man seizing an opportunity offered. But more than once—it was something different.

"This man, Croucher—he'd spoken of being by the well that night. And he's been busy going from store to store spreading rumors about Levi Weeks. The most logical explanation is that he saw something and decided to use it as a business opportunity, to extort money from Elias Ring. But—" Alexander felt like a fool even saying it, but this was Eliza, and he was too tired to dissemble. "You'll think me fanciful, but there was something diabolical about his countenance. It was the way he smiled when he thought no one was looking."

"Did he have any reason to do away with Elma Sands?"

"That's just it. I can't think of any. Elias Ring had reason enough. He has a wife and four children and a reputation to uphold among the Friends."

"This Mr. Croucher? Is he married?"

"He wasn't at the time. He just married a rich widow." Alexander straightened in his chair as the meaning of his own words was borne in upon him. "He just married a rich widow."

"So it wasn't just Mr. Ring who had something to lose," said Eliza sleepily.

"He likes fine things, Mr. Croucher." Alexander could picture him on the stand, the gleam of his ring, the rich silks and brocades. "His own means are small. He can't make that much money peddling stockings, insistent about it as he is. His desire to sell stockings makes one not want to buy stockings."

Eliza rested her head on one hand. "When did he marry his widow?"

"The day before the trial began." Yesterday. That was yesterday. Today felt as though it had been weeks long rather than hours. "He was courting his widow at the same time Levi caught him with Elma. If his widow found out about Elma—"

"She would have had reason to jilt him," Eliza supplied for him.

"And take her money with her." Alexander was turning it over in his head, fitting the bits together like a puzzle box, which would spring open when solved. "Everyone agrees that Elma was to meet someone that night. She said she was to be married. She dressed in her best clothes. Would she do that for Elias Ring? But if Richard Croucher promised her marriage..."

"He might have promised her marriage to win her affections," agreed Eliza.

"This Croucher claims to have been at the home of a Mrs. Ann Ashmore—which is also a brandy distillery." And possibly something more, although he decided he didn't need to share that with Eliza. "The well stands between the boardinghouse and the house he visited that night. He might have arranged to meet Elma there. Or he might have arranged for her to meet him at Mrs. Ashmore's and intercepted her on her way."

Of course Croucher would tell people he had been by the well that night, just in case anyone had seen him. And because he gleaned a perverse delight from taunting the law with his secret.

"I had him on the stand today—if I had known then what I suspect now—"

Eliza pushed back her chair and used her arms to lever herself upright. "Thanks to Mr. Colden's industry, you have another chance."

"I never thought I'd be grateful for a trial that ran into a second day—but I always knew enough to be grateful for you." Alexander caught Eliza's hand, looking up at her as she stood above him, with the light of the candle casting a glow about her white nightdress. "I am much more in debt to you than I can ever pay."

She shook her head at him. "This isn't your bank. There are no accounts and no lines of credit in a marriage."

"Aren't there?" Alexander said wryly. "All the same. Once this is over, I mean to pay my debt to you with a house all our own. Once he's free, Levi Weeks can design it for us and Ezra Weeks will build it."

And with any luck, his gratitude would extend to a substantial reduction in fee.

Eliza took up the candle. "Are you coming to bed?"

"Not just yet." Suddenly, the mutton seemed extremely appetizing. He was, Alexander realized, tremendously hungry. "But I'll be up shortly."

Eliza took a candle from above the hearth, lighting

it from her own. She set it down beside him, to light his way back to her.

"Don't be too long," she said. "You have important work to do tomorrow."

A woman to be avenged, a murderer to be accused, and Burr to be put entirely out of countenance when Alexander delivered one of the best speeches he had ever penned.

Outside the window, the night's black was beginning to lighten to gray. "Not tomorrow," he said. "Today."

Chapter Twenty-Eight

QUESTION BY THE ASSISTANT ATTORNEY GENERAL: Suppose, Doctor, a person had been strangled by hand, would it not have left such an appearance upon the body?

ANSWER: I think it would.

—From the testimony of Dr. Skinner at the trial of Levi Weeks

New York City
April 1, 1800

Dr. Skinner, are you not a surgeon in this city, and did not you see the body of Elma Sands after it was taken out of the well and examine it? Pray, sir, inform the court and jury."

"I follow a branch of surgery, but I do not pretend

to be a professed surgeon. I," Dr. Skinner declared proudly, "am a dentist."

Hope sat next to Caty, just as she had yesterday. Levi stood in the dock, just as he had yesterday. But everything else had changed. Yesterday, they had been here with one purpose, united in their hatred of Levi. At least, Hope had thought they were united. She had never imagined that Caty—her Caty!—could keep such secrets from her.

Hope snuck a glance at Levi in the dock and found him looking at her.

He'd left with Elma—or, rather, Caty said he had left with Elma. Once, Hope would have fought anyone who had cast doubts on her sister's word. But Caty had lied to her. She could understand why Caty would have kept the truth of Elma's miscarriage from her, as much as it made her writhe with annoyance. There were times Caty seemed to think Hope was still Rachel's age and needed to be shielded accordingly.

But Elma—and Elias!

It was impossible, it was sickening. Hope hadn't slept last night. She'd walked her room, wondering, remembering. The way Elias expanded like a toad explaining his inventions to Elma when all the rest of them had long since stopped listening, since Elias's inventions never came to anything anyway. The way

Levi had hustled Elma off to the country. To get her away from Elias.

He'd offered to marry Elma, he'd said, but not in December.

Hope felt like the room was swaying beneath her like the ferry they took up the Hudson back to Cornwall when the roads were too bad for a carriage, tipping just when she thought she had her footing.

There had been something between Levi and Elma. They all knew it. Hope had seen it with her own eyes. But what if she'd misunderstood what it was?

But there had been Levi's apprentice yesterday, speaking of Levi going downstairs in his shirt and staying away until dawn.

Only for conversation.

It was like poking at a sore tooth, but Hope couldn't seem to stop herself doing it. What if she had been wrong? What if this whole trial was wrong? They'd taken up Levi as soon as Elma's body was found; there had never been any question of anyone else hurting Elma, only of suicide, and Hope knew, with a certainty, that Elma would never have done away with herself.

Just as she'd known for a certainty that Caty had no secrets.

Hope wanted to drag Levi out of that box and

demand that he tell her the truth. But she'd tried that, hadn't she? When Elma went missing.

Everyone was lying, everyone was hiding something.

If she couldn't trust Caty, who could she trust?

The only person who could tell them the truth was Elma, and Elma wasn't here.

"I saw the corpse of the deceased twice. I had but a superficial view of it, however, as it lay in the coffin, exposed to the view of thousands. I examined such parts as were come-at-able—such as her head, neck, and breast."

The dentist was still on the stand, speaking about Elma as though she were nothing but a collection of limbs. So many contusions to be noted, a bruise here, a scrape there, just limp flesh, the abandoned casing of the soul.

"I discovered several bruises and scratches, particularly a bruise upon the forehead and chin and upon the left breast or near it. The spots on the neck were reddish, black spots which might have passed unnoticed by a common observer."

More doctors were called, all fighting over the evidence of Elma's body. Her neck was broken—or it wasn't. The spots around her neck were caused by strangulation—or immersion in water. The bruise upon her breast was the mark of violence—or of tumbling into the well.

No one seemed to know. Only Elma.

Hope wanted to shake her and demand, What happened to you? Why did you go out that night? Who did you meet?

Was it Levi, waiting in a sleigh? Or someone else?

"Was the compression that you spoke of around her neck such as might have been made by a hand?"

"My impression then was and now is that it was."

Hope's brother-in-law sat on the other side of Caty, his legs spread so that he took up more than his fair share of the bench, cramming Caty into Hope and Hope nearly off the edge. His hands rested on his thighs.

If he'd closed those hands around Elma's neck, he could have easily choked the life out of her, especially if she was tilting her head up at him, laughing, expecting a kiss and not a lethal blow.

Foolish creature, Elias had called Elma, that night she had threatened to drink the laudanum. A creature, not a person. An inconvenience to be got out of the way.

But Elias had been home that night. Or so Caty said.

One of the men who had found Elma's body took the stand. "On the second of January last, I together with Mr. Page had some business to do in breaking a horse and we went up to Andrew Blanck's and we dined there. While we were dining, two persons, Mr. Watkins and Mr. Elias Ring, came there to get hook and poles to sound the Manhattan Well for the body of a young woman who was supposed to be drowned."

Would Caty lie for Elias? Yes, Hope decided. Yes, if it meant protecting the children. Even if the weight of her conscience crushed her for it after.

"We got the poles and nails and went all together to the well, which we uncovered. I took the pole and hooked the nail in her clothes and drew her carefully to the top of the water. As soon as Mr. Ring saw her calico gown, he said it was she. He knew the gown."

Elias had claimed Elma had killed herself in a love fit. He'd had them sound the waters around Rhinelander's battery, in the opposite direction from the Manhattan Well. Hope wasn't sure if that was proof of innocence or guilt. She wasn't sure of anything.

Why had Elias brought Joseph Watkins with him to find Elma's body? Was it so there would be someone else there?

"Her hat was off, her gown torn open just above the waist, her shawl was off, and her handkerchief and shoes were gone. Her hair hung over her head."

The man's voice was rough with emotion. He had to stop and clear his throat before he went on.

"She had a white dimity petticoat on. Her stockings

were torn at the toe. Her right foot was bare and somewhat scratched. The scratches were on the upper part of the foot as if she had been dragged on the ground."

Hope knew those stockings. She could picture Elma sitting there, on her bed in her room in the third floor, stretching out her leg in her woolen stocking, pointing her toes, asking how Hope thought she would look in clocked silk. After Sunday, she'd said, she'd have silks and brocades. She'd have a grand house—a house made to Levi's designs, perhaps, she'd added archly. Nothing like this ramshackle boardinghouse with a rope bed and pegs in the wall for her two suits of clothes.

Hope had deliberately avoided Elma's confidences. Now she wished she'd asked more, had pressed her about her plans.

Could Elma have believed that Elias would provide such things? He certainly hadn't for Caty. It was true, he bragged of what their lives would be when his waterwheel was bought by the city, but his waterwheel hadn't been bought by the city. They all knew his schemes to be so much bluster.

Unless Elma hadn't.

Someone to take care of her, she'd said. She must have seen that it was Caty who did everything for Elias and not the other way around. Unless she believed that for her, it would be different. Caty and Elma never had appreciated each other; it had always been Hope who had had to play intermediary.

But no, it was all ridiculous. Elma couldn't have meant to run off with Elias.

A week ago, a day ago, she'd have said Elma would never have sacrificed her virtue to Elias, and yet, apparently, she had. In the front room.

"How did her countenance appear?" asked Mr. Colden.

"It looked like a person who had been walking against the wind." The man on the stand grimaced. "Her appearance was horrid enough—her hat and cap off, her hair hanging all over her head, her comb was yet hanging in her hair, tied with a white ribbon, her shawl was off, her gown was torn open with great violence, and her shoes were off."

If there was one thing Hope knew of her cousin, it was that Elma would have fought back. She wouldn't have gone gently. Unless her neck was broken before she could fight. It was impossible not to imagine the scene. The field, lit only by moonlight. Elma, struggling, trying to claw her attacker's hands from her neck, her shoes coming off as he dragged her across the ground toward the well.

"I went to the police and then with the officer to find the prisoner." Everyone turned to look at Levi. "I told him I was very sorry for his situation. I felt affected—I expressed it to him—he turned about and said, 'Is it the Manhattan Well she was found in?'"

One of the jurymen spoke up. "Was there any mention made of the Manhattan Well in the presence of the prisoner before he asked the question?"

"I did not hear any. I don't believe there was."

Hope looked at Levi. They were all looking at Levi, the whole courtroom, everyone sick with the image of Elma, limp and broken like a discarded doll, her hair about her face.

He had come back at eight. There was no reason for him to come back at eight and then leave again so soon, unless he had come to fetch Elma.

Colonel Burr rose. "How long before the deceased was found was the muff retrieved?"

"Blanck told me his boy found it just around Christmas," said the man on the stand.

"Objection!" protested Mr. Colden. "My learned colleagues have argued hotly against the admission of hearsay evidence."

"That's not hearsay, that's common knowledge," said Colonel Burr drily.

Was it? Hope couldn't remember when she'd heard of the muff. It was New Year's Day that someone paying a New Year's call on Mrs. Blanck had recognized Beth's muff, and the word had begun to spread that the muff Elma was carrying when she disappeared had been found.

But beyond that, Hope didn't know.

"Your Honor," said Mr. Colden, "I would like to call the owner of the muff to the stand. She can testify as to when it became commonly known that the muff she had entrusted to Elma Sands was discovered in the Manhattan Well."

"Then do so, Mr. Colden," said Justice Lansing.

"I had a *slight* acquaintance with Elma Sands." Beth Osborn had always thought she was better than they were and never bothered to hide it. "On the twenty-second of December, I lent her my muff. She came to borrow it herself, and I observed that she was very neatly dressed and she seemed to be very lively and very happy."

Mr. Colden pulled at his cravat, which was tied crookedly. "When was the muff brought home to you?"

"It was brought home the day that she was found, and it appeared as if it had been wet." From the way Beth spoke, thought Hope, anyone would think the primary tragedy was that her muff had been doused, not that a woman had been killed.

Elma would find that hilarious. Elma had done a brilliant impression of Beth Osborn, sniffing and pursing her lips.

"Did you understand the muff was found in the well?" asked Mr. Livingston.

"I did," said Beth, looking as though she smelled something unpleasant. Hope missed Elma so fiercely it was an ache in her chest.

"Did you also understand that it had been found considerably before it was brought home to you?"

"*I* only knew of it the morning it was brought home to me."

Beth had known of it only that morning—but had Levi heard?

"It's all tricks," muttered Caty. Her face was strained with lack of sleep. Her fingers were curled into claws in her lap. "They're only trying to confuse us. He knew it was in the Manhattan Well because he put her there."

A day ago, Hope would have agreed, emphatically. But now she wasn't quite so sure. She twisted on the bench, looking at Levi, at Caty, at Elias.

If Levi hadn't killed Elma, then who had?

Chapter Twenty-Nine

Some conversation arising as to when the muff was found, it was admitted by the Attorney-General that it was found some days before the body was discovered.

—From Coleman's report on the trial of Levi Weeks

New York City
April 1, 1800

"I'd say Weeks's horse is a good goer," said Mr. Cross. "He could go a mile in five minutes."

From his place at the front of the room, Cadwallader could see Hope Sands twisting in her seat. The witnesses were fidgeting, the jury getting restless. Cadwallader was so tired they seemed to double in front of him, twenty-four grumpy men instead of twelve.

Maria had sent in a pot of coffee to him that morning as he'd started nodding off over his papers. There had been an ink stain on one cheek that he'd thought he'd mostly managed to scrub off. Hopefully everyone else was so tired, they wouldn't notice either.

He'd known his medical experts were not the best they could be. The doctors who had performed the autopsy had all hemmed and hawed and said they couldn't attest to signs of violence, so Cadwallader had found other doctors who would, even if one was only a dentist.

Cadwallader hadn't thought it would matter. They all knew Elma had died in that well. He'd shown she hadn't flung herself in there of her own volition. That much, at least, he had achieved. The defense's allegations of melancholy had been thoroughly rebutted.

But as to the rest, somehow the story that had seemed so clear to Cadwallader—the seduction, the sleigh, the well—didn't seem nearly so clear to the jury. He'd seized on one last hope. He could demonstrate that Levi had known where Elma's body was before he was told. It was conclusive evidence of his guilt.

Until it wasn't.

In desperation, Cadwallader reverted to the sleigh. His prize, his pride, the center of his case. But it was past two in the afternoon, and the general reaction to Buskirk's testimony that they'd performed a sleigh trial and made it to the well and back in fifteen minutes appeared to be more irritation than awe.

Cadwallader could remember that day, the triumph he'd felt.

And here he was, cold with exhaustion, sweating with anxiety, clammy and dizzy, not sure what he'd already said and what he hadn't, calling witnesses just because they were there, even though each one seemed to have a diminishing impact.

"Do you have any other witnesses, Mr. Colden?" asked Chief Justice Lansing. "Or is the prosecution ready to rest?"

His tone implied that there was only one suitable answer.

Rest. He hadn't had anything like rest for days. On the other side of the room, he could see Hamilton, Burr, and Livingston, like greyhounds in the slip, just waiting to be let loose and cry havoc. Or was it cry havoc and let loose the dogs of war? His brain felt as cluttered as an ill-kept house. Not that Maria would ever allow an ill-kept house. He wondered if Maria would keep him.

Cadwallader reached inside the pocket where his speech should be—and pulled out a list of books he'd meant to get from the New York Society Library.

He'd taken the wrong paper.

Cadwallader cleared his throat, desperately trying to remember what he'd intended to say, all those words he'd written and scratched out and rewritten. "You see, gentlemen of the jury, we have only circumstantial evidence to offer you in this case, and you must also perceive that by its nature it admits of no other."

Cadwallader paused. His mind was blank. All he could see was little squiggles of black ink.

"The authorities agree that in a case such as this, circumstantial evidence is sufficient to warrant a conviction." Cadwallader fumbled for one of the books he'd brought with him, peppered with scraps of paper. "As Morgan tells us in his *Law of Evidence, circumstantial evidence is all that can be expected and indeed all that is necessary to substantiate such a charge. In such a case as this, it must be received because the nature of the enquiry, for the most part, does not admit of any other; and, consequently, it is the best evidence that can be given.*"

The book was solid and reassuring in his hands. Even Livingston couldn't dispute the authority of Morgan. Cadwallader knew there were other things he should be saying, could be saying. But he couldn't remember a word of it.

"The prosecution rests, Your Honor."

Colonel Burr stepped forward. Cadwallader supposed that meant he was to deliver the opening statement, and he could only be glad it wasn't Brockholst

Livingston. Although that was like being glad that one was being mauled by a mountain lion rather than devoured by a wolf.

Instead of addressing the jury, Burr turned to the bench. "Your Honor, the defense moves for permission to take the testimony of Elizabeth Watkins, who has been brought to an adjoining house but finds herself unable to be in court today."

"On what grounds?" inquired Justice Lansing.

"Mrs. Watkins was brought to bed on the sixteenth of March and has been unwell since. Mr. Watkins attests," Colonel Burr added delicately, "that her breasts are sore and do fester."

"Motion granted," said Justice Lansing hastily. "I will attend to it personally. Mr. Colden, you will come as well, of course. And for the defense—"

"I'll go with you," said General Hamilton immediately.

"Will this take long?" asked one of the jurymen. He looked considerably the worse for his night of sleeping on the floor of the picture gallery.

"Constables, if some refreshment might be found for the members of the jury? I suspect we have another long night ahead of us." Justice Lansing rose. "Court is in recess until we return."

At least this time it wasn't Cadwallader causing the

delay. He felt childish for thinking that way, but fatigue seemed to have stripped him to the most base parts of his character. Maybe Maria was right; maybe he should have tried to get some sleep. Maybe it was only exhaustion making everything seem so grim.

Cadwallader breathed deeply of the manure-scented April air. He hadn't realized just how close the atmosphere was in the courtroom, overheated with all those bodies pressed together, how long they'd been there, until he stepped outside and saw the sun already well over the midway mark.

"How is little David?" General Hamilton asked.

"Not so little anymore," admitted Cadwallader.

"Hmph," said Justice Lansing. "They think they're grown by the time they're weaned. Last week, Sally went traipsing about the house in her mother's best French heels. Nearly broke her neck."

Justice Lansing's youngest, Sally, was just David's age. Someday, Sally and David would dance together at assemblies. They might even court. Here, in the sunlight, Cadwallader felt how foolish he had been, how much he had let the unnatural atmosphere of the courtroom wear on his nerves. These men—they weren't judge and opponent. They were men he had known most of his life; their children were the age of his child. Their wives called on his wife.

The woman they had come to find turned out to be the Rings' next-door neighbor, ensconced on a sofa with a baby in her arms and a blanket over her lap.

"I would have come to court myself but the doctor said I mustn't." The baby was sleeping, a faint line of drool dripping from her slack mouth. The baby had that wonderful milky smell that Cadwallader remembered from David's infancy. "I don't like to be a bother."

"You're not a bother, Mrs. Watkins," said General Hamilton. "We're all of us men with wives and children of our own."

"This is our eighth," said Mrs. Watkins resignedly. Cadwallader thought how jealous Maria would be, festering breasts and all. They didn't need eight; they would be happy with two. Or possibly three. "But you didn't come here to hear me talk about my family. It's Elma you want to know about."

General Hamilton flipped the tails of his coat and lowered himself to a stool that had been placed beside her sofa. "Mrs. Watkins, did Mrs. Catherine Ring inform you of anything respecting Levi Weeks's character and his behavior in the family, and especially as to any person sick?"

"On Thursday evening—that was after Elma was missing—Mrs. Ring came to see me and said that Levi Weeks was one of the best, most civil, and kindhearted boarders that she ever had, and if any of the children were sick, he was as kind and attentive to them as if they were his own."

Cadwallader could feel his chest loosen. This was only more of the same, the only argument the defense had to offer, which was that Levi was a young man of good character and not the sort to push a girl down a well. There was nothing to fear here.

"I know this is difficult for you, Mrs. Watkins," said General Hamilton winningly, "but I hope you can clarify one further point."

"I'm happy to help however I can," said Mrs. Watkins, cocking an experienced eye at the baby, who was beginning to stir.

Someone had stoked up the fire for the new baby and mother. It was very warm in the house. Cadwallader could feel himself beginning to slide down in his chair, lulled by the warmth and that new baby smell. Until Hamilton asked his next question.

"Did you ever hear anything that induced you to suspect there was an improper connection between Mr. Ring and Elma?"

Chapter Thirty

Colonel Burr then addressed himself in behalf of the prisoner to the court and jury, in one of the most masterly speeches both with respect to composition and oratory which we have ever heard.

>—An Impartial Account of the Trial
>of Mr. Levi Weeks for the Supposed
>Murder of Miss Julianna Elmore Sands,
>by James Hardie A.M.

New York City
April 1, 1800

"How did he take it?" Burr and Brockholst drew around Alexander as he returned to the courtroom.

"He had no notion." Cadwallader Colden had fallen out of his chair in surprise. He'd been half-asleep, the poor boy, but that had woken him up with a vengeance.

Alexander would never forget the look of staring horror on his face.

Brockholst nodded in satisfaction. "Now we have him all hollow. Once we show that the girl was no innocent seduced, but spreading her favors generously, his case melts into air."

"I think I know who did it," said Alexander abruptly. He'd been turning and turning it over in his mind since his conversation with Eliza, and the more he thought, the more sure he was. "I think Croucher killed her."

The announcement did not garner quite the reaction he had hoped. "Yesterday you thought Ring killed her," said Brockholst, with exaggerated patience. "Who will it be tomorrow? The man who cleans the streetlights?"

"Richard Croucher, more than any other, has been busy in pointing the finger of blame at Levi Weeks," said Alexander. "He was seen embracing Elma Sands, just as he was on the verge of a marriage that would make his fortune. Why was he so keen to implicate Levi? To save himself!"

Brockholst lowered his voice, glancing over his shoulder. "We've no time for this. We have Colden ready to break. The only compelling argument he has is that Weeks knew where the body was found before being told. Once we deal with that, we've won."

Alexander dug in his heels. "Have we really won if

the murderer isn't brought to justice? If we get Croucher on the stand—"

"By all means," said Burr smoothly. "Should he confess—or should Elias Ring confess—or should the man who cleans the streetlights confess—we shall all rejoice. But in the meantime, we must proceed as planned. I believe Justice Lansing is about to call us back to order."

Brockholst glanced sideways at Burr. "You have the opening statement?"

"Oh yes," said Burr gently. "Yes, I have."

The justice's gavel pounded the table. The jurymen hastily swallowed the last of their bread and cheese. Court was back in session.

Burr rose, bowing to the judges at the bench, looking from the spectators to the jurors to the prisoner at the bar.

"Gentlemen of the jury, the patience with which you have listened to this lengthy and tedious detail of testimony is honorable to your characters."

It was a wonder to Alexander how a man who preferred to surround himself with fine things, could, when he wanted, have such a common touch. Burr's manner with the jury was rueful, solicitous, man-to-man, as if he were one with those laborers and they were one with him.

"It evinces your solicitude to discharge the awful duties which are imposed upon you and it affords a happy presage that your minds are not infected by that blind and indiscriminating prejudice that has already marked the prisoner for its victim."

Several men were scribbling away, recording their impressions, taking down the words of Burr's speech. They would appear in dozens of handbills and pamphlets across the city by the day after tomorrow.

They might be listening to Burr now, but Alexander's oration was the one they would remember. Alexander put his hand to his breast pocket and felt the comforting bulk of paper: his closing speech.

Burr's posture was relaxed, his tone frank. "You have relieved me from my greatest anxiety, for I know the unexampled industry that has been exerted to destroy the reputation of the accused and to immolate him at the shrine of persecution without the solemnity of a fair and candid trial."

Alexander could feel himself freeze, disbelieving, wondering if he'd misheard. He could have sworn those were his words Burr had just voiced.

"I know that hatred, revenge, and cruelty, all the vindictive and ferocious passions have assembled in terrible array. The thousand tongues of rumor have been steadily employed in the fabrication and dissemination of falsehoods," Burr went on, speaking without a paper, speaking as though the ideas were his, as though they had only just rolled from his mind to his tongue. "We have witnessed the extraordinary means which have been adopted to enflame the public passions and to direct the fury of popular resentment against the prisoner."

Alexander felt as though he had returned to his home to find Burr sitting at his table, wearing his clothes, embracing his wife, wearing them as of right, as if Alexander never was, never had been, as if there had never been anyone but Burr, stripping the inner recesses of Alexander's mind and wearing them like the pelts of a conquered enemy.

"Why has the body been exposed for days in the public streets in a manner most indecent and shocking? Such dreadful scenes speak powerfully to the passions: they petrify the mind with horror—congeal the blood within our veins—and excite the human bosom with irresistible but undefinable emotions."

Petrified, yes, Alexander was petrified. Burr had planned his strike brilliantly; there wasn't a thing Alexander could do. If he complained, he would only weaken their case and make himself look small. Alexander's speech weighed useless in his pocket.

Fool that he was, he'd given it to Burr. He'd had his own clerk make Burr a copy.

He didn't miss the way Burr glanced at him, such a quick look that no one else would have noticed it, but Alexander did, and it burned.

Blandly, Burr went on, "Notwithstanding there may be testimony of an intimacy between the prisoner and the deceased, we shall show you that there was nothing like real courtship, for it will be seen that she manifested equal partiality for other persons as for Mr. Weeks. We shall show you that if suspicions may attach anywhere, there are those on whom they may be fastened with more appearance of truth than on the prisoner at the bar. Certainly you are not in this place to condemn others, yet it will relieve your minds of a burden."

That wasn't part of Alexander's speech. That was Burr. It was dizzying and disorienting, this interweaving of Alexander's words with Burr's argument.

"There will be two modes of giving a solution. First, that the deceased sometimes appeared melancholy, that she was a dependent upon this family, and that a gloomy sense of her situation might have led her to destroy herself. As to the incident of the sleigh, we shall account for Mr. Weeks's whole time during that evening, except for about fifteen minutes, which was employed in walking from one house to another."

That was all Burr, pure Burr. Alexander didn't

understand how others couldn't hear the difference, couldn't know two different hands had written the words Burr spoke.

Burr paused, glancing again at Alexander before looking back to the jury, as Alexander's words oozed off his lips. "The story, you will see, is broken, disconnected, and utterly impossible. In cases depending upon a chain of circumstances, all the fabric must hang together or the whole will tumble down."

Alexander made the same mistake every time. With the Manhattan Company—a boon for the whole city, Burr had sworn, and Alexander had done all the work for him, when, in the end, it had been a boon only for Burr.

And now—this!

While Alexander stood there, sick and furious, Burr and Brockholst between them began calling the witnesses, carrying on without him, quizzing Ezra Weeks's apprentice about the sleigh and the key to the gate and the bells on the harness, coolly taking apart Colden's story about the sleigh, as if Alexander weren't here, as if it were just the two of them for the defense, following their own strategy they'd agreed upon without him.

Brockholst had known, of course. They'd planned this between them when they'd left Alexander's office the other day. He'd been a fool not to suspect something of the kind.

But, more fool he, he had thought they were all working together. For Levi. For justice.

Just as he'd thought the Manhattan Company was about bringing clean water for the city.

"It was about twelve o'clock, as near as I can recollect, on the second day of January, the day when she was found, that Levi Weeks came to our house to buy some tobacco." While Alexander was fuming, Ezra Weeks's apprentice had already been questioned and stepped down, replaced by Lorena Forrest, whose husband ran the store next to the Rings. "I asked him if there was any news of Elma. He answered no. I told him I expected Ring's family had, for they seemed much agitated."

"Did you tell him of the muff?" inquired Burr. This was Burr's courtroom now, Burr's case, Burr's triumph.

"Levi went away and in about half an hour he came in again while we sat at table, about one o'clock—I had heard before this about the muff's being found; Mrs. Ring had informed me—and I told him that Mrs. Ring had mentioned to me that the muff and handkerchief had been found in a drain near Bayard's Lane."

"Was the Manhattan Well mentioned?" called the same juryman who had asked about that before.

"There was nothing said about the Manhattan Well."

Alexander knew exactly what Burr was doing. He would prove that Levi had known where the muff had been found and use that to wrangle an acquittal and call it a win, never minding that a murderer sat in the courtroom, free to murder, and murder, and murder again.

They should be calling Joseph Watkins, they should be calling Ann Ashmore, they should be pointing the finger at the true guilty party, not quibbling over who had mentioned the Manhattan Well first.

Alexander could feel a strange energy surging through him. Burr and Brockholst had betrayed him; he owed them nothing more. But he did owe Levi Weeks—and Elma Sands.

Alexander pushed forward, claiming the attention of the witness. "Mrs. Forrest! Did you not hear Mr. Croucher say that he came near the well the evening when she was missing?"

Mrs. Forrest looked surprised at the change of subject. "Yes, he told me he did and said that he generally came that way."

Before Burr or Brockholst could intervene, Alexander called, "The defense will now call Joseph Watkins to the stand."

Alexander could see the look they exchanged. They

might not like it, but there was nothing they could do about it, any more than he could do anything about Burr stealing his closing statement.

"Mr. Watkins," demanded Alexander, "do you remember anything in the conduct of Mr. Ring that led you to suspicions of improper conduct between him and Elma?"

The question was a lightning bolt through the courtroom. There was a whispering and rustling in the galleries.

Mr. Watkins nodded slowly. "About the middle of September, Mrs. Ring being in the country, I imagined one night I heard a shaking of a bed and considerable noise there, in the second story, where Elma's bed stood. I heard a man's voice and a woman's. I am very positive the voice was not Levi's."

"Can you hear through the partition?" called one of the jury.

"Pretty distinctly." Watkins looked apologetically toward the benches where the Rings sat. "The noise of the bed continued some time and it must have been very loud to have awakened me."

Elias Ring's chin jutted out beneath the brim of his hat, his arms folded across his chest. Mrs. Ring sat bolt straight and unblinking, a figure carved from salt.

Watkins rubbed his chin. "I heard a man's voice pretty loud and lively, and joking. I said to my wife, it is Ring's voice, and I told my wife, that girl will be ruined next."

Colden found his voice. "How could you distinguish between the voice of Mr. Ring and Mr. Weeks?"

Watkins wasn't shaken. "Ring's is a high-sounding voice, that of Weeks a low, soft voice."

"Did you ever tell anybody that you thought the persons you overheard were Mr. Ring and Elma?"

"No," Watkins admitted, looking again toward the Rings.

Colden tried again. "Did you ever speak of this noise which you and your wife heard in the night to anybody else?"

Slowly, Mr. Watkins said, "I don't know but I once said to Croucher that I believed he had a hand in it."

That was just the opening Alexander needed. "Did you ever converse with Croucher about where he was the evening Elma was missing?"

"I asked him once where he was that evening, but do not remember the answer he made."

"Did you ever see Croucher busy in spreading suspicions about the prisoner?"

"The day she was laid out in the street, I saw him

very busy in attempting to make people believe the prisoner was guilty."

Alexander barreled on before his co-counsel could get in the way. "Your Honor, the defense would like to recall Lorena Forrest to the stand." Having already been sworn, she didn't need to be sworn again. He could go right to the point. "Mrs. Forrest, have you had at any time conversation with Croucher, and what was it?"

"A day or two after Elma was found, he was at our house, and he said it was a very unfortunate thing that he had not come that way just at that time, as he might have saved her life. He said he had come by that night."

"You are very well persuaded he said this?" Alexander could feel the blood singing in his ears.

"I am, very well," Mrs. Forrest confirmed.

"Repeat the terms of the conversation." Colden's voice was hoarse.

Mrs. Forrest looked at him askance, but complied. "After the young woman had been found and after the jury had sat—"

"That is fifteen days after she was lost," said Colden, his teeth clenched. "Give us the very terms, ma'am, if you please."

"Upon my telling him what he had sworn before the grand jury—"

"You mean the coroner's jury," snapped Colden.

"—he said he did come along there that evening, but not at that hour."

"Did he then say anything about Mrs. Brown or Mrs. Ashmore's house?" demanded Colden.

"He did not say anything about any house, just that he—"

"Yes, we know." Colden's voice cracked in his frustration. He scrubbed a hand over his eyes. "No further questions."

Brockholst intervened before Alexander could call his next witness. "The defense calls Dr. Prince."

"I saw no marks of violence. I saw no appearances but what might be accounted for by supposing she drowned herself," swore Dr. Prince.

Why were they wasting time suggesting the girl had committed suicide? No one believed the girl had committed suicide.

Alexander could see the jury blinking and yawning as the doctors quibbled over how much water had been in the body; whether she had been dead before she went into the water or after; if the bruising was caused by violence or by a prolonged immersion in water, leaving the jury both bored and bewildered. The sun was setting as another day waned, casting the courtroom into gloom.

If Brockholst hadn't intervened with this useless medical havering, Alexander could have pushed forward with Ring and Croucher.

He'd had Colden rattled, the jury enthralled. And then this. Alexander's old friend Hosack—to whom he would be forever grateful for saving Philip—was going on about authorities and dissection.

Alexander waited for him to pause for breath and thanked him and called Lorena Forrest's husband to the stand.

"Do you know anything of a Mr. Richard Croucher?"

"On the day after Christmas, Croucher came to my store to buy a loaf of bread. He said Ring's family was in great distress, and that being under the same roof it gave him great uneasiness. His own opinion, he said, was that the girl had made away with herself."

Alexander looked to the jury to make sure they had heard that. "Did Mr. Croucher convey any other opinions to you, regarding the prisoner at the bar?"

"On Friday last, Croucher came running into my store and said, 'What do you think of this innocent young man now? There is material evidence against him from the Jerseys, and he is taken by the high sheriff, sir, and carried to jail; he will be carried from there, sir, to the court and be tried; from there he will be carried back to jail, and from thence to court again, sir, and from thence to the place of execution, and there be hanged by the neck until he is dead.'"

The sheer malice of it came through strongly in the retelling. "Had he any particular business with you at this time?"

"He did not seem to have any but to tell me this."

Throughout the courtroom, servants were quietly circling with tapers, lighting branches of candles. They set candelabra on either side of the high bench occupied by the three judges, and on the tables set aside for the prosecution and the defense. Burr leaned over to murmur something to Brockholst.

Alexander plunged ahead with his next witness. "Mr. Dustan, you, too, keep a shop, some distance from the Ring household. Did anyone come and speak to you of Levi Weeks?"

The flickering candles cast strange shadows across the shopkeeper's face. "Last Friday morning, a man—I don't know his name—came into my store."

The candlelighters hadn't made their way to the far side of the room yet. The area where Croucher sat was shrouded in gloom, turning him to a mere shadow among shadows.

It was time to shed some light on the matter.

Alexander grabbed up the branch of candles from the defense table and strode across the courtroom, brandishing the candles in front of Croucher's startled face.

"Mr. Dustan," he demanded, "is this the man?"

Chapter Thirty-One

A careful investigation left no doubt in [Hamilton's] mind of the innocence of the accused. . . . The evidence was circumstantial, with the exception of the witness who Hamilton felt convinced was the criminal. The prolonged trial had extended far into the night . . . Hamilton advanced, placing a candle on each side of [Croucher's] face and fixed on him a piercing eye.

—*History of the Republic of the United States of America*, by John Church Hamilton

New York City
April 1, 1800

The candles carved strange hollows beneath Croucher's cheekbones.

"Mark every muscle of his face, every motion of his eye," declared Hamilton, in thrilling tones. "I conjure you to look through that man's countenance to his conscience. Was this the man you saw in your store?"

"Yes, it was," said the bemused shopkeeper.

He ought to have remembered, thought Aaron resignedly, that it was always a mistake to underestimate Alexander Hamilton.

Aaron refused to compare him to a phoenix from the flame—the man would enjoy that far too much—but it was undeniable that Hamilton had a remarkable capacity for emerging scarred but undaunted from conflagrations that ought to have reduced him to ash. The Maria Reynolds scandal should have knocked Hamilton out of politics once and for all—but here he was, a thorn in Aaron's flesh and the only real threat to the Republicans in the coming election. The purloined speech ought to have rendered him speechless for the duration of the trial, but here he was, waving candles about and creating a grand spectacle out of a simple identification.

Never mind the medical evidence, never mind the painstaking detail about the sleigh, all anyone would remember would be Hamilton and his branch of candles. Like a conjuror, Hamilton had a talent for directing the eye to what he wanted them to see. It was all bombast, but it was the sort of bombast that led successful cavalry charges and turned mad schemes into triumphs.

It made Aaron very nervous.

He preferred situations he could control. And that was the thing about Hamilton. One could maneuver him—to a point. But the very impulsiveness that made him vulnerable also made him dangerously unpredictable. Every now and again, his shots hit their mark.

Every eye in the courtroom was transfixed on Hamilton and his branch of candles, shining on the face of a man who ought to have been a minor witness and had now become Hamilton's prize villain.

"What did this man say to you?" asked Hamilton, still in those ringing tones.

The shopkeeper coughed. "He said, 'Good morning, gentlemen, Levi Weeks is taken up by the high sheriff and there is fresh evidence in from Hackensack.' He then went away and as he went out, he said, 'My name is Croucher,' and this was all the business he had with me."

Hamilton called his next witness, a voluble Scotsman with hair as red as Hamilton's, a set of well-developed jowls, and grievances which he didn't wait to air.

"I have been acquainted with this Mr. Croucher for some time but I never liked his looks," said Mr. McDougall frankly, rolling his *r*'s with abandon. "On the second of January, the day that the body was found, he was extremely busy among the crowd to spread improper insinuations and prejudices against the prisoner, who was then taken, and among other things told a story about his losing a pocketbook."

Hamilton feigned shock. "Did he claim that Mr. Weeks had robbed him of his pocketbook?"

"Not to claim, but to imply. I thought his conduct unfair and told him so plainly," said Mr. McDougall robustly. "Oh, but says he, there's the story of the pocketbook, and stopped there."

"Thank you, Mr. McDougall—" began Hamilton, but Mr. McDougall wasn't done.

"He used to bring articles of wearing apparel, such as shawls, et cetera, to dispose of, but I noticed he always came just at dinnertime," said Mr. McDougall darkly. "I told my wife that I did not like the man and desired that she would tell him that in future if he wanted anything of me, *I* would call on *him*. But did he heed me? No!"

"Tell us what he said to you, Mr. McDougall," said Hamilton, just managing to get his question in while the Scotsman paused for breath.

"Last Monday, while I was busy in my garden, he came again! Now, says he, the thing has all come out, the thing is settled, there is point-blank proof come from the Jerseys of a new fact." Mr. McDougall stuck his chin out pugnaciously. "I told him I thought it was wrong and highly improper that he should persecute Weeks in such a manner when he had a difference with him, that for my own part, I wanted some further evidence before I should condemn the man—and my wife didn't want any more shawls!"

"Objection," remonstrated Mr. Colden. "Is Mr. Croucher on trial or is Mr. Weeks?"

"The assistant attorney general will surely admit that such testimony is entirely germane to the matter of public opinion being roused against the prisoner at the bar," Aaron said silkily. Ezra Weeks looked like a kettle about to boil; it was past time to go back to the job they were here to do, proving Levi couldn't have committed the crime. "However, that point having been amply proved, the defense now calls John McComb to the stand."

After the tittle-tattle of shopkeepers, John McComb, the rising architect, was a dignified presence on the stand.

The architect had been busy: he had recently completed both a mansion for Archibald Gracie on the banks of the East River and St. Mark's church in the Bowery. But he had still found time to call on Ezra Weeks that fatal night, and it was his testimony that was crucial in placing Levi well away from the well.

Aaron put first John McComb on the stand, and

then Ezra Weeks. Hamilton held his tongue, although Aaron could feel him fidgeting. Was he trying to compose a new speech in his head? Aaron would be curious to see if even Hamilton's eloquence was up to the task.

In the meantime, Aaron patiently took his witnesses through times and whereabouts. Levi had come in just after tea and sat discussing the business of the day with his brother until the McCombs came in. He chatted with them awhile, showing no great hurry to depart, and finally left around eight. The McCombs had stayed twenty minutes more, and Ezra had taken his candle and shown them down to Rhinelander's corner. By the time he returned, Levi had come back to get his instructions for the following day, and sat there diligently taking down dimensions of doors for Mr. James Cummings's house.

All very dull, perhaps, but the very dullness was a shield, far more reliable than the haphazard slashing of Hamilton's sword, striking now at one possible culprit, now at another. If Levi had left his brother's at eight, arrived at the Ring house at ten past, and was gone, as everyone agreed, from the Ring house by a quarter past the hour, that left him only fifteen minutes, twenty at most, before he was again at his brother's hearth. And the sleigh with which he was meant to have spirited

Elma away was under lock and key, with that key in Demas Meed's pocket.

There was one last point Aaron wanted to make sure to settle. "Did your brother inform you that the muff was found prior to his arrest?"

"On the second day of January last, about two o'clock in the afternoon, I was sitting down to dinner and Levi came and told me that Mrs. Forrest had told him that the muff was found in a well near Bayard's Lane." Ezra Weeks glowered at the jury. "*I* told him that I supposed it must be the Manhattan Well."

"How came you to mention the Manhattan Well?" Colden asked suspiciously.

"The reason why the Manhattan Well came first to my recollection," said Ezra Weeks shortly, "was that I had furnished the wood materials for that well, and as my business often called me that way, I rode past the well almost every day."

"Did your brother know where the well was?"

Ezra's eyes shifted. "I believe he knew the situation to the well."

"Had he not been there before the arrest?" pressed Colden.

"Not to my knowledge. I do not think he was there until his arrest. I understood him that he was never there before the officer took him there—but I am not certain." Ezra Weeks finally stopped talking, having done more damage to his brother's case than any number of the prosecution's witnesses.

"Your Honor," said Colden feverishly, "if you permit, the people would like to call a witness germane to this point."

"The defense has witnesses yet to call," intervened Brockholst, and called Ezra Weeks's foreman.

The foreman testified that Levi had performed the business of the shop as usual the day after Elma's disappearance. Peter Fenton and Joseph Hall, who had measured the distance from the Ring house to the Manhattan Well with chains, went on the stand to say they had found it seventy-nine chains long, or just under a mile. Frederick Rhinelander opined that he couldn't have driven the road to the well in the dark on such a night. The cashier of the Bank of New York, for whom the Weeks brothers had built a house the previous year, averred that Levi was a very industrious, prudent, civil, and obliging young man.

Aaron could see each successive witness, each drip of the wax from the candles, wearing on Colden's nerves; he was in a state of nervous excitement, wild to call his witness, barely attending to the testimony of the men on the stand.

What was it that Colden thought he had?

Meanwhile, Hamilton was markedly silent. Partly, Aaron suspected, because this was the sort of dull routine that had no charm for his volatile colleague—but largely, he guessed, because as their roll of witnesses drew to a close, so did the moment when Hamilton would have to stand and improvise, delivering a speech that could only be a pale echo of Aaron's opening statement.

Aaron looked forward to that moment immensely.

"If it please Your Honor," said Colden hoarsely, after three more witnesses had attested to Levi's mild temper, "if the defense has done, the people would like to call a new witness."

The witness was a young man, a carter. He took his oath and said, "I saw a young man at the well the Sunday week before the girl was missing with a pole in his hand—"

"Do you know Levi Weeks?" Brockholst interrupted. "Should you know the person you speak of if you saw him?"

"I don't know as I should."

Colden made a vain attempt to reclaim the situation. "Take the candle and look around and see if you can pick him out."

That might have worked for Hamilton with Croucher, but Colden didn't have the same flair.

"Objection," countered Brockholst immediately. "One might assume the fact that the prisoner at the bar is standing in the dock does rather prejudice the inquiry."

There were a few snickers from such of the jury as were sufficiently alert to snicker; several of the jury appeared to have entered a state of somnolence during the long string of witnesses to Levi's good character, which was precisely what Aaron had intended. Hamilton might wish to excite the crowd; Aaron was content with exoneration by ennui. They would acquit Levi simply to be done with him.

Colden cleared his throat and tried again. "Will you undertake to swear that is the man you saw at the well?"

The man glanced nervously at Brockholst. "I cannot swear to him."

Colden said quickly, "Well, sir, tell what you saw."

"The Sunday before the young woman was missing," recited the man, "I saw a young man sounding the Manhattan Well with a pole. I went up to him and asked him what he was about. He said he made the carpenter's work, and that he wanted to know the depth of the water. He measured it in different places and found it five foot five inches, five foot eight inches, and six foot."

Colden's haggard face blazed with triumph. "How was this man dressed?"

"He had on a blue coatee, red jacket, blue breeches, and white stockings. I noticed the red jacket particularly."

Brockholst looked down his impressive Roman nose. "How do we know that Levi Weeks owns such garments? Mr. Weeks is certainly wearing no such garment now. The man was unable to identify the prisoner's face. Do we have evidence as to the contents of his wardrobe?"

Justice Lansing leaned forward. "Perhaps Mr. Ring might be recalled to speak to this point."

"I've never seen him wear a red jacket," Elias Ring said flatly. All the fight seemed to have gone out of him. Elias Ring was a broken man. He didn't even have the will to lie.

"Never?" Colden asked desperately. "Stretch your memory."

"Never."

Sitting on her bench in the front row, Catherine Ring's lips were buttoned tight, as if she were trying to keep herself from crying out.

"Perhaps the witness was mistaken—or he might have kept the jacket at his brother's—" Colden's face sagged. "If the court please, we give up this point."

Justice Lansing looked pointedly at the clock. The

hands stood at a quarter to one in the morning. "If the prosecution has no further witnesses . . ."

"Your Honors, I beg the court to reconsider your ruling on the admission of the deceased's statements," Colden pleaded. "It is not that I question the judgment of this court, but only that the complexion of the case has changed: the defense has made it a point that the deceased was melancholy—and deranged! Surely, the words of the deceased, as well as how she appeared to others, should be given in evidence in such circumstances? Without that, how are we to arrive at the truth?"

Aaron stepped forward, but Justice Lansing forestalled him.

"We are to arrive at the truth with the testimony of the seventy-five living witnesses you have already seen fit to call," said Justice Lansing drily. "You may spare us your eloquence, Colonel Burr. The court sees no reason to reconsider the point."

"In that case . . ." Colden turned, casting his eyes desperately around the room, at the assembled spectators and witnesses. "The people call Ann Ashmore to the stand!"

Hamilton's face lit up like a Roman candle.

Aaron regarded the assistant attorney general with disbelief. If the man had any sense, he would have abandoned the whole question of Croucher, left him as he was, nothing more than a scandalmonger. Like the red coat, it was a point he ought to drop. But Colden—Colden was swaying as he stood, his cravat untied, drunk with fatigue, in that state of exhaustion where it was very hard to think straight.

Not that Aaron had terribly much respect for his powers when fully rested.

Ann Ashmore nodded at Aaron as she made her way to the stand, a composed and credible witness. "On the twenty-second of December, being my little boy's birthday, I invited some of my friends to come and sup with me, and among the rest, Mr. Croucher. This was between twelve and one o'clock. Accordingly, between four and five in the evening he came, and remained there until four or five minutes after eleven."

"Could he have been absent twenty minutes during that time?"

"No, he was not," said Ann Ashmore calmly.

Feverishly, Colden called the party guests, all four of them, but none could attest positively that the party had been before, rather than after, Christmas, only that it had been on a Sunday, and to celebrate the birthday of Ann Ashmore's child.

Everyone in the courtroom was left with the impression that not only might the party have happened a week later, but even if it had occurred that Sunday, Croucher might have been traipsing through Lispenard's Meadow, murdering maidens, and they'd still swear he was there. Some quantities of brandy, it seemed, had been consumed. In a celebratory way, of course.

Colden's face had gone gray. He had made a mistake, and he knew it, but, in classic fashion, instead of doing what he ought to have done, and directing attention back to Levi, he redoubled his error and recalled Richard Croucher to the stand.

"How many times were you at Ring's on Sunday evening of the twenty-second of December?" Colden was so hoarse, his voice came out as a croak.

"Three times, and the latest about three o'clock."

"Did you ever publish the handbills about apparitions, murder, et cetera?"

"No, I never did, nor do I know who did. I was at Mrs. Wellham's and I saw one there which I asked leave to bring to Ring's, but I was not permitted and that is all I know of them or ever saw of them."

Hamilton seized his moment. "Mr. Croucher! Did you pass by the Manhattan Well that night?"

"No! I only might have said I wished I had that I might have saved the girl's life. . . . I was never near the well!"

Colden held on to the table with both hands, as if it were the only thing holding him upright. "No further questions," he said.

The hands of the clock stood at a quarter past two in the morning.

"Gentlemen of the jury." Aaron positioned himself in the center of the courtroom, letting them see him in contrast to Colden, calm, collected, unfazed. "I would call to your attention Hale's guidance on presumptive evidence—which is all the assistant attorney general has to offer you in this case. In some cases, it is true, presumptive evidences go far to prove a person guilty, though there be no express proof, but it must be warily pressed—for it is better that five guilty persons should escape unpunished than one innocent person should die."

Aaron lifted his candle and gestured with it toward Levi, putting a special emphasis on the word *innocent*.

"Your Honor." Colden swayed, bumping into one of the tables as he attempted to approach the bench. "Your Honor, I move that we adjourn until tomorrow."

"The testimony is done," said Justice Lansing. "Only the summations remain."

Colden made a sound somewhere between a laugh and a sob. "I beg of you—I have not slept since the night before the trial began. I have been awake for forty-four hours and I am sinking beneath my fatigue. I beg of you, sir, let us adjourn until tomorrow."

"I won't sleep another night on that floor!" shouted one of the jurymen. "He gets to go home to his own bed! What about us!"

"Your Honor," intervened Aaron. "These poor men have been separated from their homes and families for one night already. They have given generously of their time and attention. Must we ask of them a third day merely because the assistant attorney general failed to sleep?"

Besides, if they adjourned, it would give Hamilton time to pen a proper closing statement.

"Please—the prisoner's counsel have yet to give their closing address—it might be hours. And then I have first to make my address to the jury. It won't be until morning." Sagging like a broken toy, Colden whispered, "I have not the strength to proceed further tonight."

Hamilton strode forward. Unlike their opposing counsel, Hamilton showed no signs of fatigue. The candles stripped the years away, burnishing his hair, hiding the gray strands that had begun to appear among the red. It brought Aaron back twenty years.

Even then Hamilton had been an annoyance, General Washington's pet, always assuming his opinion mattered more than anyone else's and that any glory to be garnered should go solely to him.

"Your Honor," said Hamilton, turning all the force of his charm toward the bench, "the defense requires no labored elucidation. The testimony speaks for itself. In deference to the lateness of the hour—and the fatigue of the assistant attorney general—the defense cedes our closing statement."

It was a brilliant bit of bravado. No one would ever guess Hamilton's generosity arose solely because he had no speech to give.

"The defense rests?" asked Lansing.

Hamilton looked straight at Burr. His lips turned up in a smug smile. "The defense rests."

Chapter Thirty-Two

The jury then went out and returned in about five minutes with a verdict.

—From Coleman's account of the trial of Levi Weeks

New York City
April 2, 1800

"But—the jury should hear observations on the testimony." Mr. Colden clung to the bench like a drowning man to a spar.

"The jury has heard observations enough—more than enough," Justice Lansing said with feeling. "We cannot in good conscience keep the jury together another night without the conveniences necessary to repose. Motion denied."

Caty should have been tired—she hadn't slept at all last night after that horrible conversation with Hope, only lain awake next to the snoring bulk of Elias—but she was fired by a terrible energy.

This was what she had been waiting for these past three months, ever since Levi had been taken up: the moment when they would finally have justice, when this could finally all be done.

The chief justice peered at the jury through the wavering light of the tapers on the bench. "Gentlemen of the jury, in the normal course of affairs, the arguments of counsel would allow this court time to adjust and arrange the mass of evidence that has been brought into view."

Why couldn't he just get on with it? Caty sat bolt upright on the edge of the bench, her whole body straining for that one word: guilty.

The justice appeared to be prepared to discourse at length. "It has, unexpectedly, become my duty to charge you immediately upon the close of testimony. I have agreed to this with reluctance, and only because I am persuaded that, despite that great mass of evidence, there are only a few points on which this case ought to be decided."

On that, Caty agreed. Elma had said she was to be married to Levi. Elma had left with Levi. It was as simple as that.

Justice Lansing held up a hand. "Before I consider

those pieces of evidence, I would like to remind you of the great moment of this decision you are about to make. On your verdict depends a man's life."

Not just Levi's life, Caty wanted to cry out. It was hers and Elias's too. And Elma, who had been killed.

Justice Lansing leaned forward, his face framed by tapers. "I don't need to tell you that this matter has excited the public attention to a remarkable degree. A great many reports have been circulated, which cannot have failed to reach your ears—but you, gentlemen of the jury, by your obligation as jurors, are duty-bound to limit yourself *only* to the evidence you have heard at this trial."

Caty's nails bit into her palms through her gloves.

"The prosecution has never pretended to afford positive proof as to the commission of this murder by the prisoner. It has attempted to prove his guilt by circumstantial evidence. If it could be established, by a number of circumstances so connected as to produce a rational conviction, that Levi Weeks is the perpetrator of the crime, it would be your duty to find him guilty."

Why didn't he stop talking already and let them go and come to their verdict?

"The prosecution has failed to establish such a chain," pronounced Justice Lansing.

There was a buzzing in Caty's ears. The interplay of

flame and shadow made the room spin wildly. What in goodness' name was he saying?

"It is, as this court sees it, very doubtful whether Gulielma Sands left the house of Elias Ring in company with the prisoner."

Caty's mouth fell open; she could feel the protests jamming at the back of her throat. Of course he'd left with her! She'd told them he'd left with her! She might not have seen them, but she'd heard them. She'd heard the door.

The judge went on, in the same dry voice, "As for the testimony respecting the one-horse sleigh, if one is not satisfied by the testimony of Mrs. Susanna Broad, then it must be evident that the relations of the other witnesses respecting a sleigh and the cries of distress near the Manhattan Well can have no application to the prisoner."

No application? People had heard Elma crying murder! How had that no application simply because an old woman had been confused by clever lawyers?

Justice Lansing gestured to the shadowy confines of the dock. "The prisoner appears to be a young man of fair character and mild disposition. It is difficult to discover what inducement could have actuated the prisoner in the commission of the crime with which he is charged."

Levi Weeks stood up straighter. Caty could see his chest rise and fall as he drew in a deep breath, as if he could already scent freedom.

"The witnesses produced on his part account for the manner in which he spent his evening, excepting only a few minutes."

Ezra Weeks sat with his arms folded across his chest. Caty wanted to slap his smug face. He'd lied for his brother; they all knew he'd lied for his brother. How could the court not see it?

Justice Lansing raised his voice to be heard over the excited murmuring from the galleries. "This court is unanimously of the opinion that the proof is insufficient to warrant a verdict against the prisoner. With that charge, gentlemen of the jury, we commit the prisoner's case to your consideration."

Caty turned to Elias, who looked as shocked as she felt. "Is he allowed to say that? Can he tell them what to think?"

"They'll make up their own minds. That's what they're here to do," said Elias numbly, but he fumbled for her hand, and Caty didn't stop him.

Hope was staring at Levi with a look on her face Caty didn't like at all. Caty clutched Elias's hand, and felt him squeeze it in return.

"He did it; they have to know he did it," Caty

muttered. She turned to Hope, raising her voice so Hope would hear her. "Thee knows he did it."

Hope didn't answer; she only stared at Levi.

Caty bent her head, praying without words, praying that they'd do the right thing and come back with a verdict of guilty. If they didn't—it wasn't even to be thought of. He *was* guilty.

"Gentlemen of the jury, have you reached a verdict?"

"We have, Your Honor."

How could they be back already? They'd only just gone out. Caty clutched Elias's hand, scarcely aware of where she was or what she was doing.

The foreman cleared his throat. "The unanimous verdict of this jury is that the prisoner is NOT GUILTY."

"What?" Caty was on her feet without realizing she'd stood. "No! *No!*"

Ezra Weeks enveloped Levi in a huge hug, pounding him loudly on the back. Mr. Colden looked like he was about to faint. People were exclaiming, cheering, booing, rushing out of the room to tell the people slumped half-asleep on the floor of the corridor beyond the courtroom, waiting, waiting, waiting for the verdict.

"Not guilty!" The cry went up from mouth to mouth to the waiting crowd outside. "Weeks not guilty!"

"He is guilty!" insisted Caty hysterically. "Why do thee tell such lies? He's guilty!"

Hope tugged at her hand. "Caty, come away. Hush. . . ."

"Don't hush me! How can I hold my tongue when Elma's in her grave and her killer free? Or does thy desire outrun thy duty?"

Hope flinched as though Caty had slapped her. "Thee heard the judge, Caty. The evidence . . ."

"Thee mean Elma's words we weren't allowed to say?" Caty retorted. "Thee mean the lies paid for by Ezra Weeks's coin?"

Caty knew who was to blame. It was those lawyers, in their fancy coats with their fancy words, sowing doubt, coming up with strange rules to prevent the truth being told. She hated them all.

Levi was walking past her, walking free as day, flanked by his brother and General Hamilton. General Hamilton leaned across Levi, saying something about his plans for a house. "—in the classical style, not too large, with something like those doors Levi designed—"

"It was thy mischief!" Caty launched herself into their path. "It's thee confused their minds with false suspicions!"

"Mrs. Ring," began General Hamilton, with false sympathy.

"Thee should be ashamed of thyself! If thee dies a natural death, I shall think there is no justice in heaven!"

Someone was pulling her away, dragging her back. Elias wrapped an arm around her, turning her face into his chest, muffling her words, blocking her sight.

She could hear Ezra Weeks saying, with a coarse laugh, "I think you've just been cursed, General."

"I don't believe Quakers are allowed to do that," returned General Hamilton cheerfully. "Now about that house . . ."

She wanted to curse them. She wanted to make their man parts shrivel and their countenances turn as black as their souls.

Caty yanked herself free, but they were already gone. She could just see the glimmer of Alexander Hamilton's blue silk coat as the Weeks brothers left the courtroom. It should be purple, stained with Elma's blood.

"I'm so sorry." Mr. Colden stumbled up beside Elias, his lips gray. "I never imagined—I can't think—"

Caty rounded on him. "If thee had thought, Levi would be in prison now!"

They would never be free of this. The full magnitude of it hit Caty, making her sag against Elias. If only the court had pronounced Levi guilty, the horrible scandal of Elias and Elma wouldn't matter as much. But now—

the world would always wonder. They would wonder if Elma had killed herself. They would wonder if Caty's husband was a murderer as well as an adulterer.

Dimly, Caty was aware of someone leading her away, to Mr. Colden's carriage, as Mr. Colden went on mouthing apologies that meant nothing. She felt like Rachel's old doll, the inexpertly jointed limbs moving strangely, the head stuffed with wool.

The house was dark, Mr. Colden's maid again dozing by the fire. Caty left Hope to send the maid out to Mr. Colden's carriage. Caty spoke to no one, walking woodenly to the bedroom, her fingers clumsy on the string of her bonnet. Let someone else deal with the oats for breakfast. Let someone else make sure the fire was banked. What did it matter if the house burned down and all of them in it? Her life was ash already.

Caty's eye fell on her children, all four of them, asleep on their pallets, and her chest contracted painfully.

If the house burned, her children would die, and she couldn't bear the thought of that, of any harm befalling them.

They shouldn't suffer for their parents' sins.

Except they would. Caty stuffed her hand in her mouth to keep herself from crying out. They'd failed the children. She'd thought she was such a good wife, such a good mother, such a good neighbor, but every single one of their neighbors had testified against them. They'd all heard her husband having relations with her cousin.

And now—now they would wonder if her husband had killed her cousin. Or perhaps if Caty had, she thought wildly.

How could she live here? What would they say to the children?

Caty could feel Elias come up behind her, as he had that first day when she was on the stand and he was meant to be out of the room. It felt like years ago, back when she'd been so certain their ordeal was almost done, before the world heard all their shame and secrets.

"I didn't kill her," Elias said quietly. "I wasn't the husband to thee I should be, but I didn't kill her."

"I know." Blindly, Caty turned and leaned against him, resting her head against his chest.

After a moment, she felt his palm tentatively come to rest against the back of her head. It had been a very long time since they'd stood together like this. It had been a very long time since Elias had touched her with anything like affection.

Caty felt the sting of tears, and blinked them away before the wet could touch his shirtfront.

If this had been six months ago . . . a year ago . . .

"I should have done better by thee," he murmured against her hair.

Yes, he should have. "There's no good in *should*," Caty said wearily, moving away from him. "We can only do better from now on."

From now on, she would know better than to trust her husband too far. Her mother had made her own compromises, and Caty would have to make hers. She could feel it like a burning in her chest, the loss of her hopes, the loneliness of knowing she would always have to be the one who made all the sacrifices. Elias might feel bad now, but he couldn't be trusted to remain that way.

"We could go away somewhere," he offered.

The only place Caty wanted to go was back to New Cornwall, to the house her grandparents had built. But New Cornwall was closed to them now. Everyone there would hear; everyone would look at Elias and imagine him with Elma.

"No," she said. "No. If we go, they'll think we did something wrong."

Beds creaking in the night through the walls. Their neighbors gossiping and she'd never known.

Caty swallowed the bitterness. "We'll need new boarders. I doubt Ezra Weeks will board his journeymen here now."

"That man is capable of anything," muttered Elias.

"Yes," said Caty slowly. "He is."

That judge had said the sleigh hadn't gone out that night; that Levi's time had been all accounted for. But who had said so? The only evidence that the sleigh hadn't been out that night came from Ezra's apprentice, Demas Meed. The only evidence that Levi had been at his brother's when he claimed came from Demas and Ezra.

Caty's brain was working furiously. Ezra Weeks hadn't wanted Levi to marry Elma. Ezra Weeks's apprentice had the key to the gate. According to the people Mr. Colden had spoken to, there had been a second man in the sleigh—a man who might have untied the bells and harnessed the horse, and brought the sleigh to Levi. A man under orders from his master, prepared to lie in a court of law.

Ezra Weeks was capable of anything.

"I hope Elma haunts them," said Caty, so vehemently that Rachel sighed and rolled over and David stirred, lifting his head.

"Is it over?" he asked drowsily. "Has the bad man been punished?"

Caty looked to Elias, but Elias only shook his head. Caty had never hated her husband more than in that moment. If he had kept his hands off Elma . . . if he had refrained from spreading stories about Levi . . .

Ezra Weeks would still have paid his underlings to tell lies, she reminded herself. Elias's misdeeds had only been so much good fortune for him.

"He'll have his justice in heaven," she said in a brittle voice. "Just thee wait and see. The Lord neither slumbers nor sleeps."

"But we should," said Elias, with an attempt at heartiness that annoyed her more than anything else. "Come to bed."

Caty looked at her children, at her husband. She could hear the creaking upstairs as her boarders, returned from the trial, got themselves ready for bed.

Elma's killer was free and Elias's adultery was known to the world, but the children and the boarders would still expect to be fed.

"I've got to start the oats steeping," she said, and went to go back about the business of living.

Chapter Thirty-Three

It is next to impossible to get men of weight and influence to serve.

—Robert Troup to Rufus King on the 1800 New York elections

New York City
April 15, 1800

No one can deny that it is to the Federal party exclusively that we owe that unexampled prosperity which we have hitherto enjoyed. But beware of a blind confidence in our present situation!"

The Federalists gathered at the Tontine Coffee House cheered lustily as General Hamilton exhorted them to fight the spirit of Jacobinism. Cadwallader skulked at the back of the group, partly because his height made him an impediment, and partly because he wished he had pleaded an ague and stayed home in bed with the covers over his head.

The slate of candidates had been unveiled, with Cadwallader's name among them. A month ago, he would have been in the very height of elation at having been asked to represent the Federalist cause in the assembly; he could feel his grandfather, the esteemed colonial governor of New York, nodding in approval.

But now—Cadwallader could only feel how unworthy he was, both to win the assembly seat and to hold it.

Ebenezer Belden grabbed General Hamilton's arm. "Sir, you have the energy of Demosthenes, the ardor of Chatham, the overpowering rapidity of Fox, the logic of Pitt, and the classical imagery of Burke! You have given a new pulse to public feelings. We can only hope to see its effect among all classes of men!"

Cadwallader lurked behind Belden, waiting until he had finished his effusions, before calling General Hamilton's attention to himself with a strangled cough.

"Colden! Are you ready to lead us to victory?"

Cadwallader glanced over his shoulder, lowering his voice. "That's just what I wanted to speak with you about. Are you certain you still wish me to stand for office?"

"My dear sir, you are essential for balance. We have a ship's chandler, two grocers, a shoemaker, and a mason. You provide the aristocratic element. Your name reassures our old families that their interests haven't yet been forgotten." Hamilton grinned, looking with satisfaction at the assemblage, which had broken into small, excitedly talking groups. "There's at least one spy for the Republicans among us tonight, if not more. Let Burr say now the Federalist party doesn't stand for the common man!"

The name of Colden might once have stood for something grand, but now it represented only failure. "Are you sure my name might not be a liability?"

"Because your father was a loyalist? That was twenty years and more ago."

Cadwallader sunk his chin into his cravat. "I was thinking of the Weeks trial."

"That," said Hamilton easily, "was weeks ago. The public has moved on to new sensations."

"Only two weeks. The people haven't forgotten," said Cadwallader unhappily. "And the papers are still full of it."

Some portrayed the trial as a travesty of justice, others as a vindication of innocence. Either way, Cadwallader came out poorly.

Only the day before, the clerk of the court, William Coleman, had released a ninety-nine page account of the trial, which had sold out as soon as it arrived at Mr. Furman's shop outside City Hall. Cadwallader had known he shouldn't read it, but he couldn't help himself. He had sat up all the previous night, obsessively reading over all the testimony, trying to figure out what he had missed and how he had missed it.

There were two possibilities, neither of them good. Either he had had a murderer in the dock and so bungled his trial that he had gone free—or he had prosecuted the wrong man.

"I feel that I should withdraw my candidacy," Cadwallader said, with painful dignity. "I can only be a liability to you in my current state."

"Don't do that! Your departure would throw our slate out of balance." As an afterthought, Hamilton added, "I wouldn't have asked you to serve if I hadn't thought you were capable of it."

"Livingston and Burr had me all hollow in the courtroom. I didn't even get my precedent correct."

Hamilton looked at him with resignation. "How old are you? A score and ten?"

"Thirty-two." Old enough to know how to comport himself in a courtroom.

"Burr and Livingston and I have a decade of experience on you. That's all it is. Experience." General Hamilton's eyes shifted past Cadwallader, fixing on someone else he wanted to speak to. "When you've stood in that courtroom as often as I have, the precedents will come quick to your lips too. And now—"

"But it wasn't just that," Cadwallader burst out, desperate to have it all out. "You produced evidence I never even thought to look for."

"One of those lessons you learn with experience is that if something seems too simple, mistrust it. Probe for weaknesses as if you were your own most deadly opponent." A frown creased Hamilton's forehead. "If it makes you feel better, Livingston and Burr didn't think to look further either. They would have been content to argue that Elma Sands did away with herself. And I—I was convinced for too long that the fault lay with Elias Ring. We all make mistakes."

"It haunts me that I might have prosecuted the wrong man while the right man was before me the whole time," said Cadwallader feverishly. "I should have seen it. You saw it. But Mr. Croucher seemed so convincing when he spoke of seeing Levi and Elma together. . . . How did you guess?"

Hamilton nodded politely, preparatory to taking his leave. "I had the advantage of you—I could speak to Levi Weeks. I knew from Levi that he had seen Elma and Croucher embracing."

"There was another woman," Cadwallader blurted out. "Rose Malone. She was strangled and stuffed into a cistern. Croucher told me—he told me he had sold her stockings. He said he felt responsible for her in some way. I can't stop wondering—"

"Wondering does no good. Concentrate yourself on the present," said General Hamilton, patting him briskly on the arm. "This election—"

Cadwallader shook his head. "It haunts my sleep that Croucher might have killed both those women and I never saw it. I believed every word he told me. I believed him when he told me he only wanted justice for Elma."

"If your sin is being too trusting, that's a failing we've all had from time to time. I made the same mistake with the Manhattan Company, with far graver consequences," said General Hamilton. "I'd rather have a man at my side who is more wise than cunning, driven by good intentions rather than extreme and irregular ambitions. I have utter faith in your ability, Colden. Now, I must have a word with Philip Ten Eyck."

Quietly, Cadwallader gathered up his hat and gloves. He wasn't sure that anyone noticed him go.

It was even later than he had realized. The meeting had gone on for some considerable time. When he returned home, Maria was already tucked into bed, reading by the light of a branch of candles, her hair brushed out of its curls and pulled back in a braid, giving her face the austere beauty of the profile on a cameo.

"I didn't realize it was so late," said Cadwallader.

Without looking up from her book, Maria said, "David has gone to bed already. He asked for you."

Cadwallader felt the implicit criticism deeply. "I was at the Tontine Coffee House. General Hamilton wants me to run for state assembly."

Maria set her book down on the coverlet. "That would mean you would have to spend a great deal of time in Albany."

"Well, yes, I suppose." He hadn't really thought that far.

"There would be months when we wouldn't see you," said Maria flatly.

Cadwallader had that terrible sinking feeling of once again having said the wrong thing. "Only while the assembly is in session. Or you could come with me!" Money was no issue. They could certainly afford a second establishment. "We could buy a house. David might like the countryside around Albany. I'm sure General Schuyler would advise us."

"Did you consider that David and I might mind being either left or dragged along with you?"

Dragged seemed to be putting it a bit harshly. "I wouldn't want you to come to Albany unless you wanted to come to Albany." Oh dear. He had said something wrong again. "How could I say no? The stakes are tremendous. If we win the assembly elections, we win the country. Surely I can sacrifice my own convenience for the sake of the presidency."

"For your sake or General Hamilton's?" Maria pushed back the covers, swinging her legs over the edge of the bed. "Did you stop to think that it might not be your convenience alone? What about David? He sees you little enough as it is."

That wasn't fair. "I read to David every night! Almost every night."

"The Masons, the Manumission Society, the Federalists . . . I can't keep track of half your obligations! You might be a bachelor for all we see you. Maybe you would have been happier being a bachelor. Even when you're here, you're not." With horror, Cadwallader realized that Maria's eyes were filled with tears, her face scrunched up to keep them falling. "I don't think you hear half of what I say to you. Either you're locked in your book room or you're thinking—whatever you're thinking about! Last night, you didn't even come to bed."

"I was reading the transcript of the Weeks case," said Cadwallader in a low voice. "I was trying to figure out where I'd gone wrong."

"I should think that was clear enough." Maria turned her back on him, her voice ragged with tears.

"Don't you think I've noticed that you can hardly bear to be at home?"

"Maria." Cadwallader came up behind her. Her nightdress was of fine French lawn, embroidered with posies. He looked down at the top of her head, the white line of her scalp where the hair parted. "What are you talking about?"

"We don't need to pretend. I see the way you look at me. If you'd married anyone else," she said bitterly, "you'd have a hearth-full of children all clustered around your knees. Instead there's just David."

"David is worth a dozen other children," said Cadwallader in bewilderment. He felt as though he'd lost the thread of the conversation. Hadn't they been talking about the Weeks case?

Maria lifted her tear-ravaged face. "But he's not a dozen other children, is he? He's just the one. You would have been better off if I'd died and you might have married again and had a proper family."

"Don't say such things!" Cadwallader gripped her shoulders, as though he could keep her from the grave by force. "I love you. I love you if you have one child or ten. I thought—I thought you were regretting marrying me."

"I am—I do," she said thickly. "If you'd married someone else, you might be happier."

"I thought you were ashamed of me—that I'm not the lawyer Josiah is, or the statesman my grandfather was, or anything of note. I thought you were unhappy because you knew you'd picked a sorry fool for a husband."

"That's absurd." Maria wiped at her nose with the back of her hand. Cadwallader hunted in his pockets and produced a handkerchief for her. It was marked with his initials in a combination of Maria's hair and David's. "You're not a sorry fool."

"I saw you in the courtroom at the Weeks trial, watching as I faltered again and again and again. I wanted to make you and David proud of me, but instead I failed Elma Sands—I failed the Ring family—I failed you."

Maria blew her nose with vigor. "It was you alone against three giants! Even David in the Bible only had to defeat one."

"I wanted to defeat giants for our David—and for you. I hated to think that you were disappointed in me."

"You never had to slaughter giants for me, Cad." Maria stepped forward, leaning her head against his chest. Cadwallader wrapped his arms around her, smelling the French soap she used to wash her hair, feeling her chest rise and fall in time with his. Her voice muffled by his shirt, she said, "Don't stand for assembly. Let's go abroad, the three of us. You're always saying you want to take David to London."

He could picture driving with David and Maria down the Serpentine. David could ride his pony on Rotten Row; he and Maria might go to the theater. They could take the waters in Bath, or go bathing in Brighton, in the ingenious bathing machines set up by the water.

There would be lines of credit to arrange, servants to bring with them, trunks to pack. If he could secure passage, they could leave in a matter of weeks, tides willing. It was an immensely tempting prospect.

"I've given my word," Cadwallader said sadly. "I can't with honor withdraw."

Maria reached up, touching his cheek. "I could not love thee, dear, so much, loved I not honor more—isn't that how the poem goes? I couldn't love you so much if you weren't the man you are."

"Maybe I'll lose," said Cadwallader. "I haven't been very good at winning anything recently."

"You won me," said Maria, looking so winsome that he just had to kiss her.

"I've always worried that was a mistake," confessed Cadwallader, as the kiss ended. "My winning you, that is, and that you'd finally realized it. And then I lost the trial. . . ."

"There will be other trials," said Maria firmly.

Cadwallader bit his lip. "I asked Josiah if we could bring an action against Richard Croucher as the murderer of Elma Sands."

"What did he say?"

"He said the evidence wasn't there." Like a small boy yanking off a scab, Cadwallader said despondently, "Maria, if he's wrong—I brought charges against an innocent man. I let a killer go free."

Maria squeezed him fiercely about the waist. "You brought charges against a man the whole city believed to be a killer—with good reason! And we don't *know* Mr. Croucher had anything to do with it. He's unpleasant, certainly, and has appalling taste in waistcoats, but that doesn't mean he's a murderer."

Cadwallader thought of the way Mr. Croucher had looked, the strange, gloating note in his voice when he'd spoken of selling Rose Malone stockings for her wedding. "No, we don't know," he said slowly.

"You did what you thought was right—and if you think I'd be ashamed of you for that, then you don't know me at all," said Maria firmly. "I don't rate your worth by the number of trials you win, but by the goodness of your heart. I only feared I'd lost it awhile."

"If you think," said Cadwallader earnestly, looking down into her dear, familiar face, "that I rate your worth by the number of children you bear, then *you* don't know me at all."

Maria rose on her tiptoes to touch her lips to his. "If you go to Albany, David and I go too."

Cadwallader was torn between terror at how close they had come to losing one another and a deep feeling of gratitude that despite all of it, they had found their way back.

"Anywhere we go," said Cadwallader tenderly, "we go together."

"In that case," said Maria, taking him by the hand, "let's go to bed."

Chapter Thirty-Four

If the deceased was murdered, this at least was not the man. . . . By the evidence of the facts alone, is this young man's innocence completely established.

—*New-York Daily Advertiser*, April 3, 1800

New York City
April 23, 1800

"It's true, then. Thee are going. Elias said—he'd heard—but I didn't believe—"

On a Wednesday, Ezra Weeks's lumber yard was thrumming with the business of the shop. Apprentices carried stacks of wood and responded to barked requests for tools. But Levi wasn't among them. When Hope hurried up to the yard, doing her best to hold her skirts up out of last night's puddles, she saw him coming from the house, holding a small trunk up over his shoulder.

It was the same trunk he had brought when he came to live in the boardinghouse. Hope remembered seeing Levi carrying it in, how she and Peggy and Elma had all rushed to examine the new boarder as he climbed up the steps to the door; how Peggy had joked that this one was hers. In the first flush of summer, less than a year ago, when the greatest trouble they faced was getting the wrong ribbons to trim the hats, a new, handsome boarder had been a cause of innocent excitement.

"I'm going." Levi dropped the trunk with a thunk into the cart waiting by the gate. "You'll be rid of me for good, although not so permanently as you'd hoped."

It hadn't been she who hoped—except that it had. Hope bit her lip, remembering how sure she had been in her righteous fury. She would have seen him hang, and gladly.

"Where does thee go?" Hope asked. She could feel cold water creeping through her shoes, despite the pattens she had strapped on to raise her feet above the mud.

"Back to Massachusetts. I'm going to Bloody Brook." Levi smiled without humor. "It seems appropriate, doesn't it? Since most of the city still believes I have Elma's blood on my hands."

"Not all the city."

"No, not the people my brother paid to say otherwise." Levi leaned his hands on the side of the cart. "Did you know Ezra offered the clerk of the court fifteen hundred dollars to suppress his report of the trial? Or, if he preferred, five hundred just to add a single line saying I'd been completely exonerated."

"Fifteen hundred dollars?" Hope had never imagined such money existed.

"Oh yes. My brother is a warm man." Levi threw the words at her like a weapon. "Coleman refused. He said the city of New York hadn't money enough to buy him. Now he and Ezra are bosom friends. He consults with Coleman on his transactions. What's a mere brother to that?"

Levi made an ironic bow, sweeping his hat off his head. Where it had been, Hope could see a large scar, the stitches still visible, stretching from his hair all the way down to his left eyebrow.

"What happened to thy brow?"

Levi's hand went to his forehead. "This? Someone pried up a cobble and flung it at me when I went to Forrest's shop for tobacco." He smiled that same humorless grin. "But that's nothing strange. Three men set upon me when I had the gall to try to order a drink at Rhinelander's tavern. You did your work well."

"I didn't—"

"Your family, then," said Levi impatiently, clapping his hat back down on his head. "What does it matter? You've ruined me."

The injustice of it struck Hope. "We only told the truth."

Levi gave a derisive bark of laughter. "Oh?"

Hope could feel her cheeks heat. She'd forgotten about Elias; the thought of Elias embracing Elma made her flesh crawl. "*I* only told the truth. If thee hadn't behaved as if thee meant to court her, we might not have thought thee had. I never told thee to close thyself into Elma's bedchamber with her!"

"If every man who was ever alone with any maid was accused of her murder, the Bridewell would be bursting," said Levi bitterly. "What did I do more than any other man did? I wish I'd never set foot in your sister's house. You've been a plague upon mine. Did you know Elizabeth lost her baby?"

Hope felt a sharp pang. Elizabeth Weeks had been kind to her. There'd been a time she'd imagined she'd one day call her sister. "How does she fare? Mrs. Weeks?"

"She's recovering. Slowly. No thanks to you and yours."

"I never meant to do thee ill—or thy family." Hope

looked at Levi, trying to reconcile the man she'd known with the man standing before her. This man was leaner, marked with scars that hadn't been there before, but it was more than that. Whenever she thought of Levi, it was with the sun shining on him, smiling, laughing, quick to come to anyone's aid. She'd never known him to have a hard word for anyone. "I had hoped to see thee before thee left—to make amends."

"Why? Have you decided I didn't murder anyone after all? It's a bit late for that. It doesn't matter what that jury said. The city's decided I'm a murderer, and worse for having been acquitted. They think I dodged a noose, and every man with a few drinks in him feels it his duty to try to fit me with one—or at least black my eye."

"I am sorry, Levi." Hope had no idea what to say to make things right. "If thee are innocent, thee didn't deserve this."

"If." He repeated the syllable mockingly. "We were friends once. You might have trusted me farther."

Friends. It was a word that could imply so much or so little. Hope wasn't sure they had ever really been friends, not the way he and Elma had. "It was hard to—when thee acted so strangely."

"So you would too, if you were accused of murder." Their eyes locked. After a long moment, Levi said slowly, "You've made your amends. Now I've got the stage to catch, and I need to say farewell to my niece and nephew before I go. I need to explain to them why they won't ever see their uncle again."

Hope had been so busy grieving for Elma, she had never thought of what Levi had lost. He loved that niece and nephew of his; he had always been fashioning toys for them, speaking proudly of their exploits.

Hope's throat ached. "I wish you well in your journeys."

For a moment, she saw a glimpse of the old Levi beneath the bitter mask. "And you. You were always the best of them. If things had been different . . ."

The door of the house had opened, and Hope saw Ezra Weeks on the threshold, a child on his hip, the niece Levi might never see again.

"I'll leave thee to thy leave-taking," said Hope, and floundered off through the mud, before Ezra Weeks could send her away.

It had been so much simpler when she'd believed Levi guilty.

Now—Caty's husband had been exposed as an adulterer, Levi had been hounded out of the city. And Elma was still gone.

Back at the house, the door stuck. Elias's repairs had been no match for the April damp. Either the wood had swelled since he'd fixed it, or his repairs had been as clumsy as everything else he did.

Hope tugged at the panel until it finally gave with a long groan. Caty bustled into the hall, her face flushed from the fire, Eliza on her hip.

"Where has thee been? I've been half-distracted."

Hope wasn't going to lie. They'd had lies enough. "I went to the Weeks lumber yard to see Levi."

Caty heaved Eliza up higher. "Why would thee want to do that?"

"Did thee know he was leaving the city?"

"Good riddance," Caty said bitterly. "I shudder to think I ever indulged a favorable thought of him."

"Won't thee even consider the possibility that he might be innocent?"

"Was it innocent to try to get thee to sign a paper? Was it innocent for his brother to pay people to lie for him? All right, all right, I'll set thee down," she said to Eliza. Turning back to Hope, Caty said, "I know what I heard that night."

There was no use in arguing when Caty looked like that.

Caty had been obdurate in her conviction that Levi had killed Elma and got away with it by clever tricks in the courtroom. It was, Hope thought, just like Caty. If Levi had killed Elma, then it didn't matter as much about Elias. If Levi had killed Elma, then it didn't matter that Mr. Croucher still kept his room on the second floor, beneath the room where Levi had once slept.

Caty had always been very good at seeing the world as she wanted to see it. It was the same way she had insisted year after year that Elias was a genius just waiting for the world to appreciate him as she did, the way she insisted their father was a saint, and it was perfectly right for him to leave them for years at a time whenever the call to spread the word came upon him—which it usually did the moment things were unpleasant or difficult at home.

Hope had always prided herself on her clearheadedness. But she was beginning to wonder if the Levi she'd fancied herself in love with had ever existed, or if he had been as much a product of her imagination as Caty's Elias, a series of attributes grafted onto a handsome face and a pleasing manner.

Levi had been charming, that was true. And kind. He had always been kind. But it was the sort of kindness that took little effort on his part: a hand under her elbow to help her over a puddle, an invitation to go to the charity sermon.

All of it, the kindness, the charm, had dropped away

now, like the petals of a spring flower when the sun beat on it too hotly.

What she had taken for goodness had been only—an easy sort of complaisance. As the rest of the household settled into sleep, Hope lay awake, remembering how Levi had first flirted with Peggy, easygoing, laughing Peggy, who had made it clear she welcomed flirtation.

When Peggy had gone, Levi had walked out with Hope—but never more than honor. A pleasant way to pass the time, enjoying her obvious admiration.

And then there had been Elma. What had truly passed between them, Hope would never know, although she suspected that there, too, Levi would have taken whatever was offered.

There was that night his apprentice had seen him leave in his shirt and not come back until morning.

Whatever Levi said now, about what might have been had things been different, Hope knew, with sudden certainty, that he would never have married her. He would, in the end, have married a woman of his brother's choosing, not for love, but for advantage— and because his brother said so. He might even have persuaded himself he loved whoever it was, simply because that was easiest for everyone, but most particularly himself.

Could he have murdered Elma, if she complicated matters for him? If his brother told him so?

Hope wasn't sure. But she didn't think he had.

General Hamilton had made it clear that he thought Mr. Croucher had done it.

Outside her bedroom door, Hope heard a strange creak. Someone was going down the stairs, those stairs that had figured so largely in the trial, someone who was moving unevenly, who didn't know which steps creaked and which steps didn't.

Hope groped for the candle and flint next to her bed. All of Ezra Weeks's men had found other lodgings; even Peggy had gone. There was only Richard Van Alstine and Mr. Croucher, but Mr. Croucher spent his nights with his new bride, Mrs. Stackhaver, returning only by day to use his room as a space to display his wares for such clients as cared to come to the Ring boardinghouse.

Hope stepped silently down the closed stair in her bare feet, shading her candle with her hand. The door to the stair hung ajar; she could make out a pale figure struggling with the door, trying unsuccessfully to pull it open, her breath coming in labored, ragged gasps.

Dark hair hung down over her shoulders in wild disarray. It was a girl, but not one of Caty's girls.

"Hello?" said Hope, more curious than afraid.

The girl whirled, her back pressed against the door. Hope could see the whites of her eyes in the feeble light of the candle.

"Oh, Lord, I thought you were he. I thought you were he, come to get me. Please, please, for charity's sake, help me get away!"

"Away from whom?" There was something familiar about the girl, the thin, pale face beneath that disordered hair. As Hope stepped closer, she saw with horror that the girl's dress gaped open, the tie hanging drunkenly on one side, her shift torn. Reddish marks discolored the skin around her neck. "Did someone hurt thee?"

"He did," she whispered, her eyes lifting up, toward the stairs. She shook her head wildly, fumbling for the latch of the door. "No, no one. I only want to go home. Please, the door . . ."

"Thee are Mrs. Stackhaver's girl." Memory furnished Hope with an image of a skinny girl in that same calico dress and a white cap, standing behind the brocaded form of her mistress, sent to clean Mr. Croucher's room. Caty had been so angry. "What are thee doing here in the night?"

"He brought me here." The girl wrapped her arms around herself, making herself as small as she could. "I wouldn't have come if I'd known he meant to— He said there was a lady and gentleman coming to look at some linens he had and he wanted me to come and scrub his room for him."

"In the night?" Hope took a cautious step closer. As the small light of her candle reached the girl, she could see more bruises on her wrists, her shoulders.

The girl flinched back, away from the light. "I didn't know— He told my mamma I could sleep with a servant girl here so I could get started scrubbing early in the morning."

"Your mamma?"

"Mrs. Stackhaver—she adopted me. He wants her to get rid of me, they've no need of me now, unless I prove I can earn my keep. I only was here to scrub the room!" Her voice rose in incipient hysteria.

"Hush, hush. It's all right," said Hope nonsensically, since it clearly wasn't all right.

"I didn't know!" the girl repeated. "He took me upstairs to a room in the third story. He told me the servant girl would come and sleep with me and then he locked the door, and took me and undressed me and put me on the bed—"

Tears were streaming down her face.

"Thee poor child!" Hope hurried toward her, her mind working furiously. "It's Mr. Croucher thee speak of?"

"Yes—no—I never meant— Oh, pray—pray don't say I said!" The girl's voice rose again, the words coming out in a bubble of hiccups and snot.

"What is all this?" The door on the other side of the stair opened and Caty came out, wearing her shift with a shawl about her shoulders, squinting in the light of Hope's candle. "Hope? And who is this?"

Hope put her arm protectively around the girl, who shrank at her touch but didn't push her away. Her bones felt like twigs. In a flat, hard undertone, she said, "This is Mrs. Stackhaver's girl. Mr. Croucher took her here and robbed her of her virtue."

"Robbed her—"

"He took her upstairs and took her to bed—against her will. We need to go to the constable—now! While he sleeps. We need to go to the constable and bring him up on charges."

"No!" The girl yanked away from Hope. "No! You mustn't! You mustn't tell! I only want to go home, please let me go home. . . ."

"No one is going to the constable," said Caty soothingly. "Come, I'll get thee a warm posset and wash thee and thee can go home."

"A warm posset?" demanded Hope indignantly. "He raped her! Look at her! She looks younger than Rachel!"

"That's why," said Caty, in a low voice. "If she complains of him, the taint will follow her. . . ."

"She did nothing wrong!" Hope whirled back toward the girl. "If thee won't go to the police, go to Mr. Colden, the attorney general. He's a kind man. He'll listen to thee."

The girl shrank back, her face transformed with blank terror. "I can't."

"I'll go with thee if thee like," said Hope. "Thee needn't go alone. I will stand with thee."

"No!" The girl's eyes were dark holes in her white face. "I can't tell him. I can't tell anyone. I wouldn't have told you if—if you hadn't been here."

"But if thee go home, won't *he* be there? What if he attempts thee again?" Hope burned at the thought of that creature upstairs abusing this poor child. She wanted to whisk her away and make her safe—and see that Croucher hanged. "Won't thee at least tell thy mistress?"

"I can't! I can't tell anyone." The girl's back hit the wood of the door. With nowhere left to go, she looked from Hope to Caty. "He said—he said if I told anyone, he would do to me what was done to Elma Sands."

Chapter Thirty-Five

Quite lately I heard Croucher say he did not like her and she should not stay in the house, she was a very bad girl, and he was not going to keep a bad girl in the house; he was sure he said that she was a bad girl, he could prove it, *he knew it himself.* Then he said she was a *whore* and he could prove it. He had lain with her one night himself. He said he had heard she was a bad girl, and he was determined to know if it was so, and therefore he had lain with her one night and was satisfied it was so.

—From the trial of Richard D. Croucher
for the rape of Margaret Miller

New York City
July 8, 1800

"He used force. He did what he would, and hurt me very much, so much that I could hardly get home the next morning."

Tears streamed down Margaret Miller's thin face, the words coming out in disjointed gasps. The jury strained forward to try to catch the words. Cadwallader stood by her, trying to signal support by his very presence. It had taken some doing to get her on the stand at all; at the sight of Richard Croucher in the dock she had backed away, and it had taken Cadwallader some time to soothe her enough to get her to take her oath.

On the other side of the room, Brockholst Livingston leaned back in his chair, his arms folded across his chest, listening with a marked air of disbelief.

Brockholst had been victorious at the polls in May; Cadwallader had gone down to defeat. It was very clear Brockholst expected another easy victory today.

He'd done it before. Several years back, Livingston had won a famous—or infamous, depending on whom one asked—rape case for Henry Bedlow against Lanah Sawyer. The city had cried guilty; a civil court ruled Bedlow guilty. But Livingston, employing all his formidable powers of persuasion, had brought in a verdict of not guilty in the criminal case.

Not this time, Cadwallader swore. Not this time. This girl deserved justice. Elma Sands deserved justice. He caught sight of Maria sitting in the front row of the gallery, and her calm gaze lent him strength.

"Did you cry out and make a noise when he hurt you?"

"At first I screamed, but he said if I did not hold my tongue, he would kill me." Margaret scrubbed the tears away from her eyes, casting a fearful glance at the man in the dock. "I cried all the time, but not loud. I was afraid to."

"Was the injury repeated on you more than once that night?"

"Yes, sir, three times."

Cadwallader had learned his lesson. No elaborate theories. No scores of witnesses. Just Margaret Miller, and then two neighbors, who testified as to the girl's fear of her new stepfather—and that he'd called her a whore and sworn he'd had her.

Unlike Elma Sands, this victim was here, and able to speak for herself. The way she shrank from Croucher spoke more eloquently than any address Cadwallader might have given.

"Gentlemen." Brockholst strode to the center of the room. "No crime excites greater abhorrence or indignation than the one with which the prisoner stands charged. But—if anything of an improper nature has passed between them, I am inclined to believe that it has been with her consent. The passions may be as warm in a girl of her age as in one of more advanced years, and with very little enticement, she may have consented to become his mistress."

Cadwallader looked at Margaret Miller, skinny, flat-chested, her hair in braids, a schoolgirl who looked far younger than her actual age.

Brockholst waved a hand at his client. "You perceive the disadvantages under which the prisoner labors. The party injured is herself the principal witness—but when once it is known that a girl has had a connection with a man, there is instantly a strong bias in her own mind, and in those of her relations, that it should be proved to be done by violence. So strong indeed is the temptation to give it this color, that it is hardly possible for a girl so situated to tell the truth."

Brockholst addressed the jury man-to-man, his tone knowing, indulgent. They all knew, he seemed to imply, exactly what had gone on.

"I am not defending the conduct of that man. I will suppose he is guilty of having most shamefully seduced and ruined the girl, but seduction is not rape."

Seduction. The girl had been scarcely able to walk for two weeks after Croucher's assault.

"Gentlemen of the jury." Cadwallader could feel the anger throbbing through him. No carefully crafted speeches this time, no labored hunts through law books for precedents with which Brockholst would only quibble. Fury lent him eloquence. "This girl, finding this man paying addresses to her mother, looks on him as a father. Without hesitation she agrees to go to his lodgings, to sleep with a girl in the house—she is seduced into his room—he undresses her and treats her with violence—she calls for help—then he threatens to murder her if she does not desist, or if she ever makes a discovery of his guilt. Loose, unbuttoned, and ready for violation, with a diabolical countenance rendered ghastly by infernal lust, he lays his merciless hands upon her. She was almost torn asunder."

He paused, giving the jury time to consider that, to look at Margaret Miller, hardly a creature of unbridled lust, only a child, a vulnerable child.

It made Cadwallader sick to think of what she had endured—and all the worse for knowing that it might have been avoided. If he had fixed on Croucher as the murderer of Elma Sands, instead of pursuing Levi Weeks, if he had seen Croucher hanged, this girl would be even now at school instead of on the stand, a hunted, haunted thing.

You couldn't have known, Maria had told him.

Cadwallader looked at the jury. "It is worth remarking that a trial for murder which lately took place in this city made a strong impression on the mind of this child. She knew that the accusation was that a woman was cruelly murdered. She had learned the particulars of that trial *from the prisoner*. Is it any wonder his threats to put her away acted powerfully on her mind?"

In the dock, Richard Croucher shifted uneasily. Cadwallader remembered his lies, his gloating, his mock concern for Elma. He wasn't gloating now. He turned to murmur something to his counsel. Brockholst shook his head.

Cadwallader gestured forcibly toward Margaret. "Her age—her size—her sufferings—her appearance before you—her tears here—the very appearance of the prisoner—forbid you to believe that she could ever have consented to his embraces."

In his capacity as recorder, Richard Harison stood and addressed the jury. "The prisoner at the bar stands indicted for the commission of a rape upon Margaret Miller. The court cannot with propriety charge you, gentlemen, whether you ought or ought not to give credit to the principal witness, that is certainly your province. If upon the whole you think her worthy of credibility, you must say the prisoner at the bar is guilty. If otherwise, you are bound to acquit him."

The jury filed out, some pausing to cast last looks over their shoulder at Margaret or Croucher.

Had they been swayed by Brockholst's argument? Cadwallader hoped not. This wasn't just about justice for Margaret. It was for the shades of Elma Sands and Rose Malone.

The door opened. The jury jostled back in, not looking at the prisoner. They had been gone no longer than it took them to leave and come back again.

They had returned quickly in the Weeks case too—with a verdict of not guilty.

Cadwallader looked anxiously at Maria. When this was over, whatever happened, they were going away together, the three of them, as a family. He'd take her to London and Bath and Brighton. . . . Or possibly France. They could go to Paris and David could make friends with French donkeys in the Jardin des Tuileries.

Harison addressed the foreman. "How do you find the defendant? Guilty or not guilty?"

The foreman looked at Richard Croucher and then back at the judges, before pronouncing one word.

"Guilty."

Chapter Thirty-Six

The prisoner being brought to the bar to receive his sentence, the Recorder, in the presence of a large number of people, addressed him in the following words: RICHARD D. CROUCHER, you have been convicted, after a full impartial trial, of an offense of the most detestable nature. . . .

—From the trial of Richard D. Croucher
for the rape of Margaret Miller

New York City
July 8, 1800

"May it please the court, I have no complaint to make of Your Honors or the jury—I have no doubt I deserve punishment for my conduct—but I swear, the girl's words are all lies!"

Richard Croucher wasn't elegant now. Hope could just see from the back of the crowded, sweltering courtroom as he made a break from the dock, his cravat askew, his hair coming out of its queue. His lawyer grabbed him by the arm before he could fling himself at the bench.

Margaret Miller cried out, shrinking back. Hope would have fought her way to her—she still felt responsible; this girl had been injured in a room just upstairs from her while Hope, unwitting, had stewed over Levi Weeks below—but Mr. Colden stepped in front of Margaret, shielding her with his body.

"I never knew her!" Thwarted, Croucher pointed a finger at Margaret Miller, his whole body shaking with fear and fury. "I never had any connection with that girl!"

Mr. Harison rose from the bench, his face as stony as the cliffs above New Cornwall. "It is too late now to make protestations of this sort. Your declaration, sir, is contradicted by your own repeated confessions."

Croucher glared at Colden, at Margaret Miller, at the jury. "They've twisted my words—it's lies!"

Harison raised his voice, drowning out the prisoner's angry cries. "A jury of this country have pronounced you guilty. In several other countries a conviction of this kind would be followed by an ignominious death, but the humanity of the modern code, of this country, has instead determined that you be confined in the state prison for life. The court think themselves bound to add that it be to hard labor. You may count yourself fortunate."

When Mr. Harison said Mr. Croucher might count himself fortunate, everyone in the room knew it wasn't just Croucher's avoiding execution for the rape of Margaret Miller he was talking about.

Mr. Colden had said it out loud. A trial for murder which lately took place in this city. A trial which might have tried the wrong man.

Maybe it was for the best, Hope told herself doubtfully. Maybe Mr. Croucher would suffer more with his skin cracked and calloused, in sweat-soaked homespun that chafed his skin to sores, and lice crawling through his dirt-encrusted hair, than he would with a swift and merciful death at the end of a rope.

They couldn't prove he had killed Elma.

"Constables, take him away and see him conveyed to the state prison."

Hope watched Croucher herded from the room, pinioned between two constables. It was justice of sorts, even if not the justice they'd wanted. At least Margaret Miller had got to see her assailant punished.

It was better, Hope thought, than having a warm posset and pretending it never happened, as Caty had recommended.

Outside, the weather had turned. The day that had begun fair had turned uncomfortably sultry. Men of business hurrying their way down Broadway turned doubtful looks to the sky, which had developed the haze that heralded a summer storm. Hope's linen shift stuck clammily to her skin. A good storm would wash away the summer stench and the corruption in the streets. But summer rains also brought with them mud—and the fever.

Hope hastened her pace as the leaves of the enormous tree outside the Verplanck mansion began to shake ominously in the rising wind. She wasn't the only one; all around her, carters were urging on their mules and women with shopping baskets on their arms hurried their steps.

In the house, a fire burned in the hearth despite the heat, rendering the kitchen unbearable. Hope found Caty in the garden, resolutely weeding a row of peas, although her gown was patched with sweat and her hair hung limp beneath her cap. In the corner of the garden, by the fence, Rachel was helping little Eliza pick the first of the gooseberries, showing her how to squeeze them for ripeness and trying to get her to put them in the basket instead of her mouth.

Hope stumbled to a stop just beside her sister. The walls of the Watkins house and the Forrest house seemed to press against her, making the tiny garden feel even smaller than usual. The swollen clouds turned the sky an unpleasant orange and gray. The air was thick with smoke and the refuse of a thousand households.

Caty didn't look up from her weeding. "I won't ask where thee have been."

"I was at the courthouse." As Caty well knew. Hope had told her at breakfast where she meant to be. "They convicted him. Mr. Croucher. Mr. Colden had him convicted for the rape of Margaret Miller."

"Not in front of the children!" Caty cast a quick look at her daughters. "I don't see why thee had to go."

Hope lowered her voice, so her nieces wouldn't hear, although she suspected Rachel knew already. Rachel saw more than Caty imagined. "It happened just upstairs from me. If I had heard anything earlier that night, I might have stopped it." It was more than that. "If we hadn't been so set against Levi—"

"Are thee going to stand there gossiping all day? There's work to be done. If thy hands be idle, thee can take the berries in to boil."

"The jury didn't debate more than a minute. They knew Mr. Croucher for what he is." Unlike Hope and Caty and Elias. "He's to be sent to prison for the rest of his life."

Caty yanked at a weed, shaking dirt from the stem. "It's nice there's justice for some."

"For Elma too."

Caty straightened painfully, pressing her hands against the small of her back. "If there were justice for Elma, Levi would be in the graveyard and not in Massachusetts."

"If thee had been in court today, Caty—" Watching Richard Croucher in the courtroom, without his silks and brocades, was like peeling back the skin of a fine red apple to see the rot and worms within; he had stunk of corruption. In the witness stand he'd been bold; in the dock, he was a craven, crawling thing. "He's the very devil beneath that finery. Thee would have known, from his countenance alone."

Caty snorted. "What can one tell from a countenance? Levi's was pleasing enough, and look what was beneath it! There's no denying Mr. Croucher is an unpleasant man—"

"Unpleasant?" He'd raped a girl in their house and threatened to kill her if she told. Hope had seen her bruises.

"—and thee knows I didn't want Elias to go into business with Mr. Croucher and I never thought he was of good character, but that's nothing to what Levi did to us. If thee needs look for a devil, thee need look no farther than Levi." Caty folded her arms across her chest, daring Hope to contradict her.

Hope set her chin, feeling her temper rising. "Doesn't it seem strange to thee to think we harbored *two* devils beneath this roof?"

"Our father wouldn't wonder at it. Thee knows he thinks the world is thick with sinners, and nowhere more than here. Except perhaps Philadelphia," Caty added after a moment.

Hope wasn't going to be lured into a discussion of their father's grudge against Philadelphia. "Thee cannot expunge what happened by blaming Levi," she said, in a hard, low voice.

Caty set down her spade. "Does thee think I don't blame myself?"

"Yes, but for the wrong things!"

Over and over again, Caty lamented how she'd been bamboozled by Levi, how she had been fooled by his charm, how she ought never have let him court Elma, should never have let Elma leave with him that night . . . conveniently ignoring what the whole city knew, that her own husband had debauched Elma and then conspired with the man who might have been Elma's killer to hide his shame.

They might never know what happened to Elma

that night, but they knew what had happened to Margaret Miller, here, in this house.

How did Caty not see?

The humidity and the heat and the tension made Hope feel like she was about to burst out of her own skin. She needed to get away from this house, from Elias skulking in corners, half-ashamed, half-defiant; from Caty, working like a fury so she'd never have to stop and think; from the ghosts of Elma and Levi, which stalked Hope through the corridors of the sprawling, unhappy house. They were living a half-life, all of them, in this mockery of a garden in which only the hardiest plants survived.

At home, her mother's garden would be bursting with young lettuce and woolly sage leaves, bean vines twined around staves, the exuberant tops of carrots pushing up through the earth. In the woods, the wild raspberries would have turned from fuzz to orange buds, working their way to ripening.

Hope looked at her sister. "I'm going home to Cornwall."

"In August, when the fever season starts," Caty agreed, seizing on the change of subject with relief. "Thee can take the children for me."

"Not just for the fever season, Caty." The city had too many memories, some of them good, too many of them tainted. "Thee could come with me, with the children."

"Thee knows what happened last time I left." There was no mistaking the bitterness in Caty's voice, although she quickly put it aside again. "Elias needs me here, to help him manage."

"Close the boardinghouse," said Hope recklessly. "Why stay here after what happened? It's enough, Caty. Let's go home."

"What would we do in Cornwall, to earn our keep? We'd only be more mouths to feed." Caty tried futilely to brush the dirt from her hands. "Thee weren't to know. Mother didn't want to alarm thee, but Father—it's only right he has no time to spare for worldly things. It's not the house—we still have the house—but the rest of it, the land and the farms and the rents, he's had to deed them away to pay his debts."

"All of it?" Their grandfather had left their father a wealthy man.

"Before he left for England." Caty was wringing her hands in her agitation. "Mother does her best—but it would be hard on her if we all came home."

Last summer, Hope had been distracted daydreaming about the handsome carpenter back in Greenwich Street. Home was home, as familiar and comfortable as a pair of well-worn shoes. If the oatmeal had been thinner or the stew more vegetable than meat, she hadn't noticed. There was a great deal Hope hadn't noticed. Hope vowed to herself that she wasn't going to make that mistake again.

"She should have told me! Thee both should have told me! I have hands and a will!" Hope was sick of people protecting her, of all the well-meaning lies. Or not-so-well-meaning lies. "All the more reason to go back! Thee know I'm not afraid of work."

"Would thee trim hats for the women of New Cornwall?" Caty grimaced at her, looking almost like her old self, the sister Hope remembered before Elias.

"We could run a boardinghouse," Hope suggested. "The old house is large enough."

"Who would come to Cornwall?"

"All the folks fleeing the fever." As she said it, Hope could see the possibilities in it. "We could run a boardinghouse by summer and trim hats by winter. I've never seen thee fail at anything thee put thy mind to. And think of the children! Think how happy they are there." Hope saw Caty glance over her shoulder at the girls, and knew she was winning. "Leave Elias here in the city; let him manage however he likes."

That had been a mistake. Caty's face closed. She

shook her head. "My place is here. If thee truly wish to go, I'll send thee with my blessing. And I'll send the children to thee in August."

Hope grasped her sister's hands, dirt and all. "Come thyself."

"Perhaps." Hope knew that meant no. Caty clung to Hope in a quick, fierce hug. "I'll come when I can. Will thee—will thee tell Aunt Lizzy I'm sorry? For not taking better care. Of Elma."

"She knows." It wasn't just Caty's fault; it was all of them. Hope blamed herself as well. "But I'll tell her all the same."

"Thee aren't leaving us?" Rachel's small, anxious face looked up at her, too old for her age.

"If thee would only wait another month . . ." Caty suggested.

The wind had turned, bringing with it the reek of the glue manufactory, boiling down hides and bones to be sent to the cabinetmakers and printers, transforming dying animals hauled to the outer edges of the city into elegant tables and learned tomes to adorn the brick houses on Broadway. Beautiful, yes, but Hope knew too much now about what went into them to admire them as she used to.

Elma had died not far from the glue manufactory, her life boiled down into so much ink for the papers.

They'd had such dreams, Hope and Elma, of what their lives in the city would be, how grand they'd become, how sophisticated. Hope could feel Elma beside her, there, in the narrow garden, leaning close to whisper, *When I am married, you will come to me and wear silk and eat iced cakes.*

As soon as Hope got home, after she embraced her mother and Aunt Lizzy, she would go out into the meadow and weave a crown of summer flowers, of scarlet paintbrush and fireweed, of queen of the prairie and Turk's-cap, a chaplet for Elma.

That was how she would remember Elma. Not broken on a wooden settle, not flattened into a scandalmonger's morality tale, but with her head ablaze with wildflowers, crowned by her own hands.

"I'm not leaving thee," said Hope firmly, leaning over to kiss her niece's head. "Only going ahead a little while. I'll be waiting for thee in Cornwall."

Epilogue
What became of them after?

Levi Weeks's reputation as a murderer followed him to Massachusetts. Hounded out of first one town and then another, Levi wandered from South Deerfield, Massachusetts, to Cincinnati to Marietta, Ohio, to Lexington, Kentucky, before eventually settling in Natchez, Mississippi, where he found success as a cabinetmaker and architect and married a girl twenty years his junior, with whom he had four children before dying of an unspecified illness at the age of forty-three.

Whether Levi was happy in his exile is another question entirely. In a revealing letter to his brother written in 1812, Levi describes life in parts of Ohio and

Kentucky as "a life of penance" and refers to various of his fellow Natchez citizens as "a great horde of vagabonds."

Elias Ring and his wife, Catherine, had six more children together, but Elias took to heavy drinking. In 1816, he was expelled from the Society of Friends "for the continued intemperate use of intoxicating spirits," despite having been "tenderly labored with for a considerable time." Elias died of yellow fever in Mobile, Alabama, in 1823.

Catherine Ring and her children eventually returned to her hometown of New Cornwall, New York, where Catherine turned her childhood home into a summer boardinghouse known fondly as Rose Cottage. She lived to eighty-three, known for her good works and for the book she wrote about her father, the Quaker preacher David Sands. Local lore recalls Catherine Sands proudly coming to church on Sundays trailed by no fewer than twenty-nine grandchildren.

Hope Sands also returned to New Cornwall. In 1804, she married Charles Newbold, a New Jersey–born inventor who held the patent for a cast iron plow and predicted that someday "man would travel through the air and under water." By all accounts, they had a long and happy life together. Newbold died in 1835; Hope in 1871.

Richard Croucher was convicted of the rape of Margaret Miller on the eighth of July, 1800. Sentenced to life imprisonment, Croucher was granted a pardon on the condition that he emigrate. Instead, Croucher made his way to Virginia, where he again fell afoul of the law, this time for fraud. Exiled to his native England, Croucher was convicted and hanged for "a heinous crime."

Legend has it that Catherine Ring cursed the members of the defense team and the chief justice. The so-called Quaker's Curse took its time and its effects were felt unequally.

Aaron Burr famously shot **Alexander Hamilton** in a duel in 1804, killing his rival and his own political career. After his brief moment of glory as vice president, Burr lurched from tragedy to tragedy: in 1807, he was tried for treason; in 1813, his beloved daughter, Theodosia Burr Alston, disappeared after the shipwreck of the schooner *Patriot*, her fate still unknown. Burr lived in exile and penury, eventually returning to New York and attempting to recoup his fortunes by marrying the wealthy widow Eliza Jumel.

Jumel divorced him in 1834—hiring Alexander Hamilton Jr. as her lawyer.

Brockholst Livingston, however, appears to have evaded the Quaker's Curse. He not only survived but thrived. In 1807, he was appointed to the Supreme Court, where law students will forever remember him as the author of the idiosyncratic dissent in *Pierson v. Post*.

Justice Lansing, who delivered the charge to the jury dismissing the prosecution's evidence, became the subject of another unsolved crime. In December 1829, he was staying at the City Hotel in New York. He left to meet a friend for tea—and was never seen again. Did he drown? Was he murdered? Theories have abounded over the years, but, like Elma Sands's murder, there is no real proof.

Cadwallader Colden rose above his early defeats in both the courtroom and the polls to enjoy a distinguished career in law and public service. Pleading poor health, he took his family on an eighteen-month tour of Europe. Returning refreshed, he went on to serve as president of the New York Manumission Society, mayor of New York, a member of the New York State Senate, and a powerful proponent of canals. (Law students will note that Cadwallader Colden argued for the defense in *Pierson v. Post*. He lost—although Brockholst, in his dissent, took Colden's part.)

Elma Sands was buried in the Friends Burying Ground. In death, as in life, Elma remains elusive. The well where Elma was murdered still exists, beneath the basement of a clothing boutique at 129 Spring Street, but the Friends Burying Ground does not. Since Quakers did not believe in the use of headstones, when the bodies were moved and reinterred in the nineteenth century, the exact location of Elma's bones was lost. The murder of Elma Sands has never been conclusively solved.

Historical Note

On December 22, 1799, Elma Sands walked out of her cousin's boardinghouse at 208 Greenwich Street and never came back.

What happened to Elma Sands that night? Did she leave with Levi Weeks—or moments before him? Did the door close once or twice? Had she really planned to marry Levi Weeks that night or was that just a story her family spread to avert attention from the real culprit? Over the past two hundred years, the Manhattan Well murder has become a game of telephone, with stories being told and retold, often well removed from the original sources. Elma's murder had already drifted into legend within days after Elma's body was found, with Elizabeth De Hart Bleecker gleefully reporting misinformation in her diary and newspapers writing articles about the murder of "Julianna" Sands. With an additional two hundred years for the story to circulate, the layers of myth, legend, and misinformation have become even more confusing.

The historian, or historical novelist, attempting to claw her way back through those layers of myth does have one powerful weapon at her disposal: Coleman's transcript of the trial. Over the two long days of the trial, Coleman took down the testimony of dozens of witnesses as close to verbatim as he could, a feat made possible by his use of Byrom's *Universal English Shorthand*. The transcript runs to nearly a hundred pages, and while there are certainly discrepancies and omissions, it is an invaluable resource, providing us with a strong sense of the voices and characters of the participants. The only voice—aside from Elma's—we do not get to hear is that of Levi Weeks. Defendants did not speak in their own case. Levi's character and actions, like Elma's, are left to be inferred from the testimony of the various witnesses.

Two other accounts were published in the days immediately following the trial: James Hardie's *An Impartial Account of the Trial of Mr. Levi Weeks for the Supposed Murder of Miss Julianna Elmore Sands* and *A Brief Narrative of the Trial for the Bloody and Mysterious Murder of the Unfortunate Young Woman in the Famous Manhattan Well, Taken in Shorthand by a Gentleman of the Bar*, both considerably less thorough, with a great deal of editorializing. They make a useful cross-reference (it can be instructive to compare the differences among the three accounts), but it is really Coleman's transcript that provides the basis for any work on the Manhattan Well murder. Over the centuries, historians, journalists, and, most recently, bloggers have continued to rake through the same evidence that was presented to the jury on March 31 and April 1, 1800, trying to determine who murdered Elma Sands. One of Hamilton's biographers pointed the finger at Catherine Ring, the woman scorned. Others, including the most recent book about the case, Paul Collins's *Duel with the Devil*, incline toward Richard Croucher as Elma's assailant. Some, like Catherine Ring's granddaughter Keturah Connah, who wrote a novel based on the case, imaginatively titled *Guilty or Not Guilty: The True Story of the Manhattan Well*, felt strongly that Levi Weeks was just as guilty as the indictment claimed, escaping justice only due to the brilliance of his legal team.

Most analyses of the case, whatever their conclusion, share one striking characteristic: none bother to look closely at the background, emotions, motives, and character of the murdered woman. When writing about this case, it is all too easy to get swept up in the tactics and techniques of the flamboyant lawyers who argued for the defense—and ignore the woman at the heart of it. With all that has been written about the Manhattan Well murder over the years, remarkably little effort has been made to get the details right on Elma's parentage and childhood. Some works erroneously refer to Elma's uncle, the Quaker luminary David Sands, as her grandfather or even her father. Catherine Ring gets mislabeled as Elma's sister or her aunt. As for Elma herself, the various articles and books written about the trial tend to flatten her into archetypes: the Madonna or the whore. An innocent cruelly seduced and betrayed—or a laudanum-addicted nymphomaniac. Even Elma's name gets muddled in the retelling, with some referring to her as Julianna Elmore Sands rather than Gulielma.

Who was Elma Sands? That, I believe, ought to be the question at the heart of any discussion of this case. Attempting to find Elma is complicated by the absence of her own voice: we hear of her through the conflicting narratives of the prosecution and defense, each determined to present a specific Elma as it bears on the guilt or innocence of Levi Weeks. Even so, one starts to get a sense of Elma through the testimony of her family: "rather too gay for a Friend," her cousin Catherine calls her, although she hastily adds that Elma had modified her dress and tone to please her. Someone who teases Levi about his never asking her anywhere—and then refuses to go with him. Someone who borrows handkerchiefs without asking, because she doesn't mean to use them anyway.

I did my best to dig into Elma's background to discover the forces that shaped her. Pieces about the case often carelessly refer to her as a Quaker, raised in the home of her grandfather, the Quaker preacher David Sands. In fact, Elma, who refused to join the Quaker meeting, was the illegitimate niece of David Sands, who, as a young man, experienced a profound conversion to the Quaker faith, married the daughter of a prominent Quaker family, and founded the Cornwall Meeting in his bemused Presbyterian parents' home in New Cornwall, New York. Sands's parents and some (but not all) of his siblings converted, possibly out of conviction, and possibly because the meeting was being run out of their front room. (That house, the Sands-Ring Homestead, is now a museum.)

Sands's daughter Catherine described his ministry as having "a searching, awakening character," during which, "in the ardor of his soul to warn men against placing their affections unduly upon sublunary objects, it was not unusual for him to express himself in language which some undiscriminating hearers regarded as prophetic," but which we might call *hellfire and brimstone*. "The handwriting upon the wall is found upon all your pleasant walks, beautiful trees, fine gardens, lofty buildings, and pleasant streets . . . yea, all these things become a ruinous heap and some of you be buried in the midst of them, for . . . what sins were there committed at Sodom that are not committed here?" Such worldliness invited divine retribution. "And some of you have become vessels of wrath and displeasure in the hand of an offended God, may be swallowed up in holds in the earth, part of your bodies in and part out of it and above ground for examples or warnings to those who may see it."

Elma was born in 1777, the child of David's sister Elizabeth, who was fifteen years younger than her brother. Elizabeth Sands was sixteen when she fell pregnant with Elma. Was it a love affair? A rape? The sources are silent. We do know from the trial testimony that in 1800 Elma's father was alive, living in Charleston, and had never married her mother, but the sources never provide his name or the circumstances under which Elma was conceived. If one works on the assumption that there was, in fact, a father in Charleston (rather than that being a story to hide culpability closer to home), it seems possible that Elma's father was a soldier in one of the regiments that passed through Cornwall during the early days of the Revolutionary War.

As for Elma's name, Gulielma was the name of William Penn's wife. One wonders if Elma's teenage mother was trying to appease her outraged older brother by naming her illegitimate daughter after that pillar of the Quaker faith, but that, like so much about Elma's past, is pure speculation. If so, it didn't work. Around the same time as his sister's pregnancy began to show, David Sands felt a call to minister to the heathens of New England. He was not to return for two years and seven months, leaving his wife to cope with their small children, a pregnant sister-in-law, and angry Revolutionary soldiers who harassed the women of the Sands household as suspected loyalists. (Upon being informed of the plight of his family, David Sands's pious wish was that "the Shepherd of Israel . . . will be a father to my beloved infant children, and as a husband to thee, seeing he has ordered our separation in this trying season.")

Elma's childhood was marked by alternating periods of absence and intervention from the head of the household. When Elma was two, her uncle returned and, in addition to hosting the Cornwall Meeting, made a short-lived attempt at running a store out of his parents' house. When Elma was six, the store was robbed. David Sands escaped and ran for help while his wife was held up at bayonet-point by six soldiers. After that, he was off again, resuming his travels in New England and the mid-Atlantic, with intermittent periods at home, before succumbing to the call to visit the brethren in England in 1794. (His desire to preach abroad may have been spurred by his debts, which were considerable, leading to the deeding away of most of the family's property.) He was still abroad during the time of his niece's murder, returning in 1805, five years after Elma's death. There is no mention of Elma or her fate in his correspondence. For anyone who wishes to know more about Sands and his ministry, I recommend Catherine Ring's biography of her father, *The Journal of the Life and Gospel Labors of David Sands*.

This was the household in which Elma was raised, the illegitimate child of a disgraced sinner sister, in which the women mostly managed for themselves but were subject to the whims and rule of the peripatetic paterfamilias. We know from the trial testimony that Elma was fond of bright colors and fancy trimmings, all the snares of the world that David Sands so vehemently condemned. Despite her upbringing, Elma resisted all attempts to bring her to meeting. She was not, as Catherine admitted at the trial, a Friend, "though we wished her to be." If anything emerges of Elma from the testimony of her relations, it is that she was a woman of remarkably strong character, with something of a contrary streak.

In 1796, Elma left the Sands household in New Cornwall, where her mother still lived as an unmarried dependent, and joined her married cousin Catherine in Manhattan. The oldest of the children of David Sands and Clementine Hallock, seventeen-year-old Catherine had married thirty-one-year-old Elias Ring in 1790 in the first marriage at the new meetinghouse that the Sands family had been instrumental in building (legend has it that teenage Catherine set out alone on horseback to fetch the necessary nails). After a failed business venture in Dutchess County, they settled on Greenwich Street, where Catherine ran a millinery and boardinghouse while Elias opened a short-lived dry goods store and pushed his patent waterwheel, ads for which ran in the New York and Philadelphia papers from 1797 to 1799.

Elma's first two years with the Ring family appear to have been without incident. But in the summer of 1799, two momentous events occurred: in July, Levi Weeks came to board at 208 Greenwich Street, and in August, yellow fever struck New York. With the fever rampaging through the city, Catherine Ring whisked her sister Hope and her four young children to New Cornwall in September 1799, leaving Elma as substitute chatelaine in her absence. According to the testimony, Elma filled in for her cousin in more ways than one. The neighbors Joseph and Elizabeth Watkins attested to hearing the sound of the marriage bed through the wall, and a voice that they swore was Elias's rather than Levi's. One might argue that this was a trumped-up charge—Ezra Weeks, Levi's brother, wasn't above paying people off, and, as an ironmonger, Watkins might have relied on Ezra Weeks's custom. Weeks's building projects required a great number of nails.

Two things militate against that, the lesser of which is that Watkins was a settled, prosperous man, not a desperate man likely to commit perjury for a bribe. More convincing, however, is what my graduate school Practice of History professor, the legendary Bernard Bailyn, called "accidental evidence," the details people accidentally drop when they believe they are saying something else. If one reads the trial testimony carefully, with an eye to that accidental evidence, it becomes clear that by November and December 1799, there was something not right between Elma and Elias Ring. Again and again, if Elias enters a room,

Elma exits it. When Elma thinks Elias has come in, she steps behind a screen—but emerges when she discovers it is only Levi.

The defense team made much of Elma's threat to drink a whole bottle of laudanum, arguing that she was a melancholy laudanum addict set on self-slaughter. But in both accounts we have of that event, it is very clear that the scene Elma is playing is directed at Elias Ring. Elma puts the vial to her mouth; Elias tells her not to do so; Elma says, "I should not be afraid to drink it whole," to which Elias replies, "Why, foolish creature, it would kill thee," and Elma shoots back, "I should not be afraid." The entire episode reads not as the sign of an opium addiction but as a struggle of wills between Elma and Elias, in which Elma taunts Elias with her misery.

A woman scorned? Possibly. But I believe there was more to it than that. In mid-September, the Watkinses hear the sounds of sexual activity through the wall. In late October, Catherine returns, and Levi hustles Elma off to the docks to visit friends in the country for two weeks, even though it is no longer the season for such visits and Elma is described as reluctant to go. At some point in November, Elma returns, and in late November or early December (the exact timing is unclear from the transcript) has an illness involving cramping of the stomach so sudden and severe that Levi fears for her life, but Catherine refuses to call the doctor.

Whether the baby—if there was a baby—was Elias's or Levi's we have no way of knowing. We also have no way of knowing whether Elma suffered an inadvertent miscarriage or ingested one of the abortifacients used by women to treat "menstrual obstruction" (aka pregnancy), such as gum of guaiacum, savin, or pennyroyal. Given the Watkins testimony and Elma's charged interactions with Elias in the fall of 1799, I would be willing to wager on Elma's having lost Elias's baby, either by accident or by design.

Of course, there is no solid proof of any of this. There were no bright-line pregnancy tests in 1799, and the only people who could tell us what happened in Elma's room that night that Catherine refused to call the doctor are Elma Sands and Catherine Ring. But the timeline is highly suggestive. Catherine refers at one point to Elma having been much troubled with stomach cramps for some time, but the testimony of all of the other witnesses indicates a one-off crisis. One recent book about the murder chose to portray Elma as prone to melancholy and the odd tipple of laudanum because that was just the way she was by nature, moody and addictive. I find it far more likely that Elma, a woman of strong will with a sharp tongue, described almost universally as lively, was reeling from the emotional blow of rejection and the physical blow of a miscarriage. All accounts of laudanum date solely to that last month before Elma's death. I find it particularly telling that the only boarder to find Elma melancholy was a man who resided in the boardinghouse only during those last few weeks. Understanding Elma is key to understanding what happened that night at the Manhattan Well.

While "who was Elma?" was the largest blank in the record, there were other unexpected gaps in the narrative that needed to be filled. One of the biggest mysteries about Levi Weeks's trial—aside from who actually killed Elma—is why Alexander Hamilton joined the defense team. It makes perfect sense that Ezra Weeks would retain Brockholst Livingston and Aaron Burr. Brockholst had a brilliant record as a criminal defense attorney. Burr, although less experienced in criminal law, might well have been in debt to Weeks (he certainly was to everyone else!). Weeks had laid the pipes for the infamous Manhattan Well; the two men had an existing association. But Hamilton? Hamilton's criminal law practice was negligible, and those few cases in which he'd acted for the defense involved crimes other than murder.

The story that gets retold, usually without question, is that Hamilton took the case because he was in debt to Ezra Weeks for the building of the Grange. This sounds convincing enough, but for the fact that in January 1800, Hamilton hadn't even bought the land on which the Grange would later stand, much less engaged a contractor or an architect. It is true that Hamilton was writing about his "sweet project" as early as 1798, and had already discussed bringing logs from upstate with his father-in-law. But he certainly didn't owe money to Ezra Weeks for a house that as yet existed only in his imagination.

Julius Goebel, author of the exhaustive, multivolume study of Hamilton's law practice, noted this discrepancy and posited that perhaps Hamilton took the case because he was thinking ahead to his putative future house—and couldn't resist being part of what promised to be a cause célèbre. That seemed the most logical explanation: Hamilton, muscling his way into the defense team for his own ends. A man such as Hamilton, with the 1800 New York elections looming, certainly wouldn't want to leave the field to his two most prominent Republican opponents, Aaron Burr and Brockholst Livingston.

For such a well-documented group of men, the records are remarkably silent when it comes to Hamilton,

Burr, and Livingston's work on the Levi Weeks trial. In a world before a modern police force, where constables were charged with keeping the peace but little else, attorneys collected their own evidence. I scoured through correspondence at the New-York Historical Society, hoping to find an overlooked mention of either their investigation or their trial strategy, but came up empty-handed. None of the men left any notes about the case—at least that we know of. To fill the gap, I studied Hamilton's methods in the cases for which we do have his notes, and relied heavily on the information embedded in the trial record. For example, we know that on January 18, Hamilton went with Richard Harison to take the deposition of Elizabeth Weeks. We also know from their respective correspondence that both Burr and Hamilton were in Albany at the end of January to argue the complex and contentious commercial case *Le Guen v. Gouverneur and Kemble*, and that Hamilton returned to the city by mid-February while Burr continued elsewhere until early March, writing to his Theodosia of the vicissitudes of travel. Who discovered what, how, and when is conjecture based on what we know of the timeline and their respective personalities.

There is a legend, recounted by Burr's biographer Milton Lomask, "that in the course of an action that

Burr and Hamilton were managing conjointly, the question came up as to which of them should be the last to address the jury." To speak last was the more prestigious position, and Hamilton insisted it was his prerogative. According to Lomask, "Burr politely acquiesced," but "[i]n conferences, the two of them had discussed all aspects of the case, and when his time to speak came, Burr presented not only the points he himself had worked up, but also those Hamilton had developed. Hamilton, in consequence, was left with practically nothing to say. . . ." I chased down Lomask's sources but was unable to find any concrete indication of which case it was or when it happened. Legal historians have noted, repeatedly, how unlike Burr the opening statement in the Levi Weeks case is; stylistically, it hews more to Hamilton. However, we know, unequivocally, that it was Burr who presented the opening statement and was much lauded for it—even if it does seem to be in Hamilton's style. Putting those two items together, it seems possible that the Weeks trial was the trial in question, in which Hamilton insisted on the place of honor and Burr stole his speech, leaving him, literally, speechless.

Unfortunately for the historian, or historical novelist, Coleman, in his transcript, very seldom indicated which defense lawyer was speaking. We know Colonel

Burr and Brockholst Livingston argued Cadwallader Colden into embarrassment on the hearsay point and we know Burr delivered the very Hamiltonian opening statement. We also know that it was Hamilton who went with Justice Lansing and Colden to take Elizabeth Watkins's testimony. But aside from that, there are only rare instances in which Coleman specified which defense lawyer was asking which question. Hamilton, Burr, and Livingston were joined in defending Levi Weeks, but they were simultaneously working to tear each other to shreds at the polls. It was in Hamilton's and Burr's interests to win the case—but also to outshine each other. Added to that are their very different characters and approaches to the law. There's nothing strange about a lawyer mooting multiple theories at the same time—the partner for whom I worked during my own time as a litigator referred to it as "belt and suspenders," or sometimes "one, two, three, we win!"—but in this particular case the defense's questions jump about oddly, as if the lawyers were interrupting each other, pushing their own competing agendas. I used the push and pull between Hamilton and Burr and their competing interests to try to flesh out what actually happened in the courtroom and who was speaking when, but it is all pure speculation.

One more word about that: anyone who has previously

read about the Levi Weeks case will have heard about Hamilton's dramatic accusation of Richard Croucher. This has been largely overstated. Legend—and Hamilton's son—have it that Hamilton held the candle up to Croucher's face and declared thrillingly, "Behold, the murderer!" Other commentators over the years have ascribed the same action to Burr. Contemporary accounts whittle this moment down to something less dramatic. Hamilton did raise a candle to Croucher's face, but only to identify him as the man spreading rumors about Levi Weeks. It is debatable whether Hamilton had, in fact, fixed on Croucher as the murderer. His son John Church Hamilton insists unequivocally that he did. Lacking any contemporary notes from the principals, we can only speculate based on the direction of the questions at the trial, which do spend a great deal more time on Croucher's whereabouts the night of the murder than on anyone else with the exception of Levi Weeks.

For more about Hamilton, Burr, and their roles in both the Weeks trial and the 1800 election, I recommend the chapter on the Levi Weeks trial in Julius Goebel's *The Law Practice of Alexander Hamilton*, which is one of the more thorough and reliable examinations of the case; the seminal Ron Chernow life of Hamilton, which provides insight into his emotions and activities in the winter of 1800; Milton Lomask's gossipy biography of Burr, *The Years from Princeton to Vice President*; and Nancy Isenberg's *Fallen Founder: The Life of Aaron Burr*. Their correspondence from that period—Burr's with his daughter, Theodosia, and Hamilton's with his wife and various associates—is both entertaining and instructive.

Aside from those questions of interpretation and gaps in the narrative that could only be filled by triangulation and speculation (of which there were more than I would have liked!), I have kept as closely as I could to the details of the case as we know them. There were, however, a few places where I took liberties with known facts for the sake of the narrative, most notably with the incredibly complex timeline of Elma's last day. According to Catherine Ring, who provided the most complete account, at around four in the afternoon, Elma came downstairs to Catherine's room "not quite dressed," holding a handkerchief in each hand and asking which looked best. Hearing a footfall, Elma retreated behind a screen, but came out when she saw it was Levi, who asked her to fix his hair. She did so, but then Elias came in and Elma abruptly left. At sunset Catherine made tea, which Elma came down to drink, and Catherine began fretting about Elma catching cold and suggested Elma borrow a muff from Elizabeth

Osborn, which Elma then did. Later, at eight o'clock, as Elma was getting ready to go, Catherine followed her to her room, fussed at her a bit, and tied her gloves on for her. This was a lot of back-and-forth and would have made my opening chapter much longer than I wanted it to be, so, instead, I have Catherine follow Elma to her room, suggest she borrow the muff, Levi come to get his hair tied, and Elias come looking for Catherine, at which point Elma abruptly leaves. These were all things that happened on Elma's last day, but for simplicity's sake I changed their order, without, I hope, changing the spirit of the interactions.

As to the trial itself, all of the trial testimony is taken verbatim from the record, although I had to leave a great deal out. (Coleman's transcript ran to just shy of a hundred pages.) Elias Ring did break into the room as his wife was speaking and had to be ordered out again; poor Cadwallader Colden did suffer one embarrassment after another. Where I did deviate from the transcript was in having Hamilton, Justice Lansing, and Colden go to take Elizabeth Watkins's statement on the morning of the second day of the trial, rather than the first. Julius Goebel, the Hamiltonian legal scholar, posited that this was a transcription error on Coleman's part, that had that particular statement been taken on the first day, Colden wouldn't have been nearly as shocked or thrown off by the allegation of Elma's affair with Elias. That made far more sense, so I followed Goebel's lead and placed the Watkins deposition on the second day of the trial rather than the first.

I also substituted one Watkins daughter for another. Although it was Betsy Watkins who testified in court about her friendship with Elma Sands, Joseph Watkins did have a daughter named Frances Susannah, who appeared to sometimes go by Susannah. Frances Susannah would have been sixteen in 1799, the right age to have idolized an older, more worldly neighbor. Because there was such a superfluity of Elizas, Elizabeths, and Betsys in this book already, I decided to have Frances Susannah speak to Hamilton about Elma rather than her sister Betsy.

There is, I confess, no evidence that Richard Croucher had anything to do with the death of Rose Malone. The *New-York Daily Advertiser* reported on December 6 that the body of Rose Malone had been discovered in a cistern. Her husband was suspected, but the case against him was dropped for lack of evidence. That, sadly, is the sum total of our knowledge about the affair. We do know, thanks to the records of the Old Bailey, that Croucher had a history of violence against women in his native England; we also know that he raped and threatened to murder his stepdaughter less than a month after the Weeks trial. He was eventually convicted and executed in England due to a "heinous crime," which some have speculated was another case of rape and murder, although I wasn't able to find any evidence either supporting or refuting that claim. Nonetheless, given his history, I did not feel too much guilt in having Cadwallader Colden speculate that Croucher might be responsible for the Malone murder. Who knows? Perhaps he was. The population of New York City in 1799 was a mere sixty thousand, double the number that had resided in the city ten years previously, but minuscule by modern standards. In a city of sixty thousand, paths tended to cross and recross, and Richard Croucher's job as a peddler of women's garments gave him access to a tempting cross-section of potential victims.

Another liberty I took involves Croucher's stepdaughter, Margaret Miller. We know that on April 23, Richard Croucher brought Margaret Miller to his room at 208 Greenwich Street and repeatedly raped her. Miller recounted how she freed herself and stumbled downstairs, wanting only to go home. There is no evidence that she ran into Hope Sands or Catherine Ring at the time. That meeting—and Hope's offer to go with her to speak to Cadwallader Colden—was entirely my own invention. In reality, it was Margaret

Miller's adoptive mother, Mrs. Stackhaver, who took her to the constables to report the rape several months after it happened. Brockholst, of course, used that delay to argue that it was a false report and that Miller was a tool of her adoptive mother, who was looking for ways to divorce her new husband. For anyone wanting to know more about the Margaret Miller case, the transcript of the trial is publicly available and makes fascinating reading, as do the many articles that discuss both that case and the infamous Henry Bedlow trial. For a close look at the Henry Bedlow trial, which is referenced in both the trial of Levi Weeks and the trial of Richard Croucher, I recommend John Wood Sweet's *The Sewing Girl's Tale*. The ways in which Hamilton, Livingston, and Burr viewed the Bedlow case differ significantly from the modern perspective; any references to the case in this novel reflect their sentiments and not my own.

Those well-versed in the life of Aaron Burr might have noticed another sneaky addition to the cast of characters. In 1833, the disgraced Aaron Burr married wealthy widow Eliza Jumel. Born Elizabeth Bowen, she had moved to New York in 1798, changing her name to Eliza Brown. Eliza Brown eventually found work as an actress, catching the eye of a wealthy merchant, Stephen Jumel, whom she married in 1804. Rumors have circulated that Eliza found other ways to support herself during those missing years between arriving in New York and her appearance on the stage. Whether or not those rumors are actually true, I couldn't resist making use of them to put Eliza Brown into the story and have her briefly meet her future husband at Ann Ashmore's house. That was pure self-indulgence on my part; there is no mention of an Eliza Brown in the trial record, nor is there any proof that Ann Ashmore was running a bawdy house as well as a distillery. For anyone wanting to know more about Ann Ashmore's career as a distiller and maker of cordials following the death of her husband, I recommend the section on Ann Ashmore in A. Brandt Zipp's *Commeraw's Stoneware*.

In other errata, Levi Weeks didn't leave New York until 1802; Cadwallader Colden's European tour wasn't until 1803. I moved both of those departures to fit within the confines of the story. My apologies to both of those gentlemen for hustling them prematurely out of the city.

One last small point: although Catherine and Elias Ring and Hope Sands all used Quaker plain speech (*thee* and *thou* in place of *you*), you may have noticed that their use of *thee* and *thou* does not adhere to strict grammatical rules, where *thou* is a subject, the equivalent of the modern *you*, and *thee* is an object. In the trial testimony, all three used *thee* in places where it would be more grammatically correct to use *thou*. I attempted to replicate their speech patterns, with *thee* being the predominant pronoun, and apologize if that was jarring to any *thee* and *thou* purists.

For details about the weather in the winter and spring of 1800, I am indebted to Elizabeth De Hart Bleecker, who, in addition to recording gossip and misinformation in her diary, also kept a daily log of the day's weather, faithfully inscribing whether it was colder than yesterday, began fair but then turned rainy in the afternoon, or was sunny but cold. Had she been born centuries later, she would have made a marvelous meteorologist.

With all that out of the way, I can only end with the central question of the book: Who did kill Elma Sands? At various times, people have wagered on Catherine or Elias or even Hope, but the two most convincing suspects are Richard Croucher and Levi Weeks. Taking Levi Weeks first, legal historians agree that under the circumstances, leaving aside the propriety or impropriety of Justice Lansing's pointed summation, the jury came to the correct conclusion: there was not enough evidence to convict Levi Weeks and they acted appropriately in acquitting him. Lack of evidence, on the other hand, does not equate to innocence. Catherine

Sands believed to her dying day that Levi Weeks had dodged justice; so did many others. The trial transcript is a bit like an inkblot test. I read it and had a strong impression of Levi as a hapless man who got in over his head and found himself collateral damage in a crime he didn't commit; a good friend of mine read it and came to the opposite conclusion.

As I wrote this book, I was very aware of the fact that I could just as easily have written a version in which Levi was conclusively guilty. Even though Hope's testimony about Elma's intentions were suppressed due to hearsay rules, we know that Elma told her cousin (unless Hope was lying or misunderstood Elma) that she was leaving to be married to Levi. Levi and Elma undeniably spent considerable time together and had a strong bond, although what that bond was is open to interpretation. Susanna Broad, although she lapsed into confusion during the trial, did claim she heard Ezra's sleigh leave that night. There wasn't enough time for Levi to have gone back, hitched the horse to the sleigh, and removed the bells, but if one accepts the testimony of those witnesses who claimed to see two men and a woman, an accomplice (my vote is for Demas Meed, Ezra's apprentice) might have taken the sleigh to meet Levi and Elma at the Ring boardinghouse, which would leave plenty of time to get to the well, push Elma in, and make it home in time for Ezra to provide an alibi—assuming, of course, that Demas could be trusted to hold his tongue. In this version of the story, it seems likely that Ezra Weeks would play the part of mastermind, delegating to Demas and cleaning up after his little brother's messes.

In the end, I followed Hamilton's (supposed) lead and inclined to Richard Croucher as killer. As the police in British TV shows say, he had form. Croucher already had a history of violence toward women, and went on to offend again—and again. As Hamilton so ably illustrated at trial, from the outset, Croucher inserted himself into the case, distributing handbills, pointing the finger of suspicion at Levi, spreading rumors. He could just be a busybody, but there were other suspicious circumstances. Of all the members of that household, Croucher was nearest to the Manhattan Well that night, and his alibi was dodgy, to say the least. He waffled on whether or not he had, in fact, walked past the well that evening. And he was quick to insist that he and Elma were barely on speaking terms, because he had insulted Levi, "whom she thought an Adonis."

There's a curious little incident that tends not to be discussed in most of the pieces about the case. Croucher, when asked whether there was a quarrel between him and Levi, mentions that one day, Levi had come upon Elma in his arms, swooning. She just happened to swoon and his arms just happened to be there. Levi, Croucher insisted, had taken this the wrong way. Unless, of course, he had taken it entirely the right way. Elias, at trial, bursts out that Levi had threatened that if Elias didn't stop spreading rumors about him, he would tell "of me and Croucher." There are certainly different ways one can read that; one reading is that Levi would tell that both Elias and Croucher had been Elma's lovers.

Croucher was a merchant of women's fripperies, exactly the sort of silk stockings and trimmings that Elma craved. If my interpretation of Elma's character is correct, she was looking for an older man to replace the father she had never known, someone who could give her the place she wanted in the world, a home of her own where she was no one's charity case. Rejected by Elias, it would have been very tempting to take up with a well-dressed man of the world who could drape her in silks. To marry Croucher would be to thumb her nose at Elias. Meanwhile, Croucher, who also liked the finer things, was working on securing the hand in marriage of a wealthy widow; he might want to enjoy Elma's favors, but he wasn't going to marry her and risk losing the widow's windfall.

We know from the trial transcript that there was at least one night unaccounted for when Elma had claimed to be sleeping over at the Watkinses', but wasn't. My theory is that Elma met Richard Croucher at the home of Ann Ashmore, who may or may not have been running a bawdy house. If Croucher had arranged to meet her at Ashmore's house and from there to be married, it would have been easy for him to intercept Elma at the well, which was en route, and shove her in. Elma's behavior for the past month had been erratic. What could be easier than to speculate sadly that Elma had thrown herself into the river in a love fit? When suspicion started to point toward Levi, Croucher hastily dropped the suicide story he had begun spreading and instead vigorously worked to implicate Levi Weeks.

Did it happen that way? We may never know. Your theory might be different. I urge anyone eager to play Poirot to read Coleman's transcript, which was digitized and is publicly available. I also recommend Estelle Fox Kleiger's *The Trial of Levi Weeks*, which largely focuses on the trial testimony, but does provide background, context, and a look at the way the crime has been recounted by successive generations. Paul Collins's *Duel with the Devil* is an engaging read but should be taken with a large quantity of salt; while great fun, it is riddled with factual errors and unsupported assumptions presented as fact. Read and enjoy—but check the footnotes carefully afterward.

For more on the research that went into this book, you can find a longer bibliography on my website, www.laurenwillig.com. Please do email me through my website and tell me your theory of the crime. . . .

Acknowledgments

When I first embarked on this book, I blithely assumed that the research would be easy. After all, other writers and scholars had already done the heavy lifting. There were two nonfiction books on the case, as well as a slew of articles. And then I started reading. And digging into the footnotes. And finding gaps and anomalies and confusion and straight-up errors. Facts dissolved upon scrutiny and even simple questions, like birth dates, yielded multiple conflicting answers. What was going to be a simple literature review turned into a two-year deep dive into a wide array of sources, including wills, inventories, letters, diaries, gravestones, court records, maps, directories, and multivolume family trees produced by nineteenth-century amateur genealogists.

Acknowledgments

This book owes its existence to the generosity of archivists and librarians. First and always, my thanks go to my own Angel of the Bibliography, Vicki Parsons, Director of Standish Library, literary soulmate, and Finder of All the Things. A big thank-you to the archivists of the New-York Historical Society, who let me wallow in the papers of Brockholst Livingston, Alexander Hamilton, Aaron Burr, Richard Harison, Judge Lansing, and others. Even though no new information on the case appeared (forlorn hope!), those documents were invaluable in helping me understand the character of the participants. I'm so grateful to the New York Society Library and their "City Readers" program for making it possible to see which books Hamilton, Burr, Livingston, Colden, et al, were borrowing from the library. Hugs to the brilliant Caroline Bartels of the Yale Club of New York City, who magicked up rare books I needed, and to Emily Moog of the New York Law Institute for making me free of their Hamilton collections—and providing me with coffee while I read through it!—as well as digging into the NYLI's records to answer some of my more abstruse legal questions.

For detailed information on the changing nature of the court system in eighteenth-century New York, I am deeply indebted to the Historical Society of the New York Courts. Huge thanks to historian Katrina

Gulliver for walking me through the minutiae of crime and policing in eighteenth-century New York. I am also grateful to the brilliant ladies of Bibliophile, esq., for jumping in to help when I put out a call for legal historians who might be able to shed light on changing legal procedures in New York in the Early Republic as I tried to make sense of exactly how the court system worked at the turn of the eighteenth century and how it differed both from colonial precedent and the apparatus it has evolved into today.

My apologies and thanks go to my old grad school friends Rebecca Goetz and Richard Bell, who found themselves on the receiving end of random queries ranging from "How exactly did law enforcement in late-eighteenth-century New York work?" to "Which regiments would have passed through New Cornwall, New York, in 1776?," often by text at odd hours of the night, or while they were using archives in foreign countries in other time zones (sorry, Becky!). Huge thanks to my uncle Thomas Romich, for providing me with a wealth of sources on the geography and architecture of eighteenth-century New York, for helping me to pinpoint the exact location of Ezra Weeks's lumberyard, and for sending pictures of Brockholst Livingston's grave.

I am so grateful to my author community. Particular

thanks go to Allison Pataki, who talked me off the ledge when I was panicking about writing about real people instead of made-up ones, and to Deborah Goodrich Royce, whose thoughtful meditations on the nature of true crime guided me as I was struggling with the fact that we'll never really know what happened to Elma Sands. (Where is Poirot when you need him?) It was such a boon to have Andrea DaRif, aka Andrea Penrose, working on her Lady Hester Stanhope book at the same time I was tackling the Manhattan Well Murder: I treasured our hours in the Yale Club Lounge as we wrestled with what we owe to our historical subjects.

It's incredibly rare to have an editor who is as much of a history nerd as you are. So many thanks to Rachel Kahan, not just for her mad editing skills, but for knowing the context and the characters through and through. I am so lucky to have you as my editor—and not just because we share so many of the same costume drama crushes.

Big thanks to the whole team at William Morrow for their dedication and talent. To everyone in editorial, production, marketing, publicity, and sales: THANK YOU. I'm so grateful to you for bringing this book out into the world. I'd like to send a special shout-out to Mumtaz Mustafa, who has a genius for creating covers that perfectly capture the spirit of a story. Every time

I look at this one, I feel like I'm back in New York in December of 1799 with Elma, just before she leaves for that fateful assignation.

Thank you to my agent, Alexandra Machinist, for letting me roam down random historical alleys, for quick "just one question" phone calls that turn into hour-long gossip sessions, and for never suggesting that I write anything set in World War II.

This business has never been an easy one and it's gotten even tougher over the past decade. I would like to send my sincere gratitude to the booksellers, bookstagrammers, and bibliophiles who are the reason we authors get to do what we do. If I named names, this would stretch at least another ten pages, but I'd like to say a special thank-you to all the marvelous independent booksellers (Corner Bookstore, Litchfield Books, Fox-Tale, Book Cove, Murder by the Book, and Poisoned Pen, I'm looking at you!) who always know how to find the right book at the right time, to the bookstagrammers and bookfluencers who so generously donate their time and talent to lift up the books they love (thank you, Robin Kall, Andrea Katz, and Sharlene Martin Moore!), and to all the readers who have been with me through up and down, and thick and thin, and Pinkoramas and plagiarism. I am so, so very grateful for your enthusiasm and support.

As always, I don't know what I'd do without the friends who keep me going, particularly Nancy Flynn (setting the standard for best friends since 1982!), Claudia Brittenham (thank you for the walk 'n' whines, my dear!), and the Ladies' Caucus: Christina Bost-Seaton, Lien O'Neill, Debbie Bookstaber, and Stella Choi-Ray. Extra hugs to Justin Zaremby, Marissa Ain, Sandy Lee, and Carlos Riobo—I treasure your strong opinions. Love to my Ws, Beatriz Williams and Karen White, who are forever just a beep of the text chain away, ready to chip in with advice, support, and *Daily Mail* headlines. May the Prosecco be always in your glass.

Last but not least, to my family: to my parents, siblings, husband, and children. Thank you to my parents, who have leapt in to fill childcare gaps that would otherwise have tanked deadlines and tours. To my sister, who knows more about my characters than I do. To my husband, also known as my personal IT department. To my daughter, who appointed herself in-house Hamilton expert (which consisted largely of her singing at me), and to my son, who knows more about the details of the death of Elma Sands than any kindergartner ought to know.

None of this would be possible without you.

About the Author

LAUREN WILLIG is the *New York Times* and *USA Today* bestselling author of more than twenty-five novels, including *Band of Sisters*, *The Summer Country*, the RITA Award–winning Pink Carnation series, and five novels cowritten with Beatriz Williams and Karen White. An alumna of Yale University, she has a graduate degree in history from Harvard and a JD from Harvard Law School. She lives in New York City with her husband, two young children, and vast quantities of coffee.

HARPER LARGE PRINT

We hope you enjoyed reading
our new, comfortable print size and found it
an experience you would like to repeat.

Well – you're in luck!

Harper Large Print offers the finest in
fiction and nonfiction books in this same larger
print size and paperback format. Light and easy to read,
Harper Large Print paperbacks are for the book lovers
who want to see what they are reading without strain.

For a full listing of titles and
new releases to come, please visit our website:
www.hc.com

HARPER LARGE PRINT

SEEING IS BELIEVING!